The magician's assist... ...cked a padlock on the side of the box and flipped it open. The upper and lower halves of the box had been cut to form a small circle, enough room for a large neck—like Paul's.

Before Paul could make a move, he was seized by the magician and dropped into the box, the lid slammed shut, and the side-mounted padlock affixed with a metallic click.

"Let me out of here!" Paul screamed.

The magician leaned toward him. "And spoil the trick? No, Mr. Marat, that's not possible. We have an audience to entertain."

Seconds later Paul heard a rolling sound behind him. He tried his best to turn, but he couldn't. All he could do was stretch his neck until it hurt.

And just as the rolling sound stopped, he heard, "The sins of the fathers, Paul Marat, shall be visited upon their sons."

Moments later, a wicker basket was placed under Paul's head.

THIRST
OF THE
VAMPIRE

T. LUCIEN WRIGHT

PINNACLE BOOKS
WINDSOR PUBLISHING CORP.

DEDICATION
For my mother, Mademoiselle Marie Anne Aubin

PINNACLE BOOKS

are published by

Windsor Publishing Corp.
475 Park Avenue South
New York, NY 10016

First printing: October, 1992

Printed in the United States of America

1

The table had been lengthened by two feet for the occasion, the entire length covered by a red and white vinyl tablecloth. But even that added length could not detract from the size of this country kitchen, where several of the Marat clan had gathered for breakfast.

The relentless morning sun, tamed only nominally by the delicate curtains on the kitchen window, reflected in long, sparkling patches off freshly scrubbed, black and white linoleum. A beam of sunlight grazed a grandfather clock in the far left-hand corner of the room. Opposite the clock sat a potbellied stove, whose slumber would remain undisturbed for many months to come. It was precisely 8:00 A.M., a fact noted by the toning clock, muffling the sound of the screen door opening then banging shut. A German shepherd named Kit had nudged the door open. He would be home by noon, hungry from having chased but not caught, and thirsty from running the dusty back roads that wound through Jefferson County like twine around a baseball.

The table itself was a paragon of culinary excellence. Resting upon it were eggs that had been scrambled and hard-boiled and some over easy, and there were waffles and jams and pancakes and sausage. And there was bacon, too, pilfered from the family pig, who had donated

5

generously to the family meat coffers just two days earlier. Steaming pots of black coffee had been placed at three-foot intervals, and toward the head of the table rested a pot of tea. Aunt Sofia, eighty-three now, preferred tea. As befitting her matriarchal status, she sat at the head of the long and heavily laden table. In total, there were fifteen chairs taken this day, including Aunt Sofia's. One was still unclaimed.

Louis Marat, a large, dark-eyed man with a receding hairline and a five o'clock shadow regardless of the hour, looked up from the *Watertown Gazette*. "Did you get a chance to read this?" he asked.

His brother, George, seated beside him, and who could have been Lou's twin had he been twenty pounds heavier, slathered some margarine onto a piece of toast. "What's that?"

"In the *Gazette*. Says there're a lot of people missing from hereabouts."

George's wide brow furrowed. " 'S that right?"

Louis Marat—he preferred Lou—leaned forward slightly and turned the paper toward his brother. "Right here, bottom of page one. You didn't see it, huh?"

"How could I, Lou, you grabbed the paper soon as it got here."

Lou smiled sheepishly and ran his finger along the page. "Says that within the two-county area, that'd be Jefferson and Alleghany, I guess, says that over the last three months, the number of persons reported missing has risen dramatically."

"Yeah?"

"Word for word."

At that, the interest of two of the three assembled children was piqued. Paul Marat, Lou's twelve-year-old son, who would very much resemble his father once he attained full growth, glanced across the table at his cousin, Michel, a fair-haired, wiry boy who looked very much like his mother. Michel returned that grin while his mother, Carla, set yet another plate of steaming pancakes on the

6

table. Both mother and son had pouting lower lips, and large, light brown eyes. Carla's father, during a tantrum of sorts, chose her name. He'd hoped to have a boy—Carl Jr.—when he didn't, he simply added the vowel and told his wife something about "next time." His was the un-claimed seat. He was still in the bathroom.

Both Paul and Michel found the idea of missing people to be vastly interesting. Already coursing through their minds were questions concerning who, what, where, and when, as well as the conditions of remains. It was that thought that brought the hint of a smile to Michel's mouth, a smile that Beverly Marat, Paul's adopted sister, returned, instantly adding ten years to her thirteen. Like Paul, she had dark hair, but unlike Paul, her skin was cigarette pale, making her large green eyes appear even brighter.

"Say anything else?" George asked.

Lou scanned the rest of the article, then, "Says some-thing about that it's not just kids. You know, runaways. Says something about a sixty-five-year-old woman and a five-year-old boy . . ."

"A five-year-old boy?"

"That's what it says. Probably wandered down by Jack-son Creek and fell in."

George shook his head slowly. "Makes you sick, doesn't it? I mean a five-year-old kid! Think his parents'd keep an eye on him."

Lou shrugged. "Happens, I guess. Pass them home fries, will you, before Paul eats em' all."

In a few days the Marats would gather en force for a family reunion, which would take place on George Marat's well-appointed acre of land. Lou Marat and his family had arrived early, at the behest of Lou's brother, George, who offered a week of the best fishing and hunt-ing this side of Alaska, as Lou well knew. Lou had quickly accepted. Occupying the remaining seats were assorted cousins and aunts and uncles who, like everyone else, talked of things mundane, nothing quite as important or

7

as stimulating as the missing and presumed dead, a topic that stayed in the thoughts of Paul, Michel, and Beverly for the remainder of the day.

That night Michel, Paul, and Beverly found themselves a quarter mile from the house. From where they were the house was only a blackened outline against the dark purple sky. As they watched, a light went on in the kitchen. It was time for Michel's mother to start preparing pies for the reunion, the rhubarb and strawberry pies, the peach and apple and cherry pies, each with a thick, flaky crust and stuffed to bursting with homegrown fruit. She would prepare these desserts with skill and zeal, occasionally humming and always smiling. And although everyone would remark on the obvious merits of this pie or that—which was exactly why she prepared them with skill and zeal in the first place—the rhubarb strawberry pie would be the first to go. The Marats had uncannily similar likes in many things, especially food.

About a half mile away and off to the right, the lights of Watertown reached feebly skyward. As towns went, Watertown wasn't much. Fifty thousand people, give or take, lived in and around its limits, and the only places that stayed open past seven were movie theaters and restaurants. This wasn't Vegas, where night started at the city limits. Night lay on this town like oil on water.

Michel, leading, stopped as the moon rose like a giant bubble.

"Look at that," he said. "Looks like Aunt Connie's butt!"

Paul laughed. "Yeah," he said, "craters and everything!" Now they both laughed and Beverly crossed her arms and looked appropriately miffed, body language that again added years to her age. Connie and she were women, well, almost, and she would certainly want her aunt to defend her honor.

"Aunt Connie's got a gland problem!" she informed them.

"Yeah, saliva glands!" Paul said in a burst of inspiration.

At that, both boys laughed so hard they thought they'd throw up. Despite the fact that she, too, found Paul's remark funny, Beverly fought back a smile and continued to glare.

After the moon and their aunt's backside had been properly compared, they walked on to what was a camping area of sorts; odd-sized rocks circled a pile of burned wood. Abruptly, Michel sat down Indian-style and told the others to do the same.

"What for?" Beverly asked.

"You'll see."

Hesitantly, she sat on Michel's right, while Michel assumed what he thought to be a meditative position—he closed his eyes. Beverly swiped a liberated strand of dark hair away from her face and waited. And waited. And waited. Finally, she said, "God, Michel, this is about the dumbest thing you've ever done!"

Michel sighed and opened his eyes. "It takes time, Bev," he said.

"What takes time, Michel?"

"I'm trying to make contact with one of those missing people. You know, the ones Dad and Uncle Lou were talking about at breakfast."

"That's what we're doing here? You're trying to make contact with a bunch of missing people?"

Michel nodded.

"And just how do you expect . . ."

She left her sentence dangling. She had no choice. There was something crawling on her foot, or more properly described, slithering. Very slowly. In her mind she saw herself kick whatever it was about fifty yards, but her body would not respond. In fact, it took most of her mental fortitude to simply have a look. And what she saw then almost brought on cardiac arrest. She hated snakes.

They were sneaky and brainless and clammy. And now there was one on her leg. Actually making physical contact. And although she knew that few—if any—poisonous snakes were indigenous to the area, knowledge of that sort was hard to draw on. There was, however, one thing she could do—she could scream. That was an almost reflex response. So she did, loud enough and shrill enough and abruptly enough to actually frighten the boys. But Paul had put the snake there in the first place, so he didn't stay frightened very long. Neither boy did. After two or three seconds they laughed so hard they fell down, their sides aching from the assault. And Beverly just screamed and screamed until she stopped, when the snake slithered away and Paul scooped him up and dangled it in front of his sister's face.

"Herman, meet Beverly. Don't worry, Sis, Herm's a vegetarian," he said, which caused Beverly to scream louder still.

As Beverly slowly began to reclaim sanity, she also began to realize that even her brother wouldn't be stupid enough to actually hold a poisonous snake in his bare hands. And now the name, Herman, found a home. Herman was Michel's pet snake. He'd wanted to show it to her but she had declined. "I hate snakes," she had told him then. "They're slimy and stupid and they kill people." All in all reasons enough to not have much to do with them. And with that knowledge, she also recognized that the boys were still laughing at her. A totally intolerable situation. "Bastards!" she said, sending out a fine mist of spit.

"Bastard?" Paul said. The snake seemed content to just dangle at his side. "Why I gotta be a bastard?"

"Because I'm a lady, and a lady doesn't call anyone an asshole!"

She stood and turned toward Michel, who grinned. "You helped him, didn't you?" she said.

Well, it was his snake. But he said nothing, and the reason was simple enough; her flush-cheeked anger had generated a gentle surge of electricity in his loins, which caught him completely unaware. He chanced a quick glance at his crotch, then looked back at Beverly, wondering if she'd seen. She hadn't.

"I'm going back to the house," she announced. "You three can stay here if you want, you deserve each other!"

She turned to go, which would have cut the evening short, too short for Michel, who had, for the first time, recognized desires that had lain dormant till now, desires that screamed to be explored. "Please, Bev, don't go," he pleaded. "Not yet."

"And why not?" she asked.

He groped for something, anything. Finally, he said, "I had a . . . a vision, yeah, I saw those people!"

Beverly smiled derisively. "You've got to be kidding, Michel. You had a vision? You can do better than that."

Michel paused, feebly clutching to his lie, but at least he had succeeded in keeping her there. "Okay, so I didn't have a vision."

"Surprise!"

"But they gotta be somewhere, Bev. Maybe we can look for 'em."

"Right, you look for 'em. Not me!"

As Beverly turned to go, Michel hurriedly unfolded his mental road map and quickly scoured the two-county area, searching for anyplace a psycho might hide his handiwork. There were a few.

"Maybe the old mill on Dougan Road or . . . or the mine shaft behind the Fletcher place . . ."

Darkness had all but encircled her.

"They got to be somewhere, Bev," he yelled.

Almost out of sight now, Beverly rolled her eyes. But instead of hastening her gait, as she had intended, she stopped. Something was nearby, in the darkness, circling, looking for a way in . . . She felt a prick of pain behind her eyes . . . THE OLYMPIC. COME HAVE A LOOK, KIDS! ALL OF YOU, COME AND FIND THEM! THE OLYMPIC.

11

And then there was silence. Crickets chirped and frogs bellowed, sounds unheard by the children. And for Beverly, who was alone in the darkness, there was almost complete sensory deprivation. Her world consisted only of a woman in a window, rolling pie dough. Seconds later, the sounds of the night returned, but slowly, and Beverly heard Michel say, "The Olympic, Bev, why don't we look there?"

"Yeah, the Olympic," Paul chorused.

"Yeah," Michel interjected. "It's all closed down, but that's exactly why it would be a good place to look! I mean, if you were some sleazoid psycho . . ."

Beverly stepped into view. "I'm not going," she said evenly.

"Oh, c'mon, be a sport, Bev," Paul said.

"I'M NOT GOING!"

"Jesus, Bev, we're just tryna have some fun here."

Her lower lip began to quiver. Something was very wrong.

Michel moved to his cousin's side, and, thanking circumstances for the excuse, put his arm around her. "Hey, what gives?" he asked.

She seemed deep in thought, unable to fathom his question. Finally, she said, "What the hell's the Olympic, Michel? I've never even heard about it, but I thought about it. God, that scares me!"

Michel took it all in stride and came up with what he considered to be a logical explanation. "Maybe you don't know what it is, but I do and so does Paul. The way I look at it, we both thought about it at the same time and had a little ESP—you know, extrasensory perception—which you picked up. It's just a closed down movie theater in town, that's all. No big deal."

Beverly tried that on for size and found the seams a little tight. Still, it was an explanation, one that groped toward the supernatural, but was, nevertheless, at least negotiable.

"ESP?" she said.

"Why not?"

Paul moved closer, silently wondering when his cousin was going to take his arm off his sister's shoulder. "Yeah, Sis, why not? Happens all the time. And this'd be like a real minor case, you know?"

Beverly's jaw tightened. "Why should I go with you guys, anyway," she said. "After what you did."

Michel removed his arm and tried to appear as if his will had been broken. "You're right," he said. "There's no reason you should trust us. That was a low-down dirty trick with that snake, and I wouldn't trust us if I was you, either."

Her mood mellowed. When you got right down to it, the snake thing *was* pretty funny. She'd never screamed so loud in all her life. A pretty good trick. Not that she wouldn't get back at them, but the evening was still young, and all they'd do back at the house was watch television.

"I'm probably gonna be sorry for this," she said, "but if you wanna go, I'll go. I'm going to tell you both right now though—if this is another trick, I'll tell. I promise I'll tell everything. Agreed?"

That was as agreeable as it got, so after Michel went back and got a flashlight, they left. Michel took the lead with Beverly and Paul following behind.

To the right of the Olympic Theater sat DiVincenzo's Bakery. They could see the back of both buildings from where they were now, but even with their eyes closed they would have known about the bakery. Nothing caressed the sense of smell more delicately than the odors that wafted in and around DiVincenzo's Bakery. To the left of the Olympic, and hidden by a locust tree, was Carson's Self-Defense Emporium. Its clientele ranged from pudgy ten-year-olds who very much wanted to flatten the school bully, to housewives secure in the knowledge that every man they saw wanted to tear their clothes off and have at

13

it. Carson also taught judo and kick-boxing. Although larger than its neighbors, the Olympic was still small, as theaters go. Built in the fall of 1930 to accommodate a growing citizenry, receipts had declined along with the population. After two years in the red—deep red—the owners got what they could and tried their luck elsewhere. Rumor had it that it would open again, but nothing ever came of it.

Michel shined the light on the back door and immediately felt a surge of adrenaline. The door was open.

"Jesus," Beverly said.

"You got that right," said Michel.

Many times he'd walked through this backyard, and many times he'd stared at that back door. Every time he did he imagined a crowd of ghosts inside, munching popcorn, watching *Topper* maybe, or *Casper*. But he'd never really had the opportunity to check things out, other than the one time he'd been in there to watch *The Black Room*, another Boris Karloff movie, one his dad said was a real horror classic. Michel's critique differed considerably—a real yawner, he thought. But then, his dad liked old movies. If it was old, it was good. That was kind of a rule.

As Michel recalled, the interior of the theater was vaguely reminiscent of a huge funeral parlor. Maroon, floor to ceiling drapes hung on each side, and the seats were a plush funereal purple. That's what Michel remembered about the Olympic, and he had no reason to expect any different now, except maybe for *Topper* and *Casper*, aka The Friendly Ghost. So as they entered through that open back door, the prospect of coming face to face with Casper was not a disturbing one. It was, in fact, something he might even welcome.

They entered the theater with rising trepidation. Passing from moonlight into total darkness, Michel illuminated the stairway to the draped stage. They walked to stage center, their sneakers squeaking on the hardwood floor, and pushed through the curtains and onto the stage itself. Michel fanned his flashlight across the rows of seats, and then let the beam come to rest on the four-foot wall at the back. He envisioned people there, smoking or talking or checking out the audience (who was groping whom mainly). A vision that also supplied blue-tinted cigarette smoke rising languidly into the projector light like a spotlight through a fog.

"Wow!" Paul said, his voice echoing. "Neat!"

They first noticed the faintly acrid odor as they stepped off the stage. Michel was reminded of their kitten, Crisco. She had disappeared one rainy Saturday morning and stayed gone until they found her two Saturdays later. More exactly, she had found them. She had crawled under his dad's chair, something she wouldn't have been able to do had she been fully grown, and there she had passed on. Fourteen days passed before the smell finally worked its way out. He remembered that smell now, kind of a thick, liquidly yellow smell, he thought, both then and now.

"What the hell's that stench?" he said. He moved the light slowly along the rows of seats like an usher.

"Stinks!" Beverly agreed. She put her hand on Michel's forearm.

"Probably a dead possum or something," said Paul.

"Maybe a whole family," Michel responded.

But the melding of two truths left the trio speechless. Truth number one: people were missing, their status—living or dead—unknown. Truth number two: something, someone stunk. Miserably. So it was okay to be scared now, scared enough to turn tail and run. There were two truths to mess with here, and it was okay to be afraid. So they did run; they pushed through the curtain, then ran down the steps and out the back door. They didn't stop until they got to the dead campfire.

Winded, Michel bent over, hands on knees, and said, "Ah, wasn't that bad."

"Shit, too!" said Paul.

Beverly fell on the ground like an angel, eyes closed. After she'd caught her breath, she said, "The smell! God!

Probably just a dead animal, though, don't you think, you guys?"

No answer.

"Guys?"

Then she heard them laughing, laughter that traveled at least fifty yards through the darkness.

Alone now, Beverly pushed herself to a sitting position and looked toward town. And although she felt a modicum of fear, she felt something else as well. Something that stimulated thoughts of things awaiting and awakening. She thought of Michel then—retreating, laughing Michel—and smiled.

2

A madhouse, Michel thought two days later, that's what it is, and it ain't gonna get better any time soon. But wasn't it real peculiar that the only place the Marat clan hadn't been congregating was the kitchen? Well, maybe not so unusual, seeing's how that's where they were (Bev and Paul and Michel), where they had been for quite a while now. They'd laid first claim to the kitchen, and so far no adult(s) had kicked them out, although that just might happen, and soon. Uncle Dave, with Aunt Sofia in tow, had sauntered by just a minute or so earlier, eyeing them for a moment before they moved on. Then some grown-up cousins they'd never seen before this evening had followed just seconds later. Soon enough, someone would waltz in suggesting something about how children should be outside on such a grand evening, or didn't they have bedrooms to go to, or how long did it take to do the dishes anyway? Oh, sure, it would happen, Michel's thought continued. They could count on it.

Beverly was at the sink, washing the aforementioned dishes at the rate of about a dish an hour. Michel and Paul were sitting at the table drinking Cokes, eating Oreo cookies, and furtively eyeing a long row of six-packs—Utica Club—from Abel's Grocery in town, six-packs that were soon to be deposited into ice-filled coolers for consumption during the festivities. Abel's had run a special, two six-packs for the price of one. "Probably 'cause they can't give it away," Paul's dad had said. "Stuff tastes like stale piss!" "Then why'd you buy it?" Michel had almost asked, that and the other obvious question—how did he know what stale piss tasted like. But the role of taste was not vitally important to a couple of pubescent boys who hadn't as yet partaken of the fruit of the field. Whose minds were filled to overflowing with thoughts about what demon alcohol could do to their inhibitions. There was adventure imprisoned within those dark brown bottles with the cursively written labels.

Michel leaned slightly left, just to see if his dad was still watching "Bonanza"—he was, him and about five other people. But *his* dad wasn't the problem. The whereabouts of Paul and Bev's dad was. Last seen, he'd been on the porch reading the paper, mumbling about this and that, mostly about how he hated family reunions and wouldn't it be great if this were the last. If *he* caught them pilfering a few beers, there'd be real hell to pay. Mike's dad would just tan a few backsides; Paul and Bev's dad would have their scalps—just as an excuse!

It had been decided that removing a six-pack from the counter and then further removing it from the premises would not be as dangerous as it seemed. One out of sixteen would not be missed. Hopefully. And if the truth reared its ugly head, then so be it. A small price to pay.

Beverly, in her status as idle bystander, knew the boys were planning something. They kept looking back and forth from the beer to the living room and back to the beer. She pretended not to notice, but truth be known, she wouldn't mind socking down a beer or two herself. Just because they were boys didn't mean they had cornered the market on a little sneaky fun. She put a pan in the basin, turned and leaned against the sink, her hands clasped loosely in front of her, her legs crossed. "Well, you gonna do it or not?" she said.

Paul and Michel snapped their heads in her direction, pseudopuzzlement mapping their faces. "Do what?" Michel asked.

Beverly rolled her eyes. "Do what? What do you think, jerks? Steal some beer, that's what," she whispered.

"Steal some beer? What makes you think—"

"C'mon, you think I'm some kind of idiot? You're looking at that beer like it was Miss September!"

Paul leaned forward and looked at her crossly. "You're gonna tell, aren't you? That's how you're gonna get back at us about that snake thing, ain't it?"

"Maybe," she teased.

Paul's body lost its rigidity. He fell back into his chair. "Ah, c'mon, Bev, why would you wanta do somethin' like that? We'll give you one, wha' do ya say? A couple maybe. Two apiece?"

She let him off the hook. "And where are we gonna drink 'em, huh? Here, in the house?"

"No, not here, that'd be plenty stupid," Michel interjected. "Out in the woods maybe, I don't know. Somewhere other than here though, that's for sure. And we gotta take some Listerine, so no one can smell it on our breath later."

Another adult cousin, one who spoke only French, stopped in the doorway and smiled. They smiled back. The cousin moved on.

"They'll miss 'em, you know," Beverly offered after the coast was clear again. "Someone'll miss 'em for sure. Then you'll catch it good!"

"So?" Paul said with a shrug. "There's always a price when you want somethin' bad enough. If we get a whippin', well that's the price."

"Besides," Paul interjected, "our fathers were kids, too, they know about that kinda thing. They'd understand."

Beverly looked at Paul. What did he know about what their father understood? Maybe someday she should take him aside and tell him all about their father, where he got his pleasure. She pushed those thoughts aside. She wasn't about to let her "father" ruin this evening. Not one that held such promise. She looked at the beer, back at the boys. "It's warm, you know," she said, feeling some vague moral duty to dissuade them. "It probably tastes awful when it's warm."

"Nah," Paul said. "I heard German beer's warm, and it's 'spose to be the best beer in the whole world. That's all they drink over there, you know. Like in France they drink only wine."

"I'd hardly call Utica Club German beer, Paul," Beverly said.

"Okay, okay, cold or warm we're gonna do it, right?" Michel asked. His impatience was showing. "I mean we're just talkin' to hear ourselves talk now, that's the way I see it."

Beverly raised her eyebrows slightly and shrugged. As usual Michel was right.

Just then Paul and Beverly's dad came into the living room, said something to Michel's father, and took a recently vacated place on the couch, just out of sight. On the tube Little Joe was smiling at some pretty young thing who'd just stepped off the noon stage.

Michel looked out the window. The sun was setting. "Now's our chance," he said with a mischievous grin. "Let's just do it, okay?"

The affirmatives were given in the form of nodding heads. Michel went upstairs, pocketed a small bottle of Listerine, went back into the kitchen, quickly stuffed one warm six-pack of Utica Club into a brown paper bag, and left. Beverly and Paul followed, mouths watering in anticipation.

They chose a spot about a quarter mile from the house, a clearing they thought was probably used by hobos; the ribbon of tracks to the right glimmered dully in the glow of a half-moon. There were corpses of past fires, dead logs drawn around it, a few empty cans with the labels gone. But thankfully there were no hobos here tonight, just them, their beer, and a flashlight, which, after just one beer, Michel shoved under his chin to frighten Paul and Bev, who were already too blitzed to be scared. Paul was on his second beer by now, Bev had just started her second.

"Oh, look, it's Jack O. Lantern," said Bev, a little joke that caused her to roll onto her back like a turtle into the pine needles, gales of laughter pouring out of her.

Michel seized the moment. "I am Drocula," he said, "I have come to biiite you in the neeeck! I am not this . . . Jack O. Lantern!" His attempt at a Transylvanian accent came out slightly cockneyed.

Beverly sat up, legs crossed, smiling bewitchingly. "Bite me in the neck, huh?" she said, arching her eyebrows like she'd seen Mae West do.

"Yaass! In the neeeck!" Michel bellowed, fingers arched menacingly.

Her smile broadened. "Can't think of anyplace better than my neck, Michel?"

Michel slowly lowered the flashlight. Drunk or not, that was a ponderable question.

By now Paul had drained his second beer and was eyeing Beverly's fondly. "Had enough?" he said. His world had started a lazy, aquatic roll.

"Not by a long shot," said Beverly, pulling the beer close. She took a long swig, let a little dribble down her chin. Half the bottle was left. She looked at it, sloshing around in there like an ocean swell.

"Now you had enough?" Paul asked again.

She hugged the bottle like Chatty Cathy and made a face like a little girl. "No! Go way! It's mine!"

Michel smiled out of one corner. He was feeling light-headed, sure, but he wasn't near as far gone as Bev. She sure was a different person when she'd had something to drink.

But for Paul the night had just begun. "Let's get some more," he said with a burst of inspiration.

"Yeah, sure, where?" Michel said. "Go back to the house and get another six-pack? That'd be about as bright as a firefly."

"No, I didn't mean that. I've got some money, five or

21

six bucks. I was thinking about that old wino you told me 'bout. You know, that old fart that sleeps near the bus station?"

"Harry?"

"Yeah, Harry. Bet if we give *him* a six-pack, he'd buy them for us."

Bev giggled. "Why not?" she asked. Michel and Paul were doing the amoeba split.

Michel looked at her and smiled.

"I mean, if you're gonna do somethin'," she continued, "you might as well do it right! That's what I always heard."

"And maybe we can save it for another night, you know? Hide it or something," Paul said.

Michel gave them both a onceover. He was the oldest, he was supposed to be kind of in charge. But what the hell, you were kids for only so many years. And drinking beer wasn't like sticking a needle in your veins. And it might be kind of fun to see if they could get old Harry to get them some beer. If he could even walk.

Nighttime in Watertown was reminiscent of small town life in most places. Most shops were closed around seven, some earlier, some later. Restaurants—there were five in Watertown—stayed open 'til about nine. Pizza parlors stayed open 'til eleven. A billiards parlor stayed open 'til ten. But here, at the Bluebird bus station across the street from St. Monica's, the only business was a mom-and-pop hardware store, and it had closed at five. Except for the occasional candy wrapper blowing in the wind, the streets were deserted, and would be until the next bus arrived. The only light came from a floodlight over St. Monica's and a gasp of weak fluorescent from the hardware store, kept on in back so a patrol car could see burglars.

The only reason old Harry frequented the bus station was to panhandle from people as they stepped off the bus, a larger concentration of people than could be found almost anywhere else in Watertown.

It didn't take the kids long to peruse the bus station, it

was, after all, only one large room, but although they didn't find Harry, something did catch their attention. On the back wall was a line of photographs—Jefferson County residents who had come up missing over the last couple of months or so. There were six in all, and seemed to have been displayed in chronological and gender order. First was a dark-haired boy of seven. He was shown with his dog, a smiling black and white mix, his sluglike tongue hanging slightly akilter. The second picture was of another boy, twelve years old, according to the caption, again dark-haired, with thick glasses and crooked teeth. His was a hazy school picture. The remaining four were either girls or women, from the ages of fourteen to forty-three. All pretty, at least pretty. One, a woman of thirty-one, was absolutely incredible, from Michel's and Paul's point of view. Her name was Sarah, and she'd done some modeling for local businesses. Paul said he'd seen her in an advertising circular modeling brassieres. (Not exactly the truth. She'd been modeling swimwear.) When the kids asked the ticket agent about the pictures, he said they were up all over town, anyplace people congregated. After they'd all decided that it was kind of neat that so many people were missing in Watertown, they went around back, where the buses pulled in.

They found Harry, relieving himself on the back wheel of a bus that had arrived from Albany and other points south a half hour earlier. Harry was a short man who had once been fat, before he'd begun substituting booze for bread. His eyes were like those of a sad old bloodhound, and his skin hung like a wrinkled suit of clothes. They flanked him, waiting for him to finish up. As he went about his business, he turned his head toward Michel, on his right, and smiled that lazy half smile indigenous to drunks. Then he looked at Bev and Paul on his left, and did the same.

"Hiya, boys," he said loudly, waving with his left hand, which threw his aim off. He leaned back slightly to see

Bev, raising his trajectory from tire to wheel rim. "You, too, missy."

"Yeah, how you doin' there, Harry?" said Paul. "Lightenin' up, so's you can fill her up again, maybe?" He grinned at his little witticism.

"Sure enough," Harry quickly responded, "if I had the price. Which I ain't."

Paul looked at Michel, Michel at Paul. A smile passed between them.

"Well," Michel said, as Harry shook his Johnson off and tucked it back in, "we might be able to work something out."

Harry turned around, wiped his hands on his ratty, brown overcoat, spat to the side, and smiled knowingly. "And how might you go about that, boys?" he asked.

Paul took out his wallet and pulled out a bill. "Well, you take this fiver, go on down to Abel's, buy two six-packs, they got a special, two for one, take one, and give us the other. Simple, huh?"

Harry eyed the five a moment, reached for it, then pulled his hand back. "Oh, yeah, real simple. And what if Terry Boothman sees me? He likes to patrol down there, you know. Likes to catch the high school kids. He catches me, off I go to the calaboose, and I don't wanta go there. Huh-uh. Sorry, boys. No can do. But, how about helpin' out an old man down on his luck?"

It was then, and for the first time, that Michel and Paul saw Beverly make use of her feminine wiles. She sashayed up to Old Harry, her hands clasped behind her back, leaned toward him and said, "Oh, c'mon, Harry! Be a nice guy, wha' do ya say?" Then she smiled, which, as always, made her look considerably older than her thirteen years. Harry—although in a constant state of inebriation, which had denied him a hard-on for the last five years—was still a man, and thus as pliable as putty in the hands of a good woman. And right now, Beverly was certainly a good woman.

"I don't know, missy," he said. "That's not lawful, you know."

He was hedging.

"Neither's pissing on a bus tire, Harry," Beverly said, her smile as provocative as any thirteen-year-old's had ever been. "I think they call that indecent exposure, although from where I was standing, I'd call it pretty decent." (Another Mae West line.)

Michel couldn't help it, if Harry wasn't getting aroused, he was, although he knew the beer was doing most of Beverly's talking.

Old Harry just looked at her a moment, then returned her smile with a somewhat crooked one of his own. "Yeah, okay, okay. A six-pack. What you want, Pabst Blue Ribbon? Genny, maybe?"

"No, Harry," Paul said, unable to suppress his glee. "Utica Club. It's on special, like I told you. Two for one."

"Oh, yeah," Harry said. He held out his hand and Paul smacked the five spot into it.

They followed Harry to Abel's, way on the other side of town, and waited behind an old Volvo while Harry went inside, stumbled to the cold beer case, reached in, and withdrew two six-packs of Utica Club. One he carried, the other he stuffed under his arm.

They watched Harry walk toward the counter, but lost sight of him as he went behind a display of toilet paper. Still, they didn't dare move, someone might see them and guess what they were up to. Two minutes passed. "Probably had to wait in line," said Michel. Three minutes, then four. They finally got the message as minute five approached. And now it didn't matter who knew. They stormed into Abel's and marched to the counter. The bright lights burned into their eyes.

"Where'd he go?" Michel demanded from the clerk, a girl barely twenty, with big eyes, long, dark hair and a surprised look on her face.

"Who?" she asked.

"Harry!"

"You mean the old guy—?"

"Yes, the old guy!"

A glance gave her away. He'd gone out the back door with their beer and their change.

They arrived at an alley that led to Main Street to the right and the back of a row of dark buildings to the left. "That way," Michel said, indicating the row of buildings. "He wouldn't go back to the street. We'd have seen him." They moved in that direction as quickly as they could, each still somewhat under the influence, but not as far gone as they had been at the bus station. And although they had a vague idea where they were, they were not prepared for what they saw a minute or so later—the Olympic Theater. The back of the building was almost majestically dark. "Don't suppose he went in there, do you?" Paul asked as he took a step backward.

"Maybe," Michel whispered. He looked at his cousin. "Only one way to find out though. How bad you want your change?"

Not that bad, Paul almost answered. "It's all I got," he said instead. "Guess it won't hurt to have a quick look."

"I'm game," Michel said. "What about you, Bev?"

Bev still had a mild buzz on, but her world was turning slower than it had. "*Very* quick!" she said.

"Then it's agreed?" Michel asked.

"Yeah, I guess," Paul answered.

Luck, both kinds, intervened as they tried to gain entry into the Olympic. The back door was indeed locked, secured by a huge Master lock, the kind they'd seen withstand a direct hit from a 30-30 on TV. But while this little bit of bad luck revealed itself, Michel's bladder caught his attention. He walked behind some bushes behind the theater, relieved himself, and started back. But as he turned, he saw that a window, just to the right, had been left open a few inches. If they wanted, they could get in after all.

He stepped from behind the bushes, waved to the oth-

26

ers. "Hey, you guys, c'mere. Window's open!" he whisper-yelled.

Paul, who had now convinced himself that three dollars plus was worth more than just a quick look, was the least reluctant. He climbed up and in with the speed of a cat burglar, then stood in the open window and waved to Michel and Bev to join him. Hesitating only briefly, Michel gave Beverly a hand—firmly situated on her right cheek—and then followed. They were, they quickly discovered, in a bathroom, and apparently the johns had backed up. The nose-assaulting stench was nauseating. And the floor was slimy as well, as if someone had drilled holes in the bottoms of the urinals.

"So that's what a urinal looks like," Beverly said. She walked up to one and ran her fingers over the side.

While she did that, Michel flicked the flashlight around the room, briefly spotlighting not very creative graffiti and crude, sexually oriented artwork. He stopped on a hastily scrawled word. HELP! it said. Just the word HELP! which seemed very much out of place, surrounded as it was by overlarge penises and breasts and sexually explicit limericks. He got a picture of some kid standing there, whizzing away, while some ax murderer snuck up behind him, and all the kid had time to do was write that word. It gave him goose bumps.

"God, I think I'm gonna throw up," Beverly said. Her fascination had deteriorated to disgust.

"Me, too," Michel seconded, drawing the light away from that word, remotely thankful the others hadn't seen.

"Pretty raunchy," Paul said. "Let's get outa here!"

But as they turned to go, Michel briefly brought the light to bear on one six-pack of Utica Club just inside a stall. He went in and picked it up. Paul joined him. "Well, I'll be," he said. "Didn't leave my change, did he?"

"You're dreamin'."

Paul glanced toward the door. "Could be in there," he said, referring to the theater proper. "Matter of fact, where else could he be?"

"Maybe you should be happy with this," Michel said.

"He left this without bein' asked. I bet if we find him, he'll give us the money, too."

"You sure?" Michel said.

"Yeah, I'm sure," Paul answered.

With only mild reluctance they pushed open the door, stepped into the hallway, and stopped dead. Although cool knots of apprehension tightened their guts, their imaginations were now totally engaged. The lights were on, smokily, dreamily, but still on. Like Siamese triplets, they walked slowly into the lobby.

"Christ," Bev said. "It's open! Jesus, it's open!"

And indeed, it did appear to be, although only a few people could be seen.

"When'd it open?" Paul asked. Because the lighting made it feel as if he were in church, or maybe at a funeral, he kept his voice low.

Michel could only shrug with ignorance and disbelief.

If not for the fact that they had recently inbibed—for the very first time in their young lives—the alarms that went off inside their brains would have been louder, more blaring.

They wandered like strayed calves into the lobby, the six-pack boldly displayed at Paul's side. From here to the front, they could see a woman at the ticket window, her back to them. She wasn't passing out tickets; she was just sitting there, reading a paperback novel. They could see the gray sidewalk beyond, but the street itself was as black as old oil. They turned toward the concession stand. There was a girl there, smiling, her hands clasped together in front of her. She had on a maroon uniform with gold trim at the sleeves. Kind of scruffy-looking, Bev thought. And she was. Her dark hair was tossed and tangled; her face and hands were dirty.

"How about some Milk Duds?" she asked. Her voice was a girl's voice, but throaty. She waved her hand over the display case like an evangelist and smiled a salesgirl's smile.

28

"No, thanks," Michel said.

"Reese's Peanut Butter Cups then? They're special this evening. Two for one."

"No, we're fine," Michel said, feeling a bit unnerved. Was everything two for one tonight?

Bev leaned to him. "I know her," she whispered flatly.

"Yeah, me, too," said Paul.

They looked back at her. "Popcorn then?" she said. They looked away.

The person taking tickets at the double doors that led into the theater was also familiar, and also as unwashed as the girl selling Milk Duds. He, too, had on a maroon uniform with gold trim. A fresh yet bloodless laceration across his pink forehead looked like the first slice into the Sunday ham.

"Christ, I know him, too," Beverly said as they drew closer.

"Yeah, yeah, me, too," said Michel. "What's his name? What the hell's his name?"

The boy held out his hand as they drew closer. "Tickets?" he said cheerfully.

"No, we . . ." Michel began.

"Oh, it's you, Mr. Marat," the boy said. "Please, go on in. Compliments of the management. You and your friends."

The boy gestured toward the maroon-colored double doors. "Enjoy the show," he said.

"Show?" Beverly whispered. "What is going on here?"

Michel tried to supply an answer. "Well, near's I can tell," he said, "this place opened up all right, but they didn't really care about the kind of people they hired. But I know I've seen that kid before, I just know it!"

"The counter girl, too!" Beverly said.

Their brains dulled by alcohol or not, they still entered the darkened theater with a heightened awareness. They stood at the back a moment, waiting for their eyes to adjust, then walked down the center aisle, and sat where every kid has always wanted to sit, in the very middle. As they did, lights high up the wall on either side came on, but dimly, just barely lighting the theater enough to see the rest of the seats. There were two girls in the very front row, giggling and munching popcorn.

After a few minutes the hardened preternatural patina had softened considerably, and they had convinced themselves that the place could really be open, which was probably why the back door was locked. And as far as the john was concerned, well, someone just messed up. The ladies' john could be working, a coed thing. Something like that. And they'd gotten into the movie for nothing, compliments of the management, so what did it matter that later they'd all get wailed, but good. So they settled in, content now, and drank another beer until they got a good buzz working.

What struck them instantly—when something finally did appear on the screen—was that it was not being projected from the back of the theater. No megaphone-shaped stream of smoke-trapping light appeared above them. The lights on either side went out, and the screen simply lit up and quietly announced WELCOME TO THE OLYMPIC, ENJOY THE SHOW in a glaring white on black. As that opening faded, again throwing the theater into darkness, Paul leaned over to the others, "Yeah," he said, "I read somethin' about this in *Popular Science*, I think."

What they saw on the screen seconds later was at first perplexing, but then they realized that it was only an advertisement. The camera angle was from above, taking in the whole town. Then, with dizzying speed, the camera swooped down, zeroed in on Osgood's Department Store, and stopped. Then a woman said, "Osgood's, where the clothing is Os good as there is anywhere." A model appeared then, from a distance, and inside the store. She was standing underneath a sign that said WOMEN'S UNDRESSING ROOM. She had on one of their long, dark fur coats. The camera moved toward her.

"What the . . ." Michel began.

And as the camera got closer, her wounds became more detailed. A long slice of skin had been taken from the right side of her neck, and her left eye was completely gone, leaving only a blackened socket. As she removed her coat, revealing her naked body, they saw the rest of her injuries; a line of blood tracked from her navel into her pubic hair, her right knee attached by a ligament onto her shin, a rib stuck through the skin like a misplaced horn. She still, however, smiled prettily for the camera while the announcer continued. "And, yes, we do take all major credit cards." The model displayed one, a Master Charge, while blood dripped from the side of her mouth like runny lipstick.

Bev put her hands to her mouth. "Oh, God, oh God," she said. "It's her! God, it's *her!*"

"Who, Bev, who?" Michel asked. He could barely get the words out, his chest felt like a car had fallen on it.

"Her, dammit, *her*—the woman in the photograph!"

"Jesus," Paul said, "she's right. It is her, Michel."

Just then the fifteen-foot tall model on the screen leaned forward, blew a kiss to the camera, and said in a very masculine, very deep voice, "The sins of the fathers, children." And deep within her blackened socket of an eye, they could see just the tiniest point of light begin to expand, until a silhouette emerged. There was a guillotine and someone was kneeling, their head imprisoned.

At that, Beverly screamed as piercing a scream as she could summon. It filled the theater to capacity, and with it, Paul and Michel felt so feverish with anxiety and fear that they actually felt cold.

Everything went dark. And again, the theater was empty except for the children. And Beverly stopped screaming. The two girls who had been in the first row appeared the next row up. And although there was total darkness, the girls were still easily visible. They were necking, groping each other, and moaning and swearing like marines. After a minute or so they stopped and turned.

"Noreen," Beverly said. She looked at the other girl. "And . . . and Sheila!"

Two more of the missing.

Michel flicked the flashlight on, but nothing happened. "Oh, shit, c'mon, work you son-of-a-bitch, work!"

Noreen and Sheila started laughing.

"Oh, God, Michel, let's get out of here, let's get out of here!" Beverly pleaded tremulously.

Michel flicked the flashlight on and off, on and off, but still nothing happened. Steadily the girls' laughter filled the theater. Michel took Beverly's hand, gripped it hard. "C'mon," he said. "The back door's locked, we gotta go through the lobby."

Beverly couldn't hear him over the girls' laughter; she just followed as he ran for the double doors into the lobby. The laughter stopped once the double doors closed behind them.

The lobby was totally dark. The only shapes visible were the edges of doorways and walls, the concession stand, all lit by filtered streetlight. But halfway into the dark lobby, slow movement to the left drew their attention. They all stopped and looked. "Oh, shit!" Michel cried. There was someone standing back there, behind the darkened concession stand. Just a darker outline in the dark lobby, but still recognizable as a human form. And now they could see that it was the girl who'd tried to sell them Milk Duds. She stepped closer and then leaned against the display case. In the muted light her wounds were softened, but that didn't lessen the horror. Her lower lip hung obliquely onto her chin, the teeth on that side had fallen like slats in a white picket fence. One nostril had been removed, leaving only the sinus cavity, and the skin itself was caked with blood. Again she offered them some Milk Duds, but this time the throaty sound came out more liquidy, as if the words had fought through a thick accumulation of mucous.

A small squeal came out of Beverly when she saw her,

prompting Paul to scream as well. And now a quick look behind them, near the double doors, revealed that the other kid was still there, too. He was walking slowly toward them saying, "Tickets, please. Tickets, please!"

3

They had paid a price getting away from there. Bev twisted her ankle when she fell out the bathroom window, Paul rammed his hip into a sink, and Michel banged his head on the upper framing of the window as he pulled himself up. Nothing that wouldn't heal quickly, even Bev's twisted ankle, but still painful as hell. Running home, half-dragging Beverly, they'd all resisted the urge to look behind them, to see how close those things were. They were relying on that old standby—if you didn't see it, maybe it wasn't there, which didn't for a moment alter the notion that at any second, in mid-stride, they'd feel a hand on their collars before they were yanked backwards and dragged into the bushes. Demons, that's what they were, or ghosts maybe. The unfriendly kind. But whatever they were, they sure weren't human. Not anymore.

They took the same route going home that they had taken getting to town, just grazing the edge of the woods and the clearing where they'd each drunk their very first beer. From here they could see that the party was really going strong. Chinese lanterns surrounded the backyard, swaying in a light breeze that would get stronger later as a storm rolled in. They could hear the dull roar of conversation from here, too. Sound carries well in open country. The big band music started as they got closer. Glenn Miller. Michel's mother just loved big band music, and especially Glenn Miller. As they passed from the darkness into the glow of the lanterns and began to mingle, it became immediately apparent that almost everyone had a buzz on. There were a few, though, like his Aunt Connie and her husband, who were strikingly sober.

The kids mingled for a while among their drunken relatives, until Michel mentioned something about, "Didn't we leave the zombies back at the theater?" at which Bev and Paul laughed nervously. Then they went down to the basement and pulled up some bar stools. Michel's dad had remodeled the basement a couple years earlier, and he'd done a pretty good job. Only once had they had to tear out the carpeting because the water had gotten too high. But his dad had fixed that. He'd gotten some downstate company to waterproof around the outside. The bar was in the northwest corner, fifteen feet or so away from the stairway. There was a powder room to the right of the stairway, a wine cellar off to the left. The walls had been blacked in because the previous owner had used it as a photographic darkroom. Just to the left of the bar was a bar-sized pool table. Michel went around the bar. "What'll it be, sport?" he said to Paul.

Paul shifted on his stool and plopped his forearms onto the bar. "Bourbon up," he said.

Michel smiled at that, thinking Paul more a Kool-aid man than anything.

"And make it top shelf. Old Grand Dad," Paul added.

Michel looked at him a moment, and realized his cousin was serious. He wanted a shot of Old Grand Dad, which, Michel figured, would equal about two beers, maybe more. He'd really be sloshed then.

"Well?" Paul continued.

Michel reached under the bar, pulled out the 100 proof Old Grand Dad and poured a shot.

Beverly looked at her brother incredulously. "You're not really gonna drink that stuff, are you?"

Paul wrapped his fingers around the glass and smiled like it was Christmas morning. "It's a party, ain't it?" he said. He raised his glass to his lips and poured the golden fluid down while Bev and Michel watched. The trembles started even before it hit bottom. Paul felt like he'd swallowed flowing lava. He fanned wildly at his mouth; his eyes flooded with tears.

"God, that was stupid," Michel said. "You okay?"

"My brother, the village idiot!" Beverly announced, shaking her head in disbelief. "You gotta sip that stuff," she added. "You don't just drink it like tap water!"

"How would *you* know?" Paul somehow managed. His voice came out like Jimmy Durante's.

Beverly picked up the bottle and pointed at the label. "It's fifty percent alcohol, dummy! One hundred proof means fifty percent alcohol. God, you're a putz!"

After the effects wore off, Paul drew in a deep breath and exhaled. Then he smiled. "You're chicken," he said. "You're both chicken!"

"Yeah, right, chicken!" Michel said. "I saw what that stuff did to you. I'm not a . . . a . . . damn! What's that word?"

"Masochist?" Beverly offered.

"Yeah, that, too!"

But Paul was feeling pretty good about himself. He'd been first, no denying that, and they could razz him all they wanted. They were just jealous. He started flapping his arms up and down and squawking like a chicken.

"Now it's a double dare or something," Bev said.

Paul stopped flapping. "Okay, a double dare. I double dare you to drink a shot of that stuff. And no sipping, either. You gotta toss it down just like I did. No cheating!"

Michel and Bev exchanged glances. If they didn't take his double dare, he'd never let them live it down. He'd hold it over their heads like a bag of cement on a skinny string.

Paul, sensing reticence, started flapping his arms again, but before he could get that first squawk out, Beverly held up her hand.

"Okay, okay. But only one, that's all. Just the one!"

36

Paul smiled victoriously and looked at Michel. Michel sucked in a large breath and nodded as he let it out.

Two more shot glasses were located under the bar, and all three were placed on the bar, then filled to the top. Paul did the honors, handing one each to Beverly and Michel.

"A toast," he said. "To . . . Aunt Connie's butt!"

Michel couldn't help but smile. Beverly rolled her eyes.

"And a one and a two . . ." Paul said, just before he threw down his second shot. Beverly and Michel followed suit within a millisecond.

Carla Marat, seated in an Adirondack chair next to a distant cousin, leaned left and said to her, "I'm real glad these things don't happen more often, aren't you? I don't think my liver could take it!"

The distant cousin, a woman in her fifties with slate gray hair and pointy features, didn't seem to hear.

"Gretchen?" Carla said.

Gretchen seemed to be studying the darkness beyond the festooned Chinese lanterns. Carla tried to focus, found it difficult, looked back at Gretchen. "What is it?" she asked.

Now Gretchen heard. "I don't know," she said. "I thought I saw something. Animal maybe. I don't know."

Carla patted her arm. "It's the punch," she said. "Lou put some German stuff in it. Real strong stuff. Steinager, I think he called it."

Gretchen looked at her crossly and tilted her glass toward her. "Grape juice," she said. "That's all I've had since I got here. Just grape juice."

Carla smiled. "Oh," she said.

Party pooper, she thought, settling her gaze on the darkness beyond the lanterns, where Gretchen thought she saw something.

* * *

Three hours later Michel's head felt like it had been sawed into from front to back. He grabbed his forehead, hoping to squeeze the pain away. When he opened his eyes, the pain only slightly less, he saw that Beverly and Paul were either asleep or passed out. He was on the couch, the orange one that used to be in the living room before the cat got a hold of it. Beverly and Paul were still at the bar. He got up, saw a whole constellation of stars appear before his eyes, steadied himself, then crossed to the bar, and shook first Paul then Beverly. He got some groans and that was it.

"C'mon, you guys, wake up," he said.

Beverly's eyes fluttered open. She ran her hand through her hair and looked at him. The bottle of Old Grand Dad was right in front of her, half-gone. They'd drunk half a bottle between them. They were probably lucky to be alive. Paul woke up and worked his mouth vigorously to get rid of the cotton. His eyes were like tiny red balloons. "God, my head!" he said, turning on his stool. "Feels like shit!"

"Mine, too," said Beverly. "I can't believe we drank all that stuff, I just can't believe it!"

Just then they heard footsteps on the stairs. They sat up straight when they saw a cop's uniform descending. Then the whole body appeared. It was the county sheriff, Terry Boothman. He stopped two stairs from the bottom and just looked at them. "Jesus," he said under his breath.

Naturally, the children thought he was here for one reason and one reason only—to arrest them for underage drinking. But the look on his face said otherwise. He took his hat off, smoothed out a generous head of hair, then walked slowly toward them. "I got bad news, kids," he said. "God, how do I . . ." He paused and looked at each of them individually. "It's your parents," he began. "I'm afraid they're . . . dead."

Beverly looked at Michel first, then Paul, and then all three exchanged confused glances.

Terry Boothman didn't want to repeat himself, but it

appeared he would have to. "Did you hear me, kids? I said your parents are dead."

Michel stood and shrugged. "Yeah, we know," he said. "They died three years ago today. In a plane crash."

Terry Boothman stared at the children in disbelief.

A SHORT WHILE LATER AT THE OLYMPIC THEATER

Philippe Brissot was pleased. Over these many years his ability to manipulate minds had strengthened considerably. And everything had gone as planned, perhaps better. He remembered the blank stares on the children's faces and smiled. He would sleep well tomorrow, he and Charlotte, hidden beneath the stage of this old theater. And with luck he'd dream about the past, if dreaming was the right word. Dreams had such realism to an immortal. There were times, when he was dreaming, when he actually believed it was 1793 again. And about that, he had mixed feelings.

4

June 17, 1793, France

Something virulent had gripped the land, a madness born of drastic and violent change. No one was immune. You were either victor or vanquished, your blood spilled for the simplest of reasons, for as little as listening to antirevolutionary rhetoric. And so much blood had been spilled. There was an almost palpable sense of it, floating like pollen on the winds of revolution. Even deaf ears, it was said, could hear the sounds of revolution; heads thudding into wicker baskets, cries for mercy from the merciless, crowds chanting for more and more and more, to satisfy a blood lust not unlike that which might grip a dog that has had its first taste of red flesh. And no one knew who would be next. No one except maybe Jean Paul Marat. Men, women, even children were being taken away by the hundreds, some to be guillotined in Paris, some to suffer even worse deaths. And the rumors detailed savage atrocities; Marat's henchmen were raping women, then murdering them and tearing their guts out like slaughtered farm animals. Then, in acts that could not be believed unless actually witnessed, they would dine on strips of hacked and mutilated flesh. Those were the rumors, and Philippe Brissot knew them to be more than that. Philippe, in his position as Marat's second, had engaged in those acts. He had tasted the blood of virgins.

But no one, least of all, it seemed, those close to Marat, were immune to this insanity, which was exactly why Philippe was searching for a place to hide until the revolution was over. Someplace faraway from Paris, where even Marat couldn't find him.

His mistress, Marie, had stayed behind. She had a stomach virus. It hadn't been necessary that she come anyway. It would probably take the better part of a week to find and stock the cave. She'd just be in the way.

The cave itself was in Lascaux Hill, discovered and explored during his childhood. At the time, he had vowed to come back and pitch his family's coat of arms on the spot, but he never had. Over time he'd forgotten the exact location of the cave. But hopefully, that wouldn't be a problem. If he found it by accident once, he could probably do the same again. And although it had been almost twenty years, he remembered very well how large the cave was; how inhabitable by any number of persons, if the situation arose. The main room alone was incredibly huge, at least a hundred feet long and thirty feet wide. And there were a number of smaller rooms as well. Food wouldn't be a problem. Game was plentiful; deer, rabbit, turkey. And there was a nearby stream for fresh water. In the end his decision to first find the cave and then stay there hadn't been difficult. In Paris they ran the risk of being deemed disloyal to the cause, even if they weren't. At least in hiding they stood a decent chance of survival, if Marie's health held, which was somewhat questionable.

The trip from Paris had taken two days. His valet, Maximilien, waited at the coach while Philippe started toward Lascaux Hill on foot. His route would take him across fields of wildflowers and the stream. He needed to judge if the ground was dry enough to support the coach's weight without getting stuck. Provisioning the cave would be a lot simpler from the base of the hill.

It started to rain as he drew to within a quarter mile. A day that started promisingly had turned ugly. The rain started slowly, just moist cotton falling from the sky, but before long each cottony drop felt as if it had been encased in tin. Marble-sized hail followed, and Philippe, a tall but thin man, fell to the ground and did what he could to protect himself. Even above the storm's fury, he could hear the horses complaining. If they ran off, he'd lose everything. He'd be stranded. But thankfully, that didn't happen. The storm passed as quickly as it had begun, and Philippe stood and inspected those parts of his body that had been exposed to the onslaught. That done, he started again for the hill. A few clouds, like piles of dirty socks, remained, casting shafts of sunlight along his path, which Philippe interpreted as a good omen.

A few minutes later he stood at the bottom of Lascaux Hill. The site was dotted by scrub brush and dominated by tall, widely spaced trees; they looked like giant mushrooms, with their thick tops and straight, barren trunks. But as he scanned the hillside, it seemed that finding the entrance again would be next to impossible. Everything looked the same. There weren't any topographical features that might hint at a cave entrance, none at all, and Philippe felt disillusionment begin to settle in. But as he moved to about mid-point on the hill, small snatches of memory probed the corners of his eyes. He could see himself as a boy, climbing up the hill, stopping then starting, stopping then starting, undecided about which way to go. To the left, he quickly decided. He looked again. No, up and to the left. Yes. Of course. Up the hill a little farther, then off to the left . . . (And remember, the spot is marked by an outcropping of greenery, where the water has gathered and kept the plants moist. Look for that.) He scrabbled to the left, leaning into the wet hillside for traction, while at the same time trying to keep an eye out for the crevice that marked the cave entrance.

His search lasted only a couple more minutes, and when he found the entrance he felt as relieved as he ever had. He stopped for a moment, basking in this minor victory, then lit his torch, and started into the cave. The air grew steadily cooler, and a few minutes after he'd slipped beneath the surface of the earth, he left the tunnel and stepped into the main hall itself. He held his torch high overhead, marveling at the sheer size of this room, much larger than any home in France, except maybe for the Palace at Versailles. He could also see the dark entrances to other, smaller rooms from here. And in the distance, he could hear water dripping; the sound seemed to echo. Oh, yes, he decided, this will do nicely. Very nicely, indeed. How much longer could the revolution last anyway? A month or two, maybe. And with Marie at his side, living here would at least be tolerable.

But as he thought about Marie, he also thought about that other problem—he hadn't told her about this place, about his plans. There was a chance she'd say no—not a good chance, she did love him—but a slim chance nonetheless. And if she did say no . . . He felt his pulse quicken. Well, if she did say no . . . He'd confront that problem only if it arose, not until. He had other, more important things to worry about right now.

He saw the paintings as he turned to go. Seeing them, he remembered the brief moment of awe and mystery when he had first seen them as a child. But as a boy of ten, he hadn't been educated enough nor sophisticated enough to appreciate what he'd found. But he was now and he was fascinated.

He stepped closer to the wall and brightened the drawings with his torch. Most were of horned, cowlike beasts, some alone, some running in groups; one, on the other side of the hall, showed a man killing one of the beasts with a spear. How long had they been here? he wondered. As far as he knew, these beasts were extinct. And civilized man didn't hunt with spears. A thousand years ago, maybe, but not now. Then he had another thought. Was he the first man to see these paintings? Excitedly, he moved to the back part of the hall, crouched down, and stepped into one of the smaller chambers. The room was long and thin, but only about six feet high in the center, a couple of inches shorter than Philippe. Maybe a good bedroom, he decided. There were paintings in here, too; paintings very much like those in the outer hall. After he had inspected these paintings, he started for yet another connecting chamber toward the back. He had to bend at the waist now, but, much to his surprise, this proved to be yet another tunnel into a larger room, a room approximately half the size of the main hall. He stood and held his torch overhead, swinging it in a slow arc. He saw it then—a painting at least fifteen or twenty feet above the surface. As he stepped closer, the painting brightened a bit. He felt his skin tingle. This painting, impossibly high on the wall showed yet another of the horned, cowlike beasts, but this one was on its back, and there was a figure that looked like a man, kneeling next to it. And although the drawing was crude, he saw something else. He saw the man's long and pointed teeth, one on either side, sunk deep into the beast's neck.

Maximilien Aubin, a small, brutish man with the intellect of a ten-year-old, got down from the coach and stepped between the team of horses. A wind had came up, frightening them. Within seconds, the wind played out, and again the air was still and moist. Maximilien raised his hand to block the glare and looked in the direction his master had taken. He hoped very much that Philippe was coming back soon. He didn't like this place, and it wasn't just the funny weather. During the storm that had almost scattered the horses, he had seen something in his mind that had both frightened and confused him. He stroked each horse's neck with his stubby hands and remembered the deep, black void, the flurries of movement. He remembered slivers of light on huge, lazily flapping wings. Then he had seen a white, searing sun rise over Lascaux Hill, and the vision had ended. It was not something he cared to see again, and as he gazed toward Lascaux Hill, he found himself praying that his master would return soon. Seconds later, his prayers were answered. He could see his master on the hillside, just a dot in the distance, but it was him. He knew it was him.

Fifty feet from the cave entrance, Philippe stopped and tried to make some sense of what he had seen, and tried to determine whether or not he should change his plans. No, he thought, there was no need to change plans. The caves, save for a few bats and spiders, were empty now. The creatures that had painted those walls had died long ago. And whether or not they had the ability to fly and apparently hover in place—a power they would need to paint what he had seen in that back chamber—wasn't important now, at least not as it pertained to his survival plans. Of course, if Marie saw what he saw . . . he couldn't let that happen. He would have to concoct a way to erase or disfigure that painting before he brought her here. And lying around him was the answer to that problem. A long stick with oil or paint on it. And now he realized that was more than likely the method those ancient people had used in the first place. No winged being had hovered there and painstakingly drawn an important part of its history. They had used poles, sticks. It was as simple as that. As logical as that. Relief cascaded over him like summer rain.

Maximilien smiled a gap-toothed smile, more than a little happy to see his master. "Did monsieur find what he was looking for?" he asked.

"Yes, Maxie, I did."

"And we will live there?"

"Yes, but first we have to lay in the provisions."

And so they began to do just that. They moved the coach over the field of wildflowers to the stream, and finally to the bottom of the hill. It took them the rest of the day to finish, and they slept in the coach that night. Maximilien said he was afraid of the caves. There was something in there that shouldn't be there. Philippe laughed at his simpleminded servant, but in fact, he, too, was more inclined to spend the night in the cramped quarters of the coach, although he knew he'd have to spend many, many nights in the cave in the months to come.

Because he didn't want to take the chance that Marat would find out where he'd gone, Philippe killed his valet the next morning. He did it without remorse or hesitation. He slipped a knife into Maxie's heart, turned it once for good measure, took it out, and let Maxie fall to the floor of the cave. And as Maxie's spirit left his body, Philippe saw the eyes of a loyal dog, the confusion and terror there, but most of all, confusion. Still, his only regret was that he hadn't done it outside. Now he'd have to carry the body outside for burial. There was certainly no place to bury him in here. If he searched he might find a subterranean cliff to throw the valet over, perhaps near where Philippe had heard the dripping water, but even then the stench of decaying flesh might wend its way back to them, an odor he would just have to live with until whatever inhabited these caves disposed of the remains entirely. But Maxie was a small man and Philippe barely broke a sweat removing the body from the cave.

Maxie was buried in the hillside. When he was done burying him, Philippe said, "Goodbye, Maxie, you were such a good dog." Then he laughed heartily, went back to the coach, and pointed the team of horses toward Paris.

5

As Philippe Brissot guided the team of horses through the dark, cobblestoned streets of Paris, as his stomach rumbled acidly at the stench of this town, of garbage and human waste, of the dead lying in the streets unattended for days on end, he remembered how easily he had condemned anyone he felt needed condemning. How easy it had been to convince the rabble that anyone—virtually anyone he chose—was a traitor, no longer a true citizen of France. There was most definitely a blood urge upon the air, a cleansing attitude, and it had swept through the masses like the promise of good bread. Oh, innocents died. Searching for the bad apple at the bottom of the barrel did not necessarily mean that you could save the whole barrel.

He snapped his whip around the horses' heads. They snorted their disapproval and the carriage gained speed.

But now it was time to leave Paris, he and Marie. Even during those few days spent finding a hiding place, Marat could have signed a warrant for his arrest. His and Marie's.

THUD.

The right wheel of the carriage had sunk into a pothole. Brissot smiled.

THUD—the sound a separated head made, a simple yet resonant THUD just after the body of the recently decapitated involuntarily leapt into the air a few inches.

THUD. It was a sound he would never forget and long enjoy, because although most of those he had condemned were not necessarily disloyal to the revolution, they were still his enemies, or those who might become his enemies. Or perhaps those who knew someone who was an enemy. Whatever. And as Marat's second, it had been so easy to condemn without question. How many had he watched march up the steps to the guillotine and its awaiting blade. And although, admittedly, each had died with honor, they *had* died. And as their heads were held high for all to see, he had looked into the eyes of each and imagined that perhaps they could look back into his, if only for a little while. (A physician of some fame had told him that, at least in his opinion, a brain could stay alive for a short while, even after the supply of blood had been cut. And if the brain was alive, then certainly the eyes were, too.) He tried to put himself in the place of the deceased, his hair gripped firmly by the executioner, blood splattering from ragged edges of skin and bone. What would it be like to look down and discover that you had been separated from your body, and then, attempt to will your arms and legs to move? He had seen a few do that, he was sure of it. He had seen the horror in their eyes when their bodies didn't react to their mental commands.

He pulled back on the reins and looked up at the second floor as the horses stopped. The house was dark, Marie was in bed. He jumped down from the carriage, ran up the steps, and banged on the door, ignoring the knocker. Within a minute or so, a candle was lit. He watched while that candle, as if by itself, flickered by the window to the right of the door and then disappeared. A second or so later, the door was opened, but only slightly. (People had been taken away in the middle of the night, only to reappear at the *Place de la Révolution*, where their lives abruptly ended.)

"Yes, monsieur?" said a quavering male voice behind the candlelight.

Brissot pushed the door open. "It's me, you old fool!"

"I'm sorry, monsieur, I thought it was . . ."

Brissot snapped his head in the direction of the servant. "Have they been here?"

The servant closed the door, but not before glancing into the dark street. "No, not yet, but they have been on this street. I saw them last night. Eight of them. Mademoiselle and I saw them from mademoiselle's balcony."

Then Brissot remembered. Before he left, he'd ordered that Charles Girdoux be arrested. Girdoux lived three houses down. He smiled again. They were still following his orders, although not with great haste it seemed.

"Is mademoiselle awake?"

"Yes, monsieur."

"Good. Give me that candle."

The servant did as asked, and Philippe went up the winding stairway and then to his mistress's bedroom. She was sitting up in bed, enjoying a chocolate and spraying her blond tresses with perfume, having seen Philippe arrive.

The window facing the bed was open just enough to allow the white lace curtains gentle movement as a breeze rose. With it there also came just the hint of death, of bodies decaying.

Marie put her spray bottle down on her nightstand and swallowed what was left of her chocolate. She was a tall woman with large features accented by elegantly high cheekbones, which she accented even more with blush. She was a stunner, the talk of fashionable Paris. But she also had tunnel vision, and was unable to fully grasp that her wealth and status might eventually make her a target of the revolutionaries. But she could be forgiven her prejudices, because, plainly put, she knew no other way to think. She had never understood poverty, because she had never experienced it. And being a devout woman she had always firmly believed that the good Lord had created two classes, hers and theirs—the poverty-stricken masses—and that their suffering was just part of God's master plan.

She rose and extended enticing arms to her lover. He went to her quickly, very much longing for her touch after two days alone on the road.

"Oh how I've missed you, Philippe!" she said.

At the same time, the servant who had opened the door for Philippe discreetly closed the double doors to the bedroom.

"And I you," said Philippe. As always, her full body pressed against his aroused him. Expectantly, he pressed closer, but to his surprise, she pushed him to arm's length. "They've taken Girdoux," she said. "Do you know that?"

Brissot's member deflated like a pinpricked balloon. "No," he lied, "I didn't. Do you know what's . . ."

"The guillotine, so I've heard. Tomorrow."

"A shame. He was a good man."

Marie thought she detected a note of sarcasm.

"And he committed no crime, Philippe. None!" she said.

Philippe backed away slightly and shrugged. "None that you know of," he said.

She smiled strangely. "None that I know of? None at all!" she said with finality.

Philippe went to the window, closed it, and then closed the doors to the balcony as well. "There's a foul odor in the air," he said. "Perhaps you hadn't noticed."

She shrugged. "No worse than any other night. Or nights to come, I would suspect. Please open the doors again, Philippe. It's very warm."

He ignored her request and turned. "How are you feeling?" he asked.

She pondered that question a moment. "No better, no worse."

Philippe swallowed hard, drew in a deep breath, let it out. "Do you feel like a trip?" he almost blurted.

She moved toward him, stopped. "A trip? Where, Philippe?"

His zeal was still unchecked. "To the south, a few days'

journey. I thought we might get away for a while. Leave all this behind."

She paused a moment, regarding him. Then. "It's true."

"True? What are you talking about?"

"You *are* afraid."

"Afraid? But of what? I merely suggest that a vacation would be wise. The smell of wildflowers and fields of grain would certainly be preferable to this."

"Where is it that you would have us go exactly, Philippe?"

He hesitated for a very long time. Then he gripped her shoulders, and with a certain urgency said, "We could be next, Marie. Marat is mad. The Jacobins are mad. All of France has gone mad. I've provisioned a cave in Lascaux. There's game and fresh water. It won't be so bad. And what of Jeanette? What of our daughter?"

She looked at him curiously, and in the candlelight his normally bold and rigid features seemed to devolve. He was a child now, asking her permission, seeking her favor. She had long suspected that his part in the revolution was more than just that of an onlooker, as he had claimed. And although it was true that Marat was mad, how would it look to have his second in command arrested? How would he look to the citizens then? To her it seemed that Philippe had lost his mind. And this was the final proof. He was running away—to a cave no less—and he wanted her to go with him! Well, she wouldn't do it. She didn't fear Marat. She had done nothing to arouse suspicion among the Jacobins. And she most certainly would not subject their five-year-old daughter to such a trip.

"You may have acted hastily," she told him. "Why would Marat have you arrested? He may be your superior, Philippe, but he's also your friend. And a sick friend as well. Something about his skin, so I've heard. It . . . scales." A look of disgust passed over her face.

Philippe opened the doors to the balcony and walked onto it. The dark skyline of Paris rose into a dark purple

51

sky. To the right, a filigree of clouds passed by a quarter moon. Marie joined him, awaiting an answer. Finally, looking away from her, he said, "There have been a few . . . indiscretions."

"Indiscretions?"

"Yes."

He turned to her. Her eyes, green in the light, were dark now, but he could still see the puzzlement there. She wanted him to tell her about those indiscretions. She wouldn't be happy with just an admission of guilt. She would want a full explanation.

He gently stroked her long neck while he spoke. "Darling Marie, please don't make me explain. Just accept that I love you deeply, and that I know what's best. Especially now. Can you do that?"

She kissed the hand at her throat and smiled. "Dear Philippe. As much as I love you, I cannot go. My health won't let me, and I will not take Jeanette from this house. It's that simple."

He smiled (much as he smiled while they made love) and continued to stroke the side of her neck.

Pleasured by this, Marie closed her eyes, smiled, and moaned lightly. He could be such a gentle man. How could the stories she'd heard be true? Her Philippe would never do those awful things.

"What of Marat?" he whispered.

"Hmmmm?"

"Marat? What of Marat? What if he discovers where I've gone?"

Her eyes rolled open just a little, focusing on his for a moment. "But you've told no one, my love. How could he? And why would he care?"

A dog barked a block or so away. The sound was flat and harsh in the still night air.

Philippe pulled her closer, preferring the cloying smell of her perfume to the stench of decay, stronger here than inside.

With her ear just an inch or so away, he whispered, "As

52

I've said, Marat is mad. Who can foretell how a madman might act?"

Her tone was light, carefree. "But even if that's so, you've told no one," she whispered back.

"Dear, dear Marie. I have. Don't you see? I have."

He stroked her neck with more vigor now, and she opened her eyes a little wider and pulled away slightly. She couldn't see his eyes, not really, just shadowy circles, but he was frowning, she could see that much. His mouth was drawn down at the sides and his chin had lowered a little.

"Who?" she asked. "Who have you told?"

He began to apply a steadily growing pressure on both sides of her throat.

"Philippe?" she said, trying to smile, but failing. "You're hurting me, Philippe."

"And I don't want to, Marie, please believe me. I don't want to."

She grabbed his wrists, tried to push his hands away, but he was far too strong. His physical strength was one of the qualities that had drawn her to him. She tried to scream, but to her surprise, nothing came out. All she could manage was something guttural, almost too low for even Philippe to hear, just wet, fear-induced sounds. The noises a person makes when they're choking.

"Oh, yes," Philippe said, nodding as he spoke. "He has his ways. Believe me, dear Marie, he has his ways!"

She struggled mightily, every muscle in her body straining for life, but she knew it wouldn't take him long. Within seconds her life would be over, and the man she loved would have done it, would have killed her. But as the final darkness moved into her horizon, she heard a noise, someone yelling. And although her vision was fogged, she still managed to see her aged servant struggling with Philippe. To her surprise, Philippe let her go, pushing the servant aside as he did. But after he'd gained his balance, he started forward again. Marie shook her head and the servant stopped. Philippe looked stunned. His eyes pleaded with her. Finally he said, "I'm sorry, so sorry. Can you ever forgive me, Marie? Can you ever forgive me?"

Her hands were at her throat, massaging the abused flesh. Forgive him? Never! She would never forgive him for what he had tried to do. Never! She squeezed her eyes shut and pointed at the door. Philippe looked even more stunned. He was being dismissed from her life forever! When he didn't move, she opened her eyes and glared at him, with a hatred that traveled along his skeletal highway like rivers of ice.

Philippe looked at the servant almost as if he wanted his help, but he had a chair in his hand now, ready to hit Philippe with it, if he needed to. He looked back at Marie. Her face hadn't changed, her eyes still thrust icy daggers at him. It was over now, that much was obvious. No long-winded explanations could correct this mistake. "Someday, perhaps," he said with puzzling calmness.

"Never!" Marie replied, barely able to get the word out.

He reached out a hand, touched her cheek. "Marie, dear Marie. Forever is such a long time."

His sudden movement caused her servant to react. He started forward, the chair held high, but Philippe backed quickly away, bowed to his former lover and walked out the door.

In her room, Jeanette snapped her eyes open and stared at the dark ceiling. She'd heard a door slam. She got out of bed, opened the door, and watched as a man walked down the stairs, a man she thought might be her father, although she couldn't be sure, not in the dark. Seconds later her mother appeared in her own doorway. Jeanette, seeing that she was troubled, hurried to her. Marie lifted her into her arms.

The servant, holding a candle now, backed away slightly to allow this private family moment.

"Why are you crying, Momma?" Jeanette asked, her head nestled against her mother's neck.

Marie paused slightly, then, "I'm happy, that's all."

Jeanette looked at her. "Will you put me back to bed, Momma?" she asked, not entirely satisfied with her mother's answer, even though she did often cry when she was happy.

"Of course," Marie said. "I'll always do that. I'll always put you to bed."

6

His thoughts were as plentiful as the stars, and just as pointedly bright on this warm and clear night. He thought about Jean Paul Marat; about his daughter, Jeanette; about the cave he was going to and how long he'd have to stay there; about Marie. Especially about Marie. Hers was easily the brightest star twinkling in his heady universe. After thinking about it most of the night, he now understood why he hadn't killed Marie. And the answer had nothing to do with a newfound morality, or the fact that her servant had interceded. The reason, incredibly, was that her life, at least to him, was as important as his own. So when all was said and done, killing her would have been tantamount to taking his own life. Thinking back, he realized that he couldn't have finished the job. Even if the servant hadn't interceded, he would have let her live. But there was one lingering question to consider. Why? Why did he love her so much? She was beautiful, true. She was wealthy as well, one more truth. But she certainly was not responsive during political, philosophical, or theological discourse. He knew plenty of women who could satisfy that need. So that left only one reason— she was easily the best lover he'd had. She could arouse in him feelings and pleasure that conversation could not. Her best speeches were made in the bedroom; the boudoir was her forum. And he did love pleasures of the flesh as much as any man. More, probably. Killing her would deny him those pleasures forever. There was their daughter to consider, too. Killing Marie would have left Jeanette motherless. And he truly did love Jeanette, easily as much as Marie, but, of course, for different reasons. Besides, the chances of Marat actually arresting Marie were slim; even Marat's spies hadn't learned of the relationship between Philippe and Marie, at least the last he'd heard they hadn't. "When are you going to settle down, Philippe?" Marat had asked the last time he'd seen him. "When are you going to stop fucking every woman in Paris?" His question spoke loudly of his ignorance. Certainly Marat could have learned about their relationship since, but Philippe thought not. Hoped not. And with luck, Marie would have forgiven him this one . . . indiscretion . . . by the time the revolution was over and he had come out of hiding. He could explain that it had been the insanity of the times, that murder had diseased the air. Well, maybe not that, even she would see through that. But he'd think of something. A few months in that cave would certainly give him time enough to think of something digestible.

So, having rationalized what was a very confusing situation, Philippe Brissot laid the whip on the horses' backs, actually looking forward to those few short months in the Lascaux Hill cave.

It was almost morning when he stopped. The horses needed a rest, some food and water as well. He spotted a lonely farmhouse just off the main road, seen only as the sun rose, casting its new rays onto the thatched roofs of three outbuildings and the house itself. The fields that lay before the farm were laden with freshly bundled bales of hay, like giant gold thimbles spaced evenly over a giant gold tablecloth. From here, about a quarter mile away, he could see roosters and chickens roaming the front yard. Philippe started up the dirt road toward the farm, and one of the roosters arched its neck and trumpeted the arrival of morning. Like fat, bleary-eyed soldiers, a few pigs left one of the outbuildings and wandered aimlessly into the yard. Seconds later a boy left the main house and walked among the recently wakened animals, scattering breakfast from a basket under his arm. The boy stopped as Philippe drove up and pulled back on the reins.

"Good morning, sir," the boy said amiably, grain sifting through his fingers into the basket. He was tall and gangly, and his Adam's apple protruded like a tiny imprisoned hatchet. About fourteen or so, Philippe assumed, a guess based on the way the boy's voice seemed to search out the correct tone as he spoke.

"Good morning," Philippe said. "Is your father about?"

"No, sir. He's dead, I'm afraid. Trampled by horses a year ago. Over there." The boy nodded toward the largest of the outbuildings, one that obviously housed the horses.

Philippe got down. "Then may I take it that you are the master of this household?" he said.

"Yes, sir, that you may," the boy answered, grinning pridefully.

"Good. If you would be so kind, the horses need grain and water. As for myself, I could use some breakfast, if that's possible."

"Of course, monsieur. Times have been good. The weather has cooperated."

"Yes, I can see that," Philippe said, scanning the hayfield.

"Please, let me take care of your horses," the boy continued. My mother's awake, if you want to go inside."

"Very well, thank you . . . ?"

"Georges, monsieur."

Philippe smiled and walked to the front door of the house, which was opened as he stepped onto the porch. A tall, heavyset woman stepped out, stopped, and smiled. From just a few feet away, Philippe smiled back.

The woman looked quickly at Georges, then back at Philippe. She regarded him with only a hint of anxiety. He was dressed well, as a gentleman, and he had arrived in a handsome carriage. There was no reason for apprehension, other than that her offerings might not be worthy of someone of his obvious status. "I thought I heard Georges talking with someone," she said.

"Philippe Brissot," he said, bowing slightly.

She smiled ingratiatingly. "It's very early, monsieur."

"And for that I apologize, madam. But I've been traveling most of the night, and I'm afraid I've run out of provisions."

"Oh? Where are you going, Monsieur Brissot?"

"Limoges, actually. Government business."

She looked at him questioningly, contemplating whether she should pursue his provocative statement—especially in these troubled times—but she didn't, and an even broader smile took up tenancy on her face. "Come in, monsieur," she said. "There is bread and coffee and some boiled eggs. You're welcome to whatever we have."

"And it is most appreciated, madam . . . ?"

"Corday, monsieur. Angelique Corday."

Philippe tipped his hat and stepped past her into the house, dimly lit by oil lamps, one in back, one in front. The flames flickered as he opened the door. The house itself, although meticulous, was otherwise Spartan. Much of the furniture that he could see—chairs, a dining table, a hutch—appeared to have been made by the family themselves. But there was a coat of arms over the fireplace, which Philippe found somewhat fascinating. There were a number of socially prominent families who were otherwise financially destitute; their ruin brought on by poor management or greed or both. He racked his memory, searching for the name Corday, but although it had a familiar ring, anything more than that eluded him.

He sat down at the dining table, while Angelique Corday set about preparing him breakfast. Out a front window Philippe could see Georges Corday leading the horses to a trough and a bale of hay, talking to them like old friends.

"Your son seems to have a way with horses," he said.

Angelique Corday stopped what she was doing,

glanced out the front window, and looked at Philippe. "Yes, just like his father. He passed on last year . . ."

"Yes, Georges told me."

"Oh?"

"Yes."

She looked at Georges again. The death of her husband was not something she wanted her son to discuss with total strangers. But at least it appeared that he had come to accept his father's extremely violent and early death.

"Your only child?" he said.

"No, I have three more. All girls. Charlotte is the only one still at home. She's still asleep. She's been ill."

Angelique glanced at the stairs.

"Older or younger than Georges?"

"Much older, I'm afraid. In her late twenties." She paused then. As she understood the implications, she felt compelled to continue. "But please, don't misunderstand. She's very comely. She just hasn't found the right man as yet."

There were footfalls on the stairs then, light, wispy. Slowly, Charlotte Corday came into view. She was dressed all in white, her chestnut hair falling onto her shoulders. She saw Philippe instantly, and for ten full seconds they simply stared at each other, although neither could see the other as well as either would have liked.

Finally she cocked her head slightly and said, "You're not from around here, are you?" She took a step toward him.

"No. Paris," Philippe said, standing. Her abruptness should have been agitating. On someone less appealing it would have been.

"Charlotte!" Angelique scolded. "Monsieur Brissot is a guest in this house. You're being very rude!"

"Brissot?" she said, ignoring her mother.

"Yes. Philippe Brissot," he said.

She seemed to smile. "I've heard of you, Monsieur Brissot."

"Really? From whom?"

She didn't answer, instead she hurried over, sat down across from him, and leaned forward, resting her forearms on the table. "Have you come to have us all beheaded, Monsieur Brissot?" she asked, her eyes catching the light from the oil lamps.

Philippe released a small laugh. "Beheaded? For what, mademoiselle? I think you have mistaken me for someone I'm not."

She leaned back as her mother glared at her and placed Philippe's breakfast in front of him. Angelique had long ago given up trying to squelch her daughter's political outbursts.

"I don't think so, monsieur," Charlotte said. "No, I don't think so." She rose and stepped to the window. "Where are you going, Monsieur Brissot?"

Philippe didn't hesitate. "To the south, Limoges."

Charlotte's interest seemed piqued. "Oh? And what business have you in Limoges? More heads to be taken, perhaps?"

Brissot was intrigued by the fact that she obviously preferred an adversarial relationship. And if she was as good a conversationalist as she was beautiful . . .

"You've obviously fostered an opinion regarding the revolution," he said.

She looked at him with disdain. "Well, it certainly doesn't take a genius to make that observation. But, yes, I certainly have. And you, monsieur?"

Philippe just looked at her for a moment, fascinated by her petulant little smile. Did she need a spanking or a man's touch? And should he pursue this discussion further? If he wasn't planning an extended hiatus to wait out the revolution, he wouldn't, but this beautiful, impassioned girl probably wouldn't give him that option.

"Like everyone, I have my opinions."

Charlotte sat down again and leaned forward, waiting. Angelique had stopped what she was doing as well, and now both women awaited his reply.

"It won't last much longer," he said. "These things never do. The people are fed up—"

"It's Marat!" Charlotte yelled suddenly.

"Marat?" Philippe said, trying to force back a nervous smile.

"Jean Paul Marat!" She almost spat the name at him.

"He and his followers have done much good for the citizens of France," Philippe said.

"Oh, they have, have they? They've beheaded innocent people, monsieur. Ended lives that should not have been ended. Jean Paul Marat, monsieur, is a murderer, and anyone who follows him is a murderer as well."

Philippe shrugged. "Sometimes drastic measures must be taken to insure—"

"NO! You're wrong! Murder is never justified, *never!* We are all equal in the eyes of God. No man can dictate to another. No man can ever be allowed to take the life of another, simply to sustain an ideology."

She was an enigma, that much was obvious. Her eyes were feverish, enflamed with murderous intent, yet she spoke like a cleric. She was unlike any woman he had ever met.

"Then, if you had the chance, mademoiselle, what would you do to Jean Paul Marat? Have him tried? Imprisoned?"

Just then, Georges Corday came into the house, and Brissot's question dissolved. "Your horses have eaten, monsieur," he said. He looked questioningly at his sister. "Charlotte? I thought you were ill?"

Charlotte simply glared at her brother, looked back at Philippe, then got up and went back to her room.

"Forgive her, monsieur," Angelique said. "She has her father's temperament, I'm afraid. Someday it will be her undoing. And I venture to say that if not for that temperament, she'd be married today." She smiled and added. "One would almost think Italian blood courses through her veins."

Philippe politely returned her smile, then looked again

at the stairs, Charlotte's afterimage lingering there. In just a few minutes, she had stimulated his curiosity more than most women could, regardless of how long he sat with them. Or laid with them.

He finished his breakfast slowly, hoping Charlotte would come back down those stairs, but she didn't, and for some reason, he knew she wouldn't. He offered money as he left, but Angelique Corday flatly refused.

As he drove his carriage down the road, past the bales of newly mown hay, he thought of Charlotte, and wondered if perhaps her political passion didn't spill over into the boudoir.

7

It would be cool this evening. Tendrils of night air were already slithering down his neck and onto his chest; a fog was forming. A poet, Philippe thought, would enjoy this sunset, but I certainly don't. He'd miscalculated the time it would take to get to Montignac by about an hour. It would be full dark by the time he arrived, about fifteen or twenty minutes from here, he guessed. He could have stopped at a number of places along the way, but he didn't want to take that chance. He'd probably taken a chance by even stopping at the Cordays, although that had, admittedly, been an extraordinary half hour or so. He hadn't stopped thinking about the girl . . . well, no, she wasn't a girl, she was in her late twenties, so chronologically she wasn't a girl. But she did still project a girlish, even coquettish quality, although he wondered if she realized it. And that coquettish quality had been somehow strengthened by her sheer hatred for Marat. And she certainly did loathe Marat, a hatred manifested in her body language. What came out of her mouth seemed tame by comparison. Fascinating, utterly fascinating. Would she actually kill him though? Given the chance, would she follow her heart or her head? Now there was a thought worth pondering. And if she did kill him, if she followed her heart and not her head, wouldn't it be vastly interesting to be there while she did the deed.

The closest town, Montignac, was about two kilometers

away. With adequate provisions, he wouldn't have to pay the shopkeepers there a visit; at least if the revolution didn't last more than a half year longer, which he thought very doubtful.

It was almost totally dark by the time he got to the road parallel to the cave. Thankfully the fog had confined itself to the low, swampy areas on either side of the road, residing there like the exhalations of huge slumbering demons. As yet the moon hadn't risen, but a closer look at the sky revealed that Jupiter and Venus were separated only slightly, low in the southern sky, a planetary configuration that to him was a good omen: the heavens united in support. He left the carriage on the road and gave the horses their freedom, smacking each on the rump with the whip to send them on their way. What he did next was akin to abandoning a tall ship for a rowboat—he set fire to his carriage. (He hadn't seen a farmhouse for at least three miles, so he felt reasonably certain no one would investigate.) After he'd watched the fire for a few minutes, he started for Lascaux Hill. After only a minute or so he stopped, the lantern held away from him to lessen the glare. Now he could see the broad, elephant-back hill, black as tar in the distance; his home for who knew how long. Suddenly he seemed totally sapped of energy; his body sagged noticeably. Lonely, he thought desultorily. So lonely. "Dear Lord, why am I doing this?" he said out loud. "Why?" He looked behind him, half-hoping the fire had gone out, that the carriage had been magically saved, but the fire crackled and popped, occasionally sending an ember high into the air. The night illuminated by the fire, he could see the horses just down the road, munching on tall grass. I could take one of the horses, he thought. Go back and hope that Marat . . . No. Marat's a madman. I'd be dead within a week. I'm out of choices. It'd be easier with Marie, though. With anyone, for that matter. Lonely, so lonely. His jaw suddenly clenched, as a strong inner voice said, 'Come on, Philippe, you've got to come to terms with it: your home is inside that hill, at least until the revolution is over. You're out of options! Understand? No options!' This spirit-bolstering dialogue fortified him instantly, and he again started for the hill, firmly resolved that he had made the correct choice, that any other choice would be the end of him. But although he tried to maintain his strength and courage, he didn't feel like a man going home. He felt more like a man walking into the mouth of a huge, slumbering beast, hoping that it wouldn't wake up anytime soon.

Finding the cave in the dark was not as easy as he'd hoped. After arriving at the base of the hill, he groped around for the better part of an hour, shoving his lantern toward false openings, occasionally toward the sound of some lonely night creature. It was only blind, dumb luck that he actually did find the opening, that and poor footing. He slipped on the wet hillside, slid about ten feet and caught himself on a jutting rock, all the while athletically holding the lantern just a couple inches off the ground. After he'd inspected himself, he got up, turned and realized just how lucky he had been. The cave opening, between the roots of a dead tree, yawned back at him, dark and reproachful, the branches he'd used to cover the opening torn away as he slid by. Allowing himself the luxury of a smile, he glanced to his right, remembering his valet, Maximilien, buried about sixty feet away. "Thought I'd have to spend the night with you, old friend," he said.

He slipped into the opening with apprehension, but also with a sense of finality, sliding into a dark, lonely world. "A month, maybe less. Maybe a little more," he mumbled now, as his lantern illuminated this narrow passageway embellished by huge paintings of bulls and deer.

He moved down the narrow corridor, kicking up pebbles as he did and raising a fine dust that stayed suspended for a very long time in the cool, dank air of the cave. Now he stopped and studied a particularly interesting drawing. The hindquarters appeared to be those of a bison, the belly that of a pregnant mare. The front legs, however, looked like those of a cat. Adding to the confusion were the mottled body and two long, thin horns. Moving further he stepped into a long, high chamber, square-shaped to a height of about six feet, then almost semicircular to a height of about fifteen feet. Fat, low-bellied horses decorated the ceiling; horses the likes of which he had never seen. Walking down this hallway, each drawing revealed itself like a ghost emerging from the darkness. And regardless of the similarities in each drawing, each still engaged his imagination and awe, again provoking images of the people that had made them so long ago.

He walked beyond this hallway to a shaft that led to the room where he had stored his provisions, all stacked in the far left-hand corner, just to the side of an entryway into yet another room. Plenty of blankets, spare lanterns, lots of salted food, eating utensils, a cot. He'd worried about someone finding this cave in the few days that he'd been gone, but thankfully it appeared that no one . . . wait, wait, something was missing. Two jars of dried beef to be precise; the wood crate had been opened. A bottle of wine as well. No, no, *two* bottles of wine. A tangle of emotions rose up inside of him, and as he moved the box aside, he thought he heard something, where, he didn't know, but he had definitely heard something. He stood tall and glanced to his left, toward the other passageway. Paranoia wrapped around him like a death shroud. His eyes moistened, his legs went almost numb, his breathing became ragged and quick. Someone was behind him, he was sure of it!

"What do you want?" he said, his voice only a strangled whisper. "Please, answer me, what is it you want?" No answer. "I've got food. Take it, please. Just take it and leave me alone." His voice was stronger now, if none less pleading. Still no answer. He began a slow turn, trying to keep the lantern steady, then wheeled as quickly as he could. An afterimage of bright lantern light cast a pattern onto his eyes, but he could still see that he was alone. He sucked in a huge breath, exhaled, let his body go limp. It didn't take him long to realize that not only was no one behind him; no one had been *here,* either! The floor, save for his footprints, was undisturbed. (He'd erased the footprints left by Maximilien and himself; his way of making sure no one entered while he was gone.) But if the only footprints leading from the feeder tunnel were his—what had happened to his food? Who had taken the top off his crate and stolen the contents? That truth rose up before him like a tall, dark shadow. He stepped toward the other opening, the one that led to the next chamber. And saw them. They led from the small area behind his provisions to the tunnel opening, then continued for as far as his lantern could illuminate—a confusion of tiny footprints, as if a crowd of schoolchildren had been hiding in the furthest recesses of this cave, just waiting for him to leave so they could steal his supplies. Seeing this, his heart seemed to tickle his throat; his pulse raced. But as his mind drew a rationale from all this, he felt a little foolish. Why should he be afraid? These were children's footprints, six, maybe seven of them, but still children. And very young children, too, judging by the size of the footprints, the largest of which was only about half his size. He leaned over and held the lantern out in front of him, illuminating about forty feet of this smaller chamber and the dark entrance to another tunnel at the end.

"Where did you go, children?" he said softly. "Out of nowhere and into here?" His words echoed in a lonely tone, and when they stopped echoing he again heard the sound of water dripping. He turned his head slightly, hoping to trace the source. Yes, he thought, from beyond that tunnel. That's the source. And that's probably where the children are. Bathing maybe, or drinking my wine.

He would've started in that direction, intending to find the children and be rid of them—there were, after all, not a lot of provisions, certainly not enough for seven or eight people—but he didn't. He should get a good night's sleep first, then, in the morning he could get a fresh start. He was hungry anyway.

But as he started back to the main room, he noticed something odd. He squatted and put the lantern on the ground. Only four toes? How could that be? He inspected the remainder of the footprints and sure enough, each was like its neighbor: one big toe and three small ones. Cut off, maybe? Some kind of initiation? A ritual? He looked more closely. No, not cut off. The outside toes all seemed naturally situated. There didn't appear to be large gaps between the outside of the foot and the closest toe. These footprints had been made by children—hopefully children—with only four toes. He stood up, thought about that. Then if that's true, maybe their deformities do not stop with malformed feet. They could be outcasts. Maybe even lepers. That thought brought a vision with it that iced through his veins. Raw, meaty faces stared back at him. Discolored, runny skin hung like old, rotting meat. Features essentially unrecognizable, just the eyes, twinkling like tiny circles of tin in a vat of boiling stew. He silently but fervently hoped that they weren't lepers. Anything but lepers. He certainly wouldn't be able to avoid contact with lepers. And he couldn't take the chance that they weren't contagious, only about half were. Still, there was no reason for panic. Regardless of how many toes they had, or what other deformity they might have, they were still children, and as children, still harmless. Easily managed. Done away with. There was water; he could drown them. Once he'd figured out a way to do that without touching them. There were ways though. Traps, maybe. Something hunters used; huge holes covered over. Yes, yes, that would do nicely. A deep hole—starve them there, then cover them up to hide the stench. Yes.

Sleep, however, was elusive, as he guessed it might be. He was exhausted from his trip, but there were plenty of other factors combining forces to deny him the sleep he craved. There was lantern light for one thing, he'd always slept better when it was dark, at least as dark as he could get it. And there were the mysterious footprints, the reason he kept a lantern burning in the first place. But most of all there was Marat, idling in a heavily lit area of his consciousness, cleaning his nails and occasionally peeling off some of that scaly skin, as he told his men something about how not finding the traitor Brissot would mean that they would take his place on the guillotine. And Marie was there, too, beside Marat, answering his questions. "Some cave in the south of France, I think. Yes, I'm sure of it! Near Montignac." Marat would pull her close and smile.

For hours, all he could manage were snatches of light sleep, only minutes each, before he was yanked awake by Marat, or the footprints, or ghostly lantern light flickering in a rogue breeze.

A few hours before sunrise, he finally did manage to fall into a deep sleep. But unlike truly regenerative sleep, this sleep brought with it the strangest of dreams.

At first he couldn't tell whether he was looking at the floor or the ceiling, but he did know that he was inside a cave, probably this one. But the more he thought about it, the more he questioned whether he could actually see anything. It seemed to him that he sensed things more than actually saw them, like a blind man in highly familiar surroundings. And now he realized—sensed—something else as well. He wasn't alone. There were others here, beside him, in the dark. Seconds later, as if his eyes had adjusted, shapes began to emerge, and now he could verify what he had sensed earlier—that he wasn't alone. In the wash of this weak light, he could see them, like dark, inverted pawns on a chess board. Six or seven of them, he couldn't be sure. As he watched, each of the creatures—six that he could see—seemed to come to life. Their cone-shaped bodies opened in stuttering bursts, as if sleep were leaving them only reluctantly. Within a minute or so, each of them had awakened and detached itself from the ceiling. Now they fluttered in place, their wings moving as if they were treading water. They formed a line and flew first down and then to the right, through a very small opening in the wall that grew quickly larger. Philippe followed, seemingly without a choice. The sensation of speed was breathtaking. Course changes happened instantly, as if he had prior knowledge of this darkness, the closeness of the walls, the ceiling and floor, rock formations. The trip lasted only a minute or so, before they left the velvety darkness with a suddenness that was alarming, popping into the night like a cork leaving the neck of a champagne bottle. Philippe looked to his left, his attention drawn by a dull orange glow in the periphery of his vision—the carriage, it was there, still smoldering. Then he *was* dreaming about the cave, about leaving it in the quickest way possible—through the air. Nothing unusual about that, but what would happen now? Would he fly back to Paris, to Marie's bedroom? "It's a miracle, Marie, a miracle! I can fly! I can fly!" Then maybe he'd scoop her and Jeanette into his arms, and fly them back to this cave. It was a pleasant thought. A pity he was only dreaming, a real pity.

He followed the group as it wound its way over the hillside, the forest canopy very close, just a few feet below. Leaves fluttered with their passing. Suddenly his point of view changed . . . as he guessed was normal for dreams. Now he was leading the pack, and as he looked behind him he could see them, silhouetted against the brightening sky, their wings flapping with a kind of contrapuntal rhythm that was fascinating. But what was it he saw now? A face? An almost human face on one of these flying beasts? He looked more closely. The features were flat, as if pressed against glass, but they were still human features. He looked ahead again, amused by the twists and turns of this strange dream. A farmhouse emerged through a clearing. Cattle dotted the hillside behind it, some sleeping, some grazing. He swooped toward them, landed. One of the grazing cows turned away from its feeding to acknowledge him, looked away. Continued to graze. And his point of view changed yet again. Now he was the third in line and from what he could see, it was true—winged, humanlike creatures had alighted on this hillside. Fascinated, he watched the leader—the one he had inhabited just seconds ago—step toward the disinterested, grazing cow. What now? Philippe thought. Why should they be interested in a cow? The leader, about as tall as the cow, wrapped his small, winged arms around the beast, around its neck. Then, in a profoundly quick movement, the beast drew his head back slightly and hammered it into the cow's neck, leaving half of the beast's face covered. Even from here Philippe could see the round-eyed surprise on the cow's face, as her forelegs buckled at the moment of the attack. Then they all attacked her, and within seconds she lay on the ground, her huge brown eyes fear-rounded and glassy, her head beating up and down frantically as the beasts went about their feeding. More than anything, Philippe wanted to turn his head and have a good look at his "dinner companions," but the wishes of this dream-conjured beast and himself were, somehow, not compatible. Within a minute the cow lay dead, and again the winged, humanlike creatures took to the air.

By now the eastern horizon had brightened considerably. Morning was coming. Well, he thought, at least it's coming in my dream. But what's it really like outside? What time of night is it really?

They used the same tunnel they had used to leave the cave, and before long they were again flying through the huge rooms and passageways. But shortly after they entered the cave, his point of view changed once more. He stopped and looked to his right, at another softly illuminated tunnel opening. By now the others were out of sight. He moved toward that opening, then through it. The light grew stronger and lit yet another opening. He moved toward it, more slowly now, and stepped through.

With a slight sense of startlement, Philippe attempted to analyze this dream. There was, obviously, a kind of circuitous energy to it. His stack of provisions was there, just off to the left. And there he was, lying there on that cot, the lantern just ten feet or so away. But why had he chosen to separate himself from his body during this dream?

Dream?

For what purpose?

No, Philippe. You're not dreaming. Do you hear? Not dreaming! There's someone—something—waiting, watching . . .

Philippe snapped his eyes open, felt his blood ram through his body, threatening to violate his arteries. He rolled onto all fours and pushed himself up. With sleep-glazed eyes, he looked toward the tunnel opening. For a moment, for one silly, frightening moment, he thought he saw something standing there, its head cocked quizzically to the side, its eyes shimmering in the lantern glow. He pushed himself up fast, too fast, felt a little faint because of it, then stumbled toward the opening. His lantern, he needed his lantern! He hurried back for it, but by the time he got to the tunnel opening and raised it high, whatever had been there—if anything—was gone. He scrubbed his hand over his face and hair, smiled slightly. "Strange bedfellows, these caves," he said. "Very strange bedfellows, indeed." After another, somewhat cursory look around, he went back to his cot and pulled on his socks, convinced now that the incident had been subconsciously induced. The circumstances were ripe for that type of thing anyway. Maybe in time, after he'd grown more accustomed to his surroundings, he wouldn't dream this way. He certainly hoped so.

After he'd dined on salted pork and a glass of Bordeaux, he picked up his lantern and moved deeper into the cave, at least a quarter mile deeper than the area where he'd seen the last drawing, the one on the ceiling. Rooms were smaller here, ceilings were closer. It was also more damp and cool than it had been, and he wished he'd worn another layer of clothing. But his mission right now was to find the children. Later, after he'd planned their deaths, he'd come back and complete the job. No sense in hurrying this thing. They'd keep for a day or so.

One thing was clear, though, there was water. What had been only a drip had grown considerably in audibility. Now it almost sounded as if there were a waterfall nearby.

He stopped and held up his lantern. The area in front of him grew steadily more constricted, in another seventy feet or so he'd barely be able to stand without bending over. He looked left, right. Nothing. Just craggy, sometimes slimy walls. Other than turning around and going back, he really had no choice. A few halting steps later, he was able to make out a long, horizontal darkened area, like a hastily chiseled window looking out onto a dark night. He picked up his pace; he was going slightly uphill now, and his feet were sinking a few inches into the sandy ground. The horizontal darkened area grew lighter, and the sound of water grew louder still. Excitement began to build within him, but unfortunately, the walls and ceiling within ten feet of that opening were uncomfortably close, separated now by only eighteen inches or less. He dropped onto his stomach and pushed along the best he could, using one hand to propel himself, like a wounded crab, the other held the lantern.

A short while later, he arrived at the opening and pushed his lantern through. At first guess, he surmised that a number of lanterns would not have been able to outline the furthest boundaries of this room. It was enormous. How large, he couldn't tell, but the enormity was not what instantly struck him. There was a lake here, and of all things, a kind of beach that started at his chest and sloped toward the water at about a fifteen-degree angle. He guessed he was about halfway up one side of the room, looking in at it from this very small opening, like a squirrel looking into a bear's den. He listened. He could plainly hear the waterfall, but he couldn't see it, not yet. He'd have to move further into this huge chamber to do that.

He didn't hesitate. Once he'd moved beyond the opening, he stood and moved toward the still lake at a quick gait, moving his lantern from side to side to take in what he could, his feet again sinking a few inches into the sand of this subterranean beach. Once at the shoreline, he dipped his hand into the water, rippling his mirrorlike image. Freezing cold, as he guessed it would be, but probably potable. He pointed his lantern in both directions, and for no other reason than because he was left-handed, chose the left. How far would he have to go before he reached the natural curvature of this lake? It was obviously huge, but how large could it really be, given the fact that it was beneath the surface of the earth? He found his missing supplies just a few yards further. Both bottles lay open, the wine spilled out, tracing dark lines onto the sand. But the meat was untouched. He picked up the bottles and threw them angrily into the lake. "This is a waste," he yelled, half-hoping the thieves were listening, his words probing the furthest corners of this huge room. "To steal is one thing, but to waste is quite another!" He waited a moment, wondering if he'd get a response, then moved on, counting his steps now. At step fifty-two, the lake began a gentle, yet obvious curve to the right, but only a hundred or so feet later, the beach abruptly ended, and the lake butted up against the walls of the cave. He took a few steps into the dark, frigid water. Slowly yet steadily, the water grew deeper and deeper. He turned around once it reached thigh level, irritated at himself for having stepped into the lake. Any further exploring would obviously have to be done underwater, something he was not at all prepared to do. He started back, mildly disappointed but still energetic, still hopeful. Maybe the other direction would prove more fruitful. And the waterfalls, he guessed now, were in the other direction. He moved on, back to the L made by his footprints, stopped, and raised his lantern high overhead, hoping to gauge the height of the ceiling. His skin tingled. At least a hundred feet above him and encompassing most of the ceiling that he could see, was yet another drawing. And this one, again depicting one of the humanlike beasts at the neck of what had to be a cow, was easily sixty feet long and half as wide. Unlike the drawings in the other rooms, this drawing had been accomplished over the lake. He scampered up the sandy hillside, all the while holding his lantern high, hoping to get a closer look at that huge drawing. Fear and fascination rose simultaneously; his breath came in quick, ragged spurts. But what was it he saw there now? Dark spots within the drawing, at each point of the drawing? He stopped, very close now to where he had entered this room, and stood, raising his lantern as high as he possibly could. As he stared, one of those dark spots detached itself. With mesmerizing grace, the others quickly followed. Philippe could only watch, and as he watched, the creatures formed a line and flew directly toward him, then alighted and quietly encircled him. Philippe did a quick turn, trying frantically to see each of the beings at the same time, but he couldn't. There was always at least one of them out of view, behind him, on the other side of the circle. These were definitely the same beasts he had seen in his dream. They had the same flat, dark faces, the winged yet humanlike torsos. They were missing genitalia. Their wings rose and fell slowly, like giant birds of prey, and not a one of them made a sound. And they were going to kill him, that much was obvious. He turned faster now, like a frightened child, cursing the creatures while they slowly converged on him. He was panicking. God, he didn't want to do that, but life was not something he'd give up easily. He swung the lantern in a huge circle, not for a second believing he'd actually succeed in defending himself. But amazingly they stepped right into the swinging lantern, first one then another, then another. The swinging light created a strobe effect that detailed the creatures in varying stages of advance or withdrawal, claws raised, wings flared. But just as he started feeling a bit more secure, the lantern exploded in flame, spraying one of the creatures with burning lantern fuel. It backed away as if punched, and swatted at the flame like a child batting at a huge spider, the air alive with its ululant, bleating cry. Within seconds the creature just fell to the ground and lay perfectly still, the very picture of death. Inspired by this minor victory, the scene lit only by the burning fuel on the fallen creature's chest, Philippe continued to swing the broken lantern. In the lambent glow he could see the remaining beasts advancing then retreating, advancing then retreating. But he also realized that they would be on him as soon as the flame went out. And he couldn't run from them in the dark. Where would he go? But there were a series of minor victories then, as the flame went into its death throes. These creatures seemed weak, easily conquered, and for a moment Philippe actually considered victory to be within his grasp. But the flame went out, and in total darkness now, Philippe felt his knees go weak. He'd killed three or four, maybe even five, but others took their place; he saw them emerge from the darkness even as the others fell. They surrounded him now, so close, so very close. Resignation swept through him, and he dropped the lantern to the ground. Now, save for the rather peaceful sound of the falls, there was only silence, a silence broken within seconds by a low, guttural sound from behind him. Suddenly another grunt, and another and another, until Philippe had to cover his ears to stifle the clamorous din. But even with his ears covered, he could hear them. A tribal thing, he thought remotely. They probably won't attack until they've stopped. And they know now, they know they've got me. They probably knew all along. And that was true, all true. They did know they had him, and they didn't attack until they'd stopped their tribal-like grunting. As they converged on him, knocking him to the ground and draining him of his blood, he thought of the cow in his dream, and the look of fear and surprise on her face. If he'd been able to notice, he would have detected the earthy, blood-tinged odor that fogged about the beasts. He would have noticed the lubricated quality of their skin, or how very long and curved their nails were. Or that they did, in fact, only have four toes on each foot. But he did recognize what he thought to be human words as the creatures tore into him; *blood* was one, *water* was another, a word he thought preceded the word *drown*.

But the pain of his arteries collapsing gave birth to a series of screams that easily drowned out the noises of the creatures; the grunts of satisfaction; the occasional human word; laughter. Such a pain, fiery, lancing, as if his very marrow were being cored. A pain so intense he didn't feel himself being lifted, didn't feel his body being propelled through the air, didn't feel it smack onto the surface of the lake and then begin to sink. But in their haste to be rid of him, the creatures hadn't realized the pain-lessening properties of the cool water as it encircled him, seeking out his fresh wounds, caressing, mothering. And this sense of falling slowly into darkness was certainly preferable, oh, yes, very much so . . . as peaceful and painless a death as he could ever have hoped for . . . then why, if he was ready to die, was his brain offering him yet another dream?

There were, in this dream, what seemed like hundreds of these hideous creatures. Although similar to what had encircled him only seconds earlier, these creatures were far more human-looking. They had wings, yes, there were wings, but not as complete, perhaps not even functional. And their bodies and faces were not as dark, more closely resembling the complexions of Sicilians, swarthy but still with a pinkish cast. And they were going about what appeared to be a normal business day; there were bazaars and the attendant bartering, and the sun was high in the sky. They were existing as normally as any group of people had ever existed. There was prosperity and happiness. Normalcy. But even as he watched, the scene changed. Tension filled the air, the sun clouded over, the people panicked. They ran where they could, into doorways, under produce carts, spilling what Philippe thought to be fruits and vegetables in their haste. Fear was rampant, the sounds of it rifled through the air. One of the creatures tried to leap into the air and fly, flapping its perfunctory wings mightily, only to fall onto its hands and knees, where it curled into as tight a ball as it could. And while he watched, one of the beasts, a woman, he thought sure—this one had breasts—the sky grew steadily darker, until she slowly faded to his eyes and was gone. Then there was only darkness and the bleating of the beasts.

And the water was so cold and soothing, the music so beautiful, the light so very intense . . .

Philippe opened his eyes and panic stabbed at him. He was, after all, underwater. He felt his chest heave, a natural response, but nothing happened, the sensation of having his lungs fill with water did not happen. Although his chest moved up and down, nothing at all filled his lungs. Slowly panic retreated, and Philippe, who had been lying on the bottom of the deep, dark lake, stood. He remembered how cold the lake had been, but he didn't feel that now. He remembered the beasts tearing at his clothing, biting through his skin, sucking out his blood, but a quick inspection revealed no wounds remained. And now he realized yet another oddity. He could see. Here, beneath this lake, without a lantern to aid him to pierce the murky depths, he could see his skin. And it was milk white, just the opposite of his nails. But there were definitely no wounds. And now, he decided, he had never felt so alive in his whole life. He smiled. I'm alive after all, he thought. Somehow I've survived the attack, somehow I'm able to stay submerged without drowning.

But how? Something wasn't right. As a matter of fact, something was very, very wrong.

Paradoxically, rational thought brought with it another surge of alarm. Philippe swam frantically toward the surface, arriving there in a heartbeat, and when he had pushed through the surface, he again attempted to suck in a breath of air, expanding his lungs as much as he could.

But again he felt nothing. Whereas seconds earlier water had refused to pour into his lungs, now oxygen did the same. He swam to shore, pulled himself out, and sat on the beach in the dark. Maybe I'm having another dream, he thought. Maybe I only imagined the attack. Dreamed it. I could've fallen asleep by this lake. But then he remembered the pain, and dreams were not usually accompanied by actual physical pain. He moved his hand along his arm. It felt real enough, although it also seemed that he could see each vein, each capillary. The water. Sure, the water did that. It turned my nails black, it could do this to my skin, too. And I'm hungry. He thought about that. As hungry as I've ever been! He saw the jar of dried beef to his right, snapped it up. Once he'd pried off the lid, he dug the meat out with his fingers, shoved it into his mouth, and swallowed noisily. At first he realized a modicum of satisfaction as the food slid into his belly, so he looked back into the jar, intending to finish off the meat. But what was this? Maybe he'd eaten too fast. His stomach was rumbling, the food was coming back up. He felt it rise into his throat, press at his tongue. And he could only watch as it vaulted from his mouth and into the still water, sending out a tiny circle of ripples. He threw the jar away. "It's ruined," he said. "Tainted. I've got to go back to my supplies, and get some food, good food. Something to drink, too. Yes, something to drink. I'm so thirsty, so awfully thirsty."

He got up then and walked back through the opening, and whereas the earlier trip to the lake had taken at least a couple of hours, he found that now he was able to move with almost blinding speed. Almost as if he could will himself from one spot to another.

Within a few minutes he was back at the main room, pawing through his supplies, snapping off jar lids, decorking bottles of wine. But as he looked at each, as he had the food or drink poised, ready to eat or drink, he again felt his stomach roll. He stood, just staring at the supplies, then stumbled his way to the tunnel that led to the surface.

Philippe arrived there at twilight, the western horizon tinged by dying pastels of red and blue and orange. He stood and raised his hand against it. God, how it burned into his eyes, how it seemed to actually fuse the cells of his skin! He slipped silently back into the tunnel, intending to wait until the sky had become at least deep purple before he would again emerge. But while he waited, he discovered that his thirst was overpowering. But what was he thirsting for? The wine had seemed repugnant. Water the same.

Cow's blood, Philippe?

No, not blood.

Yes, Philippe, blood. Red and rich; flowing from another into your veins. To give you life. To nourish and provide.

No, dammit, no! You're wrong!

But, Philippe, you've drunk it before. Remember? The blood of the deflowered virgins. The blood you drank immediately after that deflowering. You and Marat. Remember, Philippe?

Now there was a thought. Perhaps a sip. A mouthful, maybe. But a cow? No, not a cow, no. A human. Another virgin!

Be reasonable, Philippe. You're hungry now. Thirsty now. Think, Philippe, think. Where would you find a virgin? No, you have a more immediate thirst. You need something now!

He snapped his head to the right. Of course, of course. In the blink of an eye he was there, on his knees, digging out the earth with blinding speed, oblivious to the fading light and its effects, which thankfully were minimal now. He'd buried Maximilien only a foot or so beneath the surface, so it didn't take long, not at all. But after he had dug up his dead valet, he did not immediately attack the decaying corpse. Instead, he hesitated. Was this a moment to be treasured? It had that feel. There was an almost religious ambiance . . . no, not religious. Certainly not that. God had nothing to do with this. But then

81

worship was not confined to the Almighty. He smiled. And this blood would not be sipped from a silver chalice. But dear God, what had he become? What manner of beast felt intense pain in even the slightest light, or had such a craving for blood? As if in answer, he remembered a word one of the beasts had used while they fed. *Lamia.* He'd heard that word before. It was Greek, he knew that much. Lamia—vampire. It meant . . . vampire.

He had become a vampire. Like those creatures. They had passed the virus to him, that was how he had survived the lake, how he could move so swiftly, why sunlight drained him so. He was a vampire. One of the undead. Immortal. Godless. Suddenly he felt an overpowering urge to make his new status known to any creature within earshot, which, considering his enriched physical abilities, was a circumference of many miles, even as far as Montignac. And the scream of new life that traveled there from so far-off was heard by more than a few, by housewives and shopkeepers, and those simply walking the streets. Not all of them stopped, shuddering at the sound of it, but most did, and most also attempted to secure themselves more tightly from it, to have it removed from their lives. And when it was over, Philippe sank to his knees and drank from his dead valet with a ferocity he had never known. And that first drop of blood, how could he define it? It was the milk of his mother, yes, the milk of his mother. From that other life, from so long ago. And wasn't it vastly interesting that he could now remember that first taste of mother's milk, could actually see himself at her breast?

When he was done he could only watch, fascinated, as the dead blood was reborn within him, turning his white skin a newborn pink, and removing the blackness from his nails, leaving them as pink as his skin. He held his hands to his face, turned them over, then back again. They were human hands again, but not human. The color was right, but the texture was wrong. Well, so be it, if someone

82

actually touched him, they would suspect, but otherwise
. . .

His valet's body, the blood now totally removed, seemed to have been crushed, deflated. Only out of some mortal habit did Philippe take the remains into the cave, to the beach, where he buried it. And some human thing, humor, he thought, prompted him to write a short note to his old friend and put it into his pocket. When that was done, he went back to the surface and gazed into the night, opening before him like the day to a mortal. He wondered as to his dominion over it, and at the same time felt only slight remorse that he would never see the sun again. But he realized full well that if he did, he would die a most hideous and painful death.

And then another thought pushed aside all others. He remembered the trip here and how he had stopped along the way. And most of all, he remembered the girl, Charlotte. Charlotte Corday.

8

July 13, 1793
Paris, France

From her bed, Charlotte Corday gazed at the eastern sky. Vague pastels customarily ruled early morning, but as her sleep-muddied vision cleared, she noticed that today's colors were not as weak or as ill-defined as in mornings past. The purples and oranges and yellows were hard and crisp, not pastels at all; colors that forced themselves onto the land like the mindless and indelicate strokes of a mad artist. She imagined a giant, glazed-eyed entity slashing paint onto his equally huge canvas, attempting, by the application of vivacious and luxurious color, to alter the mood of anyone up at this early hour. An alteration, Charlotte noted, that might lead to fleshy pursuits. A smile played along her mouth, and she ran a comb through her shoulder-length chestnut hair. Obviously God had created that brilliant and undeniable sky as a sign that her decision had been a correct one. Which is not to say, that if that sky had been bland and inconsequential, she would not have gone on with her plan. She would have. But the deliberateness and sense of purpose validated by this sky would have been lessened. Today, she concluded as she got out of bed, would be a day of great accomplishment. Today her life would have meaning.

It was 6:00 A.M. precisely, an hour she knew well. She decided to forego breakfast and started toward the nearby Palais Royal, an area of gardens and stores, where most of fashionable Paris did their shopping. On the way she again noticed the paranoia that had, in recent days, fluttered about her with vulterine persistence. She tried to dismiss the feeling, but she couldn't—she *was* on a murderous mission, after all. The night before, at dinner, the feeling had been as powerful as this morning's heavenly display. She had—and she smiled now at the very idea—even felt the tiny hairs on the back of her neck stiffen like tiny guards, an event that brought her to her feet so quickly the other diners stopped what they were doing and simply stared. After a cursory look around, she managed a weak smile of apology and sat down again, barely noticing a shadow in the doorway to her right fade and disappear. But what is paranoia, she told herself now, except shadow and innuendo and footsteps that only you can hear, all brought on by the idea of getting caught. And I know I'll be caught. I *want* to get caught. (Martyrdom was part of her plan.) Forcibly she pushed thoughts of the previous night's dinner aside and continued on.

After she arrived at the Palais Royal, she paced up and down the thoroughfare as she waited for businesses to open. Of particular interest to her was a store that specialized in the sale of cutlery, a store customarily shuttered during the night, as were most stores in the Palais Royal. A half hour or so after she arrived, the shutters to that store were removed, and the owner, a squat, almost hairless man, greeted her from behind a shy grin. "Good morning, madame," he said cheerfully. Not entirely conscious of it, he let his gaze drift over her generous curves.

Charlotte noticed, but remained silent. Under the circumstances, a display of modesty seemed somewhat ludicrous. She simply nodded, followed him inside, and watched as he hurried behind his counter.

"As you can plainly see," he said with a sweeping gesture, "I have many sizes and styles. Anything for madame's household." But as he lay out a set of five ebony-handled blades, Charlotte coolly pointed at the one with the longest blade, almost six inches in length. "Show me that one," she said.

"Yes, a good choice," the shopkeeper said. He raised the knife and held it out like a newborn for her inspection. The rising sun winked through the front window and caressed the blade, as he cunningly shifted it to accommodate the light.

Charlotte felt the hint of a smile cross her lips, as she took it from him and inspected the sharpened edge with her fingertips. "Yes, thank you," she said. "This will do nicely. And let me have that green sheath there to carry it."

"Of course, a wise choice, madame. It, uh, matches your hat."

And that it did, exactly. Charlotte smiled coyly, took the knife and sheath, and consummated their marriage with a deft and precise stroke.

Her interest in knives didn't at all alarm the shopkeeper, quite the contrary, and after she paid him and left, he gleefully counted his money and thought not of the knife, but of the buyer's unique charms.

Once outside, Charlotte bought a newspaper and sat down on a bench to read about the events of the previous day. The executioner had been kept busy of late, a fact that always fueled her anger. At a little before nine, she rose and walked quickly to a hack stand on the Place des Victoires, and confronted the first coachman in line. He was a tall man with a blemished face and arthritic hands, which made her wonder how he could possibly control his horses. "Take me to the home of Jean Paul Marat," she told him. Although she really had no idea where Marat lived, she'd heard that most Parisians did, cab drivers especially. But as she started to climb inside the hack, the driver shrugged and told her that although he certainly knew of Monsieur Marat, he had no idea where he lived.

Given to occasional fits of impatience, Charlotte

stepped down and cursed under her breath. "Come down here," she said. The driver did as he was told, and although he was close to six feet tall, they stood chin to chin. "Ask one of the other coachman," she ordered. The driver hesitated. "Go on. Ask!" she snapped.

There were three more coaches lining the thoroughfare. The driver started with the closest, while Charlotte watched. The first two drivers were as ignorant as her own, but the last driver, after much head scratching, came up with an address: 30 *rue des Cordeliers*. Her driver, embarrassed by his ignorance, sped there as fast as his horses could take him. Charlotte, jostled about as the hack rolled over cobblestone streets, didn't notice the bumpy ride. She had more important things on her mind.

Marat's home was very large for the time, eight rooms total with three carved marble fireplaces. It was set back from a courtyard, reached only after a short walk down a cobblestone alleyway. But although the house was large, it was also poorly ventilated, and during summer months trapped heat and moisture made living in such a house like living inside a well. A myriad of smells dominated: grease and human sweat primarily, with underlying hints of printer's ink and molding newspapers, which were carelessly thrown about Marat's antechambers.

Charlotte arrived there shortly before ten, only to discover that Marat was not receiving visitors, an obstacle that hadn't at all been part of her imaginings. The completion of the act, in her mind, had been a quick and exhilarating experience. She, a woman of beauty and breeding, would be allowed in immediately. There were matters to discuss, matters concerning the Revolution, a topic near and dear to Marat's heart. But Simmone Ervard, Marat's common law wife—more out of jealousy than a regard for her husband's privacy—slammed the door in her face. Charlotte knocked again, waited, tried again, and then left, wondering as she walked back to the cab, if wife and husband wouldn't enjoy spending eternity together, starting today. She went back to the *Hotel de la*

Providence and wrote Marat a note. "I'm from Caen. Your love for country should make you curious as to the plots afoot there." She gave this note to a postman, who told her it would take about an hour to deliver, and awaited Marat's reply. By six in the evening, she realized none was forthcoming. "Did you receive my letter?" she wrote back. "Might I hope for a moment's interview with you if you received it?" But she didn't give this note to the postman; she hoped to give it to one of the women of the household. Intrigued, Marat would grant her an interview, all the time she would need to complete her plan.

She arrived at Marat's home at sunset, and asked the cab to wait. But on the way to his front door, which seemed more impregnable than it had just a few hours earlier, she felt another moment of clawing paranoia. The skin at her temples seemed to stretch in response; her eyes glistened. She glanced over Marat's roof, at a dying sky, at what were indeed only weak pastels. *Be done with it,* she told herself, hoping to strengthen her resolve. *Kill the man and be done with it!* As she watched, the pastels of twilight began to fade as well. He was there again, she thought, that huge, insane artist. But now he had run out of color, real color. Soon his canvas would be awash with only dark purple and a deep, unsettling black gray. She smiled again. Not only was she paranoid—again for a very simple and good reason—but that paranoia was being strengthened by the onset of night.

Lost in her thoughts, she didn't see the door open. Jeannette Marechale, one of the ladies of Marat's household, glared at her, obviously annoyed. But as she was about to voice that annoyance, two more visitors pushed by Charlotte, stopped just long enough to be recognized, and then went inside. It was all the distraction Charlotte needed. She stepped into the dark hallway, just to the right of Jeannette Marechale, and waited while she talked with the two men. Seconds later, one of the men went into Marat's bath, while the other stayed behind. Like the clerk at the Palais Royal, he, too, was unable to keep from at least glancing at her every now and again. By now, however, Charlotte had become preoccupied. The walls in this simple hallway were closing in on her. At any second, the breath would leave her body, and she would die. Her heart drummed in her chest—surely they could hear, surely they suspected! It was all she could do to keep from running back into the courtyard, from forgetting what was probably an insane plan, anyway. But Charlotte, like her mother, had tremendous reserves of will-power. Her mission was clear. There was no turning back now. She would kill the beast. She would run him through with her knife, and quiet his traitorous heart. She took a deep breath, exhaled ever so slowly, repeated the procedure. But not until the third breath did the walls begin to recede. And slowly, her corridor to reality began to widen. Now what had been only the mindless babble of far-off birds, became the somewhat irritated voices of three women, Simmone and the remaining members of Marat's household.

"You'll have to leave, immediately. Do you understand?"

It was one of the other women, a tall woman with a hawklike nose.

No response.

"She's deaf, too!" said the hawk-nosed woman.

Charlotte squeezed her eyes shut, opened them quickly.

"I said—"

"You received my letter of this morning, didn't you?" Charlotte blurted.

All three women were startled by the sudden enormity of Charlotte's presence. "He's received many letters today," Jeannette Marechale answered. "It would be impossible to know if he's read yours."

"But there are urgent matters to discuss. I must see him!" Charlotte added with a huff.

Jeannette assumed a rigid posture, but she was a shorter woman than Charlotte and not at all pretty. She looked a little foolish and she knew it. "It's impossible. He's ill and seeing no one. Even if he could, he's in his bathtub."

Charlotte glanced toward the door, open a few inches, and saw the young man leave who had entered earlier. He stepped past her, smiled what she thought a strange smile, and left with the other man.

At about the same time, Marat called to his wife from the bathroom. He'd heard the argument in the hallway.

"It's the Corday woman," she told him. "We're trying to get rid of her."

"Corday?"

"Yes, Charlotte Corday."

Marat fumbled through his letters, let them scatter to the floor. Finally he found Charlotte's. He read it quickly, then, "Let her in, Simmone."

Simmone was nonplussed. He was sick. In his bath, too. "Is that wise?" she asked.

"And why not?" Marat answered. "Just cover me. Put my robe around my shoulders."

Filled by an inexpressible sense of impending doom, Simmone could only look into the hall, and then do as Marat had asked.

Charlotte hesitated, then pushed open the door, and went in. She was astounded by the scene that greeted her. The only light in the bath was a shaft of weak twilight entering through a window directly behind Marat's bathtub, dust motes dancing in the beam. She had a better view of him than he had of her. In this light, various shades of gray dominated, even the green fan that Charlotte worked in front of her face as she stepped toward him had a gray green tint. Marat's bathtub was itself a bit odd. To Charlotte it appeared more like a large, stub-nosed, high-backed shoe than a bathtub. A vinegar-soaked bandana had been wrapped around his forehead, and as he had requested, his bathrobe had been slung over his shoulders. An ink bottle, quill, and paper lay on a long board placed across the bathtub. Two crossed pistols hung on the wall to his left, and beneath them, written on a large cardboard poster, were the words LA MORT, the reading of which caused Charlotte's breath to quicken.

Instantly astounded by her beauty, Marat was reminded of his own younger, healthier days, when he could have had any woman he desired. But those days were long past, irretrievable. Firmly in the grasp of ill health and generally loathsome to look upon, Marat knew passion only in fantasy. He looked upon Charlotte with both desire and hate, not knowing, in those moments before his death, what fate this tall, winsome creature had planned for him.

"Please, be seated," he said politely, motioning to a stool beside his bathtub. "Now, what can I do for you?"

The answer left her mouth like finely plucked notes of a violin. "I come from Caen, Monsieur Marat. I have some interesting information to give you concerning the uprising there."

Marat seized his quill pen and frantically dipped it into ink.

"Names, give me names," he said excitedly.

Charlotte listed them effortlessly, as if she'd said them a thousand times. "Gaudet, Buzot, Barbaroux."

Smiling madly, Marat dipped his quill with each name and wrote them down quickly and boldly. When he was done, he said, "Excellent! In a few days' time, I shall have them all guillotined in Paris."

In his reverie, Marat didn't see Charlotte rise and step toward him; he didn't see her hand reach toward her breast, and then withdraw the knife from the green sheath she had purchased. And as he dipped his quill pen once more, she lifted the knife high overhead. He raised his head slowly and understood then what awaited him. She paused only briefly, and as he gazed at her in horror, Charlotte swung the knife downward, easily piercing Marat's frail chest. His aorta was severed instantly, bringing death to him scant seconds after he had weakly yelled for help. Charlotte, still cool, still unflappable, and now invigorated by the completion of what she thought her duty, looked down at Marat, dead in his tub. His arm was draped over the side, his blood draining into the bathwater, turning it a diluted shade of red that reminded Charlotte of winter sunrises. Wasn't it ironic that in death his eyes were still open. As far as she was concerned, he was blind alive or dead.

Charlotte smiled, and as she did, she felt a modicum of shame. An expression of joy at anyone's death—even Jean Paul Marat's—was not something she believed she was capable of. And although visions of Marat's death had fostered a certain sense of pride, she certainly had never smiled during those visions. Then why should she smile now, when the act had finally been completed? Contemplating that, she felt the blood push through her arteries at a furious pace, at either side of her groin, and high in both arms. At the same time, she felt a cold and sticky sweat on her body. I enjoyed this, she said to herself. Dear God, I enjoyed this! She looked at Marat as if he were capable of confirming her suspicions, as if he would at any second push himself out of the tub, his wound gushing blood, his eyes fish like, flat and expressionless. "Yes, Charlotte," he would say with ridiculous calm, "I saw it in your eyes as you stuck me, just as steel pierced flesh. At the very moment when death was no longer dismissable. What was it I saw? I saw indescribable joy. Great, blanketing pleasure. Yes, Charlotte, I'm afraid it's true. You enjoy killing just as much as anyone, just as much as the executioner enjoys it. Just as much as I enjoy it." Then he would clasp his hand over his wound, as if he'd just discovered it, and for a few seconds watch the blood slide between his fingers, but slowly, like sap, because his heart had stopped working. Then he would look back at her and continue just as calmly, just as patiently. "Don't you see, Charlotte? It's something passed on from generation to generation, like . . . like blue eyes or . . . or . . ." His face would begin to twitch, and his eyes would have lost their fishlike glaze. They would be enflamed. "Maybe the need to . . . to rut . . . to procreate . . . to fuck!" Then, smiling, he would ease himself back into the tub and regain his previous posture, that of a corpse.

No, Charlotte thought, I can't accept that. I won't leave this life knowing that I actually enjoyed taking the life of another human being. That my homicidal tendencies were only masked by my politics. I need time, she thought almost frantically. I need time to learn more about myself, to learn what I'm capable of before I die. She glanced toward the closed door. They'll be here soon, and then they'll take me away. It'll only take them a day or two, then it's off to the guillotine for the eldest of the Corday daughters, with little or no trial. With little or no time to make peace with the Almighty. And she most desperately wanted to do that now, especially now, as she realized pleasure at the death of another. And it was that prospect—of not being able to discover her motives—that caused her the most pain. She was not afraid of dying, she had long since accepted that she would do that, but to die not knowing, was not something she had foreseen.

She heard footsteps in the hallway, then a voice. "Jean Paul? Are you all right, Jean Paul?"

Marat's wife.

Charlotte wouldn't give herself up as planned, she wouldn't do that now. She couldn't do that now. She would leave quickly, maybe say something to Marat as she left, hopefully allowing her enough time to be out of sight before the body was discovered. She needed time. Lots of time.

But as she turned to go, she saw movement out of the corner of her eye, behind her and in the shadows. She turned and watched as a man took a step toward her. She was not entirely surprised to see him, more fascinated than anything, actually. He had been there in the early morning, and in the twilight. He'd had dinner with her the previous night, and he had most definitely shared the hallway with her. He was very tall and thin, and even in this meager light he looked amazingly pale. His hair was long and stringy, and his lips seemed far more red than they should have been. His eyes were barely visible, just dark circles above an aqualine nose, and his clothing, little more than rags, contrasted sharply with the expensive fabrics worn by Charlotte. But, Charlotte saw as he stepped toward her, he did not move with the humble gait of a peasant. His movements were uncannily graceful, like water in a summer stream. He held his head high, and his strangely red lips betrayed a faint amusement. He stopped short of Marat's bathtub, and in a voice as melodic as her own, said, "I mistook your intentions, Charlotte, and now it has cost me a quick and just revenge. I wanted his head, you see. I wanted to wrap these hands around his neck, and simply take his head from him. But unfortunately the dead don't know pain. What shall I do about that, Charlotte. What shall I do?"

"Take his head? But why, monsieur? Surely his death would suffice. Surely you needn't dismember the body as well."

He smiled like someone with a secret. At the same time, there came a rap at the door. He raised his eyes to it, then looked back at Charlotte. "You are extraordinary," he said. "And I've a long journey to make. Someone such as you might make that journey more enjoyable."

"Journey?"

He shrugged. "Yes, of sorts."

She smiled nervously. Never had the word journey taken on so many different meanings. She gestured loosely toward the door. "It appears that the only journey I'll be making is to the guillotine."

He laughed out loud, but it was lighthearted. "The guillotine? No, I think we should be able to keep you away from the guillotine."

He held out his hand, and she took it without hesitation. "Come with me, dear Charlotte. Assist me with my revenge. Assist me, because it is you who has denied it."

There was a flurry of movement in the hallway, feet

moving quickly over tattered carpets, mumbling, then another rap on the door, this time a demanding rap.

"Your name?" Charlotte said. "If we are to travel together, I must know your name."

"Philippe."

"It's a good name, Philippe. Where have I heard it before?"

"It was my father's."

"Where will we go, Philippe?"

"Away from here."

"And then?"

"Further away from here."

"Will you talk to me about what I have done? Will you help me determine who I really am?"

He cocked his head. "Who you are, mademoiselle? Is that important to you?"

"Very much."

"Then before we journey, we will make that determination."

There seemed to be a wellspring of truth in that answer. It seemed to her that he, somehow, would provide a trial of sorts. That the determination of her true nature was actually something that intrigued him.

Just then the door burst open, and in marched the women of the household. Philippe held up his hand and they stopped. "Ladies, what is the reason for this?" he said.

By now Simmone Ervard had discovered that her husband was dead. She knelt beside the tub, her hands over her mouth, her eyes wide with horror, while the other women could only stand by, speechless.

Philippe looked at her a moment and said, "As you can see, madame, your husband is taking a bath."

Simmone Ervard stood abruptly, glared at Brissot, and pointed rigidly at her husband. "A bath? He's dead, he's not taking a bath! And just who do you . . ." She turned slowly toward the tub again, and the look on her face, what had started as puzzlement, soon turned to glee.

"There, didn't I tell you?" said Philippe in hushed tones. "And we're disturbing him."

Simmone seemed to think a moment, then she mumbled something about being an old fool, apologized to her dead husband, herded the other women together, and followed them into the hall, shutting the door behind her.

Alone with Brissot again, Charlotte said, "How did you do that?"

He looked at her a moment, she at him, and then, as if a rope had been attached to her head, she turned toward Marat, who, she saw, was humming a tune and scrubbing his chest. Brissot continued while she watched Marat. "The mind, Charlotte, is a breeding place. What grows there needs proper nourishment. The right fertilizer, shall we say. Perhaps, in time, we can discuss what you have seen in further detail."

Marat continued with his bath as if he were alone, running the washcloth under his arms, then along his forehead.

Charlotte just stared at what she knew couldn't be true, and said flatly, "Yes, I would like that, Philippe." Then she looked back at Brissot, into his glacier-cold eyes.

"As for now, though," he said, "I think the time has come to take flight."

She couldn't help it, she looked at Marat one more time. He was dead again, as she guessed he would be. Then they left.

On the way out, Simmone Ervard smiled, bowed slightly, and wished them a pleasant journey. Then, as they closed the front door behind them, she peeked in on her husband, smiled like a mother looking in at a child, closed the door to the bathroom, and instructed the other women that her husband was not to be disturbed.

Brissot sat across from Charlotte in the carriage, and for many miles nothing at all was said. He didn't tell her where they were going, nor did she care. Anywhere faraway from Marat's house was fine with her. They left Paris within a half hour, passing by woodlands and moon-lit fields of grain, glimpsed through heavily draped windows. The ride was more comfortable now, dirt roads having replaced cobblestones, fresh air having replaced the odors of garbage and human waste. The only sounds were the clop clop of the horses' hooves on the dirt road, occasionally punctuated by a snort from one or the other. They travelled at a leisurely pace, as if they really had no place to go, which, after a while, Charlotte thought just might be the case.

Brissot never took his eyes off of her, not once that she could see. Even when she pulled back the window curtains, he still looked at her. But she didn't become at all unsettled by this prolonged study. She did, in fact, find comfort in it. And as they rolled along the dirt road, she occasionally remembered her childhood, years spent in essentially the same surroundings that she was now travelling through. She had been so devout, raised as a Christian, God-fearing and loving. Not a meal went by that she didn't say grace with her family, and not a night began that she didn't say her prayers. Even Marat's murder had been committed with one thought in mind—Marat's life was not worth hundreds, maybe thousands of others, even though she had no real assurance that taking his life would spare even one life.

And it was during this nostalgic trip that Charlotte realized something. She knew this man. She had definitely seen him before. But where? When? She stared at him, hoping the answer would magically come to her, but it didn't. All she could remember about him was that they had talked before. About . . . the revolution. Yes, about the revolution! Of course, of course, Philippe Brissot. The man who had stopped at their house the week before, who had very possibly seen the murderous intent in her eyes.

He looked at her then, smiled as if he knew what she was thinking. And as he spoke, Charlotte was sure that he did.

"My death, dear Charlotte, was painless. There were no witnesses, other than my murderers. But my resurrection, oh, my resurrection was glorious!"

He looked at her for a second longer, smiling, then looked away. But he wasn't done talking.

In her mind, Charlotte saw Philippe swimming. No, not swimming actually, he was rising toward the surface of the water. And it took such a long, long time—how could he breathe? She watched all this from just a few feet away, while he swam to shore, while he looked upwards, waiting it seemed. Which he didn't do for long, for soon he was surrounded by the most hideous, winged creatures, human-looking yet not human, animal-looking yet not animal. Then they converged on him, but he didn't seem bothered by their obvious murderous intent, and when they did attack him, he effortlessly shrugged them off, killing each one. And when he was done, they lay about him lifeless and still—their heads gone.

That scene faded then and was replaced by the buildings and cobblestone roads of Paris. Her viewpoint was from the driver's seat of the carriage as it sped along, sweat glistening on the horses' backs in the moonlight. Moments later the carriage stopped, and she watched as Philippe exited, went up the steps to the front door of a house, knocked, and then went in after the door was opened. Again the scene changed. She was standing behind Philippe, while he talked with what she thought to be a servant.

"Yesterday, I'm afraid," said the servant, obviously distraught. "They were looking for you, monsieur. They questioned mademoiselle, but she refused to answer, so they took her away."

"To the guillotine?"

"Yes, to the guillotine."

"And Jeanette? How is she?"

"Spared, thank God. She's in her room. Would you . . . ?"

"No, not now. At my own discretion."

"As you wish, monsieur. As you wish."

Philippe's eyes bored into Charlotte's. "He killed her, you see. Had her guillotined. Which was why I wanted his head. But you, dear Charlotte, you provided me with the most entertaining theater. And I do wish to return the favor."

9

The Present
Rochester, New York

For Michel Marat, who went by Mike now, the day started early and ended late. A storm born of heat and humidity, typical Rochester fare, soaked the town during the afternoon, then wandered off, leaving everything freshly scrubbed.

Mike folded his blue, London Fog raincoat over a chair, and for the first time today, entertained thoughts of his wife, Holly. Fragments of their short marriage littered the apartment; keepsakes, mementos, wedding photographs. The Rolex watch she'd given him for Christmas five years earlier—a month before her death—had been relegated to a dresser drawer, never to see the light of day, and therefore, decay. By keeping it new and unsullied, he reasoned, maybe he could also keep her memory the same. Lots of people had suggested, some less subtly than others, that maybe it was time to forget her, time to get on with his life, but he ignored them all. If he actually heeded their suggestions, the following would happen; when he got to the afterlife, he wouldn't recognize her, nor she him. That's what he believed, what he put great trust in. There was, he had long ago decided, a distinct possibility that the spirit of the dearly departed would weaken if that person was not properly remembered, if they were not occasionally thought of in human form. He had given that idea a lot of thought, and over time it had become cocooned in granite. He had explained it to only one person, Al Lopez, a friend and cop connection. (Mike was a reporter for the *Democrat and Chronicle*.) Or rather, he had tried to. "The only thing that buoys the spirit, Al, is hard and precise thought," he had said. "A spirit doesn't have a human form to sustain it, so it needs, well, a kind of prayer, I guess. A foundation."

"Like a house?" Al had asked. That made more sense than any other simile he could summon.

"Yeah, Al, just like a house."

"And that's why you're never going to forget her? Because you're afraid you won't see her on the other side if you do?"

Al had gamely attempted to hide his amusement, but Al never could hide his real feelings about anything. The phrase, "the other side" left his lips slightly upturned. He was being patronizing, and Mike knew it. Mike ended that conversation by making reference to a weak bladder, which was more or less true. When he got back to the table, he asked Al if a relief pitcher for the Red Wings had been called up to the Orioles yet. Al just looked at him for a moment, and the conversation drifted to the major leagues. Al was a good connection, and over the years he had also become a good friend. But as far as the supernatural was concerned, his mind was about as receptive as a spaghetti strainer.

Mike brushed Al from his thoughts and fried up a plate of ham and eggs. Every now and then he'd burn a burger over his tiny hibachi, but most nights he ate at Marvin's, a round-the-clock restaurant at the west end of his city block. He garnished his dinner with a line of Louisiana Red Hot Sauce, took it and a can of Coors into the living room, and sat on the window seat that overlooked the street. The sky was clear tonight. Stars flickered like sequins on a black dress. From here he could see Marvin's tacky neon sign light up a letter at a time. There were two plants close by. One was an arm of General Motors, the other Kodak. Shift workers from both plants ate at Marvin's. To the left of Mike's apartment, and jutting somewhat closer to the street, was another four-family with a porch up and a porch down. A street lamp directly in front of that building gave Mike a clear view of the upstairs porch, his own private floor show. The Puerto Rican woman—what was her name?—was there again tonight, rocking her two-month-old baby. Even from here he could see the sweat shine on her face. "Hot one all right," he said, and flipped off his overhead. He could see her now, but she couldn't see him, which made him feel a little like a voyeur. "Little private time, huh," he said. Her dark eyes sparkled like black diamonds when the rocker started backwards and the light caught her just right. Motherhood looked good on her.

Like it probably would have on Holly.

The Puerto Rican woman had a man, a skinny, angry-faced man who gesticulated endlessly and yelled at her whenever he felt like it. There were times, when the guy dumped on her or when Mike saw that blank look on her face, when he wanted to tell her, "It's okay, things . . . work out." And there were other times, like now, her baby pressed close, time more or less frozen, when he felt that she already knew that.

His attention shifted to a classic Hudson parked on his side of the street, just off to the right. It had been there for a while, but it had plates, so it was legal. Mike only noticed it because it was a Hudson, and making mental note of odd things was more or less what he did for a living. He winked at the woman, got up, took another beer from the fridge, and tuned in to a local classical station, not what he customarily listened to, but Holly had liked classical music, and it was time to buoy her spirit.

Paul Marat swung his foot off the bed from his prone position and glanced to his left at a woman he knew only as Jean; not, he thought, the sexiest of names for a woman in her profession. Maybe Marie or Simone. He smiled. Those were French names. But French women were sexier on average anyway, although names like Marie and Simone certainly did help further that sexual mystique.

He was naked; the night was humid and even warmer than the day had been. Sweat gathered in a pool between his pecs. He worked out a lot and had marvelous pecs. "Oh, my," Jean had told him earlier, "you've got nicer tits than I do!" "Pecs," he had reminded her. "Not tits, pecs." She smiled as demurely as she could, and said that pecs or tits, they were still nicer than hers. And that was true. Middle age hadn't greeted her very warmly—gravity had begun its relentless assault.

He'd approached her for a reason even older than her profession—jealousy. Kris, his wife, had cheated on him. With his partner, no less. Now he was returning the favor. He didn't feel very good about it though. Not because the woman he'd chosen was middle age and really not very attractive, but because he'd never believed in an eye for an eye, a tooth for a tooth. He'd just done this out of anger and fear and a sense of betrayal. And this hotel he'd chosen . . . well, it was the proverbial fleabag. Probably his way of keeping a safe distance from someone who might recognize him.

Jean moaned in her sleep. She was naked, too. She lay on her back; her left leg dangled off the side of the bed. The semidarkness hid her flaws, and in this light she looked almost appealing.

Paul pushed the light button on his watch: 2:38. He'd stayed out later than this, but he'd always had a good alibi. He wasn't very good at lying either. He sat up. Maybe it was time to go. Hell, maybe it was time to confront Kris about her own . . . indiscretion. Yeah, that'd be good. She'd get antagonized as hell, then she'd get moralistic, and he could just hit her with it. He'd have her then. What could she say? She'd deny it, sure. Well, maybe. He couldn't be that sure. He'd never been confronted by this kind of situation before. Never even dreamed that he would be. Well, she'd always professed her love and devotion. Extramarital affairs actually seemed to disgust her. She made fun of TV soaps and sitcoms. But maybe, he thought, Shakespeare said it best—methinks the lady doth protest too much. Classic case.

But what if—well, there was that possibility—he was wrong? What if she really hadn't had an affair with Larry? Sure, he'd seen her in a car that looked like Larry's black Mercedes. From behind though, and at night. There was a slim chance that it hadn't been her. The guy could have been someone else, too. Maybe, just maybe, he'd happened on some huge coincidence. Look-alike car, look-alike wife, look-alike partner. One colossal coincidence. Right. No way. She'd snuck around on him and probably enjoyed it. He glanced again at Jean. But then, if Kris had enjoyed it as much as he had, she really hadn't had a very good time. That was some consolation.

Nonetheless, it was time to go. He got up, dressed, dropped two twenties and a ten on the night table, and left, wondering, as he walked to the stairs, if he should have given Jean a tip.

The moist, warm outside air was decidedly refreshing after the rank atmosphere he'd just left. He drew in a hearty lungful, and started toward his car parked fifty or so yards down the two-lane street. He moved quickly, feeling somewhat exhilarated about his decision to actually confront Kris about their relationship. Just before he got to his car, a big Lincoln drove by. He watched its taillights disappear around a corner, and took out his keys. After he'd unlocked the door, he looked down the street again; something had moved into his field of vision.

What he saw startled him, and he was as perplexed as he'd ever been. Kris was sitting in the front seat of the same black Mercedes he'd seen her in last week. Larry's Mercedes. The car was parked down the street under a low-wattage streetlight, facing him. It looked like the engine was running; diesel smoke pulsed smoothly from the back. She was sitting next to a man who just *had* to be Larry. Just had to be. But again, Paul couldn't be sure. Not really. He only saw a dark figure sitting behind the wheel. "Shit!" he said. "Now what?" Which about covered the situation. He could get into his car and drive off. Sure. All that would do was postpone the inevitable. But did he want to confront Larry and Kris at the same time? He alternated glances, first his keys, then the Mercedes. Keys again. Back to his car. Then he sucked in a breath and let it out. Why, he wondered, are they just sitting there? Why the hell don't they do something? Well, if *they* aren't going to do something . . .

He started for the car.

Kris got out.

Paul stopped abruptly and Kris beckoned to him.

Paul started for her. Stopped. This didn't feel right. It did, in fact, feel wrong. He watched his wife disappear around a corner, listened as the Mercedes backed away. Now the streets were vacant. Lonely. Almost too lonely. He felt very much like he wanted to get into his car and just leave. He felt that he should. But Paul was a curious, analytical man, not given to paranoia. And leaving would certainly stoke the coals of paranoia. Logically, Kris was here to talk things over with him. Somehow, she'd had him followed—which meant she knew what he'd done—and couldn't wait for him to come home. That made sense.

"Kris?" he said and took a few steps. "Wait, Kris."

His footfalls sounded like gunshots on the sidewalk, as he quickly covered the hundred-foot distance to where he'd seen her last. He stopped as he rounded that corner. Christ, he thought, another empty street. But at least here there was a wash of weak electric light cast onto the sidewalk from a doorway: the only light on the street, save for the streetlight. He stepped into the doorway and saw a sign propped onto a stand.

AMATEUR MAGICIAN'S NIGHT
ADMISSION—FREE

An overhead light spotlighted the sign, illuminating what was an amazingly amateurish drawing depicting a rabbit being lowered into (or perhaps being raised from) a top hat. The magician had huge, green eyes drawn in crayon. Paul smiled at that. Amateur is right, he thought. But wasn't it more than a little odd that a nightclub—or whatever it was—had opened in an apartment building. And this was obviously an apartment building. Inside he saw the listings, some scrawled in longhand, some printed; Ameche, Statler, Donofrio, Shepard. People made their homes in this building for Christ's sakes! On the right was the down staircase, on the left, another door, the up stairway beyond. Probably locked, he thought. He tried the outside door—open—stepped inside and tried the door that led to the apartments. Locked. He looked down the stairs. Probably very well insulated down there, he thought. But hell. I sure wouldn't want a nightclub in the basement of my building. Rent's probably cheap though, a trade-off.

There appeared to be another door on the right at the bottom of the stairs, one with just a little, speakeasy-style window. At that moment, he had a sudden and uncontrollable urge to look behind himself. The street was supposed to be lonely, he knew that. No one walked around city streets at two-whatever in the morning. No one except him. But as he stared at the gray, cold-looking pavement, he concluded that the street had taken on a different aura altogether. It was more than just a lonely place to be. To him it looked like a painting, not real, almost surreal. As if he could step out and just disappear into some other dimension. It was—and this thought chased cold pinpricks up his back—almost as if he'd run out of options. He had to go down, he had no choice. He had to gain sanctuary from the multidimensional street. Right, he thought. A multidimensional street. He tried to

106

smile that thought away, but only half-succeeded. In truth, this whole situation had a very weird feel. Like heat on a summer morning, that took all day to form thunder-heads that rained all over your parade. And sometimes threw a bolt of lightning at you.

He laughed nervously, somewhat alleviating his grow-ing dread. But even through that rising fear, he had to admit that this was all kind of interesting. If Kris had worked this all out—and he had every reason to think so—then she'd done her usual efficient job. She was like that in everything she did. Kris, efficient as a worker ant and full of surprises. Well, he decided as he started down the stairs, let's see what other surprises you have in store for me tonight.

After he'd opened that speakeasy-style door and en-tered the club proper, he was instantly greeted by good-natured laughter and the sounds of merrymaking. Sounds he hadn't heard at the top of the stairs. Very well in-sulated and ventilated, he thought, as he tried to see through a cloud of cigarette smoke. He looked to the left, toward the stage. There was a performance in progress.

As the magician let loose a flapping dove, Paul felt someone tent their fingers around his elbow. He turned.

She was incredible. Probably the most alluring woman he had ever seen. Tall, blonde, buxom. Flashing white teeth. Blue eyes.

"Mr. Marat?" she said.

"Yes, but how—?"

"You were expected."

So Kris *had* set this up. There was no other explanation. The woman looked toward the stage, prompting Paul to do likewise. This particular magician was awfully tall. Good-looking, too, in a Mediterranean kind of way: dark hair, green eyes. Vaguely reminiscent of the magician depicted on the drawing out front. Paul watched as three doves winged their way toward the smoke-filled audi-ence—an audience still unseen by him.

Polite applause, turning to raucous. Whistles and thigh

slapping, occasionally a Bravo, which seemed very much out of place.

"He's the best," the woman yelled above the din, broadening her delicious smile.

Paul just nodded politely, more confused than anything.

The applause only whispered now. "How would you like to be part of the show?" she said.

"What do you mean?" Paul asked.

She leaned closer, and Paul felt the press of remarkably firm breasts on his arm. "Well, every night he selects someone from the audience to help him with his most difficult trick."

"Oh?"

She smiled like a lost friend. "Okay, your wife put me up to it."

Paul suddenly felt tense, but he wanted to sound light. "I thought so," he said. "Where is she?"

The woman pressed closer. "Around," she said simply.

Paul felt like someone at a surprise birthday party. "What kind of trick is it?" he asked.

"His pièce de résistance," the woman said, pride obvious in her tone.

"Well, that's a relief," Paul said with a wry smile. "No more birds out of the hat, I hope."

The woman's chin began to quiver, but her flashing eyes gave her away. "You don't like our little show?"

Paul only shrugged.

With that, she took him by the arm and prodded him forward. They walked on the left near a brick wall, and as they walked, he looked into the audience for faces looking back at him. But he didn't see any faces, just cigarette smoke rising steadily toward that unseen and unheard filtering system. He tried to see what the magician was up to; he'd stepped back, out of the spotlight. Probably getting his pièce de résistance set up, Paul thought derisively. He glanced around for Kris, half-expecting to see her near the stage, in the wings or something. But the only people he saw were the magician—at least his back—and this very beautiful woman who had him by the arm. And who, he now decided, smelled like rancid cabbage. Or was it moldy newspaper? Something equally bad.

After they had ascended three steps to the stage, she gave him a not-so-slight push forward. The applause rose as Paul stumbled closer to stage center.

The magician turned toward him, and Paul saw that the man was even taller than he'd seemed from a distance. Even taller than Paul was. He was dressed in typical magician-style, tux, top hat, cane.

"Mr. Marat," he said, turning. "Good to see you." A voice like cream flowing slowly into a rose.

Again, Paul thought. He was going to say "good to see you again." But how did he know that—and why would he think that?

The magician moved closer, sticking out an enormous hand. "Without volunteers, where would I be?" he said jocularly.

Paul shook his hand and let go abruptly, alarmed not only by the strength, but by how cold a hand it was. Christ, like shaking hands with a barracuda, he thought.

The magician only smiled, which brightened his eyes. Green eyes, Paul saw now. Almost as if crayoned in . . . Christ, what have I gotten . . .

An oblong pine box was rolled onto the stage by the very comely assistant, breaking Paul's train of thought and prompting the audience to again break into thunderous applause. Paul turned sharply, hoping to see someone now. And much to his surprise, he did, but only briefly. Rags, they were dressed in rags! he thought. Although all he had to go on was a fleeting, out of focus glimpse. He sniffed the air. Stinks in here, too. Like stale sweat and oozing mud and who knows what else. Why didn't I notice that before? The assistant stood off to the side of the box, hands clasped dutifully together in front of her. The magician's rancid-cabbage-smelling assistant, who looked so marvelous, so alluring. Who did, in fact, look very much like she was only playing a role. As if she were far more than just a magician's assistant, there only to divert attention by arousing carnal instincts.

The magician nodded. Immediately the woman unlocked a padlock on the side of the box and flipped it open. The upper and lower halves of the box had been cut to form a small circle, enough room for a large neck, like Paul's.

"Please," the magician said, hand outstretched.

Paul smiled nervously. "You want me to get in there? Christ, it looks like a goddamn coffin."

At that the crowd laughed like children, but the magician seemed not to hear. He just nodded.

"But why?" Paul continued.

"Why, Mr. Marat? So that we can get on with the show, of course. That's what we're here for, isn't it? The show?"

"Where's my wife?" Paul demanded.

The magician smiled—no, not smiled—grinned. "Resting," he said. "She tires easily."

"What the hell does that mean?"

"Most newborns tire easily, Mr. Marat. Now, if you please."

"That's it. I'm outa here."

He turned to go, but the rancid smelling yet alluring assistant stepped in his way. Paul stopped, not because she blocked his way—he could certainly handle a woman—but because a frown as malevolent as her smile had been entrancing, crossed her face. A face that was now drained of color and as white as milk. And on each side of her mouth he saw . . . tips of teeth. Oversized canines.

"Move," he ordered.

She didn't respond.

"Move or I'll move you."

As Paul saw it, what happened then happened at light speed. She was there, a good fifteen feet away, and then she was on him, gripping him by the neck and actually lifting him off the floor. Then, before he could take a

110

breath, he had been dropped into the box, the lid had been slammed shut, and the side-mounted padlock had been affixed with a metallic click.

"Let me out of here, goddammit! Let me out of here!" Paul yelled.

The magician leaned toward him. "And spoil the trick!" he said. "No, Mr. Marat. That's not possible. We have an audience to concern ourselves with. Their entertainment is of utmost importance. You understand that, don't you?"

The assistant stepped in from behind and kissed Paul squarely on the mouth. And while their lips were pressed together, his mind offered him a truly horrific vision—a head, a woman's head with thousands of maggots pouring from the open eyes and mouth like handfuls of animated rice. Paul felt his stomach rumble acidly, and the woman backed away, laughing, almost as if she knew what he had seen. He turned his head toward the audience; their help, he needed their help. This guy was crazy, something had to be done right away! Now! He thought about Michel, his cousin, Michel. But what could Mike do? What? His thoughts stopped there. What he saw, really saw, made him temporarily forget his dire situation. This was a mob of peasants, of eighteenth-century homeless, screaming and yelling at him in French, something about tyranny and anarchy and . . . Christ, something about taking his head off. Taking his goddamn head off! An old woman with a red bandana around her head, her white hair clouding out from underneath, spat on him, then laughed, displaying a row of crooked, rotted teeth. A boy with a wooden leg looked forlornly at him, while a man that looked like the boy's father shook his fist at him. Paul tried to kick his arms and legs, but of course he couldn't. All he could do was move his hands about a foot, his legs even less, certainly not enough leverage to split even this weak pine. He tried to turn his head; the only movement he could accomplish was to the left and right. And there was absolutely nothing to see to his right, just the empty stage.

111

He turned his head back to the crazed audience, to the uncontrollable eighteenth-century mob that wanted his head, and somewhere in his blizzard of thoughts, he wondered if this wasn't just part of the magician's trick. He hoped that. But as he thought that, the magician leaned over him and whispered, "No, no tricks, Monsieur Marat, no tricks. Just revenge. As we discussed so long ago. Remember? Of course, you don't remember. And you won't remember, not until I allow you to do so." Then he stood and added, "Which you may do now."

Instantly the memories flooded in Paul's mind: the massacre of his family; of heads being taken so easily, so mercilessly. The magician leaned to him once more. "No tricks, my friend, just hypnosis, that's all. A far-reaching hypnosis. And I might even attach a little pride to that accomplishment, having succeeded with three of you at the same time. Three cowering, frightened children." Then he stood again and laughed, a laugh that seemed impossible in its fury and disdain, and Paul knew that it was the last laughter he would ever hear.

"Ohhhh, Godddd!" he screamed, appealing to a higher authority that would not be at all welcome here. "Please help me, God, please help me!"

Tears stained his cheeks as he looked back toward the audience. But the audience was gone now. And he could see a thick layer of dust on the floor, the empty floor, and toward the back a rodent scurried across the neglected hardwood bar. Seconds later Paul heard a rolling sound behind him. He tried his best to turn, but he couldn't. All he could do was stretch his neck until it hurt.

And just as the rolling sound stopped, he heard, "The sins of the fathers, Paul Marat, shall be visited upon their sons."

Christ, he thought, *what does that mean? What the hell does that mean?*

Moments later, a wicker basket was placed under his head.

* * *

Mike rolled onto his stomach and covered his head with a pillow, one of three. But even that didn't work. What the hell time is it anyway? he thought. A thought that brought him closer to consciousness. He rolled onto his back and stared at the dark ceiling. That helped a little, too. But the ringing would not be dismissed. Finally, he rolled onto his side, propped his head up, and just stared at the blaring black phone on the nightstand. Who the hell would be calling at this time of night? Al, maybe? Lopez rarely called him in the middle of the night, so this could very well be front-page material.

Mike picked up the receiver with a typical beefy Marat hand; full of dark hair and knuckles the size of knots in a good-sized rope. All the Marat males had those hands, even some of the women. Every time they shook hands with someone, they had to consciously suppress the big squeeze.

"Yeah?" he said tiredly.

It was Al Lopez. "Mike? I got some bad news for you. It's your cousin, Paul . . ."

10

It immediately occurred to Mike that a display of emotion would be unwise and unprofessional. He had to remain analytical, in control. But in the face of what he saw now, control seemed elusive.

Ray Jeffers, the Medical Examiner, had flapped open the victim's wallet. Paul stared back from a license due to be renewed before the year was out. Ray knew they were related; everyone connected with the department knew. Although Paul wasn't connected with the paper, Mike had pulled a few strings and got him on the softball team. Paul, as easygoing and likeable as anyone alive, had acquired many new friends. And because teams composed of cops played teams from the *Democrat and Chronicle*, many of Paul's friends were cops.

"I'm lost for words, Mike," the M.E. said. "This defies description. Never seen anything like it."

What went through Mike's head then went through at an incalculable speed; fuzzy glimpses of the two of them doing many, many things, not one of which stood still long enough to recognize. It was as if he were being shown the parade of Paul's life.

"Mike?" Ray Jeffers said with a lot of throat.

The images stopped. Mike again saw Paul's smiling face, staring back at him from its plastic wrapping. He looked away, toward the body. It hadn't been touched. It sat on the chair, tethered by invisible strings. Paul's large hand still encircled a bottle of Budweiser. The man who had found the body—the clerk at the hotel where Paul had stayed—sat on a chair near the door, still attempting to cope with what he'd found. Time and again he repeated something about "forces he didn't understand," drawing him here—which no one believed, and which also placed him under suspicion.

"Has the . . . head been found?" Mike asked, which sounded intolerably alien to him.

"Not yet," Al Lopez answered.

"Can you make that a priority, Al," Mike said evenly. "No way I'm gonna bury Paul without it."

Out of respect, neither Ray Jeffers nor Al Lopez said anything. They all knew that after a given period of time, the body would have to be buried, regardless.

"Has Kris been notified?" he said.

"I called," Lopez answered. "No one home."

"No one home? That's pretty strange. Where could she be, Al?"

"Wish I knew, Mike."

"Can you send a black and white over there, Al?"

"Sure," Al said. He left the threesome momentarily, long enough to do as Mike had asked, then returned. "I sent Noble and Wise, best I could find on short notice."

Mike nodded absently.

Al took out a pack of wintergreen Lifesavers. He had quit smoking two weeks earlier; the Lifesavers were his latest oral fetish. He had—after listening to one too many sermons from practically everyone he knew—finally conceded that although smoking kept his weight at a manageable level, it was also killing him. He offered a Lifesaver to Mike. Mike declined with an almost imperceptible shake of his head.

After seeing the body, or rather, the ninety percent left behind, Mike had drawn an immediate conclusion as to the cause of death. It never occurred to him that anything other than the obvious could have caused his cousin's untimely and very gruesome demise. Ray Jeffers had a few surprises.

"Mike," he said. "This case is strange enough, but I'm afraid it's going to get even stranger."

"What do you mean?"

Ray Jeffers moved behind Paul and glanced about, like a professor who needed a chalkboard to make a point. Then he looked hard at where Paul's head should have been, and said, "I didn't notice it at first. Hell, when I saw . . . this," he looked at Mike with the same unflinching gaze, "I instantly drew what now appears to have been an incorrect analysis of the situation. Probably like everyone here."

An apology seemed to press on the seams of Ray's normally businesslike tone.

"Incorrect analysis? What does that mean, Ray?"

"Mike, there's no blood. None on the table, none on the floor, none on Paul. And here's the kicker, Mike. There's none in him. Not a thimble full. He's been drained. That, of course, won't be totally verified until we get him back . . ."

"Ray, his head is gone. Wouldn't the blood have gone out through his neck?"

"Not if the heart doesn't pump it out. You see, Mike, when death occurs by decapitation, the heart stops pumping almost immediately. Blood will jettison out the wound, yes, but without a pump to complete the job, only a few pints can be let. I suppose that if he had been turned upside down like a deer . . . Sorry." He paused to validate his apology, then, "Mike, the blood was pumped or drawn out, but Paul's heart did not supply the power."

All Mike could do was stare at his cousin's headless body, and try to imagine just how hideous his death had been. Had he witnessed the procedure? Had he actually watched his blood being emptied into an array of antiseptic containers? That vision tightened the skin around Mike's eyes. But if Paul had witnessed his blood being taken from him, at least he hadn't seen the blade take his head off, at least he'd been dead for *that*. That's if the killer—or killers—hadn't decapitated him before taking his blood. There was that possibility. But what about the pain of death by decapitation? He'd read somewhere that it was, if not the tidiest, at least the most painless form of death, of execution.

"Ray," he said, focused now on the level of pain Paul had endured, "did he suffer?"

Ray's answer was not quickly given. Even though he knew the answer, he didn't want to sound flippant.

"No, Mike, I don't think so. A moment, perhaps, but a fleeting moment."

"What about . . . I've heard that the brain . . ."

"Mike, that just doesn't happen. Believe me, it just doesn't happen."

What Mike'd had trouble making reference to was the possibility that the brain in a disembodied head could stay alive long enough to make a positive connection with the eyes; long enough for the victim to actually view its headless body from a totally unnatural distance. That was definitely something Mike wanted Ray to refute, which, thankfully, he did. But Ray Jeffers also realized that, theoretically at least, the brain could live for perhaps twenty seconds after a decapitation. The victim's state of mind was another question altogether. Sanity under those conditions was not an option. Maybe, Ray reasoned with lightning speed, it would be so fantastic, so beyond reality, that those twenty or so seconds would seem totally disconnected, like a really bad dream. But did he tell Mike that? Should he soothe the pain with the theoretical possibility that Paul might have actually seen his headless body, but it was okay, because he would have been insane anyway? No, Ray didn't think so.

The crime scene was crowded with officials now, all people Mike knew and had trusted in the past to do the job right. But this was different; this wasn't someone he didn't know and care about. This was his cousin, Pauly.

He heard himself say the words, but as soon as he had, he realized why he had said them and regretted it.

"Search this area until something's found. Everyone got that? No one leaves here till something is found!"

Silence, then a few remarks, "Sure, Mike," and "That's what we're here for, Mike."

Mike turned away, a little embarrassed by his outburst, and said to Al, "Sorry, guess I overstepped a little."

Al shrugged. "What the hell, you got reason."

When Mike got home, he tried to contact Beverly again. He had tried to contact her earlier, calling from a booth, but no one answered. He sure didn't want her finding out what had happened via the media. Only two of the three local channels made it a practice to make sure next of kin was notified before releasing a name over the air. He had driven over to Beverly's and left a note: *Call me as soon as you get in—it's very important!*

As he lay in bed vainly attempting to sleep, he thought about Paul and himself, but this time, Beverly was in there with them. They were children, sitting in that office again, pressed together on that plain brown sofa by more than a confining piece of office furniture. That woman with the tight gray hair and glasses was there again, too, wearing that ugly brown dress and sitting behind that huge, dark desk with her fingers laced together. Seconds later, two couples stepped into the room, and at the same time, the woman smiled and gestured toward them. Mike interrupted this vision with a thought: Isn't it strange that I should be reliving that moment in our lives when we were doled out to foster parents? But, considering what's happened, he eventually concluded, maybe it isn't so strange after all.

He rolled onto his side, tried to get comfortable, and remembered their parents, Lou and George and Carla and Louise. And then, in what was a completely unwelcome vision, he pictured what they might have looked like after the plane crash, after ignited jet fuel and a collision with the earth at mach speed had completed their unspeakable disfigurement.

11

Beverly Marat leaned to her right and flipped on a table lamp. It was 4:29. "Damn," she whispered. She glanced toward her friend, Cecile, sleeping soundly on a large sectional sofa, the deepness of that sleep verified by a snore a lumberjack might claim. She remembered rolling Cecile onto her side when they roomed together at college, a technique that worked only until Cecile rolled onto her back again. But Cecile's bone-rattling snore was music to Beverly's ears now. Sleep was a better place than reality. A reality where Stan, who liked to remind Cecile of his status in their two-person family by occasionally popping her one, as he had done eight hours ago, would not be welcome. Last night, and unlike times past, Cecile had retaliated. With homicidal fervor she had waved a very long butcher knife in his face. Stan, as surprised as a deer on the interstate, snapped up his grizzly, emblazoned hat and stomped out of the house. After one very large, nerve-settling breath, Cecile did two things. First she locked every entrance, door, and window, then she called Beverly. Beverly didn't even think about not going, although danger in the form of an irate and very large husband was just down the street at a bar called Flynn's. (And even the sight of his Jeep parked at a weird angle there—an angle that suggested a less than placid state of mind—couldn't keep her from helping her friend, or at least being there to minimize the odds should Stan decide to come home.)

But now she had another problem. Her shift started at five, and with her track record, she might just lose her job if she didn't punch in within the three minutes allotted to her.

She went into the bathroom and splashed cold water onto her oval, blemish-free face. She'd been sleeping as soundly as Cecile, a sleep unencumbered by dreams, and her brain felt like it had been stuffed with cotton. The water helped somewhat; she looked into the mirror. After sleep, her age betrayed her; there were lines under her eyes, little inverted handles. They usually disappeared by the time she left the house in the morning. She pulled down on them, made them disappear, and wondered how much longer it would be before they *didn't* disappear by the time she left the house in the morning. Forty-five maybe, fifty? But fifty was what, still thirteen years off? Little less. And she had other things to worry about right now. She ran a comb through her wavy, dark brown hair, thought about dabbing a little lipstick on, decided not to, and left the bathroom reasonably certain that Stan wouldn't be back tonight. He usually returned before midnight, if he returned at all. If not, he'd stay at a friend's house and show up the next day, flowers in hand, grinning like a little boy. But would Cecile take him back in the morning? She'd never gone as far as she had last night. She glanced at the knife; it lay on an end table near Cecile's head.

Just then Cecile moaned, a little unconscious dialogue followed, something about Stan—she was pleading with him.

"Bastard!" Beverly said under her breath. And then she left.

From the screened-in porch she could see a Volvo parked in front of her Impala. And there was another car about fifty or so feet away, on the other side, partially hidden by a newly planted red maple, wire strung halfway up the spindly young trunk to guard against a kind of deciduous curvature of the spine. There was, she saw now, someone inside the car. She pushed open the screen and stepped onto the sidewalk. The night was heavy; sweat beaded instantly on her forehead. When she reached the intersecting sidewalk, she turned as furtively as possible, satisfied herself that the person was still in the car, then continued on toward her own car. She was pleased to be in control of her emotions now, given the circumstances; a dark, humid night, a man—man?—sitting in a car just a short distance away. No one around to help if the occasion . . .

"Hello, Beverly."

She turned, looked up slightly. He was no more than five feet away, looking down upon her with feline curiosity. His deepset eyes looked like buried emeralds; his mouth, the lips cartoonishly red, slanted slightly upwards.

She looked at him questioningly, not like someone whose fear has caused their wits to abandon them.

"Visiting someone?" she asked.

"You were . . . prettier then," he said, his tone one of disappointment.

Her brow furrowed. "Do I know you?" she asked.

His smile widened. "Beverly, we're old friends, you and I. We've been through so much together. Seen *so* much! Do I know you, Beverly? I know you like pain knows disease, like death knows an undeniable stench. I know you, Beverly Marat, like I know the night. And believe me, I have long since carried on an intimate relationship with the night."

He took a step toward her, and any light was eclipsed now, taken by his bulk, his presence.

And then he changed.

He was her father, and there was a strap doubled over in his hand. She had been a bad girl, and now she would get what she so richly deserved. She shied away at first, but in some hidden reservoir of truth, she knew that she had been bad and that a just punishment was in order.

And, she told herself, she would even feel better because of it. That was the way of things. Children were bad, they got punished, and then they grew up a little. He moved toward her, slapping the strap on his hand as he did. It made a crisp snapping sound in the still night air.

"Come get what's coming to you, Beverly," he said. "Papa knows what his little girl needs. Papa knows."

He loved her, that was why he had to use the strap—out of love. Right was right and this was right. First the strap, then love. Lots of love.

"Yes, Papa," she said, "I'm coming." She reached her hand out, he took it, and now they would go into the cellar where it happened, where Papa showed her his love.

But Papa had never before held her hand so tightly, even when he was leading her to the cellar. She looked at him, wondering why he would do so now, but there was nothing in his eyes, not even the love that led him to this act. And there had always been that. Without love the beatings were without reason.

She was reminded of when she saw her father in his coffin, his eyes wide open; the life gone from them just as clearly as it had been there the day before the plane crash. His eyes were lead then, just flat, dark lead.

Like they were now.

Dead things looking back at her, mimicking life.

Pain shot through her hand; she glanced down at it. The fingers were bunched and white, like constricted pipe cleaners. They throbbed miserably.

"Remember, Beverly," he said. "Remember it all." And she did remember. And the first thing she remembered was his voice; it was her mother's heartbeat heard from the womb, her father's last words. But most of all, it was a buzzard pecking at desert carrion, affixed to the walls of memory as securely as any memory she had, just waiting to be released by that simple command. Pain like a starred windshield rose before her eyes. Through that pain she could see that her father was gone now. Her surroundings became unnaturally sharp and crisp then. It seemed to her that she could see every leaf on every tree, each blade of grass, spiders caught between storms and windows. Was this what people saw moments before they died? A preview of the afterlife? She felt his hands on the sides of her throat; one hand could encircle its circumference. Strictly as a nervous response, she wrapped her own hands around his wrist, but she was certainly powerless to keep him from doing what he intended to do.

And it was obvious what he was going to do.

"Hey, you!"

Any second now he would apply just the right amount of pressure.

"What the hell do you think you're doing?"

"Dear Marie," he said. "Dear, dear Marie."

Any second, any damned second.

"Hey, you hear me, pal?"

She wheeled away from him; her elbow hit the pavement. She grabbed at it and watched him move away. Almost as background noise, she heard: "I've got a gun, you'd better move out!"

What happened then happened very quickly, but not so quickly that Beverly couldn't find the strength to get into her car and leave. And through her rearview mirror she saw something exceedingly strange. She saw the man who had unwittingly given his own life to save hers—and only him. The vampire wasn't there. But how could that be? The dead man seemed suspended in midair; shouldn't he be lying on the ground? Shouldn't . . . The tires hit the curb, she turned the wheel sharply, brought it back, barely missing a parked car. Then she looked into the rearview mirror again. Into the rearview mirror . . . Christ, she thought, a mirror, a goddamned mirror! She brought the car to a screeching halt and turned in her seat long enough to look out the back window. As she thought would happen, the vampire reappeared, holding his victim like a lover in the streetlight glow, his head lolling about like a broken wheel, while Brissot drained his blood.

Beverly drew in a breath, held it, then turned back, and glanced again in the mirror. Again the vampire was gone, leaving only his victim, again suspended in midair. Musty mythology intruded roughly as she let her breath out: holy water and religious icons and wooden stakes. Useless mirrors. It was crazy, all so damned crazy, so unlike the world she had known all these years. So unfair! She squeezed the steering wheel until her knuckles blanched, slammed her foot onto the gas pedal, and without looking into the rearview mirror, or braking, turned at the nearest corner.

An hour later Mike stood slump-shouldered over the body. Al Lopez stood across from him holding a gray pump found nearby, a shoe that obviously did not belong to the victim. Maybe another victim, Mike thought, her neck crushed like a stalk of celery—like this guy. A crowd had gathered, rimming the scene like spectators at a prizefight. Gazing into their shadowed faces, he thought he recognized a tiny, small-featured woman wrapped in a blue cotton bathrobe. He saw more than curiosity on her face. There was fear there, too. And it seemed to Mike that she wanted his attention, but when he turned her way, she would look away, then look back to see if he was still looking. It didn't take years of experience to understand that she was hiding something. He walked toward her. She took a step backwards and stopped. As he drew closer, a name popped into his head; Seal, Cecile, maybe. Then he remembered. Bev had brought this woman to one of the softball games. She had that same expectant look on her face then, as if she were doing something she shouldn't.

"Cecile?" he said.

She smiled feebly.

"Mike, Mike Marat. Remember?"

She nodded quickly. "Oh, yeah, hi." She glanced down the street. Her gaze lingered for a moment before she looked back.

Mike turned to see what had drawn her attention, and saw a man sitting in a Jeep. More memories poured in. Bev had pulled him aside at the ballgame. "She, uh, she's . . . her husband's an asshole," she told him. Mike had seen enough cases of abuse to recognize her problem. Her left eye seemed a little darker than the other now, as if the healing process was just drawing to a close. He looked back down the street at the Jeep. Apparently the man saw him and thought he was the law. He did a U-turn and drove off.

"Significant other?" Mike said with a smile.

Cecile seemed to think a moment, then nodded.

Then he made the connection: the gray pump, Cecile. Frightened not simply by the events of this night, but by her significant other. Bev had been here. That was Bev's pump. Had she been a victim, too?

"Cecile, was Beverly here tonight?" he asked.

"Yes."

Mike called Al over, took the shoe from him. "This is hers, isn't it?" he said to Cecile.

"Uh huh."

"Did you see anything, Cecile, anything at all?"

Cecile nodded.

12

Beverly was in a phone booth, contemplating her next move. She'd spent the day hiding in a warehouse, only realizing as the sun started to set that she had been nothing short of foolish. He'd avoid sunlight, avoid it like a felon avoids a cop or maybe like a fish avoids the desert. He wasn't dangerous during the day. At night though, well, that was something different entirely. At night he was damn near invincible.

She had the quarter poised, ready to drop. She paused, asked herself a few pertinent questions. Okay, Bev, what do you tell him if he *is* home? Do you tell him how that, that . . . *bastard* implanted some kind of hideous seed in all of us, one that would grow only when he felt like giving it a little water? When the son-of-a-bitch felt like finally bringing the three of us out of our lifelong funk? And do you tell him everything right now, this minute, while it's as clear and as detailed as if it had happened just a few minutes ago?

A few minutes ago. Just a few goddamned minutes ago.

It was that thought that spurred her into action. Boldly, hopefully, she shoved the quarter into the slot, listened while it played its music of acceptance, then dialed Mike's number.

Three rings, nothing. Five rings, then six.

She started getting antsy. Maybe she was doing it wrong, maybe . . .

"Hello?"

Shit! C'mon, brain!

"All right, who's there?"

She covered the mouthpiece with her hand. Or do you do the smart thing and wait for a better time to talk about it, when you can look him square in the eye? If you live that long.

"Okay, suit yourself."

I've got to warn him though. I've just got to!

But just as Beverly was about to tell Mike everything she knew, he hung up, which caused her to rethink her earlier decision and reconsider her own set of problems.

She folded open the door to the phone booth, stepped out, and looked across the street at the warehouse. It was a huge, pale green, two-story building with a black roof, totally surrounded by a tall but useless chain link fence. Even from here she could see four large vertical openings in the chain link, easy entry onto the property. The lot itself had been long neglected: chemicals hadn't touched this ground for a decade, and a decade's worth of weeds flourished. And few windows in the warehouse had not felt the shattering effects of stones lofted from beyond the fence, a distance attainable by only a few of the local kids, those with big league aspirations. Why she was here, she didn't know. Lost in her thoughts, her sight and reason barely afloat in a flood of memories, she had pointed the car in this direction. Now, given time to remember that trip, she counted her blessings and thanked God that she was still alive. She remembered tires squealing and horns blaring, a few curses. Sleep-dulled, working class people letting her know exactly how they felt about having to get up at such an early hour, their angry retorts only sounds, nothing at all intelligible. A lot like her memories of the family reunion, she thought now. It was a thought that inspired more memories, of nights when she bolted upright in bed, bathed in sweat, her pajamas soaked, her eyes as round as pie tins. And she didn't know why, at least not back then. All she really knew was that sleep had

128

awakened something, something slumbering down there in the cellar of her mind. And when it woke up, it crawled its way out, slammed that cellar door behind it, and just stood there, smiling like some animated cadaver, looking around and feeling awfully sure of itself. And it wanted to stay, it sure wanted to stay. Which, of course, was why she woke up; that slamming door, that insistence by whatever it was that she was going to be plenty scared if she tried to stay asleep. But no matter how hard she tried, she could never remember those nightmares. They were like water trying to survive in a sieve; there momentarily, then gone entirely, leaving no residue, no clue whatsoever. But it was all clear enough now; those nightmares were of the reunion. And maybe, she thought with a blaze of insight, if I dreamt about that night now, I'd remember it when I woke up. Another blaze of insight told her that she probably wouldn't dream about it now. And that was true enough. Those little nuggets of fear, imprisoned in her subconscious all those years, were only visitable while she was unenlightened and unconscious. So maybe, her thought continued, it'd be okay to sleep now. What would a shrink say? You have to expose the nightmare, that's the first thing you do. And she'd done that, or *he*'d done that. Whatever, it had been done. And she sure could use some sleep. But then, as sleep beckoned to her like an old friend, she had yet another disturbing vision. She was asleep, smiling whimsically, at peace with herself and the world. But as she watched, her smile slowly dissipated, and then, with frightening suddenness, she woke up. He was standing over her, grinning like a Cheshire cat, spit like venom sliding gracefully along those elongated teeth. It fell onto her neck, lingered a moment, then ate through her skin like sulfuric acid, the sight momentarily rimmed by slight plumes of white-gray smoke, as a geyser of rich, dark red blood pulsed through the break. A smile appeared at his mouth then, a demon's smile, totally bereft of innocence and humor. At best the smile of a maniac, a crazed, asylum-bound maniac.

But oh so remarkably provocative.

Entrancing . . . hypnotizing . . . as warm as . . . She quickly combed her hand through her hair, and as she chased the vision away, she also recognized a need for self-chastisement. Jesus, why the hell do I do this to myself? Why? She gestured to the heavens and managed a feeble smile. Maybe sleep wouldn't be such a good place to hide after all, she decided. At least not at night.

She started toward the warehouse, glad she'd kept a pair of sneakers in the car, and thought of her job as she crossed the lonely street. She was finished there, but that was a small price to pay; she couldn't very well clock in at the right time if she were dead. She smiled at that, again seeing a vision, a corpse sidling up to the time clock, its ashen face and sunken round eyes staring hollowly, something in its dead but still somewhat functional brain telling it how foolish this was. She smiled at that vision, a smile she felt very thankful for. At least she still had her sense of humor, and a sense of humor was always a good hiding place.

She crossed the road, stepped past her car, and remembered him invisible in the rearview mirror, engaged in the act of keeping himself alive by causing the death of another. If alive was the right word.

She stepped back to the car and mindlessly ran her hand along the hood. He had seen this car, and he'd probably be able to find it. He'd cruise down this street, see the car, quickly conclude that she had hidden in the warehouse, then go inside, and kill her. She shuddered, and rubbed her hands on her arms to chase away the goose bumps. Then rational thought returned, along with a plan. If I leave the car here, she thought, and walk back to the nearest motel, one I saw on the way here . . . no, I can't do that either. Motels keep records. He can read, for Christ's sake. My best bet is to get rid of the car, then come back here. He wouldn't think of looking here. He'd think that I'd be afraid to stay in a place like this.

But first she needed some food; her fear had masked

her hunger. And now, as reason triumphed again, she realized that she was starved. She looked down the street, saw a place with a blue awning and a sign that she thought said GROCERY. But how far away do I leave the car? A mile, two miles? I could take a taxi. No, then someone would know I was here. Oh, c'mon, Bev—what's he gonna do, question every goddamn taxi driver in the city?

Maybe.

Probably.

And I could use the exercise. Two miles would be far enough. And by the time I pick up some groceries . . . glad I got a blanket in the trunk . . . it'll be dark anyway. And once I've had something to eat, maybe I can work things out.

About forty-five minutes later, after having walked exactly two miles—she measured the distance with her odometer—she stepped into the A&M Grocery store. She was greeted by the smell of limburger cheese, and an old man of Chinese descent who spoke only broken English punctuated by apologetic smiles, constantly bowing like a tall man in a short cellar. After she'd managed to relay her needs—a ham and cheese sub with gobs of mayo, a diet Coke, a flashlight and batteries—she left the A&M Grocery and went across the street to the warehouse.

Her arms full, she went to the second floor of the empty warehouse. If he wants me, at least make him climb the stairs, she reasoned. At least make him work for his prize. She smiled out of one corner of her mouth. That's if he doesn't just fly up.

She'd spent the day on the first floor, near the door, where she'd had a good view of the goings-on in this primarily minority neighborhood.

She picked a spot near the north wall of the huge, vacant second floor, swept away the dust with her hand, and spread out her blanket, one large enough to double over when it got cooler, half to sleep on, half to keep her warm. She leaned against the wall, crossed her legs, and bit into her sandwich, tearing off a huge chunk. Dying sunlight like sparkling liquid played along the edges of broken glass on the west side of the building. Layered hues of red and green and yellow played along the huge steel columns that supported the roof of the structure. When she was done eating, she went to the west-facing windows and looked out at the river, flowing languidly from right to left. There were big, ugly, square condos on the other side. The sun had just disappeared behind them. People were relaxing on their wrought iron, riverview balconies, free to stay there or go inside and watch "Jeopardy" or "Bonanza" or whatever. She envied them their freedom. Bev watched an old couple laugh and then kiss like old people do, as if too much passion might shatter those delicate old vases. A few more minor amusements, and then it was too dark to see. She went back to her blanket and lay down, using her hands as pillows. And while night began to fall, her thoughts drifted to Mike and the day he had done his Sir Lancelot impression.

Her father had never worried too much about whether anyone was in the house; discipline, as he told her, was necessary, regardless. (And wasn't it strangely coincidental that he always disciplined her while there *was* someone in the house.) That particular August day was no different. Michel and his parents were upstairs. She was in the basement with her father, who had just removed his belt. She had just removed her skirt.

He glanced upwards, let his gaze linger a moment, then looked back at Beverly. It seemed to her that his eyes reflected more light than was available, as if some fire inside was trying to burn its way out. "You know the drill," he said with absurd calmness. "Don't make me swat you in front. And put your hands down. I'm your father. I won't have you hide from me. Go on, Beverly, assume the position."

The position. God, how she hated that term. Maybe a blindfold would complete the picture.

Michel's father spoke then, and she raised her eyes to the muffled sounds. "Go on!" snapped her father. "Do it! There's no one up there who can help you. I'm the only one's gonna help you, Beverly. Teach you a little something about discipline, just like I was taught, and my father before me, and his father before him."

She turned around, but hesitantly, as always. Five lashes, that's what she'd get, exactly what she got every week. Hell, she could have done something worthy of canonization during the previous week, but that mattered little to Louis Marat. "Just because I don't know about it, doesn't mean you haven't done it," he'd told her more than once. But now, as her thirteenth birthday approached—as womanhood, like something trapped inside of her, began to stretch her skin in all the right places—she was beginning to understand something else as well. This weekly routine was not discipline. Her best interests were not what her father had in mind. (And dammit, he wasn't her father, he *wasn't!*) The removal of her skirt was for his benefit only. And what would happen when she did become a woman? Would he no longer be content to simply rub liniment on her bare backside, telling her while he did that her best interests were, indeed, all he had in mind? And would the fact that they were not blood relatives finally be the ultimate temptation? Would he eventually throw her onto the floor and rape her, all the while proclaiming her best interests? Was that what all this was leading up to?

Facing the cement wall, her palms against it, a tear wiggling down her cheek, her legs spread, she heard someone at the top of the cellar stairs call down to her.

"Bev? Say, Bev, I'm goin' outside."

A microsecond later she felt the strap slash across her backside. She cried out in pain. Another blow, even harder, and another scream of pain, louder than the first.

"Bev? You okay, Bev?"

"Go away, boy!"

"Uncle Lou?"

"I said"—he took another swing—"go away, boy!"

She was crying openly now. Her father had never been so vicious. She felt blood trickle down her thigh in thin rivulets. Seconds later she heard quick footsteps on the stairs.

She turned just in time to see Michel reach out and grab the strap, as her father started his backswing. The look of surprise on his face was something she never forgot. "Why you little shit!" he said. Then he pulled the strap away from Michel and began hitting him with it, even harder than he'd hit Bev. Poor Michel just fell against the wall and took his beating, while she yelled at her father to stop.

More footsteps. Michel's father appeared at the bottom of the stairs. "Lou? Goddamn it, Lou. What the hell do you think you're doing?"

Michel's father ran in, grabbed the strap, and threw it on the floor. Her father just looked at it, then went upstairs. Michel's father followed right behind, yelling like a crazy man.

There were no more beatings after that, thankfully. But then, her father didn't live much longer, so he didn't have many chances.

With that strangely fond memory slipping back into her subconscious, Beverly closed her eyes. As night, like a huge black mambo snake, slithered through the warehouse, sleep found her like a perfect lover.

13

After cursing those people that called and just breathed into the phone, Mike had gone back to feeding his Oscar, Clint, who looked like he might be sick. Now, an hour later, Clint hadn't touched his food, which Mike thought verified his earlier diagnosis.

Mike looked down at the darkened street from his window seat. Beverly's friend, Cecile, had witnessed Bob Rutz's death. Some guy that worked at Kodak. And she also saw Beverly's car roar off into the night. She hadn't actually seen Beverly behind the wheel, but at least she had seen the car, so there was a damn good chance that Beverly was still alive.

He looked at the phone and remembered the call of an hour ago. Maybe, just maybe that had been her. Maybe she had been trying to get a hold of him. The phone rang, startling him. He picked it up.

"Yeah?" he said tiredly.

"Hi, Mike. Al. Listen, I've, uh, got something for you."

"To do with Pauly's death?"

"Yeah, about Pauly's death."

"Well, what is it, Al?"

"Not over the phone, Mike. Can you come down to Skinny's?"

"Why don't you just come over here, Al?"

"You know me, Mike, always eating. Thought I'd buy you a sandwich."

135

Generosity was not one of Al's strong points, but Mike had suffered a loss, so maybe Al was just being nice. "Sure, okay. Give me a few minutes to clean up."

"I'll get a table."

Al hung up and stared at the phone. Now why the hell had he done that? he thought.

Because he had something new on Pauly's death.

He did?

Yes, Al, you do.

The bartender, a bald man with hound dog eyes, put the phone back under the bar and smiled at Al, who reflexively smiled back.

"Better get a booth," he said to himself. The woman beside him, a thirtyish brunette, looked at him curiously, then looked away.

"Got some news about Pauly," Al said, partly to her and partly to himself. "Better get a booth." He put his hand out in front of him. "Christ, dark as a cave in here! What's the matter, Skinny? Couldn't pay your light bill?"

He found a candle-lit booth and sat down, tracing his forefinger through the graffiti carved into the table top. Most of it had to do with rookies, when they graduated from the academy or when they made their first arrest. Things to look at down the line and get nostalgic over. His brain filtered little of that information though, and when the waitress wandered over and asked him what he wanted, Al just looked at her.

"What do you want, Al?" she repeated.

"Beer. Yeah, a beer. Don't matter. Any kind."

She propped a hand onto her hip. "No chaser this time, Al?"

"No. Mike's coming. We have to talk about Pauly."

Curiosity supplanted boredom. "Paul? I thought Paul was—"

"Dead? Yeah, he's dead. Deader'n shit! We're gonna talk about him. Me and Mike."

The waitress, an older woman named Stella, had seen it all, but she was confused and more than a little dismayed. The Al Lopez she knew would not refer to the dead with such indelicacy. As she was about to question him, he cocked his head slightly and said, "I got the English report done, Mrs. Norton, just like you asked." He looked around the booth, then looked back at Stella. "Really, I do!"

Stella, who often thought she understood human behavior—she was, after all, in a profession that saw humans at their best and their worst—decided that pursuing this conversation would be pointless. Al Lopez was obviously drunk. And starting a conversation with a drunk was like trying to get a wingless plane to fly. Neither one got off the ground. She left the booth shaking her head, privately hoping that Al hadn't finally fallen victim to his profession.

Skinny's was about a mile away from Mike's apartment, close enough to walk to, but not when time was important. Ten minutes after Al called, Mike saw the fat-lettered sign on top of the building. Mike had been here several times, mostly with Al. But this was peculiar. If you wanted to talk, you didn't go to Skinny's. Off-duty cops had a lot of pressure to dump, and there were always plenty of women hanging around, just waiting for some muscle-bound cop to buy them a drink. You could barely hear yourself think in Skinny's. So Mike had no reason to expect anything other than the usual din of merrymaking to hit him full force as soon as he opened the door. He was genuinely surprised when it didn't. He glanced around. Through a snaky haze of cigarette smoke, he could see the same guys and girls as usual, but the place was unnervingly quiet. Sure, there were conversations going on, but the machine-gun laughter and the loud, let-me-make-my-point dialogue was missing. Mike smiled nervously. What was this? A PTA confab? A church social? He shrugged.

Whatever it was, it was also a breath of fresh air. At least he'd be able to hear what Al had to say.

Glancing right, he saw Al wave to him from a back booth, just behind the silent juke box. Mike waved back and pushed through the crowd. Wasn't it odd how his apologies seemed to fall onto deaf ears? He began to wonder if maybe a cop hadn't been killed, or even a whole battalion. He asked Al about it as he sat down. Al answered only after giving the question a lot of thought.

"No, no, not that I know about, Mike. Couple guys got laid off, you know, budget-tightening bullshit, but that's about it, far as I know."

Mike looked around again and decided that being laid off would put a damper on anyone's good time. Especially a cop's. Cops identified with their jobs as much as anyone.

He looked at Al, but Al seemed preoccupied. He turned and looked in the direction Al was looking, and saw a gorgeous woman standing between two tall, young cops. He looked at her for a lingering moment and liked what he saw, from the green, shimmering, very tight-fitting dress, to the chestnut-colored, waist-length hair. She was also very tall, just an inch or so shorter than the cops beside her. He looked back at Al. "First time I've seen her here," he said. "Wonder why I didn't notice her when I came in?"

No reaction.

"Al?"

Al looked surprised. "What?" he said.

"I said this is the first time I've seen her here. You seem kind of taken with her."

Al looked back at her and Mike did the same. This time she was looking at Al. Her eyes looked like tiny lighthouses twinkling through the haze of cigarette smoke. Al smiled and looked back at Mike. But it was all Mike could do to turn away from her. When he did, he saw a look of tender reminiscence on Al's large face. His delicate tone supported that look. "Reminds me of my high school sweetheart," he said. "Same hair, same height."

If he didn't know better, Mike could have sworn he saw a tear standing in the corner of Al's eye. And that was very odd. He had never seen Al cry, for any reason. Al brushed his hair back, but Mike recognized that ploy. He had used it himself. The tear wasn't there now. He had brushed it away. And he was actually smiling.

"Remember when you got your balls mashed?" Al said. He shook his head slowly.

Mike thought he'd play along. Al could be leading up to something. Mike didn't know what, but Al rarely rambled. "Yeah, there I was digging for second base, head down, legs churning, then, all of a sudden, wham! Right in the crotch. Still hurts. And sex? Forget it!" Mike had to smile. The waitress returned. Mike ordered a Bud Light.

By now another tear had replaced the one that Al had surreptitiously whisked away. And to keep it company, a slight quiver of the chin. "You didn't know my father, did you, Mike?" Al asked, his voice vibrating slightly.

"Your father, Al?"

"He died, Mike. He died!"

"Yeah, Al, I know. Fifteen years ago, wasn't it? Al, what the hell's going on?"

"It's not how long ago, Mike, it's *how!* Don't you know how my father died, Mike?"

He remembered something about heart disease, something common like that, that took most people. Al was looking at him, waiting for his answer. "His heart, wasn't it, Al?"

Al was agitated. His eyes were round and glassy with tears. "No, dammit! It wasn't no heart problem! Jesus, Mike, can't you remember? What kind of goddamn friend . . . he got killed in a farm accident, Mike. Christ, I told you that! I goddamn to hell told you that! He fell off a tractor and it ran over him, took his head and ground it up, Mike, it took his head—"

"Al!"

Al's head drooped with alarming suddenness. And

when he looked up again, he was smiling. But now his smile seemed shaded by licentiousness.

"I remember . . . Jesus, how could I forget? I remember peeking under the Girl Scouts' tent when I was a kid. God, what I saw, Mike, what I goddamn saw! Little tiny boobs. Just getting going, Mike. God, that turned me on. I'll never forget. Never!"

Stella brought the beer and put it down in front of Mike. Then she smiled and left, momentarily diverting Mike's attention. When he looked back, Al was looking behind him again. Mike turned. The girl with the chestnut-colored hair was now two booths down, looking at Al.

Mike figured out why Al was acting so strangely. The oldest reason going. A woman—a woman who seemed to be showing some interest. And everyone who knew Al, knew that when it came to women, he hadn't left junior high school. And now the best-looking woman in the bar was sizing him up, and probably had been for a while. "Look, Al, just tell me what you got, and I'll leave," Mike said.

Again no reaction.

"Al? Did you hear me, Al?"

Al snapped his head in Mike's direction. "No," he said abruptly. "Don't go, Mike, please don't go!"

"Al, look, you said you had something about Paul. Just tell me what it is, and I'll become a shadow." He glanced behind him again. The woman was in the next booth over. A booth that had been occupied by two couples until just a moment ago. She was looking at Al. Mike looked back at Al. In his eyes Mike saw something he had never seen before. Fear. Real fear. Just as afraid as he had ever been going to his junior prom. Well, to Al this was very much like a junior prom. Mike leaned forward and allowed his hand to touch Al's. Al looked at it as if Mike's hand were a snake, then looked back at Mike. A line of sweat rolled down the side of his face.

"Al," Mike whispered, "if ever anyone felt like a fifth

wheel, it's me." He shrugged and smiled. "Now, what did you learn about Pauly?"

"Paul?"

"Yes, Al, Paul. That's why you got me here. That and the promise of a sandwich, which I'll take you up on another time."

"Oh, yeah, Paul."

"Right, Al, Paul."

"He died, Mike."

"Yes, Al, I know that."

"He was in a farm accident and he died."

Mike sensed someone standing beside their booth. He turned. The woman looked down at him and smiled.

14

Beverly looked at the ceiling, at least what she could see of it, swirling patches of dark gray. Ideally, she thought, she would have slept right through to morning light. But no, that couldn't happen, could it? As tired as she was, she still couldn't sleep through the night.

She sat up and leaned back against the wall. She looked at the east-facing windows, at the pale pink blush of morning. It would be a while before the sun rose and removed the danger . . . at least until the sun went down again.

She had a couple of options. She could close her eyes again and try to go back to sleep, or she could get up. But sleep hadn't been much of a bargain either. She'd dreamt about the Chinese grocer, the one who bowed all the time. He had been making a submarine sandwich for her, his back turned. Every now and again, he would turn to say something, just as he had when she had really been there. But once, when he turned to say something, she could swear his teeth had gotten larger—the ones on either side, the canines. And he acted like he didn't know, as if she could say, "What happened to your teeth, Chinese grocer?" And he would touch them and discover what had happened and act awfully surprised. But she didn't say anything in her dream, and he just turned around, looked back again, and they were gone. She supposed the dream was just a natural response to her continuing paranoia. She didn't trust anyone. And she *wouldn't* trust anyone. That, she thought, was a good credo to live by, to stay alive by. But she had to trust someone. And, of course, Mike was her best bet, basically the only person she could trust. One of the few people she had ever really trusted. What they could do about their mutual enemy, she didn't know, but two heads were at least better than one.

Her heart suddenly triphammered. Two heads . . . better than one. That thought gave birth to a vision, one that made her eyes tear.

So that was what she faced now. Instead of having dreams she couldn't remember, she would have visions that were all too memorable. Just the slightest provocation, the barest hint . . . She suddenly felt like all the air had been let out of her. She knew she'd never get accustomed to the abruptness with which those uninvited and unwelcome memories invaded her thoughts. She might come to know them better, but she would never get accustomed to them. She sighed. She would welcome the new day, welcome it like an old friend. And from here, as she again looked at the east-facing windows, it looked like the new day was only a few minutes away. Well, that was just peachy keen with her, just peachy . . . a noise, from the first floor. The steady *clop clop drone* of someone walking. The blood began to pound in her ears. Reflexively, she pulled the blanket up to her chin, and strained to listen, but considering the tidal-wavelike noise her blood made, that was almost impossible. She let her breath out, hoping that would help. It did. She forced herself to breathe normally, and she heard it again. Someone walking. Maybe even more than one person. Yes, she decided. There was definitely someone down there. But who? Certainly not . . . him. How could he know? A street person, sure, one of the homeless. Just someone looking for a little shelter, like her.

But did she dare move and give herself away? Chances were slim that it was him, but if it was, and if what she had read about the undead was true—that they had eyes like hawks, that their sense of smell was like that of a blood-hound, that they could hear the slightest noise—then he could probably hear her breathing. And she wasn't about to take that chance. Not that she wouldn't breathe; she had to breathe. But she sure wouldn't move, not a muscle. And she wouldn't have to stay still much longer. It would be daylight in another twenty minutes, then, if that *was* him down there, he would have to leave. He'd probably have to leave before then, just to get to wherever he stayed during the daytime.

She looked to her right, at a doorway about twenty feet away. She'd be seen if she stayed here. And if she moved, he'd hear her. The old Catch–22. But if she moved slowly enough, stealthily enough, maybe she could make it to that old, wooden, three-legged desk in the corner and use it for cover. It was worth a shot, because if he came up here—which he would probably do—then he'd see her for sure. At least in hiding, she stood half a chance. And if she could stay hidden long enough, he wouldn't have time to kill her.

It was then that she suddenly felt a little numb, almost drunk. She felt like she had been targeted, as if she were about ready to somehow receive some sort of transmission . . .

THE SINS OF THE FATHERS!

She jerked her head from right to left. Her skin prickled. Christ, she thought, what was that? What the hell was *that?* Her green eyes opened wide, like receivers of sound. But had she actually heard *something*, or had she just *thought* something? And what had she thought-heard? The sins of someone? Of someone's father?

Movement again, and now it sounded like someone was on the stairs. Panic, which had been waiting impatiently, finally found an opening. With blanket in hand, Beverly ran to the old wooden desk in the corner, not really caring how much noise she made now. She scooted

144

in behind it and pulled the blanket in after her. From where she had been, the desk had been only barely visible. As morning arrived, that would be less and less the case, but at the same time, he would be less and less dangerous. So now she waited, very much expecting to hear those footfalls grow louder and louder until her enemy stepped beyond the doorway, his eyes searching left then right. Her gaze shifted from the doorway to the windows, as she waited for the pastel pink of the sky to deepen, for morning and its accompanying sunlight to send him scurrying down the stairs for cover. But what she expected to happen, didn't happen. And although the footsteps did continue, they grew steadily softer, until finally they stopped altogether. But Beverly didn't leap from her hiding place, elated by this minor victory. Instead, she waited. What if it was a trick? He could be standing behind the doorway, waiting as patiently as a cigar store Indian. She pictured him there just seconds earlier, walking in place, trying very hard to sound like someone walking away, footfalls growing steadily softer and softer. A real smooth trick, something a human murderer might even do. But she wouldn't have to wait much longer, she knew that. Morning was close, not close enough, but getting there. So she stayed behind the desk and waited, her eyes straining for even the slightest movement at the doorway, something that would give him away. And so sure was she that he had been trying to trick her, that when something did move, her heart beat so thuddingly she actually put her hand against her chest, hoping to muffle the sound. But what she saw then, although otherwise disgusting, quieted her thudding heart. It was a rat. It had stepped beyond the door framing, its huge body curled around it. It peered in her direction and studied her for a moment. Beverly was positive he saw her, although right now a rat was certainly a far less dangerous opponent than what *had* been stalking her. And because it wasn't *him*, she even began to consider this rat a friend of sorts. She was just about to speak to him when the rat went back through the doorway with a flourish and stopped, his tail lying on the floor, visible only as he swept it from side to side. She watched it closely until it disappeared, and as it did, Beverly felt a gush of relief. A rat and a person—well, she thought, he looked like one—would not share the same doorway. They just wouldn't. Rats avoided humans. At least something that looked human. But then she swallowed yet another very large pill of fear, one that almost lodged in her throat and choked off her air. He wouldn't . . . smell human. He would smell . . . dead. And rats liked dead things. They ate dead things. Again she slunk lower behind the desk and waited, picturing him petting the rat, maybe even talking with it. She fully expected that at any second he would appear in the doorway, the rat on his shoulder like some favored feline that wanted to lick the cream from his mouth. Again that didn't happen, but it was only when she was positive that there was enough sunlight to keep him away that she finally ventured from her hiding place.

"Thank God!" she said aloud, not afraid to talk now. She moved about ten feet into the room, the blanket wrapped around her, and glanced at the crumbled white paper that had wrapped her sandwich. Her stomach rolled, speaking to her in a high-pitched voice. Hunger, she thought, that's a good sign. But she'd be damned if she'd go back and visit Wan Lee. But as she glanced around the brightening warehouse, smiling again for the first time in quite a while, she had the feeling that these walls were sentient and menacing. She even imagined that she felt the wall behind her inhale and exhale, as if she were trapped inside a giant lung. Finally, she became convinced that at any second she would hear some discarnate, booming voice. His voice, truculent and mocking. "There you are!" he'd say again. "You've led me a merry chase . . ."

She pulled the blanket tighter and moved further away from the wall. Stop breathing, dammit, stop breathing, she thought. Please die, just die! She wasn't talking to herself, she was talking to the building. She felt a little foolish asking a building to die, but slowly, the building did die, and slowly she began to rationalize this latest episode. She had dreamt about him, and now she was remembering those dreams. He had somehow hypnotized her to not remember them before, but he was a part of her now, impossible to get away from, connected just as sturdily as an arm or a leg. So when you got right down to it, he was everywhere. Like . . . God. Her own private little god. And that was why she had pictured this warehouse as being alive, with a voice large enough to be everywhere, without direction. Nowhere you could point to and say, there he is. There's the son-of-a-bitch! She smiled. Where was her sense of humor when she needed it? she wondered. What good was it if it didn't come to her rescue when she really needed it? But even Beverly's strong and reliable sense of humor had felt the strain of the last few days or so.

But her sense of humor had at least succeeded in strengthening her hold on reality, enough to let her lower the blanket, secure in the knowledge that it was over, and that it was time to get out of here. But it wasn't over. Not by a long shot. Faintly, the walls began to change color. At first she thought the cause might be the rising sun, but as she continued to watch, she realized that wasn't the reason. Instead of the dark gray that would be softer in the light, the walls were now a gay, pastel red. And as she watched, more changes took place. Paintings began to shimmer into existence, spaced every ten feet and circumventing the entire room. She looked closely at the nearest painting. It was of a man sitting sideways, dressed in what she guessed to be the clothing of the French nobility, circa 1800. A hawk-nosed man wearing a wig and a tall, blue hat, a circle of lace around the collar. And every other subject wore something different; green and red, blue and purple. So now she was faced with another, less sinister possibility. She was only dreaming. And although she had never before experienced a pinch-me-and-have-it-hurt dream, as this one had to be, she was positive this was one. She walked to the center of the room, frightened, but also strangely fascinated. It was then that the music started, something she recognized immediately. She wasn't a classical music aficionado, but she knew this music. Mozart's *Eine kleine Nachtmusik*. A little night music. She turned slowly, trying to determine where the music came from, and watched as the musicians shimmered into existence in the far left-hand corner of the room. A quintet, dressed in the finery of a bygone era, totally involved with what they were doing and nothing else. As if on cue, a dull roar of conversation followed, with, at first, no obvious source. But then, near the windows, three couples appeared. They were dancing, oblivious to her presence. And although they were near the bank of windows, wasn't it strange that the windows hadn't reverted to something from two hundred years ago? If she were dreaming, as she guessed she was, then the windows should reflect that, too. She shrugged. Dreams couldn't be trusted. The dreaming mind was like a little boy with a belly full of sugar. It could do anything it wanted at anytime it wanted, and usually did. So if the windows hadn't yet changed, they would, sooner or later. She walked over to those windows and looked down at the river, half-expecting to see the Seine, although she didn't know what it would look like. Probably bigger than the Genesee, she decided. Surprisingly, all she saw was what she had seen the last time she had stood by these windows—the Genesee River and those big, ugly condos across the way. And even at this hour, there were a few people on the wrought iron balconies. She looked at them closely and felt a chill. They were dressed like the people in the paintings. Men and women holding glasses high and laughing. She turned away and caught her breath. Now the room was filled with dancers, all doing the minuet, their elaborate costumes lit by a huge chandelier that had magically grown from the ceiling. The light from a thousand candles played on the crystal, and cast hues of red and green and blue onto the walls, the floor, the dancers themselves. The masked dancers. Now Beverly saw that not everyone was dancing. In a shadowy corner stood a man and a woman wearing masks. But unlike everyone else, they seemed to be acknowledging her. The man was awfully familiar, although she didn't know where she had seen him before, but the woman seemed even more familiar. And now Beverly understood why. The woman bore a striking resemblance to herself, same height, same chin. Take off your mask, Bev wanted to yell. Let me see who you are, if you really are me. But she didn't say anything, she simply exchanged stares across a crowded dance floor, half-expecting that any move she made would be parroted by the woman, as if she were looking into a mirror. And this latest dream nuance was particularly fascinating—was she really looking at herself in times long past? And could she be the narrator and the main character all at the same time? Then she knew who the man was. It was Mike. Even with the mask and the shadows, she recognized him. Or had she wished him here, into her dream? Maybe that was it. She was dreaming about some very romantic period in the world's history, and smack dab in the middle of it all, she had found Mike and herself standing in some shadow-strewn corner. Surprise, surprise.

She felt hands wrap her waist. She whirled.

"We're the only ones not dancing," the man said, with just the thinnest of smiles, his voice as melodic as Mozart's music.

Immediately, Beverly felt warring emotions. Fear, confusion, curiosity. He was easily half a foot taller than she, and unlike the others, his mask covered his entire face. It was a remarkably simple mask, no emotion depicted, just features painted a pale, thin burgundy color. No smile, no frown—just a face. A face from a coffin, Beverly thought. A dead face on a mask. There were holes for the eyes, and through them she saw that his eyes were dark and very deeply set. Only glimpses of color, a vibrant green, flashed out at her every now and again, as he turned his head slightly and caught the light from the chandelier. He had on a light gray wig, as did all the men.

"Shall we?" he said with a bow.

The Chinese grocer, she thought vaguely, watching him bow. Could it be? Is this only partly a dream? Is the Chinese grocer really here, and I'm imagining that he's someone else? But then, while he waited for her answer, she felt someone tug on her leg. She looked down into the eyes of a young girl, only five or so, she thought. And again, awfully familiar.

"It's time for bed," the little girl said, nodding.

Beverly just looked at her.

"I said, it's time for bed," the girl repeated.

She instantly liked this dark-haired little girl with the green eyes. She was, after all, part of her dream, and because the child was part of her dream, Bev felt some responsibility for her. She could put her to bed if the little girl wanted her to.

"And where is your bedroom?" Beverly asked, kneeling to her height.

The girl looked into her eyes, confused.

"Tell me where your bedroom is, and I'll take you there," Beverly said.

She heard her would-be dancing partner laugh lightly, amused. She looked at him. "Why are you laughing?" asked.

The man only shrugged, and Beverly looked back at the little girl. "Well, are you going to tell me?" she asked.

Suddenly the little girl's face hardened. It seemed to grow years older in just a few moments. And in a deep, disquieting voice, she said, "No, not me. You. It's time for *you* to go to bed!"

"Yes, Marie," the man ponderously seconded. "It's time for you to go to bed."

She looked at him, confused. "Marie?" she said. "No, my name's not Marie. It's Beverly. Beverly Marat."

He watched her for a moment, and then slowly raised

his hand to the mask, as if he were about to remove it. And as his fingers gripped the mask, a very bleak prospect hit Beverly like a freight train—what if standing here and looking at his mask, was like standing at the top of a dream stairway? And what if seeing behind that mask was the same as jumping and actually hitting bottom? Her heart thumped. Everyone knew what happened then. You died. That's why no one ever said they hit bottom— those that had were all dead! But try as she might, she couldn't take her eyes off of him, she just couldn't. Even though she was absolutely sure that as soon as he removed that mask she'd hit bottom, she still couldn't take her eyes off of him.

She could see his chin now. She felt her knees flex for the jump. She wanted to look away. God, how she wanted to look away! But she couldn't. His will was just too strong. Too damn powerful.

(So is yours, Beverly, said a calm yet thundering inner voice.)

No, not that strong, she quickly answered.

(Yes, Beverly, that strong.)

No, you're wrong . . .

(Stronger, Beverly, much stronger. You hear me? Much, much stronger.)

His lips were coming into view.

She felt sudden anger well inside of her like hot lava, which burgeoned her will tremendously. And a phrase she seldom used left her lips like snake venom. "Fuck you!" she said, emphasizing each word. To her surprise, he froze, and then cocked his head a little. She wouldn't get another chance, she knew that. She had fired her last salvo. She turned and walked through the crowd, pushing aside dancers who felt very real indeed. Beverly felt as exhilarated as she ever had.

Little did she know that she had only won a skirmish, and not the war. As she neared her blanket, her anger began to subside and her will began to crumble. She felt weak and afraid. Most of all, she felt compelled to turn back, to run to him, to have him take her into his arms. She wanted to feel his power, to have it released into her. She wanted to feel it throb in her veins. It would be easy to do that, so easy. So quick.

She forced herself to look down at her blanket. Was it silly to think that she could hide under it? Was it silly to think that it offered some kind of sanctuary? If this were just some kind of head game, then maybe it wasn't silly to think that way at all. Maybe she still did have a chance. All she needed was one last push, one more surge of will. She felt herself turning in his direction, could almost feel his smile warm upon her neck. But she had reserves of willpower she never knew she had. With a flourish, she fell to the floor and pulled the blanket over her. Get lost, you son-of-a-bitch, she thought, visualizing the letters in her mind, mortaring them into a brick wall. LEAVE ME ALONE! JUST LEAVE ME THE HELL ALONE! She gripped the blanket like the steering wheel of a runaway car, her facial muscles rigid, her eyes tightly closed. At any second, she expected the blanket to be ripped from her hands, expected to see him glowering down at her. But slowly, the mortar hardened, the brick wall held. And much to her surprise, *Eine kleine Nachtmusik* began to fade. It was as if there were a series of doors beyond that brick wall, each slowly closing, slowly removing him from her thoughts. And as those many doors closed, she forced herself to think about an empty, dirty warehouse, praying that her determination would rid her of this impossible dream and its unholy participants.

Eventually, the music did die, and sunlight broke through her brick wall. Warm, embracing sunlight. His worst enemy and her closest friend.

Why he had come up here, he didn't know. He was, after all, only an instinctive being, only capable of reactions based on need, for food or sex or survival. Still, he was as confused as his kind ever got. To leave the comfort zone he had created was not something he should have done. And there had been that other being, in the corner. He had smelled her fear. He wouldn't go back in there, he decided.

He started for the stairs again and stopped momentarily, warming himself in a laser beam of sunlight enhanced by a stairway window. He stayed in that beam for only a few seconds before he pitter-pattered down the stairs, moving more quickly than humans think possible, emerging onto the ground floor. To the left was a closed door, but closed doors were hardly an obstacle. Because he was double-jointed, he simply separated bone, squeezed under the door, and then negotiated the stairs to the basement. There was no light, but he felt very much at home. He was in his element. Guided by his sense of smell, he continued on to the far side of the huge basement and to his home, behind the detritus of old machinery, unused since this building had been a functioning warehouse. Once there, however, he stopped. What he had seen on the second floor, what had been standing by the door, what he had walked past, unafraid—was here. He could smell it. The odor very much like the carrion that kept his stomach full. He moved closer. It was time to eat anyway, so maybe . . .

Philippe sensed his unwanted visitor, sensed that it wanted to take a few bites out of him. He smiled, and with his eyes still closed, wrapped a huge hand around the rat's squirming body and pulled him close, so that he could feel fur against his skin. Then he threw him high beyond the machinery, against the far wall, killing the rat instantly.

Seconds later, sleep overtook Philippe, the much welcome sleep of the dead. That didn't mean that if more rats tried to satisfy their cravings they wouldn't meet with the same fate. The undead slept soundly, but not so soundly as to render them vulnerable to the machinations of rodents. The other rats in the basement, witness to the death of their companion, sensed this. They allowed the intruder his space. In fact, some even left the basement rather than risk further squabbles. And although Philippe and Charlotte were sleeping, they could both hear the footfalls of the departing rats as well as the breathing of those brave few that stayed behind.

What's more, Philippe could also hear Beverly leaving.

15

She was running. In her mind, she was running like Carl Lewis on a good day. In reality, however, she was still only walking. The message hadn't yet filtered down. And that message was this: What she had "imagined" in that warehouse, might very well have been the product of two minds. She had a great imagination, sure she did, but was it *that* good? Could she imagine that she had taken a trip back in time like that, to the eighteenth century, complete with all the subtleties and nuances of that bygone era? She didn't think so.

She walked past the A&M Grocery. The Chinese grocer was standing in the doorway, arms folded across his chest, nodding. Smiling. Tell me the truth, Chinese grocer—were you there? she wanted to say. Was that you in that mask? Tell me, dammit, tell me! She didn't return his smile. She couldn't have even if she had wanted to. She just hurried past.

So, if she hadn't been solely responsible for her imaginings, who had lent a hand? Or what? And how?

"Hey, momma, nice gams!"

"Great ass, too!"

Couple guys in a doorway, nothing to do but fantasize. She saw them, heard them, but didn't entirely process what they'd said. They were there and they weren't, just bruises on the tender skin of her thoughts. She had other things to worry about.

She started across the street. The two men lazily followed.

"Hey, beautiful, what's your hurry?"

A car whizzed past, the driver laid on the horn.

Who, dammit, who? A tear stood at the corner of her eye, a tear born of fear and confusion.

Him, Bev. That was him in there with you. That's where he stays. He probably guided you there mentally. When he saw you at Cecile's house, he probably just mentally prodded you there. Pretty good, huh? Great trick!

Now her legs were getting the information. Now they started to move more quickly. Now she realized that she had to get as far away from that warehouse as she possibly could.

But even as these truths became apparent, she knew something else as well. Wherever she went, wherever she ended up after she stopped running, could very well be someplace he wanted her to go. Just like the warehouse. He would mentally prod her to go to a place of his choosing, someplace where she would again cower in a corner or maybe pull a blanket over her, only to be removed from sanity by very real visions. Supplied by him.

Confronted by these truths, she could only stop and look around.

She stood on the other side of the street now, her body convulsing with great, racking sobs, tears she couldn't have stopped if she'd wanted to. Only vaguely did she hear one of the two men behind her.

"Sure, it's early, but I'll just bet you'd like a little drink, somethin' to put you at ease."

She saw him out of the corner of her eye, oblivious to her mental condition, a tall, thin man with a sallow complexion and an earring in his left ear.

"Hey, maybe . . . you okay, lady?" said the other man.

"Sure, she's okay," the taller man said with a leer-filled smile. "Someone looks like that can't help but be okay."

"I don't know, man. Looks kinda stressed out to me."

Their words were like small insects buzzing in her ears. All she clearly understood now was that there really was nowhere to hide. Nowhere to run. He'd know—he'd find her.

The taller man touched her on the shoulder, but to Beverly he had now become the man in the mask, the man in her dream. She wheeled, letting loose a discordant, pleading cry and running blindly into the street. A car horn blared, but distantly, barely making it into Beverly's fog-bound brain.

"What're you, crazy?" the tall man yelled after her.

"Hey, lady, you tryin' to get yourself killed or what?" the other man interjected.

Brakes squealed, a collective gasp, a scream of fear, a dull thud. More screaming. Doors slamming.

"Ah, Jesus, she just stepped right out in front of me, officer. Why'd she do that? Why?"

Beverly looked up into the circle of faces: the two men; a cop, his cap pushed back on his forehead; the Chinese grocer. And in the background, looking down, the man in the mask. The man in the mask . . .

A shaft of strong, warm sunlight probing at her cheek brought her back to consciousness. Slowly, groggily, she took inventory of her surroundings. What first caught her attention was the sterile whiteness of everything—the walls, the ceiling, her bedding. Then she saw the light gray floor and the monitors standing sentinel beside her. Seconds later she realized that there were tubes in her nose. Reflexively she grabbed at them, but stopped short of actually pulling them out; some distant voice told her they were probably necessary to her survival. Her mind replayed what had happened, and she saw the car . . . it was . . . red . . . bearing down on her. She even saw the wide, frightened eyes of the driver—a woman. Then her world fell apart like a jigsaw puzzle spilled onto the floor.

157

She did remember the circle of faces though, and seeing *him* looking down at her again—even in her mind—caused her breath to stop. But he slowly faded as she further realized that he *couldn't* have been there. It was daytime when she'd gotten hit. He couldn't have been there.

She inhaled deeply, discovered it was painful, winced, then looked around the room. It was then that she saw Mike, sitting in a chair to the right of the bed. He had fallen asleep. His arm lay over the side of the wooden chair, and his head lay propped at a thirty-degree angle. There was a copy of *Cosmopolitan* on his lap. He looked awfully uncomfortable, and she thought he must have been very tired to have fallen asleep in that position. He was lightly snoring.

"Mike?" she said softly. No sense in startling him.

No response.

"Mike?" she said a little louder.

Mike's eyes fluttered open, he caught his breath, let it out, and ran his fingers through his hair. And after all that was done, he smiled rather sheepishly.

"Hi," he said and cleared his throat. "Guess I haven't been sleeping much lately." He reached over, took a sip of water.

"Mike, where am I, what hospital?"

"Strong."

"Why have I got these things in my nose? What's wrong with me, Mike?"

There was real urgency in her tone, but Mike smiled and let his hand lay on hers easily. "Ribs," he said, hoping for a decent bedside manner. "You've got a couple cracked ribs. You were lucky as hell, Bev. Real, real lucky. The car's front tire stopped about a foot from your head."

Her pulse raced for a second as that image took focus. After it faded, she said, "But how'd you know I was here, Mike?"

"Got a call."

"Your friend on the force?"

"No, the desk sergeant. Bev, I know you're hurting, and thank God that's all that's wrong with you, but what were you doing on that side of town, anyway?"

She looked at him for only a second. She could tell him now. They were face to face. She could tell him everything.

"I was hiding, Mike."

He sat up straighter, gripped her hand more tightly. "Hiding? From who?"

"Mike . . . Mike, there was a man killed near Cecile's house, you met Cecile . . ."

"Yeah, I know Cecile. I was there with Al. We found your shoe. Jesus, Bev, I've been worried sick!"

She inhaled slightly, let it out. "Well, don't take your worry hat off yet, Mike," she said.

His brow tightened. "What the hell's that mean, Bev?"

She inhaled deeply again, realized that was a mistake, and let it out slowly. "When we were kids, Mike, something happened, something . . . unbelievable. Mike, listen closely, and please don't interrupt. Our parents, Mike, they weren't killed in a plane crash—"

Movement, to the front, in the doorway. A willowy nurse, her dark hair in a tight bun, came in and smiled. "I'm afraid visiting hours are over, sir," she said.

"Just a few minutes more," Bev pleaded. "Please, just a few more minutes. Have a heart!"

The nurse seemed to stand taller, and her smile dissolved into something official. "I'm sorry," she said, "I really can't. There are rules."

"Please, it's important. Very, very important."

"Look, if it were up to me—"

"That's all right," Mike said, standing. "I'll come back. Six, right?" he asked the nurse.

Her smile warmed slightly. "That's right, sir. Visiting hours are from six to eight."

Mike took a step toward her. "Listen, uh, can I talk to you a second?"

Mike made an almost imperceptible gesture toward the

hallway. The nurse seemed confused a moment, then smiled her broadest smile yet. "Oh, she's just fine, sir," she said. "There's nothing that need be said in private. As soon as her ribs heal, she can go."

Mike was a little perturbed, but he didn't want Bev to know that. He knew very well that Beverly was okay physically, he'd confirmed that with the attending physician earlier. What he was concerned about now, was her mental condition. Maybe she'd sustained a head injury or something. Why else would she say what she had just said? That thing about her parents. He decided to let it go for now. Tonight, maybe, when he came back for another visit, when the attending physician was back on duty, maybe he'd question her then. For now, however, the best thing for Bev was sleep.

"Hold that thought 'til later," he said to Bev, as he went back and kissed her on the cheek, a kiss that Beverly thought too siblinglike, even patriarchal.

"Maybe you're right," she said. "Maybe I should gather my thoughts properly first. But promise me you'll come back this evening. Promise! It's important, Mike!"

"I promise."

He smiled at her again, and she watched him walk out the door, the nurse following. True to her word, as soon as he was gone, she began gathering her thoughts for their next meeting.

It was around five and Mike was making supper: a couple of burgers with cheese and a few slices of crisp bacon. He flipped the burgers. They were getting there, just a little pink left inside. The bacon, nuked in his Sharp microwave, lay on a piece of paper towel. The cheese was still wrapped. Al would love these things. Mike looked up, distracted by thoughts of the other night, when they had been together at Skinny's. It occurred to him that he hadn't heard from Al since then, which wasn't any big deal, but what *was* a big deal was the strange behavior Al had exhibited. Sure, the lady was a stunner, but even Al had never before acted that weird around beautiful women. She sure had been drawn to him though. Soon as he got up, she sat down across from Al, as oblivious to Mike as she might be to a cockroach under the floor. He'd felt a stab of jealousy at that, but then, she wasn't really his type. Too uptown, too much like a professional, which she could have been, but he didn't think so.

The burgers were done. He flipped them onto toasted rolls, unwrapped the cheese, laid it on top, then took out a can of Coors Light, and sat down in his chair that overlooked the street.

Al was still there, in his mind. And he wouldn't leave.

Beverly was watching the news and wondering vaguely how painful her ribs would be if it weren't for the painkillers. Sure would be easy to become a dope fiend, she thought. The euphoria was amazing!

She looked into the hallway, a kind of square, silver white tube where it seemed no human had walked for the last half hour or so, even though it was now feeding time here at the Strong zoo. Hospitals were like that. Probably getting you ready for the grave, her thought continued. Get you a little more accustomed to all that quiet. All that loneliness. As if on cue, a cart laden with plates of food squeaked by, pushed by a bored-looking candy striper who didn't even bother to glance in Beverly's direction.

The squeaking sound stopped a second later, and she heard someone—probably the candy striper, Beverly thought—say, "Well, sir, visiting hours don't start . . ." A pause. "Oh, okay. She's right in there, room 412. I think she's awake, sergeant."

412, that was her room. Who? Just then Al Lopez stepped into the room, displaying a badge. "Sergeant Lopez," he said in an oddly official voice.

Beverly smiled. "Oh, c'mon, Al," she said.

Al looked at her confusedly.

"I know it's you, Al, don't be so official."

Al smiled like a puppet, put away his badge. "Mike, he, uh, he wanted me to come over and see how you were doing. How you doing?"

"Other than I can't breathe, you mean?"

Another puppetlike smile. "Yeah, other than that."

"Okay, I guess. Great drugs around here."

Al responded, but out of rhythm, as if her joke had to travel a long way to get to where it could be processed.

"I, uh, he . . . that is Mike . . ."

"Yes, what about Mike, Al?"

"He thought maybe you'd be more comfortable at Ridgeview, private room and all that. Said he'd take care of it. The bill, I mean."

Beverly smiled lopsidedly. "Mike wants you to take me to Ridgeview? Are you sure?"

"Yeah. That's what he said. You wanta call him?"

Beverly looked at the phone, back at Al. Maybe she should call Mike. Al was a cop, but he sure was acting strangely.

"Yeah, think I will," she said. "I mean I just got here, and he knows I'm in no shape to travel."

She picked up the phone, dialed his number. Al just watched, a ludicrous little smile pasted on his sweating face, his hands clasped together between his legs. And wouldn't you know it, Mike wasn't home. Probably on his way here, she thought as she hung up.

"No answer?" Al asked.

"No. Listen, Al, I don't think I should leave. Really. And to be very truthful, I don't think Mike would ask me to."

Al looked very confused now. He cocked his head slightly, his brow knotted. Then he said, "You know, you're right. Mike didn't ask me to tell you that at all. Now who was it that asked me to . . . oh, yeah, I remember. It was *him*, that's right. Him. Yeah, that's right, he asked me to come over here and say that, so that I could take you to him. You know, trick you. I guess it was some kind of test or something. For me, I mean. Anyway, will you come? I sure don't want to flunk the test. Please say you'll come, Bev. Okay?"

She almost pinched herself, just to make sure she wasn't still dreaming. But she wasn't dreaming. Al was as real as pain. He stood up, moved toward her. " 'If she doesn't come willingly,' he said, 'just bring her.' That's what he said. So that's what I'm going to do, because you aren't going to come willingly, are you, Beverly? I know I wouldn't."

Beverly moved quickly to the left, away from him, but even the slightest movement caused her ribs to scream. She fell onto the floor near the monitors, clutching her ribs as best she could, but that didn't help much. She bit her lip to help transfer the pain, that didn't help either. The tubes that had been in her nose swung back and forth, dangling free. Though pain fogged her vision, she managed to look up at Al. And the last thing she saw before she lost consciousness was Al's right hand, poised like there should have been a tennis racket in it, ready to slam a backhand at his opponent. That and the completely flat and unconcerned look in his eyes.

The candy striper saw him first. At first she thought that there was probably a good reason why the police sergeant had the occupant of room 412 slung over his shoulder like an overcoat. He was a cop after all, and cops always had reasons for doing things, even if they didn't make a lot of sense to other people. But as she watched him walk down the hall with passive indifference, she gradually concluded that even cops wouldn't do something like that. She felt a demand press into her throat, something like "Stop," or "What do you think you're doing?" but she knew that wouldn't do any good, so she ran into another room, where one of the doctors was, and grabbed him by the arm.

He wheeled, agitated. Mrs. Willoughby's IV had come out, when the candy striper yanked on his arm.

"Look what you've done!" he said. "What's your name?"

"Doctor, the lady in 412, there's a cop, he's taking her! Christ, I mean he's got her slung over his shoulder and he's—"

At that, the doctor, a second-year resident named Southly, ran from the room just in time to verify what the candy striper had said. But all he had time to do before the previous occupant of 412 and the very large man who had her—as the candy striper had said, slung over his shoulder—stepped onto the elevator and allowed it to close, was yell, "Stop! Orderly, stop that man!"

Panic and confusion reigned then. The hallway was a beehive of activity; just the opposite of the way it had been just a minute or so earlier.

The orderlies, three of them, ran frantically to the closing elevator, slammed on the buttons out of blind helplessness, then ran to the stairway. They were all very young, very quick. Adrenaline pushed them down the stairs at a furious pace, each of them smiling just slightly, totally exhilarated by what they were doing. And they did, all three, manage to get to the first floor before the elevator. They watched the numbers go down from two to one, then watched as the doors opened. Al Lopez just looked at them, then stepped off the elevator. "Step aside, please, police business," he said. "There are penalties for interfering in police business."

The smallest of the three, a Latino about thirty, with dark hair and skin, stepped in front of Al and stopped. Beverly moaned.

"This ain't no police business, pal," the Latino said. "And you know it! Now just give the lady to us, and we'll let you walk out of here. Deal?"

Al looked at the three men, one at a time.

"Three against one," one of them said. "Odds ain't real big in your favor."

At that Al put Beverly down very gingerly, reached into his coat, pulled out his gun, and shot all three men in the forehead. And each man, as surprised as they had ever been, just stood there and allowed it to happen. Logically, this was not happening, so there was really no reason to run, to do anything. Which made them very easy targets. As each lay sprawled over the other like pick-up sticks, Al repocketed his gun, picked up Beverly, again slung her over his shoulder, and walked out the door to his car. Once there he opened the back door, put her inside, and drove away.

A small army of people gathered in the parking lot and just watched as Al threw on his blinker and turned right, onto the main road. As he drove out of sight, none of them really noticed how he dutifully obeyed the posted speed limits.

16

The first thing Beverly thought after she woke up was, So that's how cops drive. She was leaning against the car door, Al beside her, his hands at ten and two, his back straight, his gaze flitting from the rearview mirror, to the road, to the side mirrors. He could have been taking his driving test.

The pain came when she tried to sit up. Instantly her ribs yelled at her to stop that, and a sound like a huge, steel door closing on rusty hinges squeezed through her grinding teeth. All she could do then was fall back against the car door.

She looked at Al—teary-eyed vision made him look blurry—and pressed her hand against her side, actually drawing blood as she sunk her teeth into her lower lip. "Why, Al? Why?" she managed.

Al, however, would not be persuaded to divide his attention. Beverly, realizing this now, just got as comfortable as she could, which was about as comfortable as leaning onto a spear. She would, she decided, do her best to tolerate the pain, a pain very much exacerbated by the beefed-up suspension in this standard issue Ford Galaxie 500. But game as she was, there was little she could do when the right front tire slammed into a deep pothole. The pain flashed into her side like a bolt of electricity, and she saw lines of red and orange wink across her field of vision. Seconds later she passed out.

It was almost dark when she woke up, except around a streetlight about eighty feet away. The western horizon was a dull, burnt orange. Al was still sitting beside her, hands at ten and two, eyes fixed on the road, which to her seemed very odd; the car was parked after all. But as she woke up, he turned to her, his face lit softly yellow from the glow of the streetlamp, and held out his hand. "Go ahead," he said. She held out her hand, palm up, and felt two pills drop into it. She drew them close. They looked black, although color was hard to tell in this light.

"Take them," Al said. "For the pain." He actually sounded concerned.

Beverly hesitated at first, but the pain wouldn't let her hesitate for very long. And if Al had wanted to kill her, he probably would have done so by now.

"Water, I'll need some water," she said.

"Sorry," Al said.

She'd never taken pills without water, she didn't even know if it was possible. They were small though, about the size of baby peas. She placed them as far back in her throat as she could, and swallowed. They only scraped a little on the way down.

"Give them about five minutes," Al said nonchalantly. "At least that's how long they take on me. I got them from a snitch. Great for migraines. I get migraines."

"What are they?" Beverly asked.

"Nothing that will hurt you."

She looked at him a moment, wishing like hell she could see more than just a fuzzy yellow sideview. "What about you, Al," she said finally, "are you going to hurt me?"

"Me?" he said right away. "No, of course not."

She had expected him to hesitate before answering, as if the answer were obvious, leaving only the timing to consider.

"But you hit me, Al, you hit me!"

"Well, yes, I did, and I'm sorry for that. But it was necessary, I'm afraid. If I hadn't, you'd have raised a big stink. Just business, you know." Another pause. Then, as if to solidify that answer, he added, "Police business."

By now Beverly had more or less satisfied herself that Al was not going to kill her, at least not yet. But she was also quite sure that he wouldn't just let her walk away either. She wondered if that was even possible in her present condition. So, satisfied now that he wasn't going to kill her, her next topic of interest had a lot to do with where he had taken her. Her eyes panned left, right, and then stopped when she saw a sign in the passenger side mirror. She squinted, trying to make it out. When she realized what the sign said, she sucked in a huge breath, which again acted like a spear in the side. The A&M Grocery. They were near the warehouse again. For some insane reason, he had taken her back to the warehouse! She forced herself to breathe normally, then said, "Why are we here, Al?" She felt a certain pride in having asked that question so calmly. She even tried to smile.

"Orders," Al said flippantly.

She felt her face flush, but again she intentionally kept her voice low, her question hopefully undemanding. "From who?"

Al said nothing, he just looked at his watch, then at the sky, then at Beverly.

"Who, Al?" Beverly said again.

Al only smiled and got out, came around to the other side. "I can carry you if you want," he said, as he opened the door.

Beverly leaned out and looked up and down the street, hoping to see someone, anyone, maybe a car. She saw no one. They were alone, almost as if Al had ordered it. But her inner alarm was not blaring, not yet. He had given her pain pills, he had apologized for hitting her. It was, at least, something to hold onto.

"Help me out, Al," she said. "I'll see if I can walk."

Al was very gentle. And much to her surprise, the pain had dulled considerably. The pills, she thought remotely. They're working. With his help, she discovered that she *could* walk. Al gestured to the right like a doorman, and they moved very slowly toward the warehouse.

Philippe Brissot was pulled to consciousness by the mental image of Beverly and the cop walking side by side. Opening his eyes he looked to his left at Charlotte. She opened her eyes and looked at him. "He's done well," he said to her.

"I had a dream," Charlotte said. Her eyes sparkled. "I dreamed he killed three men. Did you dream that, too?"

Brissot smiled. "Yes. Yes, I did. Shall we greet our guests?"

Charlotte returned his smile and extended her hand. Brissot took it, and together they went to the bottom of the stairs.

Beverly, her hand on Al's forearm to steady her, moved like someone going to the gas chamber, hoping that at any second the governor would call with a pardon. But if anyone could pardon her, it was Al. Obviously her old nemesis was here, waiting, and by now she'd figured out that Al had done his bidding. But would Al stand idly by and let him kill her? He was still a cop, after all, still sworn to uphold the law. And she and Al were friends, not close friends but friends nonetheless. But as they moved closer to the warehouse, stepping beyond the fence and onto the property itself, she began to wonder why he—the vampire—hadn't killed her before now. He'd had his chances. He could've easily done it at Cecile's, and at the time it seemed that he had tried. But looking back, she wondered if she hadn't misunderstood his intentions. He'd killed that man so quickly, so mercilessly, he certainly could have done the same to her, just as mercilessly, just as quickly. And he could've come right into the hospital and killed her, rather than having Al kidnap her. Her heart didn't leap at these thoughts, these possibilities, but it did do a little tap dance. But when her thoughts continued, when she realized that he could have something else planned for her, something far worse than death, something that even transcended death, the tap dancing stopped, and her heart felt like it was being pressed between two slabs of granite. She stopped, her chin quivering. Tears previously held back by sheer force of will, began to flow. "Please, Al, don't do this. Please don't do this!" she pleaded.

She almost fell down then, but Al put his hands under her arms and held her up. "Come along now," he said, sounding very much like someone tending to the physical and spiritual needs of the condemned. "Just come along."

Her legs moved, but it was purely a mechanical thing. She knew very well that if she didn't move, he'd just pick her up and carry her. She wouldn't go in there that way, she just wouldn't! She'd lost almost all hope, and she was crying like a newborn, but she'd go in there under her own power, she wouldn't be dragged in there! There was no way she'd let that happen.

"Just a little bit further," Al said. "Watch your step there."

She took a step up then and watched as Al took out a small flashlight, flicked it on with his left hand, and swung open a steel door with his right. He let the light play through the interior for a moment, and then beckoned to her like some kid going into a haunted house. She stepped past him and stood inside, while he closed the door before he joined her. "Just over there," he said as he pointed the beam to the left. Beverly, now overcome by the finality of the moment, started walking backwards, away from the door illuminated by the flashlight beam. She shook her head savagely and held her hands defensively out in front of her, like someone groping for a doorknob in the dark. "No, please, no," she said, her gaze flitting about the otherwise darkened warehouse. Al stepped toward her. "Help me, someone please help me!" she yelled, her pleas echoing throughout the rambling structure. But just a few steps later, she stopped, really having no choice. The breath was almost gone out of her from her effort, and her knees felt like clay. All she could do now was simply stand there and weep, while Al put an arm around her and guided her toward the doorway.

He pushed the door open as they arrived at the top of the stairs. For the longest time, Beverly kept her eyes tightly shut. Al stepped back, although she wished he hadn't. She needed someone to lean on right now. She didn't at all trust her own equilibrium. But as she reached a hand behind her, feeling for Al, she heard, "Beverly, so good of you to come."

His voice was so tender, so sweet. So unlike what she remembered. She turned toward the sound with a smile. She had to see him, she just had to.

No!

"There is much to talk about," he continued.

She felt like she'd been immersed in a hot bath. The pain withdrew almost entirely.

It's a trick, Beverly, a trick!

No, you're wrong. So wrong!

She opened her eyes then and looked down. And although it was dark, she could see him there. There was a woman beside him, a woman who looked vaguely familiar. Wasn't it strange, this sensation, this fear, yes, fear, but also this utter and indescribable joy. How had she missed it before? He was beautiful, beautiful beyond words! There was an aura about him. Warm, so warm. So compelling. Her pain withdrew entirely, and she felt her blood surge through her veins, almost as an offering. A salute. He reached out his hand and ascended the stairs toward her, while she simply stood there, waiting. When he was only three steps away, while she looked into eyes so beguiling, so filled with silent love, she felt a swoon coming on, but she didn't feel light-headed from pain or fear. It was great, unfathomable happiness that caused her heart to race, that caused her to fall silently into his waiting arms.

* * *

When she awoke, Beverly discovered that she was lying on her side on a mattress. She didn't remember what she had felt at the top of the stairs, she only remembered the pain caused by sudden movement. She sat up very slowly, then leaned back against the wall. There was a lit candle on the floor to her right about ten feet away. Beyond that she saw two mounds of dirt piled on the cement floor like giant molehills, which did seem odd, but not distractingly so. In front of her she saw what looked like machinery, something big and ugly and cumbersome, almost a wall itself; to the left, another wall. It was then that she had a terrible thought. She ran her fingers over her neck, near the carotid. Thank God, thank God! No wounds, nothing to indicate . . . movement then, from the mounds of earth. Philippe rose. Seconds later, Charlotte did the same. They moved toward her with such grace, such joy of movement. Philippe held out his hand. "Are you up to a walk, my dear Marie?" he said.

There, he called her that name again. But why?

"Where?" she asked, choosing not to question him about why he had called her Marie.

"There are things to straighten out."

"I don't understand."

"You will, Marie, you will. And a question will be answered."

"A question? But I don't . . ."

"One lingering question, perhaps? One that has been tormenting you. About this love you have for Michel." He punctuated that dialogue with a salacious grin.

She smiled weakly. "Love for Michel?"

"But that will change, believe me, that will change."

He held out his hand and she was compelled to take it, if only because doing so meant that an answer to that particular question would be forthcoming. How warm his hand was, how relaxed she felt.

He took her to the first floor. Tall support columns cast

weak, angled shadows onto the litter-strewn floor. Prison bars, she thought desultorily. They moved into the doorway and stood there for a very long time, looking out onto creamily moonlit fields of weeds. She looked at him, a gaze he did not return. Then just the whisper of a smile crossed his face, and without looking at her, he said, "We'll have a visitor soon, Marie. Won't that be nice?"

He nodded to Charlotte and he and Beverly watched as Charlotte walked away, toward the road and to the waiting Mercedes.

Charlotte was familiar with this social phenomena. During her mortal years this kind of business thrived, and had thrived for thousands of years. In Paris during the late eighteenth century, however, these types of women did not present their favors so blatantly. Things were more reserved then, at least in the fashionable areas of Paris. True, in those poverty stricken areas where survival was day to day, ladies of the night weren't quite as furtive, but this atmosphere was very much removed from the Paris slums of the 1790's.

She was sitting alone at a table, outfitted in the garb of the day, jeans and a loose-fitting white blouse. (She preferred the clothing of her mortal period. Only when she had to walk among humans did she hesitantly wear contemporary clothing.) Because she didn't want to be mistaken for a hooker, she'd opted for somewhat puritanical dress, nothing suggestive or too tight-fitting. She'd tied her chestnut-colored hair back in a bun, and she'd donned glasses, which she didn't at all need. She thought she probably looked like a schoolteacher. Occasionally men walked toward her table, smiling what they thought to be boyishly handsome smiles. (Why had men reverted so? she wondered. Why was sensitivity so important now? It was all so ridiculous. Couldn't the women of this time recognize that?) It was simple enough to alter what these men saw from afar, simple enough to add minor skin eruptions to a flawless complexion, or twenty or thirty pounds to a splendid figure. Seeing this, or more aptly, thinking they saw this, they would politely excuse themselves, saying something about mistaking her for someone else or even saying nothing at all.

The women in the bar, the hookers, did not congregate as those who worked the street did. And wasn't it interesting that there seemed to be a healthy sense of competition among these women. Charlotte saw that easily, in sideways glances or tight smiles, the occasional wink. Of course, she recognized the "professional ladies" immediately, and by her count only two of fifteen were not pros, and one of those was a waitress. It was Charlotte's job to choose one, based on Philippe's description, then return with her to the warehouse. But that description—was it possible? Would such a woman actually attempt to make a living selling sexual favors? Well, she decided now, after having sat here for the better part of a half hour, if such a woman exists, it's not here, not in this bar.

But there were more bars along this stretch of road. Plenty more places to find the woman Philippe had described.

Charlotte got up and started for the door, choosing not to disguise her beauty as she passed a table full of gawking, leering men, some of whom spoke to her, one of whom actually reached out and touched her on the forearm. She turned and glared at him, and that first touch, as cold as the surface of the moon, caught the man very much unaware. He let her go and just stared at her, his eyes flat with trepidation. Charlotte simply smiled at him, then leaned over, and kissed his cheek. His friends broke loose with catcalls and gales of laughter, but the man seemed frozen. During that kiss Charlotte presented to him a far more grotesque image than she had shown to the others (those who had approached her only to find a face full of blemishes or a woman badly overweight). To him she was horribly diseased; open, runny sores covered every inch of her face, leaving only a pair of sparkling, piercing eyes.

Charlotte laughed wildly as the man ran into the bathroom, holding his hand over his mouth, his friends yelling and calling his name as he rounded a corner and disappeared. Then she left.

While she was on the sidewalk, walking toward the next bar, a place called Flynn's, choosing to leave the black Mercedes where it was, she saw a car drive up to the curb, a long, white Lincoln Continental. The passenger door on the curb side was opened, and a woman was shoved out onto the sidewalk. The car sped off immediately, a flurry of crumpled bills helicoptering to the pavement in its wake. The woman was on all fours when Charlotte approached her, offering a hand. The woman took it, looked at her a moment, then got up, and brushed herself off.

"Bastards!" she said.

Charlotte smiled, adjusted her glasses. "What was that all about?" she asked.

The woman stared after the retreating car, then looked at Charlotte. "Business . . . say, you ain't a cop, are you?"

Charlotte almost laughed aloud. She remembered the time she had accommodated her thirst by allowing her victim, a young boy, fair of hair and pale, to believe she was, indeed, a cop. Thinking back, she wondered how much longer he would have lasted had she not taken him that winter night, finding him lost and alone. Why, she wondered now, had she drawn only enough blood to replenish herself? Why had she allowed him the eternal gift? Had she actually felt something for the boy, something she had not felt for so very long? Compassion, perhaps? Or did she actually realize then that the boy could not survive much longer, and that the gift of immortality was the only gift she could give? Tantalizing.

"Well, are you?" the woman said.

Pulled rudely from what she considered interesting thoughts, Charlotte put one of her hands over the other. "A cop? No, of course not. What makes you think I'm a cop?"

" 'Cause if you are, and you said you weren't, that

would be entrapment. I know the law!" the woman responded, ignoring Charlotte's question.

"Well, rest assured, I am not a cop."

Charlotte studied her further while the woman took inventory of her injuries, which were minor. She was patently ugly and very thin, with a swarthy complexion. Lips thin enough to be almost nonexistent. Dirt-colored hair. Nose humped, the nostrils flared. She was short as well, and very possibly diseased. Charlotte could smell the beginnings of something virulent on her skin. Quite reminiscent, Charlotte thought, of that witch in *The Wizard of Oz*. How any man could pay for this woman's charms was something Charlotte found vastly interesting, although there *was* a specific type for every man, that much she knew very well. Surely, she decided, this woman's ugliness could not be matched or even duplicated, at least not on short notice.

"Here, let me help you," Charlotte said, and began gathering the ten-dollar bills thrown from the car. She gave them to the woman, who took them eagerly.

"Stiffed me again, dammit!" she said, shoving the bills into a flower print purse. She looked at Charlotte. "Why you bein' so nice to me, anyway?" she asked, snapping the purse closed.

"Why not?" Charlotte replied lightly.

The woman shrugged that off.

"Can I give you a lift?" Charlotte asked, as the woman turned to go.

The woman turned and looked at her suspiciously. "And what would you be wantin'?" she asked.

"Why, nothing." Charlotte smiled widely at her. "You are paranoid, aren't you? But I can certainly see why. Look, what's your name?"

The woman hesitated a moment, then, "Bertha. Friends call me Berty."

"Berty, such a pretty name. Berty, listen, all I want to do is give you a ride, if you need one. If you don't, I'll just leave. Fair enough?"

Charlotte could have mentally manipulated her, she knew that. But this was more fun, more challenging, like assuming the role of the policeman.

"Well, I was going to call it a night," the woman started. She looked at Charlotte closely, her face a study in concentration. Finally her face softened, as much as was possible. "You wouldn't be going near the Cadillac Hotel, would you?" she asked.

"Well, to be truthful I'm not, but it wouldn't be a bother, really, none at all."

For the first time, the woman smiled. Charlotte returned that smile and together they walked to the Mercedes and got in.

"I must confess," Charlotte said, as they pulled onto the highway. "I do have an ulterior motive."

"A what?" the woman said.

Charlotte smiled inwardly. Most of all, language had suffered. "Something else in mind."

"I figured as much. And what might that 'ulterior motive' be?"

Charlotte took a right, onto River Road. "Feel up to maybe one more job, Berty?"

The woman laughed. "I knew it, I just knew it."

"Five hundred dollars?" Charlotte asked.

The woman sat up straight and smiled at her benefactor, as she smoothed out the front of her black dress. "Five hundred dollars! What I gotta do," she asked, "blow a Doberman?" She laughed, very much pleased with her little joke.

Charlotte forced a smile. Mortals could be so vulgar. "No, nothing like that. Straight sex. You and a very handsome man."

The woman smiled like she'd discovered a secret. "You're gonna watch, aren't you? That's how you get your kicks, ain't it?" She poked Charlotte with her finger.

Charlotte thought she'd play along. She smiled and raised her eyebrows.

"Hah, thought so, thought so. I see it all the time,

177

looker like you don't like it straight, always something kinky. Well, that's okay with me. But I'll tell you a little secret, sweetie, for five hundred dollars, I just might hum a Doberman."

At that, she laughed a screeching, piercing laugh, and Charlotte jammed her foot down onto the accelerator.

17

In some remote area of Al's brain, in the place where duty and honor and right stood poised like stony palace guards, a battle was going on. Someone had broken in to tempt the guards, to tickle their privates, and to tell them there was more to life than honor and right and being unflinchable. Go on, matey, this cerebral felon was saying, take a long walk on the wild side. Do what you have really always wanted to do! Unfortunately, if Al had been thinking clearly—as clearly as Al could think—he would've had to admit that the palace guards were losing, and losing badly. How many battles dictated a war, no one knew, but Al did know that he'd lost some skirmishes of late. The battle for Beverly's right to stay in the hospital—lost. The battle to let those orderlies continue their lives—lost. The battle to allow Beverly to run away, to fend for herself—lost. So now, standing here with Charlotte and Philippe and this woman he'd never seen before—who smelled of lilacs and who kept asking where her five hundred dollars were—he wondered about the next battleground. And he wondered how many battles were normally fought in this kind of war. This head war.

Charlotte moved toward him and stopped a foot or so away. To Al, however, it seemed that she was right on top of him. He looked into eyes that were flat and toneless, like marbles in a puddle, but he didn't see muddy marbles. He saw gaiety and vibrancy and the very model of womanhood. And she was smiling, exposing a long row of milky-white teeth. Looking into her eyes, Al felt like a rutting teenager; seeing that smile, he felt like a small boy who's pleased his mother.

"Let's find a private place and talk," Charlotte said.

Al looked at her, his eyes sparkless, his thoughts chaotic. Conversation would be difficult. He hadn't done well with conversations lately. His brain seemed to have slipped into neutral. But he had nothing better to do, no battles to fight.

"Okay," he said, his smile expanding, until he realized he didn't know why he was smiling.

He took her hand and followed just a step behind as they left the warehouse, emerging into a warm, moon-filled night. Mosquitoes rallied as they tramped through the weeds. They ignored Charlotte. Drawing close to the street now, Al saw the black Mercedes.

"Are we going to talk in there?" he asked, as they stepped onto the sidewalk.

"Yes, Al, we are."

"Oh, okay." His mind suddenly filled with things obscene and nasty, things that happened in cars at night on lonely streets. His penis twitched. "Yeah, I like to talk," he added. But then, and with alarming suddenness, one of his palace guards called his comrades to order. Al turned and looked back at the warehouse. Without looking at Charlotte, he said, "I sure would like to talk in the car, but I'm a little worried about Beverly."

She squeezed his hand a little harder. "And that's very commendable, Al. She's got a good friend in you. I can see that much. But I don't want you to worry, Al. Let Philippe worry for you, okay?"

Al rubbed his hands on his thighs and tapped his forehead with the heel of his hand a few times. Why couldn't he think? Why the hell couldn't he make a decision? He turned back to Charlotte, hoping that perhaps she could give him an answer. While he'd been turned away, she had opened the door, and that, Al thought, was a very nice thing to do.

He smiled, said, "Oh, thanks," and stepped into the car. The scent of leather was overwhelming, the sound of it like paper burning as he settled down.

Charlotte slid in next to him and closed the door behind her. She pressed close and Al felt a surge of hormones. Again he saw kids in the backseats of cars, petting and groping and sweating, typical kids doing typical things. They were frenching, and the boy had his hand on her tit. Al could read the boy's mind though, he wanted more than that! Much more! Al felt a blush coming on, but it was dark enough, so she wouldn't see. "What are you thinking, Al?" Charlotte asked in a velvety smooth voice. The seat made that burning paper sound again as she moved closer.

"About kids," Al said. "I'm thinking about kids." He hoped she couldn't see him smile.

"What about them, Al?"

What was that smell? Rancid meat?

"Al?"

"What?"

"What about the kids."

"The kids? Oh, yeah. Well, they're . . . they like each other."

"Are you sure, Al?"

"Yes, oh, yes, they're . . ."

Charlotte turned and looked into the rearview mirror, prompting Al to do the same. The kids had left his mind; they were in the mirror now. And if Al hadn't been under a power he didn't understand, he would have reacted differently. He would have separated himself from this scene, and with cool detachment, tried to understand just what the hell was going on. But as it was, he simply felt like a voyeur. The girl in the mirror sneaked a glance at him, and Al felt the heat of a blush around his collar. He leaned back in the seat, further into the shadows, and the girl went back to what she was doing. But as he watched, that changed, too. The skin on Al's face felt suddenly heavy; he leaned forward again to get a better look. Like a fish on the side of an aquarium, the girl had stretched her mouth impossibly wide, completely covering the boy's cheek. And while Al watched, the boy started to convulse, then his eyes rolled back, his head lolling about as if the muscles in his neck had suddenly atrophied. Finally, with one giant effort, one that made the vein in the middle of the girl's forehead throb wildly, she sucked his cheek right off his face. That done, she pulled back, and with passive indifference, chewed what she had cannibalized while the boy just lay his head back against the seat and died.

"What were you saying, Al?" Charlotte asked.

Battle's on! Al thought. Oh God, oh God, the battle's on. He grabbed the door handle, but before he could turn it, Charlotte grasped his forearm and said, "Just a little entertainment, Al. See." She nodded toward the mirror. Reluctantly Al looked. All he saw now was his own reflection. Then he smiled.

"How'd you do that?" he asked.

"Just a parlor trick, Al, that's all. But let's not talk about me. I'd much rather hear about you. Tell me, what's it like being a cop? Are you a good cop?"

Al sat up a little straighter. "Yes, I am, a very good cop!"

"How good, Al?"

The windows had begun to fog.

"How good? Well, I've got awards . . ."

"Yes, I'm sure you do, Al. But how's it been going lately? I mean, have you been as good a cop lately as you were in the past?"

"Lately? Well, lately . . ." Al got a mental picture of the hospital massacre, the total surprise on the face of each orderly as a bullet ended their lives. "Could be I'm in a little trouble."

"You mean about those orderlies you shot, Al?"

Reviewing the scene again, Al felt the heat of remorse, but then he reminded himself that he was just doing his job, and he *had* warned them. "I told them," he said. "I told them, so it wasn't my fault!"

"Well, of course, it wasn't your fault, Al. You had every right to blow their heads off. But a good cop brings more to the dance than a big gun. Tell me, Al, what makes you such a good cop, other than your streak of pure violence?"

Al's pulse hit a high note when she said that, but he ignored it. "Well, I don't like to brag . . ."

"Please, I want to know."

"Well, I got a way with people who hurt. You know, people who've lost a loved one. Not everyone's good with people like that, you know. It's a talent. I could probably go back to those orderlies' families and make it right. Maybe I should. You think I should do that, Charlotte?"

"You've got a big heart, is that it, Al? Your strongest asset is your big heart. In the good-cop, bad-cop scenario, you could play both roles."

Al thought about that and nodded. "Yeah, I guess you could put it that way." He smiled broadly.

"I've always admired men with big hearts, Al. Would you show me yours?"

Al laughed. "Well, it's not something you can show people. I mean you can't just—"

Charlotte reached into the holder on the back of the seat and took out a long knife. She tested the blade with her finger, then held it out to him. "Show me, Al. Show me what a big heart you have. I want to see. Show me."

Al saw this in his mind: A hairy-chested man lying on a gleaming steel table, and a doctor wearing a mask standing over him with a scalpel in his hand. With agonizing slowness the scalpel was brought down onto the (cadaver's) man's chest and a long, thin line was drawn. A nurse reached in and padded up the oozing blood. This vision was important to Al; the man did not scream in pain, he didn't jump off the table fearing for his life, so apparently, he was okay. Apparently, a person, engaged in conversation, could show that other person what a big heart they had, if only to prove a point. He looked at the knife, then back at Charlotte. "Will it hurt?" he asked.

She nodded. "Oh, yes, Al. It will hurt. Very much."

He'd tried to trick her, tried to get her to say it wouldn't hurt, when he knew damn well it would. If she had said it wouldn't hurt, when he knew it would, then he'd know something was up. "I thought so," he said with a sly smile.

He took the knife, undid his shirt, exposing his ample chest, and after pausing for just a moment, pushed the knife in an inch or so.

"That's good, Al," Charlotte said, although not with the degree of enthusiasm Al would have liked.

A line of blood flowed down his chest and gathered in the folds of fat on his belly, first drowning his belly button, then blossoming out slightly and staining his new shirt.

Inside of him, of course, the palace guards were in a full state of panic. The battle had been joined, and there was a damn good chance that this battle could decide the war. He giggled, tickled by the flow, then looked closely at Charlotte, hoping his efforts would be rewarded with a smile. They weren't. Well, he thought, if he didn't speed this thing up, she'd be . . . annoyed. And so far, he had only made a small puncture wound, certainly not large enough a wound to show her his large, cop heart. He grabbed the handle with both hands and pushed it in a little further. The pain, although substantial, was not yet debilitating. In actuality, he'd had paper cuts that were more painful.

"Good, Al, good," Charlotte said with alacrity. She stroked his cheek, and Al rewarded her with an inch more.

Now the wound was gaping, the blood flow about equal to a half-turn on the faucet.

Charlotte was very pleased; she ran a finger through the blood, then stuck the finger into her mouth. Hearing her sigh with contentment, Al cut feverishly. Charlotte dipped time and again into the ever-expanding well of blood, very much unconcerned with table manners. But, of course, she couldn't be blamed, the sight and the smell of blood caused her to react very much like a dog who'd discovered a fresh and meaty bone. By the time Al had carved a six-inch wide square on his chest, Charlotte's face and hands were covered in blood, her clothing splattered with it. But for Al, there was certainly a bountiful harvest of (sexually) contented sighs to spur him on, more than enough to kill off the palace guards one by one. Finally all that was left was Al's overwhelming desire to show this so very appealing woman—whose hands and face were covered with his precious blood—his big cop heart.

But alas, he was foiled in his final attempt. After he'd peeled the skin back, he discovered that his heart was very well protected by a stout ribcage. He touched those ribs, his world spinning now, and told her the problem.

"The ribs," he said. "Guess I can't go any farther."

Charlotte, lost in immortal ecstasy, let go with a ululating wail, reached out, snapped those confining ribs, one at a time, then reached in, and fulfilled her needs.

Al Lopez, perhaps unlucky in one sense, was lucky in another. He was dead before his heart was taken.

18

Mike was at the money machine, wallet flapped open, fingering through the clutter. "Where's that damn access card?" he muttered. "Where the hell . . . there you are!"

If he was going to search for Beverly, he needed cash. For what he didn't know, gas maybe, but he knew he'd need it.

Hidden behind his access card was a wallet-sized photograph of Al, grinning ear to ear. The shot had been taken at a softball game. Al was seated on the bench, leaning forward, forearms on thighs, the middle finger on his left hand straight and proud. Seeing this photo again, a wave of sadness rushed through Mike. "Jesus, Al," he said. "Why'd you do it? What the hell would make you do something like that?"

There was an old woman dressed in a black wool coat and hat standing next to him. "I'm sorry, what did you say?" she asked. Her machine spit two twenties and a ten at her. She scooped up the cash without a glance.

Mike looked at her and just shook his head, one of those mechanical, reserved-for-stranger-smiles pasted onto his mouth. "Just thinking aloud," he told her.

The woman glanced at the snapshot in his hand and went about her business, while Mike pushed his access card into the slot.

While he waited, he rethought what he'd learned at the hospital, what had been so damn difficult to pry out of the cops there, at least until he found one he knew. "We have reason to suspect that Al, Sgt. Lopez, killed three hospital orderlies, Mike. And that's not all. He had Beverly with him when he left. Unconscious, too. At least that's the report we got." Mike asked him which way they went. "South, toward the river area," the cop told him. "We've got a dragnet out, we'll get him." He didn't sound over-zealous about this one, as he might have about an ax murderer or a dope dealer. This time it was one of their own.

The cop, feeling inclined to somehow explain Al's behavior, continued, saying something about job stress and how Al sure had to be crazy to do what he had done, if the reports were true, which he really doubted, knowing Al as he did. Brain tumor, maybe, he added with a sage nod. He'd heard that brain tumors made people do crazy, extremely violent things. He ended his explanation by adding that he hoped to hell that Al was still alive by the time they found him, that he prayed to God that Al hadn't turned his service revolver on himself. Self-destructive behavior was normal in brain tumor cases, too. It seemed to Mike that the cop put a lot of stock in the possibility that Al had a brain tumor, as if job stress alone wouldn't do the trick. Mike excused himself and headed south, which was why he was here now, at this Wegman's grocery store, taking money from his checking account.

With a mechanical hum the machine showed him half his card; reflexively Mike tried to snap it out before that annoying little buzzer came on, but he failed again. He pocketed his cash and card and went back to his car. But before he could open the door, he saw three cops speed past, their flashing red lights lighting up the night. Either there was, coincidentally, something else going on, or they had found Al Lopez. Mike hurried into his car, started it up, backed out, and slammed his foot onto the gas pedal, barely missing a woman and her young son.

He followed as best he could, but while other traffic pulled over for the cops, they pulled out on him. Just trying to keep up meant laying on the horn constantly. Some people obliged him, maybe thinking he was a cop, too, but most people shot him the bird or beeped obnoxiously back at him.

Their route took him alongside the river, onto appropriately named River Road, and much to his surprise, he did manage to keep the patrol cars in sight without loss of life or limb. It was after they'd raced through a short commercial district that the cop cars finally screeched to a stop, one in front, one behind, and one to the side of what had to be Al's car, surrounding it on three of four sides. Mike parked down the street, across from the A&M Grocery, got out, and walked cautiously toward the scene, thoughts of brain tumors and the accompanying irrational and violent behavior running through his mind.

"Yeah, it's Al's, all right," he thought he heard one of the cops say after the sirens were turned off. "No one inside, though."

Mike continued walking and stopped in the middle of the road, fifteen feet or so from Al's car. The cops seemed oblivious to him, and he just watched while one pair of cops went in one direction, toward the warehouse, and the other went across the street, toward an alley. Within seconds the only people left at the scene were himself, one uniformed cop sitting inside his patrol car, speaking into his car radio, and that cop's partner, walking around Al's car and taking notes. The driver's door of the occupied cop car was open, the cop had one foot inside the car and one foot on the pavement. Mike listened.

"The vehicle has been located, suspect and victim unaccounted for. Request backups. Suspect may still be in the area."

As Mike approached the car, the cop suddenly lost his officially placid demeanor. "Just send everything you got, Janet! He's around here somewhere, just do it, okay?"

Mike stopped, startled by the cop's outburst.

The cop saw him and seemed equally startled.

"Listen, I . . . what can I do?" Mike asked sheepishly.

He wanted to do something, anything. He felt so helpless.

Mike recognized this guy, at least his face, but obviously the cop didn't recognize him. The cop got out of the car and stepped toward him. "Sir, this is a homicide investigation, you'll have to leave," he said.

Leave? Mike thought. No, no, I can't leave, not now! They're around here somewhere, I just know it!

"Sir? Did you hear me? You'll have to leave!"

The cop took another step toward him. This guy was obviously ready to make him leave. Mike held his hand out in front of him, palm out. "No problem, pal. I'm parked just down the road. I'm outa here."

"Yes, sir. See that you are."

Mike went back to his car, intending to drive out of sight and just wait, but the cop obliged him by going about his business almost as soon as Mike started walking away.

Mike sat in his car and watched the proceedings, which seemed to take forever to unfold. The backups arrived within minutes, four more patrol cars, eight more uniformed cops, and two detectives. The canine patrol arrived a little later; the dogs sniffing at everything as soon as they jumped out of the van, their eyes flashing. For two and a half hours they searched, not caring how much noise they made or didn't make. Lights came on everywhere, and people leaned out their windows for a better look. A few cops stopped and questioned Mike, but as soon as he was recognized, they left him alone. He didn't know what to expect, not really. If Al had actually killed three orderlies to kidnap Beverly, there was no telling what he was capable of. Of course, if Al had wanted Beverly dead, he could have done that in the hospital. He wouldn't drag her off and waste three people; unless he was a pervert or a sociopath, which Mike didn't think at all possible. He'd known Al for several years, that serious character flaw would have shown itself by now. What about what that other cop had said, something about a brain tumor? That was the best possibility. Al had been acting awfully strange of late, at the bar especially. But wasn't it weird, this detachment Mike felt. This kind of show-me attitude. Maybe that was why he wasn't feeling any real concern for Al, maybe . . . no, that wasn't it at all. His concern was all used up. He was worried like crazy about Beverly; he just didn't have time to worry about Al too. And all along, while those cops went about their business, two images kept playing through his mind: Beverly's dead body lying in the weeds, or caught up in the superstructure of the bridge just down the street, like that kid who'd been found last month. As he envisioned these things, Mike wondered what he really felt for Beverly, whether he could tap into his real feelings or not. But then, he'd been wondering the same thing for a long, long time.

At a little past midnight, the search ended. One at a time the cops left, even Al's car was towed away. A patrol car stopped next to Mike's car. The cop in the passenger seat rolled down his window. "Sorry, Mike," he said. "Nothin'. Not a clue. Go figure." Mike thanked him and the cop drove off, leaving Mike alone with his thoughts. The show now over, windows were closed, lights were turned off, people went back to bed. But Mike wasn't the least bit satisfied. They were here; he'd never been more sure about anything. He flipped open his glove compartment and took out a flashlight. He could see the black bulk of the warehouse from his car, rising against the skyline. "Damn thing's huge," he said. "Absolutely huge! Be damn easy to miss someone in there, even with dogs." His breath fogged the window and he wiped it clean.

Of course, he knew he was going to go in there. Even before he parked the car and saw the warehouse looming in the distance, he knew he would search the place. And he also knew that although the cops would give it their best shot, they'd come up short. He didn't know these things consciously, but intuitively, that second cousin to déjà vu. Even as he got out of his car, he didn't realize this. He thought he was going in there on his own, that the Lone Ranger was on his way.

What struck him as he neared the warehouse, was the realization that fear was not part of his emotional repertoire. A certain apprehension had come along for the ride, but not anything as blatant or as helpful as fear. There was something else overriding fear, something . . . titillating. So he walked faster through the archipelago of night, the flashlight beam bobbing up and down in concert with the undulations of the ground, tall weeds and broken glass coming into and then out of the circle of light with dreamlike quickness. He could hear himself breathing, could hear his feet crunch on the hard ground, like someone walking on aluminum foil.

When he got to the warehouse, he walked along the front of the building looking for a door. Finding none, he went around to the right. He could hear the river from here, nourished by a recent storm, a sound he would have found relaxing under different circumstances. After he found a door—thankfully open—he went inside and swung the door closed behind him. But shutting off the sounds of the river raised his level of apprehension. For a very long time all he could do was stand very still, drinking in the vast emptiness, playing his light up and down the roof supports and along the floor. What little light there was strained to filter through windows caked with dirt, but at least here the windows were all intact, unlike the street side of this walled-off structure.

Not really knowing what to do, he did the first thing that came to mind, he bellowed, "Beverlyyy!" Mike beamed the flashlight from right to left as the sound echoed and bounced and came back to him. He felt a little foolish about calling out to her—she was probably tied up and gagged, maybe even unconscious—but frustration makes people do foolish things.

He dropped the flashlight. As he bent down to pick it up, he shouted again, "Beverlyyy!" He got up, concentrating on the search.

He turned to the left, toward a wide stairway. He climbed the L-shaped stairway cautiously, imagining someone—something—stepping into the junction of the L at any moment. Maybe Al, maybe Bev. He was prepared for Beverly, but not for Al. But he saw nothing as he rounded that junction and stepped onto the second-floor landing, the light barely grazing the litter-strewn floor as he pointed it toward the back. Suddenly he picked up something out of the corner of his eye; his skin tingled, his breath quit. He swung the light quickly to the right, leaving a burning afterimage—and watched as a rat raced into a corner and rose onto its hind legs. Mike let the breath out and smiled—poor thing looked more scared than scary.

He started walking again, flicking the flashlight from right to left. Behind him, the rat scurried down the vacant stairway, his feet making little clicking noises on the wood.

There appeared to be a hallway toward the back. When he got there, he discovered rooms on both sides. He pushed open the door on the left and stepped inside. A john. White tile everywhere and filthy as hell, filled with graffiti. Four urinals toward the back, three stalls on the right. Three sinks. Briefly he remembered something about graffiti on a bathroom wall, something from when he was a kid. Him and Bev and Paul had been doing something . . . what though? What?

HELP!

That word tore through his brain at light speed, much too fast to catch, even stealing his balance for a moment. He reached a hand to the right and steadied himself against the wall. "Jesus, what the hell was that all about?" he said. His head felt like something had scampered through it, tearing up brain tissue along the way. It took him a while, but after he'd regained his bearings, he stepped back into the hall. He looked at the door on the right with a wary eye, not at all wishing to duplicate the episode in the john. Still, he felt compelled to go inside, so he reached out and pushed. As the door swung open, he heard a woman say, "Michel?"

From the middle of the second floor—where Beverly had spent the previous night, where she had visualized so much—she watched Mike step across the small hallway and into the other room. She wanted to call out his name, more than anything she wanted to do that, but nothing would come out, nothing at all.

"Watch closely now," Brissot whispered. "Watch the man you love." Again his tone distracted her, comforted her. He stood behind her, his huge hands wrapped around her waist, guiding her forward. He leaned and kissed her on the right side of her throat. What should have felt like the press of very cold meat, did not. Quite the opposite. "A rutting pig, that's all!" he said with whispered disgust. "An animal in heat! Who could love a man like that? Certainly not my dear, dear Marie."

Beverly said nothing as she and Brissot simply continued toward that back room.

Mike stood just inside the room, his light fixed on a woman sitting on a plain wood chair. The circle of light explored her face. But who . . . was it Beverly? "Bev?" he said hopefully, taking a cautious step forward.

"If you want," the woman quickly replied.

It certainly sounded like Beverly.

The woman lowered the right side of her strapless dress, revealing the breast. Mike lowered the beam onto it. "Whatever you want, dearest," she continued.

The woman stared longingly at him and slowly removed her dress. It certainly did appear to be Beverly. But there was something . . . he couldn't quite make it out. Maybe it was the light that made her change like that, made her into such a hag for just the blink of an eye. Like a hologram, he thought.

He stepped toward her. "Bev, what are you doing?" he asked, a nervous smile in his voice.

The woman stood and approached him, letting the dress fall to the floor. She was naked beneath. Again the light explored her, all the right parts, which she certainly did have. "You have to ask?" she said.

Mike was perplexed. He was ecstatic, yes, very much so. He'd found Beverly! But this purely physical response—he was as stiff as a board—why? What would cause something like that? The circumstances weren't right, not at all. He'd always wanted Beverly, he knew that. He guessed he'd always known that. But here, now, after what they'd both been through? And she was hurt, too. Her ribs . . .

The woman wrapped her arms around his neck and kissed him. "Beverly today, Berty tomorrow," she said. "Doesn't matter to me." She pressed close, rotating her pelvis against him, running her hands over his chest (having unbuttoned his shirt with practiced speed).

Mike tried, he tried like crazy, but he had never been this aroused, never experienced this insane lack of control. He responded in kind, letting his fingers play through her hair, whispering to her and trying so desperately to be gentle. She would want him to be gentle. But he was failing at that. His hands moved gruffly over her; deep throaty sounds of passion came out of him.

"And you're a handsome one all right, just like she said," Berty whispered.

His amour suddenly short-circuited. That was not Beverly's voice! He pushed her away and looked at her closely, at least what he could see in the reflected light of the flashlight, lying at an angle on the floor, dropped there in the fire of his abrupt and overpowering need. For a millisecond, Beverly looked back at him, then she changed. The hag was there. "This is crazy, so goddamned crazy!" Mike said. "What's going on here, Bev? What the hell's going on here?"

The woman started kissing him again; face, neck, chest.

She started toward his groin. "Better'n a Doberman, I'll bet," she said, as she wrapped him, stroking briskly. Revulsion started to swell within him. This wasn't Beverly! Somehow his mind had played a trick on him. Somehow he'd let his passion run wild.

Laughter, hollow and derisive, came from behind him. He pushed the woman away and turned. She came back to him instantly. "Hold on there, sweetie," she said, "I gotta do this right, or I don't get my money!" Distracted, he pushed her again. This time she fell backwards and hit her head on the chair, sending it slamming against the back wall and then clattering to the tile floor. Ignoring the woman, who appeared to be unconscious, Mike started for the doorway. When he got there, he shined the light to the left into the warehouse. Beverly was there, about fifty feet away, but there was someone with her, behind her.

"This what you're looking for?" the man asked.

"Mike!" Beverly screamed, "please help me, Mike, please help me!"

Brissot laughed. "Help you? Dear, dear Marie, that's not what he's interested in. He came here to get fucked. Isn't that right, Michel? Tell me, isn't that right? You want to spread your seed, that's all! What's the old joke? Spread your seed and hope for a crop failure?"

He laughed again.

So many emotions, tearing him apart. Apologize, yes, yes, he had to do that, right now, right away! She'd seen! She'd seen him and that . . . woman. Jesus, she'd seen! But she needed his help, too. She needed him to rescue her from . . . but that wasn't Al. Who the hell . . . ?

"Who are you, dammit?" he said, moving toward them. "Who the hell are you?"

"In time," Brissot said. "All in good time. As for your detective friend. Let me see, ah, yes, a riddle. Humans do so love riddles. On an elephant, it's hollow, and on a tree, it's vertical. Now let's see where this 'exploration' takes you."

With that, Brissot laughed madly, took Beverly into his arms, and ran down the stairs, Mike in hot pursuit. By the time he got outside, however, they were gone. Silence, save for the sound of the river, prevailed.

19

As empty as the warehouse had been just minutes earlier, the opposite was true now. There were cops everywhere, all trying to find something to go on. They had Berty, but she was in no shape to talk. She'd taken a severe blow to the head, and although she wasn't unconscious, she might as well have been. She was in an ambulance receiving treatment. Mike was standing near the side entrance with Al's boss, Lt. Anthony Siragusa, a short, thin man with a dark mustache and penetrating blue eyes. What the lieutenant wanted to know, right now, was how his men could have missed so much. There appeared to have been a conspiracy of sorts, at least if what Mike said was true—that it wasn't Al who had run off with Beverly in his arms! And if what the second kidnapper said was true, something about Al being in the trunk of a car, then Al had been a dupe in all this. Somehow, he had been conned into not only kidnapping Beverly, but killing three people as well. (After Mike told Siragusa what the second kidnapper had said, both he and Mike quickly concluded that Al had been killed and left in the trunk of a car. The clues were obvious, what's vertical on a tree and hollow on an elephant? A trunk.) But Al hadn't been stuffed into the trunk of his own car, they'd checked. The hell of it was, there were thousands of car trunks in this town; they couldn't search them all.

There was definitely something else going on, some part of this clue that wasn't so easily deciphered.

"Did he say anything else, Mike?" Siragusa asked. "Anything at all?"

"You mean other than 'let's see where your explorations take you'? No, Tony, he didn't."

Mike was getting a little tired of being constantly grilled like this, and it showed in his tone.

"Okay, okay," Siragusa said. "Can you tell me anything about what we found in the basement?"

"The dirt, you mean?"

"Yes, the dirt! Or maybe you can tell us what that hooker was doing here? Or how she got that huge knot on the back of her skull?"

Looking into Siragusa's probing eyes, Mike almost told him about his tête à tête with Berty, but he held back. What good could it do? Other than cast him in a light he definitely did not want to be cast in. Before he called, he had decided to tell Siragusa only those things he thought he could use, like why he was here. He'd come back to assure himself that Siragusa's men hadn't missed something. Just to lend a helping hand. And they had most definitely missed something.

"No, I have no idea what she was doing here, nor do I know anything about those piles of dirt in the basement," Mike said.

"And you don't know which way the guy went?"

"No, when I got down here they were gone."

Siragusa's frustration was showing. He inhaled mightily, then let it out. "Let me get this straight, Mike. You were right behind them, but when you got to this door, they were nowhere to be seen. Am I following you on this?"

Mike shrugged. "That's about it, Tony."

Siragusa did a circle, then confronted Mike again. "We found a paper bag, Mike, upstairs. Had the name of that grocery store on it—the A&M Grocery, I think it was. Anyway, the owner lives above the store, so we woke him up and showed him a picture of your cousin. He recognized her right off. We found her car a couple miles away. The way I see it, Mike, based on the fact that we found a sandwich bag that at one time had her sandwich in it, she first stashed her car, then came back here to hide. You got any idea why she'd do that, Mike? Why she'd be so damn scared, she'd hide her car, walk a couple miles, and hide out in a place like this? A dump like this? Why she wouldn't go to the cops?"

"None, Lieutenant, wish I did."

Siragusa shook his head in bewilderment. "This is as strange as it gets, Mike. Fresh dirt in the basement, a hooker upstairs, you looking for your cousin, and then having them just disappear into thin air. Strange!"

Mike was going to say something about not knowing the half of it, but he didn't. Instead he asked Siragusa if he could go. Grudgingly, Siragusa said he could.

The last thing Mike thought he'd do that night was fall asleep. But fall asleep he did, as deep a sleep as he had ever experienced. The dream began about three in the morning, and based on the dress of the main character, the dream was set during the Civil War. Mike had a bird's eye view, literally. But even from that vantage point, he knew everything the soldier was thinking.

"Damn things are as big as barns!" he whispered as a mosquito bit his neck, whispered because anything above a whisper might be heard by someone holed up in that house not more than fifty yards away. It did look deserted though. More than one cannonball had ripped open the roof, and even at night he could see the shell holes above the porch. Still, the rebel he was after might've stopped here, maybe even more than the one he'd seen from his guard position. And that possibility—that more than one of the enemy was in there—gave him pause. But then, he did want to set things right with his captain. At Cold Harbor the week before, he'd hesitated with a rebel dead in his sights, not more than ten feet away. Hesitated because that rebel was only fourteen or so, maybe fifteen, and he'd never killed a man that young, who probably hadn't been with a woman yet. War or not, that seemed wrong. A man should know of things like that before he died. But his captain, who fancied a higher rank, thought otherwise. While that poor rebel just stood there, hands raised like he wanted to give himself up, the captain lifted his sidearm and blew the top of his head off. He'd seen men die, but not like that. "He who hesitates is lost," the captain said to him right after, while that boy's spirit was probably just leaving his body. "You'd do well to remember that."

He gripped his Sharpes carbine and wondered what the hell he was doing here anyway. He shouldn't have left his watch. Rebels sometimes attacked at night, they'd done that before, although he couldn't remember where, but he was sure they did. He was at the edge of a woods, out of eyesight, but well within earshot, which was why he'd whispered in complaint about the mosquitoes. Once he stepped out of the woods though, the rebels would see him, if there were any of them at the windows, or just behind, out of sight. He looked behind him, although he couldn't see anything really, just an obscenely dark expanse of woods that stretched about a half mile. The battalion had set up tents in another clearing another half mile or so away, on the other side of those woods. There weren't supposed to be any gray coats out here, not of regiment or even battalion size, but that didn't mean there weren't pockets of them, two to twenty who maybe struck out on their own, as they sometimes did. But what he'd seen hadn't been two or twenty, he'd only seen the one. Well, more to the point, maybe he—the rebel—had seen *him*. He'd waved to him, after all. Gestured like he actually wanted him to follow. But they were like that. Bold as raccoons and twice as smart. Which was why he hesitated now. He could just picture a ball going through his forehead the second he exposed himself. That would take a sharpshooter's skill, surely, but the rebels had their share of sharpshooters. He could skirt the house, go around the woods, keeping them behind him all the while. Or he could get onto his belly and crawl. Either way was good, really.

In his bed, Mike started to feel uncomfortable with this dream. Although he realized he was only dreaming, there was a realistic patina that was unnerving, as if he had somehow gone back in time to actually witness a Civil War event. And wasn't it peculiar that he should think in the parlance of the time? But although he had become apprehensive, he didn't force himself to wake up. His interest was aroused too much to do that.

As he was about to fall onto his belly, he saw an arm reach out a first-floor window of the two-story building. Waving to him, like before. Beckoning slowly, as if the person waving wasn't in any big hurry.

"So he wants to have at it hand to hand, does he?" he said, an option that was very much to his liking, being highly skilled in that area.

Suddenly, he heard, "I'm unarmed, Yankee. You scared of an unarmed rebel?"

And at that moment, perhaps because there was a strange calm in the man's voice, he became frightened. But if nothing else, rebels had pride, and if that reb said he was unarmed, he probably was. And if *he* didn't go in there right now and see to things, then maybe he was a coward after all, just like his captain probably thought. How could he look his captain in the eye then?

"What about the others?" he said.

"There are no others. Just me, Yankee," came the prompt reply.

"I'm supposed to believe you?"

"You do what you think is best. Just like you did the other day at Cold Harbor."

At that he felt like a frozen iron rod had pierced his body from top to bottom. How could this rebel know about that? How could he? Maybe . . .

Mike's apprehension was slowly strengthening. As the dream progressed, he grew closer and closer to the soldier. He was only twenty feet or so above him now. He could see what he looked like, and he looked awfully familiar . . .

"You mean how we whipped your Southern asses?"

Strange laughter came from the house. Sardonic and arrogant. The soldier scowled at that, then considered it. His breath quickened and the blood raced through him. This Johnny Reb was playing games with him, making him look the fool. And he wouldn't tolerate that. Not for a second! Wasn't no reb gonna make him look the fool.

"Okay, you son-of-a-bitch, you got me, and I hope you're ready, 'cause I'm gonna take you apart with my bare hands!"

Without hesitation, he laid down his carbine and walked briskly toward the house, scanning each of the four windows as he drew nearer. He didn't think so, but a sharpshooter could still be in there, just waiting to get off a clean shot. He wouldn't even hear the shot; his head would just explode, and that'd be it.

But suddenly, this very strange confrontation became even more strange. Standing in the doorway of that bombed-out building was a woman, and she *was* a looker. He slowed his pace and drank her in. Although she was still about thirty feet away, he could swear that her eyes were visible, every aspect of those eyes, the warm and comforting blue of them, the roundness, the way they seemed to drain him of strength, actually making him far more submissive than he had ever wanted to be. (And again there was laughter from inside the house, low and guttural, jeering and hateful. Laughter he did and did not hear.) Only remotely did he notice that the woman was dressed in a long, white, puffed sleeve dress, and that her chestnut hair was tied together and dangling behind her head. All he really did notice were her eyes. He stopped then and just stared at her, and she at him, but seconds later she turned, and with a whoosh of skirts and a small gleeful laugh, disappeared inside the house. Almost immediately the soldier's head began to clear, and again he knew why he was here. He slapped at another mosquito, this one on his cheek—an action that further cleared his thoughts—and moved toward the bottom of three steps. The front door was closed. He looked back toward the dark woods where his carbine lay. Right now he wished he hadn't left it, but his pride had been wounded, and a real man didn't let that happen without retaliation. No, he was here, and he was going to see this thing through. He opened the door slowly and stepped inside. Dark as a goddamn tomb, he thought. How'm I gonna fight this rebel in the dark?

"Let's you and me take it outside," he yelled.

No answer.

"You hear me? I said—"

The strangeness of what then happened chilled him to the marrow. He would have been easily overpowered by a real rebel, lost in his thoughts as he was, his brain unable to fathom the queerness of what he heard.

The words were spoken in perfect French, a language he knew moderately well, because his parents were French and he'd lived with them for twelve of his twenty-one years. "The sins of the fathers," he heard, which of course made no sense at all. He tried gallantly to decipher what had just happened, but he couldn't. All he could do was ask his opponent where he was, which he repeated time and time again, receiving no answer. So, receiving no answer, he stood near the front door and just listened, expecting that at any moment the rebel would jump him, or maybe run him through with a bayonet. Just because he didn't have a carbine, didn't mean he hadn't kept his bayonet. But why had he spoken to him in French? And even more, why had he said what he'd said? *The sins of the fathers.* What did that mean? What did anything mean right now?

Movement from behind, subtle and almost noiseless, like a bird floating on a gentle current of wind.

". . . Shall be visited upon their sons!" he heard then.

He was close, right behind him, no more than a few feet . . .

A small, weak sound came out of the soldier as he wheeled, his eyes round, probing. He fully expected to see his enemy, or maybe the glint of steel as a bayonet went into his belly, but he didn't see either.

"Jesus!" he said, and did a quick circle of the dark room. "Where you at, boy? Come on out and stop playing games."

On his right, there was someone on his right! But as he turned that way, he heard again, "The sins of the fathers shall be visited upon their sons."

He stumbled backwards. "Goddamn it all to hell! What kind of rebel are you?" he said.

"Rebel?" he heard from behind him.

He turned quickly and struck out with his fist, connecting with flesh and bone. The force of the blow—a prodigious one at that, considering how large a man he was—couldn't make his enemy lose balance. Or even budge.

"Christ Jesus!" he said as he backed toward the door. God, how he wished he hadn't left his carbine back there!

Suddenly, a huge, powerful hand wrapped his throat, and then—impossibly—he was lifted into the air. He kicked his feet and grabbed the man's arm, but even as he struggled, he knew there was nothing he could do, except, hopefully, prolong his life a few minutes.

Within seconds, his eyes began to glaze over, mostly from fear and lack of oxygen. Then he felt the sensation of movement.

He could hear himself gurgle as he was carried away by the throat. Every now and then a syllable worked out of him, but anything else was impossible.

They passed into another room—his feet hit against a doorjamb—and seconds later he felt his cheek mash against something. A table, he thought vaguely, because from his stomach up he felt something solid, beneath that his legs dangled, and his feet, from his ankles up, scraped along the floor. He tried to turn his head, but the man had him pinned to the table. He tried to see something, anything, but all he saw was light glinting off unseen objects. And, oh, how frightened he was. As frightened as he had ever been during any battle, even more so. This wasn't war, not like he knew war, this was . . . personal.

It was then he felt a remarkable flash of focused pain at the back of his neck, just above where the man held him. Then he felt warm and thick liquid slide down the sides of his neck.

Blood. His blood.

Tears streamed down his cheeks and he kicked his feet wildly, but the man only tightened his grip. More pain followed, then a sawing sound.

And he experienced a pain very few have felt.

His head was being sawed off! What's more, he knew it. All he could think about were all those limbs he'd seen taken off by the battalion surgeon. And the reb was doing it slowly, precisely, so he knew—knew exactly—what was happening. Each stroke was as methodical as the one that preceded it, cutting into the bone just slightly, flopping the side of his head from side to side with each downward stroke so hard that his ear started to bleed . . .

Mike snapped up in bed, his eyes glassy, his body lathered by sweat, his breathing labored and quick. Muttering, he ran his hands through his hair and got out of bed. He went into the bathroom and splashed cold water onto his face. Once his heart regained normal rhythm, he looked at himself in the mirror. "You know that man," he said to his weakened reflection—three of the four lights above the sink were blown. "You've seen him before. But where, dammit? Where?"

As he thought about that, he realized something. He was bleeding. There was blood on his neck, just below the chin line, long fingers of it just now spreading downward.

out, and he had closed them. "I told them," he said. "I
told them, and it wasn't my fault."

20

At sunrise Mike was sitting in his window seat watching
the sky change. He'd stanched the bleeding, deciding that
he'd simply reopened an old shaving wound. Beside him
lay the photograph given to him by his grandmother years
earlier, taken by Matthew Brady himself during the Civil
War. He'd fished it out of a scrapbook kept in the bedroom closet. The photo was of a platoon of Union soldiers, the Albany Volunteers, under McClelland. A
soldier in the back row stood out, not only because of his
height—he was a head taller than everyone else—but
because of the remarkable resemblance he bore to Mike.
Mike's grandmother, a steadfast believer in reincarnation,
had always insisted that Mike was the reincarnation of
that soldier—Ernest Marat. Until now, Mike had lent
little credence to that theory.

But after a long and sleepless night, he'd finally put the
dream on the back burner, at least for the time being.
He'd started thinking about Al again, and where he might
be. Or maybe, where his body might be hidden.

He went into the kitchen to make himself a cup of
coffee. "Damn riddles," he mumbled, as he ran water into
the coffeepot. "No sleep doesn't help much, either."

With coffee in hand, he went back into the living room
and reclaimed his window seat. "Al's in the trunk of a
car," he said. "That much I know." He took a sip of
coffee while visualizing that. Then he remembered what

had been said in the warehouse, "Let's see where those explorations take you." He looked at his Oscar, Clint. "What the hell's that mean?" he said.

There was a dog on the sidewalk, a white, mixed breed with orange stripes, moseying along as dogs are wont to do, sniffing anything with potential. The dog squatted and marked the spot, then turned her attention to the other side of the sidewalk, specifically, the old Hudson that had been there for so long.

Something clicked in Mike's brain.

The dog walked over to the car and sniffed the front tire, then worked its way back.

"See where those *explorations* take you," Mike said.

The dog suddenly let loose with a howl and started scratching frantically on the trunk. Mike hesitated only a moment before he ran from his apartment and into the street. Running through his brain were the words *explorations* and *Hudson*. Following thereafter was the grotesque image of Al shoved unceremoniously into the trunk of this old car.

Book Two
Watertown and Points East

21

Propped against the car door as she was, Beverly would probably have felt a few of the bumps, had she been aware enough to notice bumps in the road. But right now her state of awareness was such that even the deepest ruts went unnoticed, especially in this late model Mercedes, the kind that ate bumpy pavement for breakfast.

At times, when she had the wherewithal to actually consider her state of mind, she got more than a little worried. A swirling vortex of past and near past events fluttered before her eyes, competing with what really surrounded her. Even full consciousness was no bargain. The low, dull headache that preceded snatches of full consciousness was highly reminiscent of how she'd felt coming out of anesthesia, when she'd groped like hell for reality, only to have it slip back and forth like oil on a teeter-totter. And along with that full consciousness, came an overwhelming sense of obedience that made her feel oh-so-sure that she would do anything her captors wanted, anything at all. All of which made her wonder if semiconsciousness wasn't the better choice.

But although her tether to reality was frayed at best, one thing she did know, they were going way too fast. Every now and then she caught a glimpse of the digital readout speedometer: eighty-five a constant eighty-five. But where were they going at that speed? All she saw out the window were trees, evergreens mainly, coming into and then out of the headlights in a faded green blur. But it didn't really matter where they were going. She would be dead soon, or worse, so what did it matter? This overpriced German luxury car could very well be a hearse for all she knew—or cared. She felt her eyes well up; this was too much to handle. She was physically spent, mentally drained. A real Section Eight mess! But as she had done before, she somehow found the strength to fight back her tears. Tears, she quietly decided, were definitely a sign of defeat. Well, she thought, sniffling and clenching her jaw, she hadn't given up yet, and she wasn't about to anytime soon.

She dabbed at her eyes as if to push back the lake of tears, then forced herself to sit up. As she did, pain said a loud hello. But pain was almost welcome right now, at least more welcome than all that mental confusion. The woman she had seen at the warehouse turned and smiled at her, her face lit softly green in the glow of the dashboard lights. Beverly considered her astonishing beauty.

Charlotte smiled as if she'd read her thoughts, which, in fact, she had. "You're awake," she said in a feather-light voice.

"Where are you taking me?" Beverly demanded with a tight snarl.

The woman ignored her and looked at the driver. "Philippe, Beverly would like to know where we're taking her. Should I tell her?"

Silence, long and infuriating. Then, "Home," Philippe said. "Circuitously."

"Where am I going to stay?" Mike said to himself, competing with the latest from the Judds, blaring from the stereo. "There's probably a million conventions going on." He smiled. "Well, maybe not in Watertown."

He'd decided to make the trip for one reason and one reason only—from all indications, that's where Beverly had been taken. Bev and a very important part of Al's anatomy. Light from the headlights made an excellent stage. Staring at the road, he saw himself opening the trunk of the Hudson and staring in horror at Al's chest, which was pretty much gone, as was his heart. In slow motion, he saw that skinny mongrel dog scrabble wild-eyed into the trunk and begin lapping up the half-coagulated puddles of blood that had settled into the concavities. There was blood everywhere. When he first opened the trunk, he wasn't sure if it was Al, there was so much blood. Then he saw himself grabbing that dog by the scruff of the neck and throwing it onto the sidewalk, staring blankly at it while it silently slinked off. Only when the car veered too far to the right, onto the shoulder, did his vision fade.

After the coroner arrived to verify that Al's heart had, indeed, been cut out, they also found a note. It said, HOME is where the HEART is. "Another riddle," Siragusa said, "another goddamn riddle! But at least this one's easy enough to figure out. Topeka, that's where your cousin's at. Al was born in Topeka, so it's my guess that's where the killer's taken her." The first thing Siragusa did was notify the authorities in Topeka. But Mike didn't think it was that simple. This wasn't about Al. Al had only been part of the puzzle. This was about Beverly and Mike. Topeka didn't have a thing to do with this. This had all been done for *his* benefit. That's why the killer chose that Hudson parked in front of his apartment, why he'd told him that riddle about tree trunks and dead explorers. Home, as in HOME is where the HEART is, referred to *his* hometown, not Al's. And his hometown was Watertown, New York. He didn't tell Siragusa this, because he didn't want to be stumbling over FBI agents and local cops. And there was something else at work here, anyway. Something that went beyond routine investigatory procedure. That hooker, whom he mistook for Beverly, was the best proof of that; followed closely by those perplexing mounds of earth in the basement and the remarkable dream of the night before. The killer, more

213

than likely the guy who had Beverly, had stashed Al's heart in Watertown somewhere. And now the killer wanted him to go there and find it. Beverly was just part of the deal. No heart, no Beverly.

With that highly unpleasant memory tucked away for a while, he remembered what Beverly had said in the hospital, that their parents hadn't died in a plane crash. While that was obviously not true, the look on her face made it clear that she was totally committed to that possibility, and that persuading her otherwise would be next to impossible. Why she would think that, he didn't know, but maybe in Watertown, he could check into it, have a chat with the shrink who'd taken care of their minds during the weeks following the incident, or maybe even go back to the house. Of course, he could just be grabbing at straws, but it was all he had right now.

The sign said Route 81, Watertown, 1/2 mile. Mike eased the car into the gentle curve that eventually pointed him north, and settled in. He was still fifty miles away, but at sixty-five, he'd be there in about forty-five minutes. And traffic was light, as it usually was on 81 North. He wished he hadn't gotten such a late start, but Siragusa had gotten some local felons together for him to look at. None even came close. Siragusa had even thrown in a couple cops, Mike recognized one.

He turned the station. Country and western was fine for an hour or so, about how long he had been on the road, but not for the long haul. He found some easy-listening station. If it put him to sleep, so be it.

While humming along with an old Beatles standard, a big Mercedes roared past. Mike looked at his speedometer. "Jesus, pal, where you goin'?" he said. "This ain't the autobahn, you know! Probably see you a couple miles up the road, pulled over by the local gendarmes." He smiled. He always wished that on speeders, but rarely did he get his wish.

* * *

214

Beverly turned and looked out the rear window. "Mike! Mike!" she yelled, waving her hands furiously. "Mike, it's me, Beverly! Please, Mike, please!"

She was positive it was him. Even whizzing by as fast as they had, she'd recognized first the car and then Mike. But she realized something then that harpooned her spirits. Their windows were deeply tinted. She could see out, but no one could see in. She watched Mike's headlights fade and fade and then pop into nonexistence, and her body felt like it weighed a thousand pounds.

22

As he got off the expressway, Mike silently concluded that things hadn't changed. Towns like Watertown rarely changed. There was just enough going on here to sustain the existing business climate, and not much else. People lived here, loved here, died here, and probably didn't much care what happened beyond the Jefferson County line.

It was almost nine, but finding a place to stay, despite his earlier worries, wasn't very difficult. He stopped at a Ramada Inn about a half mile from downtown and got a room. This particular Ramada Inn had been built on a huge parcel of land with woods flanking the mostly empty parking lots. There was a nip in the air, fairly normal for summer this far north, but he was prepared. He had on a blue wool pullover with red trim at the neck and wrists, his favorite. After he'd checked in, he put his lone suitcase into his room, went down to the restaurant and had a late supper. Then he went back to his room.

The trip had made him drowsy; the food made him feel like a caterpillar crawling along baking asphalt. But there was just too much going on inside his head right now to sleep. He lay down on the bed and turned on the television.

Ten minutes later he clicked the TV off, sat up, then went to the window, and pulled the curtain back. He thought about the house and the night of the family reunion. Peculiarly enough, he had an instant and very strong desire to go out there, and to hell with what time it was. There was, he quickly rationalized, really nothing better to do anyway. He dropped the curtain, shut off the lights, and left his room feeling strangely exhilarated, almost like a man with a mission.

On the way there, he thought about a couple things; why he was going out there at this time of night, and could he get inside, but he didn't have any answers.

When he got to the house, he stopped right out front. The brakes squeaked, and he wondered if anybody had heard.

Except for a thin, horizontal shaft of light from an upstairs bedroom, the house was dark. These people were getting ready for bed. Sitting here watching this dark house—this particular dark house—was like someone with pointy little teeth biting into his nerve endings. I should try to get in there, he thought. I really need to get in there. There are more important things going on than these people sleeping. He grabbed the door handle—and froze. What the hell would he tell these people after they opened the door? What *could* he tell them? That was definitely the final Jeopardy question, one he didn't have an answer for. He slumped, as the tension that had built up from the prospect of impending action drifted away.

Scant seconds after he'd stopped the car, a few mosquitoes flew in the barely open window. Their steady, high whine—softer then louder as they buzzed his ears—was maddening. Mike cranked the window closed, flicked on the dome light, and did in the interlopers with a flourish. That done he flicked off the light and moved the car about a hundred feet, just down an incline. From here all he could see of the house was the roof, but they wouldn't be able to see him at all. And he still had a good view of the backyard area, and the black hulk of the woods a quarter mile off. Even the city lights, haloed against the black dome of the sky, were nominally bright from here. Sure, he could keep an eye on things, he could

. . . an eye on what, Mike? Who? What in the world are you doing here? He pondered that question a moment, then shrugged it off as being too hard to answer, and laid his head back against the headrest. Jesus, that's uncomfortable, he thought almost immediately. He scooched down into a modified fetal position and laid his head on his fisted hands. In less than a minute, he was fast asleep, snoring ever so lightly, contentedly. But in lying down, he had also moved the window crank slightly, just enough to let a few mosquitoes into the car, advance scouts who went back and got the whole army. As the hours passed, they had a glorious and memorable feast.

An earthquake. They were having an earthquake! Mike sat up like he'd been shot from a cannon, leaving his senses behind. His muscles seemed to flutter. A blanket of white light dropped before his eyes; he rubbed them vigorously with the palms of his hands. The earthquake grew even louder, and he snapped his head to the left toward the sound. The bright red of what appeared to be a very new tractor reflecting the morning sun cut into his eyes like a laser. He squinted and raised his arm for protection. A man who looked to be in his sixties, with deeply tanned and furrowed skin and light blue eyes, leaned over slightly to get a look at him. Mike looked back, waved the half wave of someone who had been caught, and actually smiled. The man, however, frowned, and Mike watched as the tractor lumbered past and then pulled into his lane. At the bottom of the incline, the tractor turned right into a wheat field. It was then that Mike got a glimpse of himself in the rearview mirror, and what he saw made his breath quit. The right side of his face was a mass of mosquito bites. Anywhere they could bite, they had. The little bastards had attacked without mercy. But why only the right side of his face? Then it dawned on him. He'd spent the last seven hours or so in one position, with the left side of his face resting on the back of his right hand.

218

The little sonsabitches hadn't been able to get at the other side. But wasn't it amazing that he hadn't woken up? Something like that should have jerked him awake right away. Boy, I must have been out! he thought. He started scratching. Really out! But what do I do about these damn bites? Concentrating his efforts, he moved his hand away. "Don't itch them, for one thing!" he said to his reflection. "You'll have a real mess then! And you certainly can't knock on that door looking like this!"

He leaned closer to the mirror to get a better look at himself. The best thing to do, he decided, would be to go back to his room, call a pharmacy then wait 'til the swelling went down. "Face it, Mike," he said, "you're going to have to put your hunt on hold for a while, maybe until the end of the day, maybe even until tomorrow." He slumped back against the seat and suddenly realized why he hadn't woken up during the onslaught: he hadn't wanted to. An incident he had too easily dismissed from his conscious mind had come back for a visit while he slept. He had been dreaming about the warehouse, and about making love to Beverly in that little room. And all the while they made love, that old whore, Berty, just stood behind them chuckling and telling them they weren't doing it right. "Little more hip action there, Mikey! Come on, Beverly, don't be a slacker." He should have been totally repulsed, but he hadn't been. He didn't even tell himself to wake up, he just went on making love to Beverly while Berty chuckled away. It had been that tractor-earthquake that finally brought him around, out of Beverly's willing arms.

He started the car and drove into town. Because it was only a little before seven, he went back to his room and closed the door behind him, feeling a little like the Phantom of the Opera.

At nine precisely, he called a drugstore and almost begged them to deliver a bottle of calamine lotion. The woman on the other end hesitated, but eventually she agreed, and a half hour later, Mike got what he wanted. He spent the rest of the day in his room watching soaps, waiting for the swelling to go down, and fighting a very strong urge to go back out to the house, even looking as bad as he did. But fight it, he did, and by the time the sun started to set, he thought he looked reasonable enough to venture outside.

23

It was about 9:30, dusk, and Mike wondered if they weren't already in bed. He reminded himself to keep his bad side turned away as much as possible, and walked to the bright green front door. It opened almost as soon as he pressed the doorbell; someone had seen him coming up the walk.

"Yes?" said a cheerful, older woman with gentle, curving features. She looked at him closely, and Mike thought he saw her tense a little. He backed away slightly. "Can I help you?" she continued, less cheerfully.

She could see the chalky white mask sculpted from calamine lotion, he was sure about that, but Mike took a bold step forward anyway. How could he protect them if he wasn't bold? She looked a little stunned, but that quickly changed to sadness. Much to Mike's relief, she smiled. "Poison ivy?" she asked.

"Mosquitoes," Mike said, somewhat relieved. "I . . . it's a long story."

"Looks painful."

"Itches like crazy," he said with a shy grin. His hand twitched toward the abused area, but he stopped it.

There was a comfortable pause, then the woman asked, "Are you a friend of Ethan's?"

"Ethan?"

"My husband."

"He doesn't own a tractor, does he? A new one, very red?"

"No, that's Bill Tibetts, down the road. We just have a small garden, no need for a tractor. Then if you don't know Ethan . . ."

"I used to live here. I was in the area, and I thought I'd come by. I hope it's all right."

"Live here? But the only people who lived here was that family . . ."

"My parents."

She chose her words carefully. "Then you must be one of the . . . children."

Mike didn't know what to say, and he suddenly felt very foolish about being here.

"Excuse me," she said, "but I don't understand. Why would anyone . . . I mean the memories alone—?"

Memories? Mike wanted to say. I have no memories, not really. We were all stoned that night, blitzed into unconsciousness. But that, he knew, wouldn't do, not at all. "Therapy," he said. "You know, confront your problem head on. Look it straight in the eye, that kind of thing? My therapist told me it'd do me a world of good."

She thought about that for a very long time, and during the lull Mike thought he'd ask the obvious. "Look, maybe I'm a little outa line—"

"Why'd we buy the place, that's what you want to know, isn't it? Why anyone would want to buy a place like this?"

"Seems like a good question."

She smiled a tight smile, and for a moment Mike thought she was going to shut the door in his face. "That's simple," she said finally. "The house was, well, affordable. And having just put two kids through college, we needed something like this. And we weren't about to move away from the area. We love it here, Mr. Marat. And to be frank, we don't believe in ghosts, and we don't believe that lightning strikes twice in the same place. The evil had already happened here, Mr. Marat. We considered that."

He didn't ask her how she knew his name. Everyone knew what had happened here all those years ago, and the name of the family it had happened to.

He smiled, he hoped not wryly, and said, "And so did we, ma'am. So did we."

Finally, he thought he might have said the right thing, something that drenched pure, honest reaction. He watched her face, saw it brighten slowly but surely. Then she smiled and said, "Carolyn Fetchit, Mr. Marat. Ethan's in the study watching a baseball game. Please, won't you come in?"

Mike smiled absently and said, "Mike," as he entered.

Simply stepping into this house renewed emotions he wasn't sure he wanted renewed. It wasn't paranoia that he felt, paranoia only suggested that he was being watched. Stepping into this house made him feel more like someone whose body is suddenly not their own. As if he were being guided.

". . . Yankees and the Red Sox."

"Oh, I'm sorry," Mike said, turning.

Carolyn Fetchit looked at him and smiled knowingly. "Here I'm rambling, and I'm sure you just want to have a look around. Please, make yourself at home, Mr. Marat. I'll just go in and watch the game with Ethan."

She walked away, and Mike was stunned by how trusting she was. Or maybe she was simply being empathetic. Whatever, he decided that he liked her.

He went into the kitchen. The floor and cabinets were new. Cherry cabinets, a light-colored floor. Looked nice. He looked at the counter and imagined all those six-packs of beer sitting there next to a trio of dark brown canisters: sugar, flour, tea. The table and chairs were a lot like they'd had, which made it doubly easy to imagine the three of them sitting there working out a plan to steal that beer. For a second he actually thought he saw them doing just that. He passed that off as an hallucination born out of his surroundings, worked up a smile of fond reminiscence, then went into the dining room. Again he won-

223

dered why he was here, why he'd slept in his car all night. And again he couldn't come up with an answer. The only thing he did know for sure was that he absolutely had to go into the basement.

Although he barely recognized the rest of the house, it appeared the new owners didn't even know they had a basement. For all he knew those stairs could have been a time portal. Even the arrangement of the balls on the pool table looked the same. (And wasn't it odd that he would remember exactly where the balls were on the table.) What he'd felt upon entering this house had changed. He felt very much at ease now, almost as if whatever were guiding him had decided to leave. Feeling unusually refreshed, he walked over to the bar, sat down, and did a couple of quick three-sixties, like a kid. When he stopped, he saw that the walls were still speckled with carved coconut heads. His parents had collected carved coconut heads. Every time they went to the Florida Keys on vacation, they brought a couple back, and they went to the Keys as a vacation rule. As far as he could tell, these could very well be the same heads. Most of them were intended to be humorous, but some were a little scary, at least to a kid. Looking at them now made him feel like a kid again. They peered back at him from three sides, hairy and neckless and grotesque. One big one, carved into the head of a boar, tusks included, had stains beneath it, running down the wall like a V-shaped beard.

He glanced to his left, toward the darkroom, wondering if they still used it. Then he looked just to the right of the darkroom, toward the powder room. Oh the power of suggestion. He hesitated, wondering if he should ask permission, and decided that probably wasn't necessary.

After he had peed, flushed, and washed, he stepped back into the basement. What he saw then made his legs rubbery. They weren't ghosts; they couldn't be. Well, one could. Paul was dead after all. But he and Beverly were still alive, at least as far as Mike knew.

Beverly and Paul were seated at the bar, drinking shots of Old Grand Dad. He was behind the bar, pouring. What he saw were not transparent apparitions, and yet they weren't solid, either. The surroundings—the bar, the table, the floor, and walls—were only black and white shapes, that seemed very much removed from the colorful and very real apparitions socking down shots of good old Kentucky bourbon.

Mike stepped around the pool table and watched from a distance of about ten feet. He thought of his thirteen-year-old counterpart as Michel, not as Mike, the bastardization that had happened when he was about twenty.

The bottle was about half-gone, and from the looks of things, so were they. The tingling, weak-legged sensation had slowly subsided, merging into an intense interest in the goings-on.

He watched Michel refill the glasses. Beverly was definitely wasted. She wobbled like a deckhand on the high seas during a hurricane, and Paul laughed. He watched Michel tilt his neck back and throw down another shot. A couple of shots apiece later, the bottle was almost empty, or at least at the level it was at when they woke up that night, so long ago. Won't be long now, he thought. Just thinking about how their heads had felt back then made him grimace. And although this little show was quite strange, he'd been witness to stranger things of late. When all was said and done, it made more than a little sense that his mind should conjure this up for him now. Hell, he told himself, maybe I was right after all. Maybe I did come here for therapy.

Beverly swayed front to back and almost fell off her stool. Now they'd all pass out, just like before. He went to the bar and stood very close to Paul, half-expecting one of them to turn and say something to him. He leaned forward. "Go on," he said to Michel, "you've had your fill. Time to go night-night."

"I don't feel so good," Paul said.

Mike looked at him. Funny how he could see that little mole behind his left ear.

Beverly winced. "My gut feels like something's alive down there."

As if cued, she slumped off the chair, fell to her hands and knees, shakily got up, then stumbled into the bathroom, and threw up. He could see her rump as she leaned over the bowl. He smiled. "I don't remember you doing that."

Paul and Michel pointed at her and laughed like wild men. Seconds later Beverly came back in and sat down again. Paul waved at his nose. "God, you stink, Bev!"

"Shut up!" Beverly sleepily responded.

Out of the corner of his eye, Mike saw Michel turn toward the cellar window. "Must be playing some kind of game," Michel said, half-smiling.

"What?" Beverly asked. She ran her hand through her hair. Her eyes were half-closed.

"Out there," Michel said, without taking his eyes off the cellar window. "They must be playing tag or something. Look."

Paul got up and drifted over to the window. He could reach the interior ledge, but he couldn't pull himself up. He looked around, found a chair, then moved it under the window, laughing all the while. "Tag!" he said. "Can you see Aunt Connie playing tag? Be like a weather balloon that can't get off the ground."

He stepped onto the chair and slowly his expression changed from that of a clown to someone in ever-increasing pain. He looked back at Beverly and Michel, and for a moment it looked like he was going to say something; his mouth opened, he shook his head slightly. Finally, he closed his mouth, his face red now, his chin aquiver. If he wanted to say something, he couldn't get it out.

Mike stepped over to the window and looked closely at Paul, while Michel got up and promptly banged his hip into a corner of the pool table. "Ahhh, shit, that hurts!"

Paul didn't seem to notice. He got down from the chair

nd stumble-ran toward the stairs. "MOM! MOM!" he
elled, his voice liquid and pleading. By now the obvious
eriousness of what was going on had brought Beverly
ack to dim consciousness. She reached out to Paul as he
vent past, and grabbed his arm. He pulled free, yelled,
'Mom, they're after Mom!" and ran up the stairs.

Beverly put a hand on the railing and continued to
vatch, even after Paul was long gone. She did her best to
naintain her composure, but her face transformed as
nuch as Paul's had. Finally, not really knowing what to
lo, she yelled, "Michel!"

No response.

She started toward him. "Michel, something's wrong.
God, something's really wrong!"

Michel turned and looked at her.

"Outside," she said. "Something outside. Paul ran out
here. He said something about Mom. Michel, I'm
cared. God, I'm really scared!"

Mike watched all this from the cellar window. He
lidn't want to look away, they'd disappear then, some-
now they'd just disappear. Something was happening that
e didn't at all remember, and it wouldn't if they disap-
eared. Still, he couldn't help but glance outside, and
vhen he did, all he saw were arms and legs and feet
urrying past the small, rectangular window. While he
vatched, he heard Michel say, "We gotta do something,
ve gotta go out there, Bev. We got no choice."

Mike turned away from the window and watched while
3everly and Michel simply looked at each other, then
quietly got up, went to the stairs, and began their ascent.
He ran across the cellar, but they were out of sight now.
'Michel, Beverly, stop. Please come back!" He stopped at
he bottom of the stairs and looked upwards; the door was
ppening, they were leaving. The door closed behind
hem. "No, come back, come back!"

He took the stairs two at a time, threw open the door,
nd burst into the kitchen. He looked left. Nothing.

Looked right. And there stood Carolyn Fetchit, a worried look on her face. "Something wrong, Mr. Marat?"

His eyes were wild, frantic. "No, I—"

Movement to his left. He wheeled. They were still there. Michel and Bev were just now opening the screen door that led into the backyard. Light. Weird colors.

"I'm going to have to ask you to leave now," said Carolyn Fetchit.

He heard her, but only from a distance. She grabbed him by the arm, distracting him with her amazingly strong grip. He looked at her, and only half-realized that she, too, was colorless. At the same time, Michel and Bev stepped into the backyard, letting the screen door slam closed behind them. He jerked toward the sound.

Didn't you hear that? he wanted to say.

"Mr. Marat, did you hear me? I said you'll have to leave now."

Ethan Fetchit stepped into the kitchen. "What's the problem?"

What to do, what to do? Mike's mind raced. He could barely see Beverly, and Michel was gone. It looked like the wind had picked up. But now he heard other voices from out back, yelling, pleading. Appealing for mercy.

He turned to the Fetchits. "Didn't you see them?" he asked. He looked closely at them. "No, you couldn't have seen them. They're the ones that're real, not you."

"Just what do you mean—not real?" Ethan Fetchit asked. His rising anxiety brought on a smile.

"Mr. Marat," said Carolyn Fetchit, "what is going on here?"

Mike turned toward the back door.

"Mr. Marat, I'm talking to you!"

He started to walk away. "It's all right. You're not real, so it's all right. And even if you are real . . . but you can't be. You're black and white. So how can you be real? They're real though. They're real!"

Ethan Fetchit stepped toward him, but his wife put her hand on his arm. He looked at her, she at him, and both watched as Mike opened the screen door that led into the backyard and stepped out.

Mike didn't hear the door close behind him, nor did he hear the bolt being thrown. There were other things for him to see and hear.

24

What first caught Mike's attention were the Chinese lanterns swaying in the wind, etching brightly colored smiles onto the dark background of night. From there his attention was naturally drawn to a body lying lengthwise on a redwood picnic table, a fat woman wearing a flower print dress. The wind had whipped her dress unceremoniously over her waist. She had on a girdle, and she was on her stomach, her right hand behind her back at an impossible angle, the other hand thrown to the side, palm up. Her face was turned away. Her long, dark hair covered most of it.

His Aunt Connie.

Around her on the table were soiled paper plates, half-eaten burgers and potato salad and fried chicken. Gobs of ketchup and mustard. Plastic spoons and forks. Part of a plate stuck out from under Connie's body, like the curve of a big, white belt buckle. In front of her, seated in the middle of the bench, was her husband, Al. Big man, almost two-fifty. Arms like a lumberjack. He had on his Hawaiian shirt. His big, hairy hands were folded onto his lap, fingers laced. His legs were spread. His head was gone.

Mike thought of Paul.

From mid-chest up, Al's Hawaiian shirt was drenched in blood; had to be blood. His head was gone, so it had to be, although at night it looked more like tar. When the anterns moved, Mike could see colors reflect in the blood. For some reason he thought of the word festive.

He moved toward them, ignoring the people around him trying to get away, and said, "Aunt Connie? Uncle Al?" His voice was low, reverent.

The closer he got, the stronger the old fear became. His muscles tensed, his pulse pounded high in his arms. And as he reached out to them, tears streaming down his face, as he reached out to touch his uncle on the shoulder, he saw Michel out of the corner of his eye, reaching and crying as he moved toward them from a dark area off to the right, where the Chinese lanterns had been busted.

From the doorway, Carolyn Fetchit watched the crazy man while her husband dialed the sheriff's office from the kitchen.

"Not real, huh, I'll show you who's not real! WHAT'S HE DOING NOW, CAROLYN?"

Carolyn squinted. She couldn't see him very well. It was pitch-dark out back, and the bulb was blown. She wouldn't have turned it on anyway, even if it had been working. "DUNNO. WAIT! LOOKING, JUST LOOKING AT SOMETHING. Why'd I let him in, Ethan? WHY'D I DO THAT? 'Specially since last night."

Ethan put his hand over the mouthpiece. "DO WHAT?"

"LET HIM IN! WHY'D I LET HIM IN?"

"WASN'T YOUR FAULT, CAROLYN. YOU WERE TRYING TO BE NICE, THAT'S ALL. AND WHAT YOU HEARD LAST NIGHT COULD HAVE BEEN ANYTHING. JUST KEEP WATCHING. DOORS ARE LOCKED, FRONT AND BACK. DON'T YOU WORRY, HE CAN'T GET BACK IN. BUT DON'T LET HIM—"

"Sheriff's office."

"Yeah, I gotta speak to the sheriff. And make it snappy."

"He's at home, sir."

"Home? Dammit! Well, send someone out here. We got a problem . . ."

Michel stood on the other side of the table, gently jostling his aunt. "Aunt Connie? Wake up, Aunt Connie, please wake up!"

Mike wanted to tell him she wasn't going to do that. Look at her husband, Michel. His head's gone. And look at her arm. It's busted and she doesn't care. For chrissake, she can't care!

Misery and hope. Close relatives.

Michel moved away from the picnic table, shaking his head. Unbelieving. He'd always liked Connie and Al. They teased, but he had always liked them. This couldn't have happened, it just couldn't! This was not what he remembered! His parents had died in a plane crash, his aunt and uncle in a fire. No one had died here that night, no one!

Mike looked to the left. Beverly was just standing there, her hands over her face, crying. Michel moved toward her, Mike followed like a shadow. He could see Paul in the darkness along the side of the house, away from the glow of the Chinese lanterns.

Beside Beverly, seated in folding chairs, were his Aunt Sofia and Gretchen, the distant cousin. Except for the fact that their heads were too far back and their eyes were glassy, they could have been alive. Mike could see the lanterns reflected in their eyes, swaying, swaying.

By now the backyard was quiet. Everyone who wanted to get away, had. Mike just stood there and counted bodies; six that he could see; Al, Connie, Gretchen, Sofia, two men propped against the house near the back door. He didn't know who they were. Their heads were gone, too. Why, he wondered, were the men the only ones whose heads were taken off?

Paul stepped out of the shadows. "Over there," he said quietly. "They're over there."

So passive. Michel and Beverly followed Paul. They went into the darkness and almost disappeared. Mike just watched from where he was. He didn't want to go over there. He could see the three of them kneel, at least their dark forms. There were more bodies propped against the side of the house. He could make them out now, not who they were, just that they were there. They could have been bags of potatoes.

Mike's chest tightened; his breath came in quick, shallow volleys.

Mom? Dad?

Movement was difficult, but he managed. Gretchen's and Sofia's eyes seemed to follow.

The Chinese lanterns were fading; the party was ending. But along the side of the house, in the shadows, everything was the same.

Michel? Bev? Paul? What is it? What'd you find?

Stupid question.

He watched them stand up and hold each other, just a big, dark blob. He thought he heard them crying. A big, dark blob crying in the night.

This is what happened, Mike thought. Really happened. We forgot. Didn't want to remember.

The big, dark blob separated slightly and started for him. They were holding each other, arms wrapped. Crying openly. They walked right past him. He watched as they stepped toward Gretchen and Sofia, then stopped, stepped toward Connie and Al, and stopped again. It didn't matter which direction they took.

Movement—from the darkness and into the fading lantern light.

Mike watched the children out of the corner of his eye, more interested now in the two people who had stepped out of the darkness, who were now moving steadily toward them. Who are they? I don't know them—who are they?

233

One was a woman, the other a man, both tall and well formed, their clothing splattered with blood. But it was not their blood-splattered clothing he first noticed, it was their freedom of movement; like fog under the influence of a gentle breeze, but even that description fell short, for the movements of these two seemed totally uninfluenced, as if the background were shifting and they were simply walking in place. And their expressions, given the circumstances, were decidedly strange. Indifference is what Mike saw; and something more as well. A kind of subdued glee. Especially on the face of the man. He held out his hand, the woman stopped and looked at him. Mike looked back at the children. Involved with their grief, they hadn't noticed the pair, not yet. The woman stopped and the man smiled at her and stepped closer to the children. That was when Paul noticed the man. His eyes wide, pleading, he broke away from the group, moving only a few feet before he stumbled and fell down. Now the others saw him, too, his slow, yet inexorable approach, his arms swaying like metronomes. Although they did seem startled, that reaction changed quickly, almost mirroring the indifference on the face of the man, who stopped and gestured toward the back door. The children moved in that direction without hesitation.

"Wait," Mike said. His voice sounded flat and toneless.

The man opened the door; the children entered. The man followed.

"Wait, dammit, wait!" Again his voice seemed capable of reaching only a few feet, no echo, no resonance, as if he'd yelled into empty space.

The door closed softly. As Mike moved toward it, so did the woman. Mike hesitated, but he knew exactly what was going on here. She couldn't hurt him. Just the opposite of how things appeared. He and the Fetchits, this house—all real, black and white, yes, but still real. This woman, although extraordinary, although as filled with luxuriant color as any rainbow, was not real. He moved toward her; half-expecting her to look at him, almost wishing she would. But she didn't look at him, nor did she fade with his closing proximity. Finally, resisting the urge to step through her, he stepped around her—and looked into the very frightened, pale face of Carolyn Fetchit.

"Ethan, Ethan!" She stepped back and let the curtain fall.

Ethan stepped behind her. "Not to worry," he said. "He can't get in."

The door rattled as Mike grabbed the handle and shook it. "Let me in, please, please, let me in!"

"Go away, mister!" Ethan yelled.

"Please, it's very important. Please!"

Ethan and Carolyn moved further away from the door; the door rattled once more, then there was only silence.

Mike turned. They were in the basement. The children had been taken into the basement! The Chinese lanterns were gone now. "Too late," he muttered, glancing toward the dark woods. "God, I hope it's not too late!"

He ran to the left and fell onto his stomach. He could see into the cellar from here. Some things were black and white, others had color. But they weren't there! They weren't there!

Then, as if on cue, Michel, then Paul, then Beverly appeared at the bottom of the stairs. They stepped back a few feet, their collective gaze drawn to the stairway. Within seconds, Mike saw the man's feet, then the whole man. But then the children started to fade.

"No, don't go, don't go! Show me more. I have to see more!" The resonance had returned to his voice.

They vanished, and what had been black and white in the cellar regained color. Hope almost gone now, Mike pushed himself up and ran toward the back door again.

"YOU SEEN ENOUGH, PAL?"

Mike grabbed the doorknob, shook it violently.

"I SAID, YOU SEEN ENOUGH?"

Mike let go of the doorknob and turned; reality returned in a rush. There was a man carrying a flashlight coming down the hill toward the backyard; the beam bobbed up and down as he tried to keep his balance.

Mike stepped away from the door and onto the grass.

The man stopped, just twenty or so feet away. "Get down," he ordered.

Mike raised his arm to deflect the light. "Wait, you don't understand."

"Get down or I'll make you get down!"

Small man, wearing a hat. Gun in his other hand.

Mike dropped to his knees.

The man stepped closer. "On your stomach, I'm sure you've done this before, pal. Don't play cute."

"Before?"

"Just *do* it!"

Mike did as he was told. He wondered if he'd gotten any blood on him. He looked at the back door while the man pulled his hands behind his back and cuffed him. Through the window he saw Ethan and Carolyn Fetchit looking at him. Their fear had been replaced by relief.

25

The deputy pulled the car onto the main road. Mike was in the backseat.

"Look, this is all a big mistake. Can't you see that?"

"That's not my judgment."

"I used to live there, I told you that. I told them that. That's why I was there!"

"And when I found you, you were peeking in the window."

"You saw my ID. I am who I say I am."

"Your name is Marat. That's all I know. That don't mean you used to live there."

The deputy got on the radio. An electric crackle, then, "Deputy Sorles, over."

"Dispatch, over."

"Suspect in custody. ETA, five minutes. Over."

"Copy. Over and out."

Suspect, Mike thought. Jesus, now I'm a common peeper! Mirandized and cuffed. What next?

"Look, deputy, you think I could see a judge tonight?"

"That wouldn't be up to me. Sheriff's the only one—"

"Him, then."

"I'm not sure I want to call Sheriff Boothman in on this tonight."

"Boothman? You mean Terry Boothman's still the sheriff?"

The deputy peered quizzically into the rearview mirror. "You know Sheriff Boothman?"

"Yes. I know him."

The deputy seemed skeptical. "You sure? I'll get in real trouble if you're lying to me. I don't want to call him and find out you lied to me."

"No, dammit, I'm not lying to you! He investigated that night."

"That night?"

"When my parents were killed."

"I still got to take you in."

"Fine, take me in, but call Boothman. Can you do that, please?"

"I guess I can do that," the deputy said. "But if you're lying to me . . ."

Mike was fingerprinted, photographed, then put into a cell. There was another man next cell over, sound asleep. Through a small window in the metal door that led into the outer offices, Mike could see Deputy Sorles every now and again as he walked by. A half hour passed, then an hour. He was beginning to think that Sorles had let him down. Ten minutes later, Boothman arrived.

Carolyn and Ethan Fetchit stayed up and watched television. They were too scared to go to bed. Again Carolyn Fetchit asked, "Why did I let him in, Ethan? Why?"

Ethan just patted her hand for comfort. He knew how it went. She'd dismissed what she'd heard last night, down in the cellar. He hadn't heard it, but she had. She'd woken him up. "Ethan! Ethan! I hear something! Wake up, I hear something!" So he woke up and the two of them just sat up in bed and listened to the sounds of the house, waiting to hear something mysterious. They didn't, not after he woke up, just the sump pump coming on and that crazy woodpecker trying to build a home in the corner of the big window on the first floor. She'd let the man in because he looked pretty harmless, and he had lived here. Ethan hadn't seen anything wrong in that. Everyone liked to go home. How were they to know he was one of them crazies? Who could tell? At least he hadn't stolen anything. He thought about that. Least nothing up here. There were things of value in the basement though. He could've taken something from down there. A knickknack, maybe. His elephant statuary. A coconut head. He smiled thinly. Marat could have all those coconut heads if he wanted. Only reason he kept them was because Carolyn liked them. Still, maybe he should go down and check. They had the guy locked up. If he stole something, he probably still had it. They could get it back with a phone call.

"I'll be back," he said to Carolyn. He got up.

"Where you going?"

"Basement. Just going to check things out, make sure he didn't steal anything."

"You think he stole something, Ethan?"

"I don't know. Maybe. I'll just check."

He didn't know why he was doing this. The chance that the guy had stolen something was pretty remote. He was just a little crazy; he wasn't a thief.

Ethan rolled the cue ball back and forth across the pool table and looked around. Knickknacks were all there. He went around the bar. Two bottles of Chivas Regal, one of Jim Beam. Still there. He remembered the man using the bathroom and felt funny about that.

Coconut heads all still there, near as he could tell. He squinted. The rheostat was low, so he turned it up. What the hell? Water leak? He walked around the pool table to the other side of the basement, and inspected the V-shaped, beardlike stain beneath the boar's head coconut.

"What the . . ."

He touched the stain. It came off red. Thick. His heart thumped a couple of times. "Jesus!"

He lifted the head off the wall, and as he did, something

239

fell to the floor with a liquidy splat, leaving a slimy trail.

Ethan knelt and looked at it. He didn't know what it was, but he did know that he didn't want Carolyn to see it.

Not knowing what else to do, he went into the powder room, dug under the sink, and came up with an old dustpan and a whisk broom, then he swept up the mess and flushed it down the toilet. A couple minutes later the wall and carpet were at least cleaner than they had been; tomorrow he'd come down and scrub it good. After a last look around, he went back upstairs.

"Nothing," he said as he sat down next to his wife.

"Well, that sets my mind at ease."

"Thought it would. What's on?"

" 'Love Boat.' "

Sitting here watching television, Ethan couldn't help but wonder about what he had found. Animal something or other, probably. He thought about the *Godfather* movie and the horse's head and shook his head with bewilderment and outrage. Someone had played a mean, dirty trick on them.

Liver, maybe.

No, livers were darker, soaked with blood.

Heart? He tried to think of what a heart looked like, not the Valentine's Day kind, the real kind. Yeah, he concluded, probably a heart. Pig's heart, maybe. Could be a cow's. He pictured some satanist sneaking down there and leaving a pig's heart behind that boar's head coconut. Maybe he should tell the sheriff about what he'd found. Or maybe he should just lock the doors from now on. Of course, that guy could have put it there. A survivor from what happened here probably carried weird shit around with him, in his mind.

That conclusion had a more reassuring feel than cult members sneaking around in his basement.

"I hate 'The Love Boat,' " said Carolyn Fetchit with a disgusted sigh.

Ethan settled in and watched, and while the normal

240

clutch of bikini-clad young women gathered around "The Love Boat" pool, cow's hearts and satanists slipped silently from his thoughts.

Terry Boothman closed the door behind him and gestured to a straight-back, armless, wood chair in front of his desk. He was bigger now than Mike remembered. The good life showed, like half his belt buckle when he stood up. He was almost bald, just a little gray left on the sides. His scalp was light red, as were his cheeks. His eyes were still bright and kind though. Lots of laugh lines. Mike remembered that about him. The priesthood might have been his second choice as a profession. Boothman tented his fingers on the desk; his forearms were still huge, lots of hair on his nicotine-stained fingers.

Mike had quit smoking years earlier. Still, he wondered what the cigarette sticking out of a pack of Carltons on the green blotter would taste like.

"Michel—"

"Mike, if that's okay?"

"Mike. I got three people telling me you were acting awfully strange; Ethan and Carolyn Fetchit and Deputy Sorles. Now I know you used to live there, and I certainly know about what happened there, but Mike, I got a community to protect. You can't go around scaring people like that, peeking in their windows."

"Sheriff, I didn't mean to scare anyone—"

"Well, you did. And Carolyn Fetchit's got a weak heart—"

"It's just that I saw some things."

"Things?"

"Things I didn't remember."

"Such as?"

Mike hesitated.

"Mike, I'm tired. Now I can sympathize, but like I said—"

"I saw my parents killed."

Boothman's eyes, tired earlier, brightened. "You saw your parents killed?"

"Yes."

The sheriff just looked at him. Then, "What do you mean when you say you 'saw them killed'?"

"It came back to me. I mean, that's natural."

"Wait, I don't understand. Now I know it's natural. Hell, that's what Samuelson said, but . . . wait a sec, I want to read you something."

Boothman got up and called in Deputy Sorles, spoke at a whisper. Sorles left and Boothman sat down again. Nothing was said until Sorles came back, a brown file folder in his hand. He gave it to Boothman, who flipped it open, glanced at a few pages, then stopped and let his finger run down to the middle of the page.

" 'All three children, Paul, Beverly, and Michel Marat, have been referred to Dr. Joshua Samuelson, on staff at Watertown General. For reasons unknown they seem to believe that their parents died in a plane crash three years ago. Our efforts at convincing them otherwise have been fruitless. Furthermore, it is their belief that nothing happened here tonight.' Uh, by tonight I mean . . ."

"I know."

"You do?"

"Of course, the night of the massacre."

Boothman put the file down. "That's just what I'm getting at, Mike. You and the others, well, you just wouldn't accept it, I mean that there *was* a massacre. We took you to the morgue, showed you the bodies—I was against that, by the way, but Samuelson said it was our best shot."

"I remember. And I remember seeing my mother's body, too. I assume you didn't let me see my father because he had been decapitated. Is that right?"

Boothman nodded and said, "Yeah. Samuelson agreed with me on that. We sat you all down and tried to tell you what happened, but you just looked at us with these blank stares like we were speaking some foreign language or something. We even took one kid at a time, but that didn't work either. In a way I guess it was okay, I mean you'd already done your grieving. You thought your parents had died in a plane crash years earlier, so you'd already been through it. But, Christ, I knew it'd come back to you someday, I just knew it! Samuelson knew it, too, but there wasn't a thing we could do about it. I'll bet you came back here 'cause it started coming back, right?"

"Yeah, in a dream. A nightmare."

Boothman looped his fingers together on the desk and shook his head in commiseration. Then he looked hard at Mike. "What about the others? Them, too?"

"No, they . . . Paul's dead, so . . ."

"Ah, Jesus. How?"

"Accident."

"Drunk driver probably, huh? What about the girl?"

"I don't know, I haven't seen her for a while. Lost touch a little, I guess."

"You know, I saw something between you two back then. You acted really protective of her."

Mike smiled politely.

"Guess I'm a little surprised to hear you lost touch."

"Well, I got married. My wife died."

Boothman shook his head with more vigor. "Ain't life a bitch? So what you got planned now, Mike? I mean, you got this thing purged, so what do you plan on doing now? Be kind of like a new start and all, I guess, huh?"

"No plans. I'm a reporter. I guess this revelation doesn't affect that too much. Does seem like a real weight's been lifted though."

"Yeah, I can just imagine."

"So, I'm free to go then?"

"Sure, why not. No crime done here that I can see. Just promise me that you won't go back out there. Can you do that? It won't do you much good anyway."

"No, I won't go back out there, Sheriff. I have no reason. I can go then?"

"Sure. One thing though, Mike. How long you gonna be in town?"

"Not long."

"That's good. Real good."

"Sheriff, what about my car?"

"It's out front." He reached into his front pocket. "Here." He threw Mike the keys they'd taken from him while he was being booked.

"Sheriff," Mike said, "you never arrested anyone, did you?" He spoke rhetorically.

"No. We had the usual crap. One guy came all the way up from North Carolina to confess, some goddamn student doing some psychology paper. Jesus. But no, we didn't arrest nobody. Oh we had descriptions, you know, but every one of the survivors had something different to say. Nothing jived. Real mishmash. And that was *très* strange, as they say."

"No prints?"

"Oh, sure, plenty of prints, on the bar in the basement, on the railing going down, on those . . . whatchamacallum . . . Adirondack chairs outside, on the picnic table. We got some prints in blood, you know, dried blood. We had more fuckin' prints than we needed, but there wasn't anything on file. State police came up empty, too.

"You know, Mike, I always wondered about the case, why all those descriptions, why you and the other kids insisted no one died that night. I asked Dr. Samuelson about it, too. He said that if he didn't know better, he'd swear there'd been a case of mass hypnosis. That's pretty farfetched, I know, but I sure wish to hell there was another explanation. You ain't got one, do you, Mike? I mean you're seeing all this through new eyes so to speak, so . . ."

"No."

"Well, no harm in asking."

"No, no harm in asking."

"Then you'll let me know . . ."

"You'll be the first, Sheriff."

* * *

After Mike drove away from the station, he pulled over to the side of the road and let the engine idle. Given time to think now, he finally realized what had happened. All these years he had been convinced that nothing did happen that night. And although he had always remembered sitting down with Samuelson and Boothman, what they talked about had nothing to do with a backyard, family-reunion massacre. The pain of their parents' deaths, they said, had been so intense that regular sessions had been needed to help them through their grief. And the bodies in the morgue were, again until tonight, just other people; clinical attempts at helping them wade through that thick puddle of grief. Now, of course, he knew that was all a lie. With his mind's eye he could see his mother on that cold slab. And he knew damn well that his father was in there somewhere, too. Hidden. So it was all coming together now. The reason Al Lopez, sworn to uphold the law, would kill three people. Why Mike in some immensely shallow, animalistic moment, got aroused by some old whore, an old whore he could have sworn was Beverly. And why he'd spent twenty years thinking the wrong thing. Everything. Boothman had nailed it—they'd been hypnotized! Probably given a posthypnotic suggestion to believe one thing, while something else altogether had gone on. And who had done it was no mystery either; it had been that guy in the backyard, the man who had taken them down into the basement, the man who had sat them all down and told them what he wanted them to believe, not the way it was. But wasn't it a bitch that he couldn't for a moment remember what the guy looked like? And where Al's heart had been stashed was still a mystery, too. But if Al's heart was here, in Watertown, then Beverly was probably here, too. Still, he wasn't entirely positive that he was right and Siragusa was wrong. Beverly could be in Topeka or Toledo, or wherever the hell Al was from. Shit, what made him think he was right

245

and Siragusa was wrong? Siragusa *was* the detective, after all. Mike was just a reporter. What did he know?

He sat up, inhaled, let it out. Of course, he's here, Mike. Why do you think you had those visions at the house? You think you did that to yourself? Not on your life!

"Christ," he said aloud, "I need a beer. Maybe a chaser, too."

26

Mike pulled onto the highway and drove aimlessly through the city streets. Once he got to the town limits, he slowed down. There was a bar on the right. He pulled into a parking place between an old red Camaro sporting a bumper sticker that said Snow Capital of the Free World, and a white pickup truck with bundled hay in the back. The bar was called The Lonely Bull; the sign had a picture of a bull with a tear wiggling down its face. Mike went in and sat at the bar.

"Yeah?" said the bartender, a tall, corpulent man with a red face. He had on a white shirt and a white, spotted apron.

"Bud."

"Comin' up."

Mike turned on his stool and looked around. There was an old couple on his left, at the far end of the bar, staring into their beer. Two women in their twenties sat a couple seats down drinking margaritas and smoking Chesterfield cigarettes. They'd left the pack on the bar. Elvis blared from the juke box. Just behind the old couple, Mike saw a pool table. It reminded him of the basement at the house. He watched a short guy in his thirties come around to the end to line up a shot. At the same time, the bartender put Mike's beer on the bar in front of him.

Mike turned and looked at him blankly. "Oh, fuck!" he said.

The bartender leaned in, "Hey, pal, you wanta watch the language, there's ladies—"

"Where's the phone?"

"D'you hear me?"

"Where's the phone, dammit?"

The bartender backed away. " 'Cross from the john."

"Where's the john?"

"End of the bar, on the right."

"Phone book there, too?"

"Yeah, there's a phone book."

The phone book hung on a chain. Mike flipped it open and looked up the number, listed under both names, then dialed. After five rings, he started to get concerned. On six he got an answer.

"Hello?"

"Mr. Fetchit, listen very carefully. There may be something in your basement, something very important—"

"Wait a minute here, just one damn minute! You're the fella that put that thing down there, aren't you?"

"Then you found something? What, Mr. Fetchit? What did you find? It's very important!"

"You know Carolyn would have had a heart attack if she'd seen that! You know that? What kind of terrible thing is that to do to someone?"

"What was it, Mr. Fetchit? What did you find?"

"Don't give me that crap! You know damn well what I found! I wasn't gonna call the sheriff about this, but I just might now. You've got a real nerve calling here. Real nerve!"

"Whatever it was, Mr. Fetchit, I did not put it there. Believe me, I did not put it there. Now please, just tell me what you found."

Ethan Fetchit hung up with a noisy flourish.

Mike held the phone in his hand a second, then put it back on the hook. At the same time, he sensed someone standing behind him. He turned and looked into the face of a large, middle-aged woman with bleached blond hair and tiny, dull blue eyes. A cigarette dangled between her fingers like a growth.

"If you're done, I'd like to make a call," she said nasally. She took a drag on the cigarette and exhaled through her nose like a steam engine.

Mike stepped aside, stood there a moment, drawing in the somewhat teasing smell of cigarette smoke, then went back to his car. He sat there for a very long time, not really knowing what to do. Finally, he drove into town, just down the street from the Olympic Theater. His car was spotlit by a streetlamp; light spilled onto the sidewalk from a video arcade two doors down. There had to have been lots of noise, but with his windows shut, Mike couldn't hear a thing.

He ran his fingers through his hair and shook his head desultorily. How could he fight this . . . monstrosity? This preternatural creature? And why in the world was he playing these head games with Mike? The overwhelming futility of his task suddenly fell upon him with all the mercilessness of a hawk clamping onto a field mouse. There he was, that scared little mouse, screeching and crying and being lifted far, far away from its home, alive, sure, but for how long? When would that hawk settle in and dine on its tasty morsel? And where. Here, in Watertown? And was there even the slimmest chance that he could eventually save Beverly from the same fate Paul and Al had met? Not to mention his own fate. Ah, but that seemed less important now. Far less important. He leaned his forehead lightly onto the steering wheel and closed his eyes. A good night's sleep right now seemed like something Ed McMahon might offer in lieu of ten million dollars.

Beverly looked out the front window of the Mercedes and imagined herself running down the street and pulling open Mike's door. But imagining was one thing; action was quite another. Charlotte and Philippe, as she had come to know them, had a firm grip on her ability to even move across the backseat of her own volition. They were in the front seat, passive, restrained, just watching Mike's car. How far away was he? A hundred feet, maybe even less? She wondered if Mike knew this car was here, and thought not. Although he had parked beneath a street-light, they hadn't. And this car was black. She could see the video arcade and the theater, the Olympic, just beyond where Mike was parked. It looked closed now, as it had probably been for decades.

Sometime ago, she had decided that she wasn't in any immediate physical danger. Psychological injury, how-ever, seemed imminent. The mind control they were ex-erting had left her feeling defeated and alone. Totally at their mercy. Every minute it seemed she sank further and further into the depths of irretrievable depression; suicide, hovering at reality's door, had become an option. If she ever got the chance. Her only hope, it seemed, was the strength she had garnered from the love she felt for Mike, love she had allowed to remain dormant all these years, love brought out of its hibernation quite unwittingly by what she had seen at the warehouse—Mike and that woman together. The event tugged at her, and she had come to the conclusion that Mike had not been responsi-ble, that Philippe, through some far-flung mental gymnas-tics, had managed to manipulate Mike. Just as he had manipulated Beverly into believing that the warehouse was an eighteenth-century ballroom. She told herself that from here on she'd try her damndest to look at whatever happened with a discerning, questioning eye. Separating reality from fiction wasn't going to be easy, considering her steadily declining mental state, but it was all she had, that and her faith in Mike.

One side effect of her mental imprisonment was that her pain was minimized. As if she'd been given a local anesthetic. Unfortunately, it had worked on her tear ducts as well, and she thought she'd feel a whole lot better right now if she could just cry.

* * *

Philippe, although mentally engaged, had caught a few of Beverly's thoughts. And although sympathy and understanding were not part of his emotional repertoire, he did remember that he *had* felt them at one time, long ago. For Marie, for his daughter, Jeanette. But what those emotions actually felt like, he didn't remember. Of course, remembering these pseudoemotions also rekindled thoughts of his "life" up to now, most of which had involved his revenge, a revenge whose gleam had not dulled over the centuries. He was beginning to wonder how he would feel when his revenge was complete, a revenge made unique by his peculiar powers. At times he cursed that power, even more developed than in other immortals, those who had been made by different races of vampires. And wasn't humankind foolish to believe that vampires were of only one genus. Given their own varied and diverse origins, couldn't they begin to understand that vampires were also begotten from diverse and varied origins? Some blessed, some not as blessed. Some, once transformed, stronger physically or perhaps brighter, their particular peculiarity genetically traceable to the clan of vampire that had made them.

Looking out the windshield at Michel Marat, Philippe almost pitied him. Such a short life—and certainly not to be lengthened by him. To allow him the gift—never. It did seem strange at times though, the reason for his revenge. Love. That feeling was alien to him now. Unremembered. What burned in its place was revenge. Soon to be complete. Surely immortality was worth the price.

He smiled, remembering how he had hobnobbed with mortal men, those of greatness. Napoleon at Waterloo, speaking with him at length the night before. Lee at Appomatox Courthouse, begging him not to surrender, extolling the virtues and necessity for slavery, for which Philippe was quickly rebuffed. Hitler in the bunkers, seconds before he killed both himself and his mistress, Eva

Braun. He remembered Charlie Manson, given to evil but not to the extent necessary to murder, not until they had "talked." And wouldn't the world be amazed and totally confused when it came time for Charlie to die, when his eighty-odd years was up and he simply continued. As yet they hadn't begun to notice that Charlie hadn't aged. They would, though. Someday. And Charlie, who understood the gift as much as any mortal ever had, refused to escape from his prison. "The joke's the thing," he told Philippe, that murderous grin affixed to his mouth, that unforgettable glint in his eyes.

He glanced at Charlotte. She had been with him during those meetings, but of late she seemed aloof, as if she had grown weary of his thirst for revenge. Or did she sense something more as well? The "feelings" he had for the woman in the backseat. Perhaps she felt threatened. Charlotte caught him looking. It wasn't love that passed between them, but confusion.

Funny, Charlotte thought, how over the centuries people haven't changed. She studied Philippe's face, undistinguished as a mortal, but hauntingly beautiful now. Even she, as an immortal, could see as much. She wondered how Beverly felt looking at him. Did it, as it had done to Charlotte all those years ago, beguile her to the point of total distraction? Would looking upon it allow Beverly total peace and sublimation at the moment of making? But he had made so few, far fewer than she. Charlotte thought about that, about the giving nature of the female, mortal or immortal. She remembered the boy, and how she had assumed the role of a policewoman. Was it something that followed you all your days? And nights? Somehow she hoped that were true. Certainly she had killed to satisfy her innate and indescribable thirst. Yes, she had; Al Lopez came to mind. But she had also made when it hadn't been necessary. Unlike Philippe. In Los Angeles he had made. A woman, naturally. The woman had somehow seen through his mental firestorm, had seen that he did not lust but thirsted, and she had fetchingly taunted him to make her, too. She hadn't begged for mercy. She hadn't screamed God's name. Just the reverse. Like him, she had proclaimed an affinity to the dark one. That which humans called the devil. So in a moment of compassion—was there no other word?—he had allowed her the gift. He had made her. No such proclamation had ever been necessary with Charlotte. If she was recognized for what she was prior to the blooding, and if the human did request it, then she would make them. Philippe, at times, angered by her female nature perhaps, would immediately undo what she had done. But she had managed to make many without him knowing. Just as he had so readily made her.

There was a Methodist Church across the street. Seeing it now reminded Charlotte of the time just before her making, while she lay in a death sleep, allowing his seed to germinate within her. He had taken her to the cave, to the furthest reaches beyond the lake. She remembered the grunts from around them as he first talked with her, telling her about her trip to immortality, how they would travel the world together, experience things she had never dreamt about. And then the making itself. How he had first embraced her with such delicacy, such devotion. And the surge that followed, of her blood being drained into him. She remembered how her eyes had rolled back in their sockets and how she had actually been aware of the blood roaring through her veins and arteries. Her pleasure had been so great, it took her a while to realize that she was, as legend said, looking down upon her body. Philippe stood over her, her blood upon his mouth. She circled there for so long, then beyond, even beyond the hillside that housed his cave.

She remembered the earth as a sphere, the stars so unbelievably bright against the blackest of skies. And so she thought the legend would continue, that a radiant, undeniable light would appear, and she would be drawn to it, forever alive. Reborn. That would be his gift.

But no light appeared. Beings did appear, yes, against the starlit backdrop. And they were familiar; there was her father, beckoning. Aunts and uncles and friends who had been guillotined, their heads magically rejoined to their bodies. All beckoning. But although she tried mightily to go to them, she could not. Her legs would not move. And then, from behind her, she sensed another presence. She turned. It was Philippe, there in the sky. "We can never go there, Charlotte," he told her. "That is not a place for you or me." Then she realized that it was true, what she feared was all true. She was a murderer, judged so and cast off.

She turned away. Her father had begun a slow retreat, as had the others. No longer were they offering her sanctuary, eternal rest. They shunned her now. They loathed her now, what she had become. She had no choice. And as they disappeared, she understood and she turned. After all life eternal was hers. Philippe had done that for her.

Looking at him now, however, with God's house so near, she wondered again if she had been forever barred from eternal rest. With quiet desperation, she hoped not.

"I think he's going in," Philippe said.

In the backseat, Beverly moved ever so slightly.

Charlotte looked at the car parked down the street. The driver's door was opening.

27

Mike stopped and looked inside the video arcade. It sounded like a war was going on. But while he stood there, mentally commenting on the whimsy of it all, something else even more whimsical caught his attention. The marquee lights at the Olympic Theater were blinking on. He smiled crookedly, amazed by what he saw. He had intended on simply walking by the place, maybe going around back to see if a window might have been left open. But obviously that wasn't necessary. The sounds of horns blaring and the occasional obscenity, as drivers fought for diagonal parking spots out front, confirmed that. He saw the red Camaro with the Snow Capital of the Free World bumper sticker pull in, and wondered about the pickup truck with hay bundled in the back. But while the pickup truck wasn't here, it appeared that most of the rest of the town was. While he watched, tens of people exited their vehicles. The chatter of small talk only lightly bruised the tender fabric of night.

But even amidst this screaming normalcy, caution prevailed. This could be another trick. A tall, thin man paired with a woman at least a foot shorter, strolled past. On impulse, Mike purposely bumped into him, wondering if they might simply pass through each other. But that didn't happen this time. This time flesh met flesh with a dull thud, and the tall, thin man got a little pissed.

"Jesus, pal, you blind or what?" he yelled.

. Mike smiled apologetically and backed away. "Sorry, I thought . . . (you weren't real) . . . sorry."

The man grudgingly backed off, making a show of it for his confused girlfriend. "Maybe you are real," Mike muttered as he walked away. "And maybe this theater really is open."

But he wasn't quite convinced, not yet. His enemy's power might be limitless, or at least strong enough to make him think he really *had* bumped into someone, although he certainly couldn't go around bumping into people all night just to find that out.

He decided to wait in the ticket line. An older woman sporting a modified beehive smiled at him from behind the glass ticket booth as he approached. "What time's the next show?" he asked, bending over to speak into the half-moon opening.

"Ten thirty, sir. *The Rocky Horror Picture Show,*" she said in a high, whiny soprano.

"Still hangin' around, is it?"

The woman smiled politely. "Cult classics have a way of doing that." She leaned left and looked at the line behind him. "Would you like a ticket, sir?"

Mike hesitated.

"Sir?"

"Yeah, I guess. How much?"

"Two-fifty. There's audience participation, you know."

"Yeah, I know." He looked behind him; the line had gotten longer. They all looked normal enough, he thought, not like the weirdos he'd heard routinely went to this movie. Someone said, "Move it, buster!" and Mike hurriedly handed the ticket taker a five-dollar bill. "Quite a crowd tonight," he said.

"There always is. Enjoy the show."

She handed Mike his change and he went inside, entering the theater with mild apprehension, like a vacationer in a fringe motel. He half-expected to see the same kids he and Paul and Beverly had seen all those years ago, behind

256

the counter and taking tickets. The people doing those jobs now could have been their parents.

He waited his turn at the refreshment stand, asked for a Mallo Cup, then went inside.

Feeling very much like a moviegoer and not someone frantically in search of a dear friend, he chose a seat in the middle of the theater and opened up his candy.

Within minutes, the theater was packed with cultists, all in the costume of their favorite Rocky Horror character. The lights went off right on time; a trio of teenaged girls to his right tittered and within seconds of the lights going off, the crowd became quiet. Inexplicably so. Probably preparing themselves for the opening scene, Mike thought. Soon as the screen lights up, they'll let out with a noise that'll probably scare the bejesus out of me. Thinking that to be true, he even prepared himself for that contingency. But after a couple more minutes of silence, his anxiety got the better of him. He turned and looked toward the back. Never fails, he thought. Some jerk in there doesn't know how to run a projector. He squinted, hoping to see the guy walk by the little window, but no one did. He couldn't even see the little window. After five minutes passed, he discovered that he was getting a little angry, and crowds like this wouldn't stay quiet for very long. He leaned left, and although he couldn't see the girl next to him, said, "Are they always this slow?"

No answer.

He waited a second and with a little laugh, added, "Any time now, huh?"

Again he got no answer.

He pushed himself up, his gaze flitting from side to side, hoping to catch someone's attention. But still he couldn't see a thing. "What the hell's going on here?" he said under his breath. He waited a second longer, then fumbled in his pocket for a book of matches, the same book he'd been carrying around with him since he quit smoking. He struck one; the smell of sulfur made his eyes water. The flame danced a moment, then settled. As it did, he

257

held the match at arm's length and did a slow circle. The theater, at least the twenty or so seats he could see in all directions, was deserted. He was alone.

Panic knocked once, then left. He smiled. Just as he thought, another trick. He heard something then, like someone yelling underwater, thick, muffled sounds. In his mind's eye he saw Beverly tied and gagged. "Bev?" he yelled, unable to control himself. The match went out; he lit another. "Bev? Where are you, Bev?" Frantically now.

More muffled sounds, but he couldn't pinpoint the location. They seemed to come from everywhere, from every seat. She's underneath one of those seats, he thought, but which one, where the hell . . . No, Mike. Calm down, just calm down. He did a quick circle. The match went out again. "Shit!" he said and lit another. Instantly the sounds were back, but as he did another circle, he decided that he should look somewhere else—maybe the john. The match went out, but instead of lighting another, he just stood there. Sure, the john, he decided. He remembered what had been written on the wall so long ago—HELP! He remembered the six-pack left in one of the stalls.

He went into the lobby, lit softly yellow by the street-light, and stopped to look back at the double, swinging doors. Funny, he thought, I can't hear those sounds now. I can't hear anything. Funny.

The darkness inside the men's john was cloying, suf-focating. He lit another match and looked around. It was as he remembered, filthy, smelly, graffiti everywhere. He looked into a stall. Empty. But as he started for the one beside it, the toilet flushed. Mike froze. Someone was in there. Good God, there was someone in there!

He stepped toward the closed stall door; the orange, flickering flame had almost reached his fingertips. He stepped closer, but just as he got to the door, he had to throw the match away. He quickly lit another; holding it in his left hand, he put his right on the door. Water filled the bowl, and then the drain closed off with a loud me-

258

chanical *pop*. Following that, there was only silence. Mike drew in a deep breath and pushed the stall door open.

Empty. Relief washed over him, and he exhaled the breath he hadn't realized he was holding. A smile appeared on his lips.

But while he stood there, water suddenly gurgled in the bowl, causing him to catch his breath again. When it stopped, he saw that there was something in there. As he stepped into the stall, the thick, muffled sounds he'd heard in the theater started yet again. Then the match went out. He lit another, even more quickly than before, and looked in the bowl.

Half-submerged was Paul's head, bobbing around as water churned around the edges. The skin was a thin purple color, the eyes half-closed, the lower jaw open to reveal a mouth teeming with insects—millipedes and roaches, a few squat potato bugs. And while he watched, unable to look away, Paul's mouth moved; he was trying to speak.

Mike felt a high-pitched wail leave his mouth and he fell backwards, banging his shoulder on the door, causing him to drop the match. He spun away, toward the back wall, running blindly into it, forehead first. A huge knot rose on his head and he slumped to the floor, fighting for consciousness. A line of blood dripped into his eyes. "Oh, Christ, Pauly," he said desperately.

While he lay on the floor in the dark, grieving for his dead cousin, he suddenly heard more thick, muffled sounds. And with them he saw light. Overhead fluorescents winked on, casting the john in a bright white glow. Mike tried to get up, but before he could, he heard, "You fucking pervert!" Then the door opened and out stepped a middle-aged man, glaring as he yanked up his jeans and pulled up his zipper. "What the hell you think you're doing? The goddamn door was closed! How'd you like it if I busted in on you?" His tone changed when he saw the blood on Mike's face, but only slightly. "Jesus, man!"

Shakily, Mike got to his feet. He touched his head, then

pulled his hand away and looked at the blood. "I didn't know . . ."

The man washed his hands and sniffed his fingers. "Yeah, well, you oughta get that checked out." That said, he stomped out the door.

Mike washed his wound at the sink and looked in the mirror. "Jesus, you're a sight," he said to his reflection. "Chasing windmills again. When are you gonna stop that?"

He tore off a section of paper toweling and dried his face and hair. "Pauly's head in the toilet! Boy, you fell for that one good!"

Then he realized something. The theater really was open. He ran back into the lobby. Just as it was earlier—the girl selling candy, the guy taking tickets. Open. Doing business. He went back into the theater. *The Rocky Horror Picture Show* was in full swing.

From his right, he heard, "Hey, pal, I thought you left."

Mike turned. The usher trained the flashlight onto his face. "No, I went to the bathroom. What's the problem?"

"You know what the problem is—you can't light matches in a theater. You wanna start a fire or something?"

Mike quickly puzzled it all through. The thick, muffled sounds he'd heard were people yelling at him. That was all, just pissed-off people.

"Sorry, I didn't mean . . ."

"Yeah, well, I can't let you back in."

"Please, I've got to find something."

"Find something? Look, mister, just wait outside. After the movie's over, we'll both look for whatever it is you lost, but now you gotta go. You understand that, or do I got to call the cops?"

Mike went back to his car, waited a few minutes, then went back to his hotel room. Then he stripped and took a shower. The warm water felt fantastic.

After he'd toweled off, he went back into the room and

put on his shorts. As he did, he saw something on the floor. He picked it up—the points coupon from the Mallo Cup. He smiled and was about to toss it away when he noticed something. In fine print below the point total —5— was this message:

A WINNER—WE HAVE A WINNER
YOU, MICHEL MARAT, HAVE WON AN
ALL-EXPENSE PAID VACATION
TO
PARIS, FRANCE—WHILE THERE
VISIT LASCAUX. THE ARTWORK IS
FASCINATING

And then, before his very eyes, the card simply disappeared.

28

City of Light—so appropriate, Beverly thought.

She was looking down upon the city from Philippe's private plane. It was night now, the shades were up, the sun was hiding on the other side of the world. Philippe was flying the plane himself. The daytime pilot—typical of his kind, tall, gray-haired, handsome, his tie still knotted—sat across from her, reading something by Peter Straub. Charlotte sat to her right, on the other side of the aisle, gazing down at the city as the plane banked right to position itself for landing.

Beverly's mental anguish and physical pain had suddenly subsided about halfway across the Atlantic, as if Charlotte or Philippe or both had turned some mental key and allowed her to leave her cell. But she also fully realized that although she had been allowed out of her cell, the front gates of her prison were still locked. If she tried to escape, she'd be killed. Plain and simple. But suicide was no longer her only option, and that, she thought, could only work in her favor.

The plane taxied to a stop; the gangway was lowered. The air inside the plane had been lightly scented. On the concrete of DeGaulle Airport, walking toward the terminal, there was a faint odor of jet fuel in the air. They'd parked a distance away from commercial traffic, but the whine of jets made it difficult to talk and be heard.

'Where are we going now?" she asked Charlotte, walking beside her.

"I'm just as much in the dark as you are," Charlotte answered.

They walked through the terminal building, past crowds of people, and not once did Beverly have to resist the urge to yell for help. She knew how foolish that would be. Nothing had been done to her. She wasn't being mugged or attacked. To yell out that she had been kidnapped by vampires would be a sure way of making herself a laughingstock.

They exited the brightly lit terminal and got into yet another black Mercedes, waiting for them at the curb. Beverly sat in back with Charlotte while Philippe drove. He seemed to like to be in control. She gazed forlornly at a gendarme directing traffic, but he didn't notice, and before long the airport was behind them.

Fifteen minutes later, having negotiated the car through very heavy traffic, they arrived at the Champs de Mars, home of the Eiffel Tower, rising huge and foreboding into the night sky. As it came into view, Beverly whispered, "I've seen pictures, but I never imagined . . . !"

"I'm told it looks larger at night," Charlotte said.

It dawned on Beverly then that Charlotte had nothing to compare night viewing to. "Night has that property," Charlotte continued, her tone nostalgic, which somewhat confused Beverly. "I remember running through the woods as a child. Everything seemed to fly by."

Beverly turned and just looked at her. Charlotte had spoken to Beverly like she might to a fellow traveler. Having read her thoughts, Charlotte smiled.

It was then that Philippe stopped the car and announced, "I've something to tend to." Then, before Charlotte could respond—or perhaps he hadn't allowed her to—he went into the night.

What he had to tend to began to take shape in Beverly's mind; she saw some unwary tourist being carried into a dark alley, thinking perhaps that he was going to be robbed; she saw some cab driver dead behind the wheel, tiny punctures at his throat. She didn't dwell on these thoughts though; she didn't want to concern herself with either of her captors, at least not now. She was here, in Paris, and maybe, just maybe, Charlotte would allow her to see some of the sights. A new side to their relationship had been hinted at.

Having read her thoughts yet again, Charlotte, sounding very much like a parent who has weighed favorably the behavior of a child, said, "We have some time. Would you like to see Paris?"

They started at the Champs de Mars, and there was so much to see here beyond *La Tour Eiffel*. Children's rides and puppet shows. Merry-go-rounds. Watching the children clinging tightly to the necks of horses or giggling side by side in the huge belly of a swan, Beverly decided that merry-go-rounds would forever be a child's favorite. And children seemed so important to this great city.

Her attention was drawn to the fountain behind the merry-go-round. Two children were there, splashing and laughing, a pigtailed girl about eight and a boy just a little older.

Beverly smiled. "Never fails," she told Charlotte.

Charlotte looked at her quizzically.

"Water. You know? I gotta pee."

"Oh. Don't be long, there's much to see."

Beverly actually smiled, went into the ladie's room, peed, then came back out.

For a moment she thought she was alone, Charlotte was nowhere to be seen. But before she could arouse enough courage to run, Charlotte reappeared from the darkness. "Ready?" she asked.

"Ready."

They drove past Bourbon Palace then across the Seine river to the Tuileries, where they got out of the car and strolled, their path lined by statues, the air alive with the fragrance of splendidly kept gardens, redolent with the delicate aroma of so many varieties of flowers. There Beverly's attention was momentarily drawn to a hotel across the Rue de Rivoli. Why, she didn't know. It was easily a quarter mile away, yet she had seen someone . . .

The laughter of bright-faced children playing with toy boats in the fountains pierced her thoughts. And when Charlotte spoke, Beverly's interest in that someone across the Rue de Rivoli waned entirely.

"Children," Charlotte said, "are so delightful."

Further on they found more puppet shows, where they stopped again.

"I've never seen anything quite like this," Beverly said.

"And you won't, at least not in the States. It's called Punch and Judy. An English import. Charming, don't you think?"

After watching the show in its entirety, Beverly concluded that charming was definitely not the right word. The show featured three puppets, Punch, his wife, Judy, and their child, whose only role was to be beaten senseless by Punch, who then, in a homicidal rage, killed his wife. And although justice was speedy, Punch ultimately evaded imprisonment by using trickery. The children, seated in a semicircle around the stage, loved it immensely.

After Punch had been granted his freedom, Beverly and Charlotte walked back to the car and continued down the Rue de Rivoli past the Louvre. From there it was a short drive to the bridge that led to the Île de la Cité, the island in the Seine where Paris had been founded two thousand years earlier. Île de la Cité was also the home of Notre Dame Cathedral, swathed in white light. So huge, Beverly thought. It totally dominates the island. They parked the car and walked toward the cathedral at an economical gait. A warm breeze blew across the Seine. It was there, within the floodlit glow of Notre Dame, where Beverly boldly asked, "Charlotte, I want to go inside. Will you let me?"

Charlotte cocked her head slightly. The wind blew her hair and she seemed to enjoy it. As Charlotte looked at the cathedral, Beverly saw a blend of emotions appear on her face—revulsion, longing. Fear.

"I can't go in there," Charlotte said. "I'd be as helpless in there as you are here, with me."

"You think I'd run away?"

"Run away? No. Where would you go? But you might hide in there. I'd do that, if I were you."

"Charlotte, please don't do this. I'm going to die soon, I know that, so please don't deny me this. Never, in my wildest dreams, did I ever think I'd get to Paris. But I made it, I'm here! Can't you just please trust me?"

Silence for a moment, then, "You think you're going to die soon?"

Beverly hesitated.

"*Do* you?"

"Yes. Or worse."

"I still can't let you go in there."

The light seemed to shift then. Angles changed, shadows grew softer.

"You have my word, I give you my word."

"Your word. Beverly, right now, right at this very moment, you really think you'd keep that promise. But once you got inside, that would change. It would, believe me. You'd feel safe and untouchable, and you *would* be safe and untouchable, at least untouchable by me. And Philippe. You'd feel as if you could reach out and touch God's face. And in a way . . . His crown of thorns is kept in there, did you know that? At least what's left of it, the remnants. No, I won't let you. I can't let you."

Although Beverly was tremendously disappointed, Charlotte's tone intrigued her. "You've been in there, haven't you? And you want to go in again. You do, don't you?"

Charlotte answered without hesitation. "Yes, a long time ago. It was one of the most beautiful experiences of my life. And you're right. I guess I would like to go in there again. But even here, at least a hundred feet away, I feel pain. It glows inside me. No, I can't go in there. I won't go in there. It's not allowed."

It was then that Beverly actually tried to touch her. She reached out, and with her hand almost on Charlotte's, said, "I can't believe—"

Charlotte withdrew her hand quickly. "You can't believe what? That I am what I am? That I walk the night in search of blood, of nourishment? Why can't you believe that, Beverly? Do I seem human to you? Do I act like I've actually got a conscience?"

And that was exactly what Beverly thought. Listening to Charlotte talk about Notre Dame, about the beautiful experience it had been for her, could leave her thinking no other way. And Charlotte's face, so filled with human compassion and warmth, so radiant when she spoke of the cathedral.

"Yes, Charlotte, that *is* what I think. Maybe this is just some kind of . . . sickness. Maybe you can get some help. You know, professional help."

"Professional help? What do you think I am, Beverly, some lonely teenager seeking cult comfort? Is that what you think? Then tell me what you think of this, dear Beverly." She moved closer, just inches away. "You think my skin is radiant, that it has a healthy glow. Feel it then. You wanted to feel it, so feel it!"

Beverly raised her suddenly trembling hand and stroked Charlotte's face. It was as hard as marble and just as cold. Startled, she withdrew her hand quickly.

Charlotte couldn't help but laugh. "What's the matter, Beverly, never touched the dead before? But it is radiant, isn't it, just as you thought. Glowing. In bloom. Do you want to know why? Do you? Well, let me tell you why. While you made use of the facilities at the Champs de Mars, I dined. That's right, Beverly, I was hungry, so I ate. That's what you do, isn't it? When you're hungry, you eat. While you were inside peeing, I prompted that young girl off the merry-go-round. You remember, the one with the pigtails, the one who was so bubbly and vivacious and filled with the joy of living? It was very easy, you know. All I said was, 'Your mother's over there, she has an ice cream for you.' And would you believe it, her brother wanted to come, too. Well, I was famished, but not that famished, so I told him that there had been only enough money for one ice cream, and that his sister would gladly share when she got back. She followed me to the darkness behind the facilities, and there I took her. Let me tell you, Beverly, there is no blood like the blood of the young—rather like veal I would think. I could hear you peeing while I dined, while I drained that little girl of her most precious blood. I could hear your bodily fluids wash from you, while another's bodily fluids washed into me. And do you know what I did with the remains, Beverly? I just left them there, behind the facilities. The child's mother should be finding her corpse about now. Such a pity, don't you think? Such a shame. I've lost count, you know. But you figure it out. One a day, or more, for almost two hundred years. What does that come to, Beverly? Eighty thousand or so? So tell me, is that humane? I was a human, yes, I was at one time, but I'm not human now. I can't cry now! Understand this and understand it well—I don't want your pity, I don't want your friendship! So, if you think I won't stop you from going in there, if you think for a moment that I care what happens to you—you're wrong. If you don't believe me, then go, start walking. And see what happens to you."

Through a haze of revulsion and fear, Beverly saw something on Charlotte's face, in her eyes. Pain perhaps, masked by anger. A spark of decency, which seemed ludicrous considering that she had just killed a little girl. But Beverly chose not to test her. Not yet at least.

When Beverly didn't respond, Charlotte said, "There's something I want you to see."

They stopped at the Comédie-Française, where the work of Moliere was being staged, then continued down the Champs Elysses to the Place de la Concorde, perhaps the busiest plaza in all of Paris.

"Do you know what happened here?" Charlotte asked.

"No . . . should I?"

"Well, you claim to love Paris. I'm surprised you don't know what happened here. This, Beverly, is where many hundreds, perhaps thousands of innocent people were beheaded. Louis XVI, Marie Antoinette, Robespierre. Why? Simply because their political views differed. This is where I would have been taken."

That pronouncement piqued Beverly's interest. "What do you mean, where you would have been taken?"

Charlotte smiled lightly. "You don't know, do you? After all that's happened, you still don't know. I am Charlotte Corday, Beverly. Anyone who knows Paris, who loves Paris and its past, knows the name Charlotte Corday."

Beverly searched her mind, then, "Jean Paul Marat. You . . . but how? I don't understand."

"I was 'made' almost two hundred years ago, Beverly. I am a product of the eighteenth century. From what I understand, two hundred years is not very old for our kind."

Beverly had always liked history, how one event prompted another larger event. But like most people, events of the eighteenth century seemed very much out of focus. There was no pictorial history of the period, unlike the Civil War; nothing she could look at and say, "Yes, this is real, those people were real." But standing before her now was a woman who had helped create history, a woman who, by rights, should be only a skeleton in the Montmarte Cemetery. But she wasn't a skeleton, she was real, very real. Although she did feel dead. Looking at her Beverly wondered mightily about what Charlotte had been like when she was mortal. And although she'd read accounts of the murder of Jean Paul Marat, they were nothing when compared with actually hearing about it from the murderess herself.

Charlotte smiled before Beverly could speak. "I see the details interest you," she said. "All in good time, all in good time. I've shown you what I wanted to show you. There are just too many memories for me here."

A minute or so later, Beverly saw the Arc De Triomphe, Napoleon's brainchild, rising skyward. Traffic was heavy, but Charlotte maneuvered the car skillfully. They stopped within a half mile of the Arc de Triomphe, at one of the many sidewalk cafes where tourists ate and drank but mostly people-watched, a Paris tradition.

And looking over at her as she glanced around at the walkers and diners, wasn't it peculiar that she felt no threat from Charlotte now, despite her earlier proclamation.

Charlotte turned to her. "What would you like?" she asked.

Her smile seemed so genuine.

"Something cold, I think. Seems appropriate."

Charlotte responded to that by raising one eyebrow before she called the waiter over. She spoke with him in French, and after he left, she said, "I've ordered a bottle of Dom Perignon. I hope that will suffice."

"Dom Perignon? Yes, that would be nice. Thank you."

"You're welcome," said Charlotte.

They looked into each other's eyes then and Beverly said, "Would you have?"

"At Notre Dame?"

"Yes."

"Without a second thought."

"You only take Visa or Master Card?" Mike asked. He was at the front desk of the Louvre Concorde Hotel, an immediate neighbor to the Tuileries and the Louvre. The Comédie-Française was across the street. The hotel's cocktail lounge was crowded.

The clerk was being polite, but in the French, politeness sometimes comes off as rudeness.

"Oui, monsieur," said the clerk. His upper lip, Mike noticed, was almost nonexistent, which looked, as Boothman would say, *très* weird, considering that his lower lip looked like it had been injected with collagen.

"Look, I've got Diner's Club and American Express. Lemme see, Mobil. You take Mobil?"

The clerk only smiled politely, rudely.

"Shit," Mike said.

"Excuse me, monsieur?"

"Look, it's been a rough coupla days, can you cut me some slack here? You took American Express the last time I was here."

He had come here on assignment three years earlier. He had obtained an international driver's license at that time. He was glad he had it now. He didn't want to use the Metro.

"We do take cash, monsieur."

"Cash—what a concept! Look, if I give you cash, I won't have a lot left."

"Perhaps tomorrow you can go to an American Express office, monsieur?"

That obvious solution made Mike feel a little embarrassed.

"How much?"

"In francs, sir?"

"Yeah, francs."

"Eight hundred, monsieur."

"Eight hundred!" Mike slapped the money on the counter, signed in, got his key, and went to his room feeling like he'd been had.

"Well, here I am," he said as he unpacked his suitcase. "What now? Off to Lascaux?"

Would that be wise though? Beverly's kidnapper was definitely playing games with him, so maybe he had some time to prepare, find out as much about the cave as he could. He looked at his watch. Almost ten. There wasn't much he could do tonight except get something to eat. First though, he thought he'd take a very long and very

271

warm shower. The air-conditioning in this room was on full blast. A warm shower would feel wonderful. Might even stoke his appetite. He went into the bathroom, undressed, and stepped in.

29

"Have you heard of the Moulin Rouge?" Charlotte asked.

"Sure, hasn't everyone? The height of debauchery and all that. Topless a go-go."

Charlotte smiled. "Yes, there is that, but there is more. There is the mystique, the pervading sensuality."

Beverly took a sip of her Dom Perignon, which wasn't quite as tasty as she'd hoped. "Oh, *that* Moulin Rouge," she said.

"You're being petty. It doesn't become you."

"Why do you ask?"

"I thought we might go there. What do you think?"

"I doubt I'm dressed for it." She had on jeans and a red turtleneck sweater.

Charlotte rose and laid the equivalent of one hundred dollars in French francs on the table. "Come with me," she said.

"Where?"

"I have an apartment nearby."

"You're joking!"

"Why would I joke about that?"

"Well, I just thought, I mean . . ."

"You assumed that our kind sleep in caves perhaps, or beneath the ground somehow?"

"Well, don't you?"

Charlotte shrugged her shoulders. "Sometimes. Now

273

come, let's find you something appropriate to wear, if you think it's necessary."

Charlotte's apartment in the Latin Quarter was located on the second floor of a squat, dull-looking building, whose architecture could have been influenced by inner-city America, not romantic, refined Paris, and accessed only by a claustrophobia-inducing, windowless stairway, where the odor of stale urine hung suspended in the damp, stagnant air. Beverly stood on a lower stair while Charlotte unlocked the door.

"Wait a second," Charlotte said with a glance. She pushed the door open and went inside. Beverly waited in the doorway, while Charlotte walked across the room and pulled a heavy blanket back from a window, allowing lambent streetlight to enter. The window faced north, struck only infrequently by direct sunlight.

"I apologize, Beverly. If I'd known I was going to have a guest, I would have bought a lamp or something. I'll light a few candles."

Considering the grace and beauty and total involvement with image that seemed so important to Charlotte, what Beverly expected, she did not get. From where she stood, she could see only two rooms, the kitchen just off to the right, and the living room, both now lit only by streetlight and a large candle on a table to the right of the sofa. What was nauseatingly apparent and immediately abhorrent was the odor of blood; not as if the furniture and floor were soaked with it, but simply as an aftertaste for the nose. A not so delicate reminder of what Charlotte had become. She could easily imagine Charlotte here, feeding on some kidnapped child or maybe a vagrant. Someone she had seduced. The furniture, dark, early French Provincial, was tattered and worn, and there even appeared to be claw marks on the legs of the sofa and chair.

"Excuse me," Charlotte said.

She went down the hall to what Beverly assumed was a bedroom.

Just after Charlotte stepped from view, Beverly heard a window open and then the padding of many tiny feet. Seconds later a quintet of large cats sauntered regally down the hallway and took a left at the kitchen, Charlotte right behind.

"Madame Chevard takes care of them while I'm away, but they're acting like they haven't been fed for a while. They get lazy roaming rooftops."

Charlotte shook a bag of food into a large bowl. The cats encircled it and ate ravenously; their collective purr sounding like a small car.

While they ate, and while Charlotte went back into the bedroom, Beverly stepped into the living room. There was an oriental rug on the floor, the wood beneath visible in spots. Beverly's first thought was that the rug and the furniture could have been here for the last two hundred years, barely used except perhaps by cats, by the hundreds and hundreds of cats who had called this apartment home during that time.

There was a painting on the west wall, above the sofa. Beverly stepped closer. A portrait of Charlotte done by Renoir. She was seated on a credenza, dressed in a purple dress, circa 1870 or so. Her fingers were laced together on her lap, her back straight, her hair piled atop her head. She was smiling. But even though she was smiling, Beverly felt a chill scamper up her spine. Done in his fine, impressionistic style, Beverly thought Renoir had ably captured Charlotte's inner turmoil, the subdued demon that sat so patiently for this French genius, who seemed to know very well what manner of being he had chosen as a subject.

"This painting," Beverly yelled. "It's a Renoir."

"Yes, a gift. From the painter himself. Fantastic lover, for a mortal. Even with his hands crippled. But, of course, hands have little to do with the art of lovemaking."

Charlotte stepped out of the bedroom and into view. She was holding a long, blue, sequined dress that shimmered even in this meager glow. "It should fit," she said, holding it up to Beverly. "We're the same size, so it should fit."

Beverly saw the dress, but she was more interested in what Charlotte had just said. "You made love with Renoir?"

Charlotte smiled crookedly. "Yes, I did. Very creative man. I've allowed only creative men to touch me over the last two hundred odd years."

While Charlotte inspected the dress, Beverly stepped closer to her. "I guess I don't understand. You've actually made love to humans?"

Charlotte's brow furrowed. "Well, perhaps love isn't precise. Call it . . . experimentation."

"Experimentation?"

"Yes, I wanted to compare these creative geniuses with Philippe. Here." She handed Beverly the dress.

Beverly took it from her and Charlotte stepped back. "Yes, with your dark hair and green eyes, that color definitely suits you."

Beverly lowered the dress. "And?"

"And what?"

Beverly smiled. "How did he compare, Charlotte?"

"Oh, not very favorably, I'm afraid. Now please, get dressed. I'm anxious to go."

So Beverly changed, and as she looked in the bathroom mirror, her candle-lit image looked back at her like someone she had never seen. It's the dress, she thought. It belongs to . . . her, so . . .

"Ready?" Charlotte called from the living room.

"Just a moment. Do you have any lipstick?"

Charlotte laughed.

"Guess not, huh," Beverly said under her breath. She looked again at her image. She was, she had to admit, stunning. Her long, dark hair had somehow acquired a luxuriant sheen, her skin was flawless and creamy, her body seemed perfect for this dress. She actually felt like a woman again. A very appealing woman, indeed. Despite everything, she had to smile, and it was then, while she

276

looked into the mirror, a pleased smile on her mouth, that Beverly felt pressure on both shoulders, as if someone were kneading her tired muscles. The blood suddenly drummed in her ears, and upon closer examination, she could actually see the fabric of the dress rise and fall as the kneading continued. Frightened, she started to turn, but the pressure grew stronger, stopping her.

Then a whispered voice, "Look into the mirror, Beverly. What do you see?"

"Charlotte? Is that you, Charlotte?"

"What do you see, Beverly?"

She looked into the mirror, but there was nothing *to* see, only her candle-lit image staring back. What else was there? What else could there be? Nothing, nothing at all, just . . . and there was Mike, but not just his upper torso, as she saw herself, but the whole man, far away, his image only points of light that slowly coalesced. He moved toward her and she caught her breath, and held it until he stopped right behind her, just to the left. Then he cupped his hands lightly around her arms and kissed the nape of her neck. "Mmmmm," he said, "it's been too long."

"No, it's not you. I know it's not you!"

A sly little smile. "Lovemaking should always make a woman feel as if she's just slid into a warm bath."

She tried to turn again—this wasn't real. It couldn't be real. But again she was stopped.

"A gift, Beverly. From me to you."

"Charlotte?"

"Look in the mirror, Beverly. Relax and just look into the mirror. Allow pleasure to guide you."

"NO!"

He ran the back of his hand over her cheek, then along her temples, allowing his fingers to linger, to feel the blood pulse there, his touch lighter than seemed possible.

"No. Please, Mike. No."

"Time is unimportant to immortals," he whispered. "How would you like to be stroked like this for hours on end? Every wonderful, tantalizing inch of you."

The phrase, I'm going to die soon, began to form on an empty wall of her mind.

"Why, Mike? Why are you doing this?"

"It's what lovers do, Beverly."

He continued to caress her, and as he did, her will began to crumble. The pleasure was too draining, too hard to resist. And if it were true, if she was really going to die soon, then . . .

"What . . . lovers do, Beverly!"

Her body went limp, submissive; and in the mirror, Mike smiled. Inch by alluring inch, he worked his way down, first her arms, then onto her breasts, his hands poised ever so close. She felt compelled to lean forward, to actually feel his hands on her breasts, but he was making such grand progress; he seemed to know exactly what to do. She looked at those hands. She'd never before noticed how huge they were. She put her hand on his and pushed it forward just enough . . . He smiled more broadly now, she could see him smile. He had wanted her to do that.

"Your breasts. I've always thought they were perfect."

"Mmmmm."

She wanted—needed—just a little more pressure now. Mike responded instantly, teasing her nipples with his fingertips, gently flicking them through the satiny fabric. He bent slightly and again kissed the nape of her neck, and at the same time, unzipped the back of her dress. Then, as if his fingertips had turned to smoke, ran them over the downlike hair on the small of her back. His breath was warm between her shoulder blades, his tongue moist as it traced the length of her backbone. Her body quivered and she arched her neck backwards. His hand moved to the front, onto her belly and then lower, his fingers entwining her pubic hair.

You may, she wanted to say. Just a little lower . . .

"Please, Mike," she whispered.

He looked at her reflection and smiled. "I want to make you, Beverly. I want to give you that."

Charlotte?

"This gift and more. Pleasures unimaginable."

She thought she heard a cat meow. Something brushed her calf, she glanced down quickly; the cat ran off. She looked into the mirror again. Mike was still there, smiling, but there, on either side of his mouth . . . and his eyes, shot with blood.

"Let go, Beverly, just let go," he whispered.

His eyes! God, they were the wrong color! The wrong color!

"CHARLOTTE!" Philippe bellowed from the door-way.

A large volume of air left Beverly, and her legs almost gave out. She grabbed the sink and looked again into the mirror. But there was no one there, no one . . . she turned and barely got a glimpse of Philippe and Charlotte leaving. She almost followed, but the realization of what had almost happened gorged her with new fear. Charlotte hadn't wanted to befriend her—she'd told her as much at the church—she'd wanted to kill her. To make her like her. And Philippe—of all people—had stopped her!

He had saved her life.

She slumped to the floor between the wall and the toilet and cried, and didn't hear the one-sided argument going on in the other room.

"Have you no control, Charlotte? Her time will come, but it won't be here—and it won't be done by you! Understand that well, not by *you!*"

Later, after Philippe left, Charlotte came into the bathroom.

"Get up. We have to go. You do still want to go, don't you?"

Confused, Beverly looked up at her with a tear-stained face. "Leave me alone. Please, just leave me alone!"

Charlotte looked surprised. She knelt beside her and stroked her hair. "You enjoyed those moments with Mike, didn't you? I gave you that. So much more than what Philippe gave you. Trust me."

Trust her? Why should she trust Charlotte? She tried to . . . No, she wouldn't trust her, she couldn't trust her! The only trust she had left was reserved for Mike, and maybe . . . dear God, did she dare even think it? Maybe even Philippe.

They went to the Moulin Rouge, but Beverly didn't at all want to be here. She didn't want to be in Paris. She wanted to be home, in the States. She wanted to be back there helping Cecile. At least Cecile's husband was human. So unlike the woman seated next to her, dressed in a green version of what she was wearing, laughing and clapping and carrying on as if nothing had happened. Or would happen.

Charlotte looked at her. "Drink your drink, Beverly."

Beverly looked at the drink. Hell, she thought, maybe I will. And not just one. She raised the glass to her lips and drank half of it. The alcohol left her throat feeling parched, but that didn't stop her. Within seconds she finished the drink and asked for another. And another . . . and another . . .

30

"The Caveau de Chevillards is at One Rue St. Hyacinthe, right?"

Mike wished his French was better. He really felt like a tourist.

The clerk smiled, his demeanor a bit less patronizing than it had been when Mike checked in. *"Oui, monsieur,* One Rue St. Hyacinthe. Go down Rue de Rivoli about one half of a mile. It's just east of Place Vendome."

"Thanks."

"You're very welcome, monsieur."

"And you say they're still seating?"

"I can call if you like."

"No, no, that's okay. Thanks."

Mike drove his rented Renault down Rue de Rivoli half a mile, turned right onto Place Vendome, then left onto Rue St. Hyacinthe. The Caveau de Chevillards Restaurant was at the other end of this well-lit street, a street crowded with seventeenth- and eighteenth-century homes, each with colorful gardens and ornate fencing. The loom of these tall, graceful homes provided him with an instant sense of time. How easy to imagine dirt roads and gas lights, tail coats and top hats, bouffant hairstyles and beauty marks, carefully placed upon alabaster white cheeks. The Caveau de Chevillards Restaurant itself was in the vaulted cellar of one of these fine old homes.

He parked in the small, well-lit parking lot, his car one

of only a few at this late hour. The lot was enclosed by an elaborate and very tall, black, wrought iron fence, embedded into a stone wall. Climbing red roses added a colorful harmony. The front steps were covered by an awning. An older couple, locked arm in arm and babbling on in French, pushed open the double doors and waited, holding the door open for Mike. He thanked them with a nod and a smile and went inside, noticing first the menu on the wall. Pricey kind of place, he thought. Real pricey. The air here smelled faintly like sawdust in the sun. He glanced down the red-carpeted stairway. A floor-to-ceiling potted plant sat in the corner opposite the left side. There was a painting on the wall in front of him at the bottom of the stairs, what might have been an original by Paul Cezanne. But he thought not, not here where it could have been easily stolen. He started down, stopped again. Five hundred francs was a lot of money for dinner, but he really had no choice, most places were closed by now, even the hotel restaurant. And this place did take American Express.

He went inside and was greeted by a short, slim man with a pencil-thin mustache.

"You're still seating, aren't you?" Mike asked.

"*Oui*, monsieur. Till eleven. Table for one?"

"Yes, just one."

The air seemed a battleground for strange and wonderful aromas. Sauces mainly, the mainstay of French cooking. Mike's salivary glands were working overtime.

The restaurant was splendidly decorated, candles on each table, huge, dark, Louis the XIII chairs. The walls were gray stone, almost completely covered by paintings, some, Mike thought, probably original. To Mike's surprise, however, there was an aura of intimacy that fought through the elegance.

He was seated toward the back at a table for two. A large red candle sat in the middle of a simple white tablecloth with the name of the restaurant embroidered into it. He counted four other occupied tables, three couples and a woman. The woman's back was to him; he saw only her long, black hair. Oddly, he didn't feel ill at ease about eating alone, as he usually did at home. None of the patrons had so much as glanced at him, while the maitre'd walked him back to his table.

"I am Henri," said his waiter. Henri was tall and blond, dressed in black and white, barely twenty, his voice as smooth as silk.

"Might I recommend, monsieur?"

"I was hoping you might, my French . . ."

"*Oui*. You might open your meal with lobster-caviar salad, and for an entrée, perhaps seafood mousse? The garlic-scented lamb is exquisite, also. And the wine, perhaps, a Gamay Beaujolais with the lamb, or if you prefer the seafood mousse, house sauvignon blanc."

"You speak very good English."

"Thank you, monsieur."

"I guess I'll have the lobster-caviar salad and the lamb."

"Very good, monsieur." Henri smiled, bowed slightly, said he'd bring the wine with dinner, and left.

While Mike waited, patrons at two of the four tables left, leaving only himself, the woman, and a very well-dressed older couple, he with a cloud of white hair and she the same. They looked tremendously happy together, entwining arms and sipping wine from each other's glass. Watching them, Mike felt a wave of melancholy. What was he doing here while Beverly was being subjected to physical and mental torture? He should be out there right now, and to hell with the time, and to hell with his gut and its need to be satisfied! He should be out there looking for her!

His thoughts were suddenly interrupted as the woman eating alone turned. To his great and complete surprise, there was a baby at her bare breast. She began to rock slightly while offering a motherly smile to the baby. Then she looked at Mike, and her smile mysteriously faded.

"You're alone, monsieur?"

Her hair was short now and dingy brown, her face unwashed, her eyes blank with despair.

"Monsieur?"

Mike turned so fast he got dizzy. The man on the other side of the table, just to the right of the chair, seemed to sway slightly.

"What? Who are you?"

The man smiled delicately before he spoke. "I asked if you were dining alone. I'm sorry if I startled you."

Mike glanced back at the woman, but all he saw now was a fall of glistening black hair.

Imagination?

He looked again at the man. He was impeccably dressed: gray suit, white shirt, and blue tie. His brown-blond hair was combed straight back and tied in a three-inch ponytail, noticeable as he glanced to his right to perhaps see what Mike was looking at. His eyes were small yet brilliant, reflecting the candlelight, and his smile revealed a row of perfect teeth. The fingers of his right hand were stuck into his coat pocket, thumb exposed. Mike had never been given to homophobia, but he couldn't help but think along those lines now.

"Well, no, I'm waiting for someone, actually," he lied.

The man's smile seemed to say, I caught you. "Really? Well, that's too bad. I do so hate to eat alone. Don't you?"

Mike hesitated, probing the man's eyes for intent. "Well, yeah, I do," he finally answered. "I guess if they haven't showed up yet . . . Please." Mike gestured to the chair across from him.

The man sat down with noticeable grace, then leaned back, his hands on his lap. He glanced around for a moment, then looked back at Mike.

"This building, this house, has been here for a very long time. Hundreds of years. Did you know that?"

"Yes, well, not the exact age, but I knew it was old. Hundreds of years, huh?"

"Sixteen forty-seven, to be precise." The man smiled expansively. "Do you think it's haunted?"

Mike returned his smile and mentally pictured the breast-feeding woman. "Haunted? I don't know. Maybe. You tell me. You seem to know a lot about this building. You come here a lot?"

"Yes, yes, I do. As a matter of fact, I was born here."

"Oh, really? How interesting. Then I guess your parents owned this house?"

"Well, no, my mother worked here. For the lady of the house."

"And the present owners bought it from her, I mean from the lady of the house?"

"Not quite." The man leaned forward. Candlelight played on his face. "It might interest you to know that this house was also a kind of underground railroad during the French Revolution. Many people hid here rather than risk the guillotine. Tell me, do you know very much about our revolution?"

"No, not very much, only what I learned in school. I probably should learn more. I understand I have a descendant who figured quite prominently—"

"Oh, really?"

"Yes, Jean Paul Marat. Have you—?"

"Heard of him? Oh, yes. He was a madman, you know. There were lots of madmen during the revolution. Marat was the maddest. He—perhaps more than anyone else in history—enjoyed killing. And not only by the prescribed method of execution, either. Not only by the guillotine. People were drawn and quartered, burned in oil, eviscerated, and then burned in oil. Blood was the predominate smell back then. It laid over the city like a shroud. At least, so I've read. Tell me, how do you feel about being a descendant of a madman and a murderer?"

"Well, I don't know . . ."

"There was a woman, a very beautiful, very delicate creature. Somewhat simpleminded, that's true, but harmless nonetheless. She was killed simply because she refused to tell Marat where someone was hiding. His lieutenant."

Anxiety had begun to hover.

285

"Well, that happens in any war."

"War!"

"Well, a revolution is a war. I've always thought of revolution being war."

"They were lovers, you know. Marie and Philippe. Philippe Brissot, Marat's lieutenant. And Marat had her killed. Tell me, should Jean Paul Marat pay for that sin?"

Mike thought, Present tense?

"Well, he's been dead for what, a couple hundred years?"

"Yes, almost. Killed by Charlotte Corday while he bathed. Killed by a friend of the people. But Philippe never got the chance to avenge his beloved. And that was the tragedy."

The man leaned back again and smiled. "Romantic, isn't it? The French Revolution has always intrigued me. And who knows, perhaps someday poor Marie's death will finally be avenged. Then she'll rest peacefully. Blissfully. Finally."

The man rose with alarming quickness. "Well, I've suddenly remembered that I have a pressing engagement. Tell me, are you here on business, or is this a pleasure trip?"

"Business."

"Too bad. There's so much to see in Paris. France as well. Have you ever heard of the famous Lascaux Cave near the town of Montignac?"

"Lascaux? Funny you—"

"In the south. Two days' journey by horse. It's there where time stands still. Rites of passage are restricted, but if a boy can find it, so can you. Well, good evening to you, sir. Enjoy your meal and your stay."

Mike watched him walk away, and in his periphery Mike saw people that hadn't been there, men, women, children, some walking quickly or crying or holding each other, moving through and around the tables, walking through walls, seated, standing.

"Your wine, monsieur."

They began to fade.

"Sir?"

Mike snapped his head to the sound of the voice. Henri's voice. "What?"

"Your wine. You looked thirsty, so I thought—"

"Didn't you see them?"

"Monsieur?"

Mike just stared at him a moment, then, "Nothing. Just leave it. Thanks."

Henri did as asked, and Mike poured the wine and raised it to his mouth. As he did, he saw the man who had supposedly left, standing at the woman's table. He was looking down at her, reaching out to stroke the head of the baby pressed close to the woman's breast.

31

Mike bolted upright in bed, his body filmed with sweat. Fear worked down from his chest and into his belly; his stomach grumbled. He pulled the sheet off and went to the window. He gazed at the moonlit rooftops of Paris, appearing more like a dreamscape than not. He stood there naked, but what did it matter? Something trivial and true about everyone being naked came to mind, and a capricious wind, as if sent by an embarrassed night, lifted the lacy white curtains and covered him. Somewhere far-off a threatened cat meowed. The sound echoed and Paris seemed to flinch.

After a few minutes, Mike left the window, sat on the bed, and again considered the utter futility of what he was trying to do. David and Goliath came to mind.

In his dream he had been at the restaurant again, speaking with the man who had appeared and disappeared under equally bizarre circumstances. But this time the restaurant was crowded, not with patrons, but with the dead. All animated by his subconscious, sitting there and enjoying fine nouvelle cuisine. Forks poked into holes beneath lips, into blown-open foreheads, into bellies teeming with maggot-infested entrails, into heads perched on empty chairs, fed by the headless body. They all smiled so pleasantly, and told him all about the sights of Paris and its environs and how they wished they, too, could enjoy the sights, but they were dead, you see. Quite dead.

Beyond repair and all that. But the nouvelle cuisine—magnificent! And they'd kiss their bunched purply fingers and continue to dine. He knew these people, too. They were his relatives, those who had been killed at the Marat family massacre. Connie, Al, Mom, and Pop. And in the background, standing there all prim and proper and ready to be seated, stood Beverly. Radiant in a blue, sequined dress, her black hair shimmering, her skin as white as snow. Tears streamed down her cheeks and gathered in a huge, dream-exaggerated puddle at her feet.

Seeing her, his dining companion rose and kissed her hand. It was then that Mike woke up.

Now, reviewing their conversation and the ghostly sightings, it became clear that the man sitting across from him was his enemy. Disguised again, but the same man he'd seen at the warehouse, the same man he'd seen take Beverly, himself, and Paul into the basement. So if that were true, then everything he had said had meaning: places—Lascaux Cave, people—Philippe Brissot. He should learn what he could about Lascaux Cave and Philippe Brissot. He couldn't do extensive research—there wasn't time—but he had to learn more. The guy was dangerous. Crazy, too. And with his kind of power, that ability to manipulate minds . . .

Mike lay down and tried not to think about that.

32

Morning brought a sense of purpose, of possibility. Mike ate only because the Paris Library—Bibliothèque Nationale—wouldn't open till nine. The library was housed in eighteenth-century buildings behind the Palais Royal, not far from his hotel. He left at about 8:45, emerging into a bright, sunlit Paris day.

Bibliothèque Nationale was cavernous. The woman at the information desk, middle-aged with short black hair and tanned skin, looked up long before Mike stopped walking. She crossed her hands on the light oak desk and smiled. Mike felt suddenly self-conscious.

Closer now, he saw small diamonds in the outer corners of her dark-rimmed glasses. The glasses were on a chain, imprisoning her dark brown eyes.

"I need some information on Lascaux Cave."

"Of course, monsieur."

"Oh, and a figure from the revolution, the French Revolution. Philippe Brissot? Him, too."

She stared at a small crystal book on her desk for a moment, then looked up. *"Oui,* Brissot," she said, "Philippe Brissot. From the French Revolution. Yes, okay. I'm sure we have that information."

She did a quarter turn and typed those references into her computer. The screen lit up, blocks of gold highlighting the available text. There were many. After a minute or so, the printer chattered away. A half minute later, she handed Mike the list.

"You may use the cross-reference file there." She pointed to a small desk against a wall, upon which sat a black, loose-leaf binder. "If we have the magazine or the periodical, then it will be listed. Books are in the card file. After you have cross-referenced, take your list to the check-out desk, and the magazines will be located for you. You will have to research them here. We do not allow them to be taken out."

"Sure, all right. Thanks. Listen, they have tours of the cave, right?"

She looked at him quizzically. "No, monsieur. Lascaux Cave is closed to the public."

Mike felt the skin around his eyes heat up. Closed to the public! She might as well have shoved a knife into Beverly's heart. There had to be a mistake.

"Closed." A hopeful smile. "You mean for maintenance or something?"

"Maintenance? No, monsieur. To the public at large. Lascaux is open only to researchers, and then only under special circumstances."

Mike's composure had begun to unravel at the seams, causing his tone to rise an octave. "But why? I don't understand!"

"Monsieur," she whispered, "caves are very . . . delicate. They have their own, what is the word? Atmospheres. Too many people can . . . disturb the atmosphere. Do you understand?"

"No, I don't understand! Look, it's very important. Is there anyone——?"

"Monsieur, please understand. There was a fungus on the walls, on the paintings. They were deteriorating. They are the property of mankind, monsieur. They could not be allowed to disintegrate. It took two years for scientists to reverse what all the tourists had done."

Defeat made Mike feel as though they'd have to scrape him off the floor. Closed to the public. To him. Closed.

Beverly dead. These things went together. Brissot had only been playing games with him, leading him on, giving him false hope. If Brissot had, in fact, taken Beverly to Lascaux Cave, then there was nothing Mike could do. Hope had all but vanished.

"And I suppose they guard the place, too?"

With a suspicious eye, she nodded. "*Oui*, monsieur. It is very well guarded."

Mike half-expected armed gendarmes to leap from the shadows. "Yes, well I, uh . . . thanks, I'll just . . . go. See what I can find."

But hope hadn't vanished entirely. As he sat down and blindly paged through the black loose-leaf binder, he concluded that Brissot would not end the game this way. Too much had gone on to end it so anticlimactically. Lascaux might be closed to the public, but there was another way in. And if Brissot *was* the same man who had been at the warehouse, the same man who had written HOME is where the HEART is, then he had probably provided him with another clue.

His thoughts went back to the night before, to dinner. Focus came easily. Their conversation echoed through the corridors of his mind. He could see his dinner companion seated across from him, jabbering on. He tried to read his lips. Saw those lips very close. Saw them form words. His face suddenly brightened. Of course, of course! But what were his exact words? He ran his fingers through his hair. Christ, where the hell was his memory when he needed it most? Something about visiting Lascaux, then . . . sure! Rites of passage and a . . . a boy! But that was only a part of it. Half the sentence. There was more. C'mon, brain! C'mon! His brain wouldn't cooperate.

"SHIT!"

He slammed the book closed; it sounded like a gun going off. He noticed people glaring at him. He glared back.

More nebulous bullshit to decipher. He opened the black book again and started cross-referencing. Pour over these periodicals. See what they have to say. Something's there. Got to be. Just got to be!

The list on Lascaux Cave was long, everything from *Archeology Digest* to *National Geographic*, and something titled, "Strange hiding place: an arms cache in the Lascaux Grotto." Of course, these things would give him the facts; dimensions, dates, etc, etc. But what he thought he might need was something more in depth, something perhaps not found in *Archeology Digest* or *National Geographic*. Or maybe not. Maybe the answer was right there in front of him. Like the Hudson.

He made a short list, compiled from cross-referencing, and took it to the check-out desk. A young man took the list, disappeared for five minutes, and returned.

"These are all we have. You have circled one that's too old."

He handed Mike an October '88 issue of *National Geographic* and the June '87 *Scientific American*. Mike took them to a reading desk and opened the *National Geographic* first. The story opened in a smooth first-person narrative, but by the end of the first page, the writer had slipped to third person, present tense. Here the story drew his interest. It was about four youths who, in September of 1940, explored a deep, dark hole noticed a week earlier. The hole lay between the roots of a dead tree. The story went on to say that the boys entered the hole only after tossing a stone into the hole to judge depth. The stone fell for a very long time. The boys, three in their mid-teens and one only twelve, guarded their secret for a whole week, finally confiding in their schoolmaster, who notified the proper authorities. One of the boys, the story went on to say, was the cave's chief guide, or had been until the cave closed. His name was Jacques Marsal.

"Rites of passage are restricted, but if a boy can find it, so can you."

Mike snapped to attention and stared at the wall in front of him. That's it! That's what Brissot had said. Exactly what he had said. "Rites of passage are restricted,

293

but if a boy found it, so can you." There was a picture of Jacques Marsal, a handsome man with a full head of gray hair, wide, expressive eyes. Did he know something? Mike studied the face, the eyes. You know, don't you, Jacques Marsal? You have my ticket, my Rite of passage. If anyone—other than Brissot—knows a way in, it's you. Mike looked hard at the picture. "And you're going to tell me. You and I are going to share a bottle of good French wine and have a chat, and you're going to tell me everything you know about Lascaux Cave."

33

The urge to immediately find Jacques Marsal was almost overwhelming, but he fought it. There was more research to do. He needed to find out what he could about Philippe Brissot. He went to the card file, looked under Fra-Ga and found a number of books on the French Revolution. In the racks now, he pulled a couple of books and sat down again, turning to the index of a book entitled *The French Revolution—Paris in Terror*.

There was an artist's rendering of Philippe Brissot on page 232. A small portrait, but very lifelike, almost photographic. The longer Mike looked at it, the heavier his breathing became. And without knowing it, he had begun to shake his head slowly in denial. The man in the painting bore an uncanny resemblance to the man who had sat down with him at dinner the night before.

But logic had been a friend to Mike all his life, and it didn't let him down now. The man staring back at him could not be the same man who'd sat down with him. That was an impossibility. The resemblance—especially in the eyes—was frighteningly close, but there was a matter of two hundred years to consider. The more plausible, more acceptable reasoning, had the man a descendant of Philippe Brissot, as he'd thought earlier. Simple enough. Just a descendant.

He waited until his breathing returned to normal, then took the open book to the librarian who had helped him earlier, determined to find out as much as he could about Philippe Brissot. "This man," he said, "was he important? I mean, can you tell me anything more about him? This really isn't very extensive."

The woman gave Mike another suspicious look before she adjusted her glasses and studied the picture. "Like most French men and women, I am a student of the revolution," she said. She ran her finger quickly from left to right down the article. When she was done, she looked up, took off her glasses, and let them fall around her neck. "He's, what is the word? My English is good, but—an enigma. Enigma?"

"Puzzle? You mean a puzzle?"

"Yes, yes, a puzzle. A very big puzzle." She turned the book around and pointed at the death date listed beneath the picture. "As you can see, monsieur, there is a question mark."

"That doesn't seem too unusual."

"That is part of the puzzle. No one knows when or how Philippe Brissot died. There has been speculation, rumor, conjecture." She smiled again, pleased with her sudden command of the language. "Some people think he was beheaded—guillotined—but revolutionary scholars doubt that. Wait a minute, please. If we are lucky, Madame Petain . . . wait here."

She got up from behind her desk and walked past the stacks to an office. A minute or so later she reappeared with a bent old woman, her white hair tied back tightly, her nose hawkish. The librarian had cupped a hand under the old woman's elbow. She looked, Mike thought, like Golda Meir. Both women stopped outside the door to the office and looked in Mike's direction. The librarian waved him over.

Mike exchanged glances with her before she spoke; the sparkle of youth was still present when she smiled. "You are interested in Philippe Brissot, monsieur?"

"Yes, very much."

She held out her hand. "My name is Madame Petain, and you are?"

"Mike, Mike Marat." Her handshake was surprisingly firm.

"Marat, not any relation . . ."

"So I'm told."

"Well, isn't that delightful? Just delightful! Well, Monsieur Marat, Philippe Brissot and Jean Paul Marat have been a hobby of mine for many years." She looked at the book in Mike's hand and dismissed it with a small wave of her hand. "These books are competent, but there is more to know. Things that cannot be substantiated, true, but I assume that's why you came to me—you want to know more than what books have to say."

"If there is more, I'd certainly like to know it."

"Good, come into my office then. Do you drink cognac?"

"Well, it's kind of . . . sure, why not?"

"Good. Very good. Come."

She walked back into her office, her step a little more deliberate now, and poured two shot glasses of Remy cognac. That done, she handed a glass of the golden fluid to Mike and pulled up a blue-cushioned chair beside his, gesturing that he should sit in its twin. Closer now, Mike noticed that her breath smelled vaguely of tobacco.

"Monsieur Marat, I cannot believe my good luck." She downed the cognac with barely a squint. "A descendant of Jean Paul Marat himself. How fortunate."

The sudden adoration somewhat unnerved Mike. The old woman seemed to sense as much. "But you are here about Philippe Brissot," she said. "Where should we start? Perhaps with his death . . ."

"As good a place as any. There does seem to be some confusion about the date."

"The date? Yes, but *how* he died might be of more interest." She continued the conversation almost conspiratorially. "Speculation has it that he, too, may have

297

been killed by Charlotte Corday. That cannot be verified, yes, but Brissot was Marat's second in command."

"Charlotte Corday?"

"Yes—your ancestor's murderer. Comely woman. Ravishing."

"Really?"

"Yes. Very beau—"

"I meant, did she really kill Marat?"

Her eyes lit up. "With a knife, while he bathed."

"And did she get away with it?"

"Even more speculation. History tells us that she was tried and beheaded, but there are those—I among them—who believe that a double was used. Someone who took the blame. If that is true, then yes, she did, as you say, monsieur, get away with it. There are those who speculate that she died a horrible death in the south of France. In the caves of Lascaux. But then, there's been much ado about Lascaux."

"Really? How so?"

"Have you studied Lascaux, monsieur?"

"A little. Discovered in 1940, closed now. Well, that's what the librarian told me."

"Yes, closed. The caves, unfortunately, were dying. But there is legend surrounding the cave. Myth and wild superstition. Some say that evil lurks in that cave, beyond those boundaries mapped by man. There are rumors of other passages where evil ones dwell. It is believed that they leave in the dark of night to feed upon livestock, and if there is no livestock to be found, they feed upon humans."

She began to smile, then she chuckled.

"Forgive me, monsieur. Whenever I speak of these foolish things, my funny bones get tickled."

"What do you mean, evil ones?"

She got up, poured another cognac for herself, and raised the bottle to ask if he'd like to join her. To his surprise, Mike said he would. She sat down again, thought a moment, slugged down the whole glass, and said, "May

I assume you know what vampires are, monsieur Marat?"

"Vampires?"

"Yes, vampires. Bloodsuckers if you like."

"Well, sure. Everyone knows about vampires, but what do they have to do . . ."

"They reside in the cave. That's the evil I speak of, monsieur. Vampires. And there's more. Some believe that Philippe Brissot himself is a vampire."

"You mean people really believe in that kinda thing?"

"With every fiber of their beings. And more myth as well. Some people believe that Philippe Brissot himself spirited Charlotte Corday away and gave her the gift."

"The gift?"

"Immortality, monsieur."

"In the caves."

"*Oui,* in the caves."

"But why? Why would he do that?"

"No one knows. Perhaps to gain a companion. Perhaps as punishment for killing Jean Paul Marat. Who knows?"

"As punishment?"

"Think of it. Eternal life, monsieur. To live forever. As for myself, at the age of eighty-two, I have begun to accept the afterlife. Immortality to me would be a punishment."

Mike had never thought of it quite that way, but then he was barely half this woman's age.

"But punishment for what?"

"Marat had his mistress beheaded, leaving their daughter motherless. He never forgave Jean Paul Marat for that. And as a vampire, he could certainly avenge Marie for a very long time."

"What do you mean?"

"Through his ancestors, monsieur. Vampires are immortal. And if what you say is true . . ."

"If what I say is true, then, then he's after me, too."

Madame Petain forced a smile. "But, of course, it can't be. Vampires! It is ridiculous, yes?"

"But you don't understand, madame, something *is* going on. People *have* been killed."

Her smile vanished. "Oh, my! How terrible. But surely you don't think . . . ?"

"What else can you tell me? You said he had a daughter?"

"Yes, her name was Jeanette. Many years ago I followed the line. There are many old records in the basement of this building. It may interest you to know that Jeanette's direct descendant lives in Paris."

Anything concerning Brissot was of interest; his life, his death, his ancestry. This old woman had said so much, revealed so much. And although most of it—vampires especially—was fantastical and highly improbable, the fantastical was only a small step beyond what had happened thus far. He found himself very much interested in this Jeanette Brissot and her descendants.

"Where?" he asked.

"Let me think, let me think. Yes. On Rue de Mabeuqe. Do you know it? Just a small street."

"Yes, yes, I do. I was there last night, well, I drove by there. What number?"

"Thirteen Rue de Mabeuqe."

He would have liked to have taken the picture of Philippe Brissot, but he didn't have a library card, a bit of red tape that seemed totally ludicrous considering the circumstances. The best they could do was a photostat. It was on the seat, positioned so that he could look at it.

A car horn, slamming of brakes. He looked up, a Citröen was stopped about a foot from his bumper. The driver was shaking his fist out the window. The Citröen honked long and hard and pulled around him. Mike could only shrug an apology.

He parked on the street at 13 Rue de Mabeuqe. The house looked to be fairly new, in comparison to those on either side. Nineteenth century, Mike thought. There was a gently curved walkway lined by peonies and alyssum. The gray house, with black shutters and dark gray trim, looked smaller from the street. The knocker had the name Goden etched into it. Mike raised it, let it fall. The door was opened very quickly, but only a foot or so. The woman looking at him was in her early sixties, salt and pepper hair, green-blue eyes, and a creamy complexion. She was wearing a robe. She smiled statically and mindlessly fussed with her hair.

"*Oui?*"

"Hello, my name is Mike, Mike Marat."

"Marat?" Her smile disappeared.

"You don't speak English, do you?"

"English? *Oui.* A teeny bit."

"Can I come in?"

The woman hesitated, then, "My husband, he is out. To come home soon."

Mike smiled. She was frightened of him. No matter where you went, women were afraid of strange men at their door.

"It's a nice morning, maybe you'd like to come out on the porch?"

"What do you want?"

"I need to ask you about your ancestor, Philippe Brissot."

"Philippe Brissot? You wish to question me about Philippe Brissot?"

"Yes, for just a moment."

The woman studied him a moment longer, stuck her head out the door, and looked in both directions, wondering if the neighbors had seen. Then she stepped back, waved Mike inside, and quickly shut the door behind him.

The interior of the house was amazingly dark; the smell of old wood and varnish was overwhelming. Mike stood in the foyer and mentally pictured someone in the basement refinishing furniture. From here he could see the living room; the dark drapes were drawn. A thin beam of sunlight shone through and lanced the floor. Dust motes frolicked in the beam. What struck him immediately were the photographs that graced each and every piece of furniture that wasn't used for sitting. Frames of silver and gold plate, all feebly reflecting what light there was. The woman gestured toward the living room. Mike followed her there.

She took a seat on a French Provincial sofa, and Mike sat down across from her on a plain wooden chair.

"Can you tell me anything about him? For instance, do you know how he died or maybe where?"

"Why do you want to know? And why, Monsieur Marat, do you think he is my ancestor?"

Mike decided to lie. "I'm doing research for a book on the French Revolution. And Madame Petain at the library—"

"Madame Petain is a busybody. Monsieur, there is no one who can say that Brissot is my family. No one."

She's denying him, Mike thought. Why?

"Madame Petain seemed to think, well, she's pretty convinced that your great great great grandmother was Brissot's mistress, and that she had a daughter, who had a daughter, who had a daughter. Do you understand?"

"And you think I am the last of these daughters?"

"I don't know, are you?"

She stared at him for the longest time, then, "This book. Which publisher?"

"Simon and Schuster."

"Yes, I have heard of them." She sat up straighter. All prim and proper now. "Will you pay me?"

The bottom line. Money. It was all about money, the great communicator. But what would he be paying for? Verification that Brissot was her great great great grandad? Or was there more? He pulled out his wallet and set it on the table between them. "One hundred francs."

The woman sat up even straighter. "Two hundred and fifty."

"One hundred and fifty."

"Yes, okay, one hundred and seventy-five."

Mike smiled and gave her the money. The woman stuck it into her robe pocket, got up, went to a table in back, and returned with a photograph in a wood frame. The picture was of a baby, probably not yet a year old. "I am not the last. This is the last. I gave her up for adoption a very long time ago."

Mike took the picture from her and studied it. The photograph was in black and white and showed a smiling baby on a white blanket, sucking on the big toe of her right foot. There was a black cross around her neck.

"When was this taken?"

"I don't know. Sometime in the fifties."

"Then she'd be about forty now, maybe a little younger." He was talking to himself. "The family that adopted her, what was their name?"

The woman smiled again, a puzzling smile. "That is perhaps why I let you in. The family's name was Marat. Like your own."

34

There was sadness on Charlotte's face. Darkness couldn't disguise it, and moonlight only deepened the shadows. Beverly had never seen sadness on Charlotte's face. It made her smile.

They were driving up a dirt road; overgrown weeds slapped against the sides of the car. Up ahead she could barely make out three buildings caught in the headlights' glow.

Timorously, she asked where they were.

Charlotte turned her head. "Home," she said.

Philippe stopped the car in the middle of the yard, then he and Charlotte got out. Beverly stayed in the car, peering out like a frightened cat. Even in the moonlight, she could tell that the house and the two outbuildings were in an advanced state of decay.

Charlotte motioned to her.

"NO, DAMMIT, NO!" Beverly shouted, shaking her head wildly.

Charlotte opened the door and took her hand. "Nothing's going to happen to you, not . . . I've just got to get something."

Not here, Beverly thought. That's what Charlotte had meant to say. Nothing would happen to her *here*.

"Please," Charlotte said.

Hesitantly, Beverly stepped out of the car, her attention immediately drawn to the house. Going inside would not be wise. "This is where you lived, isn't it? Where you grew up," she said to Charlotte.

"Hm hmm."

Beverly pictured her as a child running out the front door, perhaps playing with the animals, maybe feeding them. A glaring sun overhead.

Charlotte smiled at Philippe. "It's where Philippe and I first met two hundred years ago. Quite by accident, I might add."

Philippe seemed impatient, as if he were uncomfortable riding this nostalgic wave.

"Get it," he said to Charlotte.

"Get what?" Beverly asked.

"Come with me, Beverly. I want to show you the house where I grew up."

Beverly smiled wryly. "Oh, no! I'm not going anywhere with you."

Charlotte's face hardened. She grabbed Beverly by the arm. "Do as I say!"

No choice. None.

They went inside; the darkness here like a huge, expanding black bubble. Charlotte had her by the hand.

The appreciable mustiness made Beverly sneeze; her eyes teared. Most of all, being here played havoc with her sense of time. It wouldn't take much to convince her that it was not 1992, not much at all.

"Where are we going? Where are you taking me?"

"Upstairs, that's all. Just upstairs."

Her eyes had begun to adjust. She saw an L-shaped stairway in front of her. As she ascended now, the runners complained loudly under her weight. But wasn't it odd how easily those runners coped with Charlotte's weight?

The room at the top of the stairs was surprisingly large. Moonlight entered through a half-boarded-over window and illuminated a bed in front of another window, the light soft, creamy, inviting. To the right of the bed stood a cupboard, easily six foot tall. Charlotte let go of her hand and opened the doors. Dust flew about, and Beverly waved it away from her nose.

Oddly, the house was in remarkably good condition. Although deserted, it appeared that vandals had avoided this property.

Charlotte reached into the cupboard and seemed to smile. "There is myth surrounding this house," she said. "About a vampire and his lady. People—humans—don't come here. Ever. Myths make such marvelous watchdogs."

She brought the dress over to Beverly. "You seem so taken by fine clothing," she said. "Yes, this suits you. You do like old things, don't you?"

Beverly looked at the dress. Although it was old, it was also beautiful; pale green, with ruffled, dark green shoulders and skirt. But appearance and reality were at odds here. The dress gave off an odor reminiscent of raked-over dirt in mid-August.

"Why are you giving it to me?" Beverly asked.

"It was Philippe's idea, actually. History repeating itself and all that. Try it on."

Reluctantly, Beverly did try it on, and as it went on, time did a back flip. She looked at Charlotte. How easy to imagine them here so long ago, trying on dresses and laughing.

A noise, from behind. Beverly turned slowly, elegantly, and looked at Philippe standing in the dark doorway, shadowy. There was something in his hand. He stepped toward her and held it out. A fan. Beverly took it, smiled, and only half-pretended to be a radiant, desirable lady, waiting for her betrothed to arrive in his four-horse carriage.

And wasn't it peculiar that the air was no longer musty, no longer stale and old and dead.

Seeing Beverly fan herself, a coy smile playing along her mouth, Philippe was pleased.

35

For another fifty francs, Mike was able to purchase the photograph of the baby. Why he bought it, he wasn't sure, but when he saw it, he knew he had to have it. Was it the coincidence—that the adoptive parents had the same name as he? Or was it something more? Being separated from it, he couldn't be sure, so he bought it. She, Marie-Therese Goden was her name, had feigned insult that mere money could make her part with the photograph. But in truth, she had parted with the child, so why not the photograph of the child?

Mike had all the information he needed now, or at least as much as time would allow him to gather. He had heard a story that under other circumstances would be laughable—that Philippe Brissot and Charlotte Corday were very possibly vampires. And although these stories were probably only superstitious nonsense, he had, before beginning the trip to Montignac, decided that he would attend the vagaries of these legends with caution. To do otherwise would be foolhardy.

It was night now. The trip had taken about five hours. Montignac, a small town in stasis since the almost-religious fervor surrounding Lascaux had diminished in the early sixties, was very old, like all French towns. Hanging flowers cascaded down stone walls that rose over narrow, cobblestone streets; horse-drawn carts competed with modern-day conveyances. Depending on where you were in Montignac, it could be either this century or the last.

A fog had begun to gather, caressing the town, providing cover perhaps. His hotel, The Lafayette, was located in the middle of town. He had called for reservations before he left Paris.

The top two floors of the Lafayette were shrouded in fog, leaving only the bottom three floors visible; turquoise shutters, white stone, and clinging ivy. Very touristy.

The Lafayette, although small by French standards, treated its guests like kings and queens. Mike was greeted by the rotund, rosy-cheeked owner and given a glass of a local cabernet, wonderful stuff. After a few minutes of small talk, he was led to his room by the owner's wife, an ample woman in her forties, who smelled like freshly baked bread and insisted upon carrying his bag. The room was at the northern end of a long, bare hallway, number 23. The woman smiled very broadly, displaying what had to be false teeth, and handed him his key.

"A nice hot bath, perhaps?" she suggested.

"Sounds great," Mike said, just to be polite. "Tell me, madame," he continued, "do you know of a man named Jacques Marsal?"

"Oui, everyone knows Jacques. Such a nice man."

"I'd like to meet him, maybe you can arrange it?"

"Meet him?"

"Yes, to talk about the caves. I understand he was the chief guide when they were open."

"Oh, yes, certainly, monsieur. Many people like to talk to Jacques. The caves are unfortunately closed, but Jacques very much likes to talk with tourists."

"Can you tell me where he lives, maybe—"

"He lives on a farm outside of Montignac, monsieur, but if he is not there, then you can find him at the Cafe de la Paix—"

"Cafe de la Paix? Isn't that in Paris?"

"Oui, yes, but we also have a Cafe de la Paix. Ours is more intimate. We southern French enjoy intimacy more than Parisians."

She was flirting with him. Her eyes were working a mile a minute, and she was flirting with him! Mike was a little embarrassed.

"Is the cafe close by?"

She seemed somewhat disappointed. "Two doors down, monsieur." She raised her wrist to within six inches of her face, necessary in the ill-lit hallway. "It is still early. Perhaps he is there now. Perhaps not. He has many children, you see, and sometimes a man with many children enjoys the cafe a little more than a man with fewer children." She smiled coyly and nudged him with her elbow. "Or perhaps such a man enjoys being home more? Eh?"

Mike grinned. "Lots of kids, huh?"

"*Oui*, nine. And twins on the way. But the Marsals are self-sufficient, as are many Frenchmen. They have pigs and vegetables and grapes for wine. Jacques sometimes lectures about the caves."

"Knows a lot about them, does he?"

"*Oui*, Jacques knows more about the caves than any man." She seemed proud of that.

"Then I look forward to talking with him."

"First a bath?"

She seemed insistent that he bathe. Maybe he smelled. He resisted the urge to raise an arm to see what kind of odor escaped.

"Maybe. I'd really like to talk with Jacques Marsal though."

The woman nodded, said, "*Oui*," turned, and left, humming a tune as she walked down the hall.

The room was slightly disappointing. There were paintings, but they were all cheaply done reproductions; banal scenes of French life, peasants in the fields, and Paris street scenes. The pastel green bedspread smelled slightly moldy and there was a spider feverishly working on a web in a corner. What's more, there was no shower, only a tub, a black one shaped like a stub-nosed, high-back shoe. Mike ran his hand over the pebbly surface.

Quite the relic, he thought. Maybe that's part of the charm though. Maybe Louis XVI himself bathed in this thing. Thinking that, he imagined Louis in there, and then a host of French nobility. He smiled lopsidedly. If nothing else, perhaps he could say he used a tub fit for a king. And he really could use a bath.

He started to undress, turning to the sink mirror to see if he needed a shave. He could see the tub out of the corner of his eye. Something caught his attention. He turned, focused as best he could, then dropped to one knee for a closer look. There was a thick, red-colored liquid, dripping down the side of the tub.

Charlotte stopped and picked a few wildflowers from the side of the road. "For your hair," she told Beverly. She arranged the flowers precisely, provocatively. "Mike will like them. I know he will."

Montignac lay just ahead, fog-shrouded, the sounds of light traffic magnified in the still, night air. The woods all around were quiet. Fireflies blinked on and off. Charlotte and Beverly were alone.

"He'll be glad to see me," Beverly said.

"Very glad," Charlotte responded.

"And I'll be very glad to see him." She looked hard at Charlotte. "I will, won't I?"

"But, of course, Beverly."

"Then why . . ." She looked down at the green sheath that so complemented her dress.

"Authenticity," Charlotte told her.

Mike stood, grinning. What he at first thought to be blood was just shampoo. A small tube, set on the edge with conditioner and small, round, blue soaps, had spilled, dripping down the side of the tub. Blood, he thought, mildly scolding himself. Why the hell would there be blood in there?

He stood, no longer grinning, realizing how illogical his actions of the last few minutes had been. Beverly was out there somewhere, waiting for him. She could be dead. Go find Marsal, he told himself. Find him and make him take you to the cave! If he won't do it on his own, then *make* him go!

And Mike very much wanted to do that, but he was—he had to admit—very tired, his energy level as low as it had been for a long time. Maybe, he thought, a bath would revive him, but even as he thought that, he realized that he was still thinking illogically. His next rationalization had something to do with taking a short nap in the tub; all the stimulus he needed. He finished undressing and turned on the faucets.

The steady, monotonous flow only added to his lethargy, and as he listened to the sound of the water running into the tub, he felt compelled to watch. The wine, he thought. It's the wine that made him feel this way; so light-headed and weak. Naked, he sat on the side of the tub and simply stared at the rising, roiling water, steam building around him.

It was then that a pair of eyes seemed to rise through the foam—flat, blue, lifeless eyes.

"Armand," said the Hotel Lafayette's owner's fat wife, "did you hear something?"

Armand was in their living room watching an old Jerry Lewis movie. "What?" he called, a bit annoyed. His wife knew not to disturb him while he was watching Jerry Lewis.

She appeared in the doorway. "I thought I heard someone crying, Armand."

Armand looked at his wife. "Crying? But there aren't any children here tonight."

"No, Armand, not a child. A woman, I think. A woman crying."

When will it stop? Mike wondered. He lifted the blue soaps out of the tub and turned off the faucets. Eyes, he actually thought the soaps were eyes! He tested the water with his hand to see if it was cool enough, then got in.

The water seemed a panacea for his withering spirits. Sitting here, eyes half-closed, he allowed his thoughts to drift. He was back in Watertown, he and Beverly, but they weren't children, they were adults, seated together on a porch swing. The night was starlit and warm, their kisses light and probing. They got up and went into the living room, to the couch, where they talked and kissed some more, speaking of the future and how they would spend it together, always together. Glancing around, he noticed how beautifully she had decorated; colors, textures, fabrics. And paintings on every wall, not just commercial copies, but works that echoed their individual personalities. No velvet Elvises here.

Nice. Real nice.

Smiling, he took notice of her latest acquisition, a wall hanging with a French phrase.

LA MORT.

He looked back into her eyes, his smile fading. How odd, he wanted to say. It's really out of place, Beverly. The rest of the house is so nicely decorated, why . . . ? Mike chopped his hand onto the surface of the water— SPLAT—then pushed himself up and snapped his eyes open. Now he knew why he had daydreamed what he had. On the wall to the right of the tub, was the wall hanging he had envisioned on the wall in Beverly's living room.

LA MORT.

And now he saw that the wallpaper had changed in here as well. The simple black and white stripes had been replaced by a floral pattern of red and green, and in the corner, on an ornate wooden table, stood a purple vase filled with huge black orchids. He sat up even further in the tub, his neck bristling. A glance at the mirror—LA MORT reflected back at him from the opposing wall. Another glance, just to the right, toward the door.

It's opening, he thought. The damn thing is opening!

From the outer room, he heard a woman's soft cry, not of remorse or grief, but of defeat. The light was so weak, though, he couldn't see. Who was it? Who the hell was it? The door swung silently open and Mike sat up further still. He didn't want to get out of the tub, not yet—what if it was the woman who had showed him the room? "Madame?" he said.

But what about the wallpaper?

"Is that you, madame?"

And what about that wall hanging?

"Please, madame, I'm in the tub." A nervous laugh. "Just as you suggested."

He saw her now, but all he could see was that she was a tall woman, taller than his hostess, a fan held in her left hand, covering her face, something glittering weakly in the other.

Fear glowed in Mike's belly; his temples began to throb. "Who are you?" he asked, lifting his left leg over the side and propping himself up.

More crying, steady and low. Now it had taken on a grieving tone.

A knife, Mike thought, staring at the woman's hand. She's got a knife! He pushed himself up, his butt on the edge of the tub, left leg out, right leg in. But in his haste to get out, his trailing foot slipped. He went down hard, his right hand slapping at the water, the left side of his head slamming against the back of the tub. Pain rifled through his skull as he fell back into the tub, bathwater streaming into his mouth and nose. He flailed away, resisting the urge to grab his wound, knowing only that he had to get up, he had to get out. But as he surfaced, he discovered that he was too weak to do anything but gasp for air and watch helplessly, as the woman moved toward him, the knife raised high in her right hand, the fan in the other, still covering her face.

Beverly? Was it Beverly?

"Mike, oh, Mike. I'm so sorry, Mike!"

Christ oh Christ—it was her—it *was* her!

He tried to scrabble out of the tub, but he couldn't. He'd been hurt, he was weak, he couldn't move. His head blazed with pain.

She lowered the fan and he saw her now; the red, tear-stained face, the green on green dress. Closer she came, almost on him now, her face suddenly hardened with resolve. She raised the knife higher still, ready to plunge it into him, ready to take his life . . . but then, from behind, a huge hand appeared, and Philippe Brissot, one hand around Beverly's waist, the other now holding her wrist, looked scornfully down upon his naked, injured enemy.

"Not yet," he said, the air suddenly burdened by the sour odor of blood. "Not yet. But you'll continue, oh yes, you will. And that will make it all the better for me. See you in hell, monsieur."

That said, he pulled Beverly out of the already changing room; laughter, callous and hate-filled trailed behind him.

Summoning every ounce of strength he could, Mike lifted himself out of the tub and promptly fell, ramming his elbow into the floor. Wincing, he grabbed at it.

"Bev!" he hollered. "Come back! Please come back!"

More strength now, just to get up. And the room was spinning, wheeling. A goddamn kaleidoscope! He stumbled after them, slamming into the bathroom doorframe. "SHIT!" Into the hall now, and there they were, at the end, just standing there laughing.

Focus, where was his focus? "LET HER GO, DAMN YOU! LET HER GO!"

Brissot's head rolled back and laughter poured out. "All in good time, Monsieur Marat."

Down the stairs they went, Mike in hot pursuit, pinballing off the walls. A door opened to his right; something was said in French, something about a naked man, and then a startled yelp.

Turning right now, into the stairway. Dizzy, so damn dizzy! Get a grip! Just get a grip. Going down too fast, way too fast!

"Bev! BEV!"

"See you in hell, monsieur. In hellll!"

Spinning, spinning. Falling . . .

"Monsieur!"

Gone. They were gone. Follow, he had to follow. He had to get up! But he couldn't. The pain was too much. There was nothing he could do. Really having no choice, he rolled onto his back, concerned faces around him, peering down.

Then Armand's fat wife said, "Monsieur Marat—you are naked!"

Before he passed out, Mike felt a blanket wrap around him, and he heard something about blood on the back of his head.

36

Jacques Marsal raised his glass with his fellows and saluted the waitress's large bosom, drooped between him and his good friend, Antoine, as she leaned in to remove some of the empty beer bottles from the table. As always, she took offense, but again as always, she kept silent. Times had been difficult, and tips were important. They looked, these men, they made crude remarks, but they never touched.

During the last three hours, the four friends seated at the round wooden table had saluted everything from good weather to the soccer skills of Jacques's youngest son. And although they had raised their glasses in salute many times, they would never lack for something to raise their glasses to. There was always something to toast, some reason to imbibe far too much, which Jacques did with great zeal and continuing pleasure.

The Cafe de la Paix was but a small establishment, ten round wooden tables, a long, highly polished bar, waitresses hired purely for their glandular appeal, and drinks that were one price for locals and another for tourists. Montignac was a small town; tourists were easily recognized, easily swindled. In the air there hung a puzzle of tobacco smoke; cigars, pipes, American cigarettes. Marlboro was the brand of choice. Two women played darts, an English import.

In one of those minor coincidences, the wooden double doors opened at precisely the same moment a dart found the bull's eye. For a brief time, the din of social interaction quieted. A tourist had arrived. A tall man who moved into the room and then to the bar with an undulating sensuality that was close to mesmerizing. Yet there was also a brassiness about him that the patrons, Jacques included, instantly disliked.

The man laid one hand on the bar and waggled a finger of the other at the bartender, a stout man with a stouter stomach and a bald head.

"Yes?" said the bartender, choosing to stay near the cash register.

"Jacques Marsal, is he here?"

The bartender moved closer, his fat stomach pressed into the bar. "And who is asking?"

"A lover of caves."

The bartender's gaze drifted momentarily, and the man followed that gaze to the table in the corner. Four men stared back at him.

"And who are you?" asked Antoine, the short, dark-haired friend of Jacques Marsal.

"Are you Jacques?"

"Answer my question."

Antoine had been Jacques's friend for forty years. Because Jacques had once saved him from drowning, Antoine felt a continuing need to return the favor, as he was doing now. For reasons Antoine was unable to fathom, this man seemed to pose a threat to his old friend.

The man left the bar and stood close to Antoine.

"I'll ask again," the man said, his voice unnervingly calm.

"Antoine," Jacques said, "calm down. I'm sure he just wants to talk about the caves. It's all right."

Hoping to appear threatening, Antoine sneered at the man glowering down at him. The man's expression didn't change.

"You are Jacques Marsal?" said the man. They locked gazes.

"Yes, I am Jacques Marsal."

The man's smile seemed out of place. "Good, I wish to talk with you."

37

"Monsieur, you can go nowhere like that. You have been concussed!"

Mike looked at her suspiciously, wondering how these French-speaking people had learned to speak such remarkably good English.

"I've got a concussion?"

"*Oui*, you do!"

"Shit!"

"Monsieur, please!"

Mike was in his room. Someone had dressed his wound. There was a cotton swath around his head, and he had on pajamas. He looked at Armand's wife. She'd put the pajamas on him, he was sure about that.

"Look, I may be . . . concussed, but I've got to see Jacques Marsal tonight. Now! It's a matter of life and death!"

"Monsieur, it will be *your* death, if you leave this bed. You could pass out in front of a car and be killed. Whose life and death?"

"A friend. She's been . . ." He looked at the woman and her husband, both leaning closer now. Should he bring them in on this or not? He didn't think so. The fewer people who knew about this the better. Involving this couple would most assuredly involve the police as well. Then he'd never get into Lascaux Cave. "It's my wife. I followed her here from the States. I think you know the rest."

Armand and his wife looked at each other and shook their heads knowingly. An affair of the heart was most certainly a matter of life and death.

"Tomorrow you can find your wife, monsieur, tonight you must rest. But tell me, why did you wish to speak with Jacques?"

Mike looked at her a moment, his brain doing its best to supply him with something believable. "I'm ashamed to say that during our last visit, she and Jacques . . . well, you know."

More knowing shakes of the head. "And you wish to harm Jacques Marsal?"

"Oh, no. Not at all. Just talk to him, that's all. Just talk."

They had more questions to ask, he could see as much on their faces, the first question being what he was doing running through the lobby of their hotel buck-naked. But they left without asking.

Staring at the ceiling now, a little afraid to go to sleep, and just as afraid to walk the streets in his weakened condition, Mike wondered about Beverly, and whether she really would have killed him if Brissot hadn't interceded. And he also wondered about where she was now—if she was still alive.

Beverly consciously tried to control her respiration; it had become too quick, labored. She could hyperventilate. She discovered that although it wasn't easy, she *was* able to control her respiration, even finding some pride in that accomplishment. But then she substituted one reaction for another. She began to hum, eventually breaking into an old Beatles tune, "Hey Jude."

A tear wiggled down her cheek, another joined it. She wiped them away. "C'mon, Bev," she said aloud, "you've done pretty well up to now, don't spoil it. Just 'cause you

can't see anything, just because you . . . almost killed
Mike."

NO!

Yes, you did, Beverly.

No, I didn't. I wouldn't. Never. Never!

She rocked harder now, creating a deep concavity in
the sand, her arms wrapped around her knees. More
tears. She swiped at them angrily, then buried her head
in the hollowed-out area between her knees and chest,
closed her eyes, and sang the last line from "Hey Jude."

There was a certain degree of comfort to be had in the
gentle rocking motion she had begun a minute or so after
they had sat her down here, on the sand. "Don't move,"
Philippe had ordered. "If you do, you will die." His voice
seemed to encircle her; was he in front of her, behind,
standing off to the side? Funny, she thought now, how
Brissot had sounded so much like a doting parent. "Don't
go too far into the lake or you'll drown." "Don't go too
near the road, you'll get run over." Of course, Mom or
Pop wouldn't be the ones doing the drowning; they
wouldn't be the ones running her over. Charlotte had
been somewhere close. She hadn't said anything, but
Beverly had sensed her presence. There was a certain
odor . . .

A few minutes later she raised her head, and silently
noted that her eyes still hadn't adjusted. She still couldn't
see a thing, not a damn thing. By now, she thought, she
should have been able to see something. Was she blind,
actually blind? That was entirely possible, although she
didn't know how that could have happened. She didn't
have any pain; she didn't remember sustaining any specific injury. No, she wasn't blind. There was just no light
for her eyes to adjust to, that was why she couldn't see.
And so it held that if there was nothing to listen to, then
she wouldn't be able to hear either. And if there was
nothing to touch . . . Okay, she hadn't suffered complete
sensory deprivation. And odds were, she could still see,
too. This sudden lucidity of thought both surprised and

delighted her, and she decided to actively compete with the darkness. She thought about the blind, about what weapons . . . her sense of smell! Was it stronger now that she couldn't see? She could smell water as well as hear it, as it cascaded down a waterfall far-off to the right. And even here, as in the house they'd stopped at, there was a decidedly old smell. Slightly rancid, slightly putrid, like what might waft out when a mummy's coffin was opened. Even older than the smell she had encountered at Charlotte's house. But she was in a cave—she knew that much—so why shouldn't it smell old? Everything in here was old. Everything except her. And she'd never get old. Never. She was going to die in here. Then whatever lived in here would eat her rotting flesh, and her bones would get old and shiny and . . . Shit, do something! Dammit, Bev, do something! Don't just sit here feeling sorry for yourself. Get up, look around, feel around. Find a way out! Just sitting here won't get you anywhere but dead. And that's nowhere!

She couldn't. They'd told her not to move. They'd told her she would die!

But what did she think would happen if she continued to just sit here?

That made some kind of twisted sense.

She raised her head and scanned the darkness, silently praying for light. There had to be some, at least a little. Her singing had echoed after all, so this had to be a very large chamber.

She felt her palms press on the sand. "Don't kill me!" she whispered to the darkness, as she pushed herself up. She cleaned her hands on her dress, just now realizing that she still had it on. "Please, I don't want to be blind," she pleaded. Surely they wouldn't kill her for not wanting to be blind! That wasn't a reason to kill someone.

She moved one foot forward, stopped. Took a few more steps. She knew she was on the side of a hill, but how high a hill? And how deep was the water? What was on the other side? So many questions—too many to answer.

f only she could see—just enough to walk. The darkness was unlined, unrelieved. She wondered if maybe she couldn't just suck it all into her lungs, and exhale only light.

She clenched her jaw, steeling her determination, and started down.

After only a few steps she kicked something, creating a metallic clatter. She stood stock-still for a moment, trying to gauge direction, then got down on all fours, and searched for whatever it was she had kicked. Seconds later, she found it. She sat up and ran her fingers over the surface. A lantern! A lantern! She'd be able to see! Thank God, she'd be able to see!

But depression coursed through her like a quick virus. She didn't have any matches. She couldn't very well light this lantern without matches!

With a yelp of frustration and anger, she threw the lantern as far as she could. The crisp SPLAT created as the lantern struck water startled her.

She started down again, and within a few yards, the ground leveled off. A few yards later, the sand became soggy underfoot, and she knew she was near the water's edge. Cautiously she stepped closer, then, despite the rigid cold, walked into the water up to her ankles. She stopped, backed away. It wouldn't do any good to go in here. She'd just freeze to death. The damn water was like ice. She turned her head to the left, then to the right, trying to determine which direction she should take. She chose right, walking very slowly, her hands out in front of her. The sound of the falls grew steadily louder and fueled her anticipation—just moving toward something was itself a minor victory. She kept the shoreline just to her left and picked up her pace.

What was that?

She stopped and squinted. Light? Either her brain was playing a very cruel trick on her, or she could actually see a semicircle of light up ahead. Throwing caution aside, she picked up her pace. Light—validation that she wasn't blind after all! It had to be, just had to be! She started a kind of groping trot, hands outstretched, face turned— just in case. But now she was sure she saw light, and there, off to the left, the falls. The water glittered ever so feebly, like a cluster of subterranean falling stars. She ran faster, straying a little into the water, then out again. Light! Could it be? Was this the way out? Had she caught a glimpse of sunlight?

She broke into a fast trot; the semicircle of light had grown brighter, summoning, beckoning. She started to laugh gleefully. She was going to beat them! She was going to get away!

She slowed to a walk. There was light, yes, but it radiated from below, from a hole in the ground. Not from above. Still hopeful, she went to the edge of the hole and peered into it. About four feet across, she guessed. The light appeared to come from an area about fifteen feet down and off to the right. But the walls of the hole were rock. At least she'd have something to hold onto. Well, she thought, if I've got to go down to get out of this blasted place, so be it.

She went into the hole feet first, her chest against the wall. She descended slowly, her fingers constantly looking for a grip, her toes curling, searching for cavities. She stopped and looked behind her often, half-thinking that someone or something would look back at her: nothing ever did.

Once down, she surveyed her surroundings. Here the light was definitely brighter, although now it was apparent that it was not a steady light. There were variations in intensity, not much, but enough to notice.

There were only two ways out of this hole; she could climb back out, or use the tunnel that acted as a kind of light funnel. She bent at the waist—the tunnel was about three feet high—and entered. As she bent down, she could see that the tunnel was only ten feet long or so. She traveled that distance quickly and emerged into a much larger chamber. The variations of light were more pronounced here, but thankfully the light was more intense as well. A fire, maybe, she thought. If it was a fire, then maybe there were people. Humans. Her heart leaped at that possibility, and she crossed the forty-foot expanse of this chamber quickly, passing through yet another tunnel, this one at least seven feet high. She stopped at the neck of the tunnel, lit only by what had to be a fire. It was off to the right slightly, burning from a large hole in the ground. "Hello? Anyone here?"

No answer.

But someone had to have started the fire.

It was then that she noticed huge drawings overhead and on the walls, fascinating drawings of winged beasts, some alone, some in groups, some seen looking down upon what she thought were farm animals. And further, more drawings, of what had to be fire rising from a pit and a man looking down into that pit. She stepped nearer to these drawings and looked at them more closely. They were crude, yes, but . . . she felt a chill . . . God in heaven, that could be Philippe. She backed off, unable to look away. Yes, that *was* Philippe, she was sure of it. Even in the drawings, the eyes were unmistakable. The drawings encircled the room, and each was remarkably similar to its neighbor. Fire rose from a hole in the ground to surround the feet of a man who bore an uncanny resemblance to Philippe Brissot. But what had the artist meant? Had those fires been real or imaginery? What's more, had Philippe actually started those fires? And if he had, for what reason? Despite everything, she was fascinated, utterly fascinated, drawn almost totally into the world created on these calcinate walls, imagining herself in the place of the man, of Philippe, as he stared down into the pit. What was there? What could fill his face with such . . . madness? Such happiness? Oh, dear God, she didn't want this experience. She didn't want to know what he felt looking into the fire, but she did know, remotely. Truth had been brought to her on the wings of history, provided to her by Philippe, whose thoughts were mostly uncontrollable in these caves. What she read in those thoughts was denial, a denial of heritage. That's what the fire was for—denial. Denial of truth. And the attempt to destroy that truth. To burn it into oblivion . . .

The fire suddenly crackled and hissed, startling her. Sparks leapt into the air. She stepped closer. She could feel the heat of the fire now, dry, refreshing, more intense the closer she got. A few steps away and afraid that she might actually fall in, she dropped to her hands and knees and crawled to the edge.

And terror filled her.

There were . . . beings in there. Four of them; one alone, the others piled atop one another like pick-up-sticks. Not people, but beings. And they were burning. They had wings and long arms, and they were small, very small, and they were all burning. The fire, as fires are shamelessly wont to do, burned bright blue at the tips of their extremities, their ears and hands, their wings. As Beverly watched, the small body of the one off by itself seemed to suddenly convulse. Then, incredibly, it turned its head and looked at her, and in a remarkably feeble gesture, raised one winged arm and opened its wide, fanged mouth, releasing a keening cry into the dry, heated air.

Beverly rolled onto her back and squeezed her eyes shut. She didn't want to see this! She didn't want to hear this! But still she saw it, even with her eyes closed. There was nothing she could do to remove the image from her eyelids, the image of that burning, dying beast crying for help. Tears flowed freely, pressing through the tails of her tightly closed eyes, as great, wracking sobs of fear and denial filled the tomb. She thought of Philippe—how could she not, glaring down at the burning beasts, taunting, chiding . . .

It was then that she felt stone cold hands upon her tear-stained cheeks.

38

The day had started warm, innocuous; the sun sat poised just beneath a bank of thin clouds on the horizon. But if things went well, Mike would spend the remainder of this day in Lascaux Cave, the weather above unimportant to him. But hopefully his head would have stopped throbbing by then. A concussion—of all things to happen! Well, he'd have to deal with it the best he could.

Walking up the narrow path to the front door of the Marsal farmhouse, Mike wondered if it wasn't too early, even for farm folk. He glanced at the bare windows, hoping to see movement beyond, but there was none. He glanced around at the outbuildings, of which there were many; only a few chickens could be seen. Four large pigs were gathered around a trough next to one of the outbuildings. Someone had to have fed them. He walked onto the porch, rapped on the door, waited. Nine children, that's what Armand's wife had said. And twins baking. There should be some noise, some indicator. He knocked again, then moved slightly left to look in the window. He saw what he thought to be a child, but only for a moment. The door was opened. He moved back to it and stared into the eyes of a woman of uncommon beauty. Her face was vaguely V-shaped and tanned, blemish-free, her tousled hair long and radiant, streaked with gray, and her eyes were a deep, almost unsettling blue.

Quietly appraising Mike, she knotted her robe around

her large belly. "It is so early, what do you want?" she asked in French.

Mike understood some but not all of what she'd said. He smiled weakly. "Do you speak English? I'm afraid my French . . ."

She wouldn't let him finish. She frowned noticeably and spoke this time in English. "What do you want? It is very early."

"I'd like to speak with your husband. Is he up?"

A doe-eyed girl of about eight appeared in the doorway. The woman put a protective arm around her, and the girl nudged in closer, gazing questioningly up at the stranger.

"He's sleeping," the woman said. "He doesn't feel well. Come back later."

She attempted to close the door, but Mike put his hand against it and smiled his best smile. "Please. It's very important. It's about the caves."

"What can be so important about the caves that it cannot wait?"

"Please."

The woman inhaled deeply and let it out. "What is your name?"

Mike told her.

"It is against my better judgment, he was drinking you see . . ." Another long look, then she spoke to the little girl in French and patted the child on the backside as she ran off.

It seemed to Mike that only a few seconds passed before Jacques Marsal appeared at the door, rubbing the back of his neck, a weak smile affixed to his mouth. "Too much drink," he said. He looked at Mike for a moment, then stepped aside. "Come in. Please, come in, Monsieur Marat."

Mike stepped inside and the door was closed behind him. All nine children, varying in age from five to twenty, were gathered around the table toward the back of the house, the scene framed by a large, multipaned window

328

that opened onto the backyard and its stunning array of flowers and green plants. Each child seemed quite intent on getting as close a look at this American as they possibly could. Their mother made small circles with her forefinger, a gesture they obeyed with what Mike thought to be refreshing speed.

"Come, sit down," said Jacques Marsal. "You have come about the caves?"

"Yes, about the caves."

They sat in opposing chairs in front of a huge fieldstone fireplace. Marsal lit a pipe, releasing a raft of smoke that rose sinuously toward the ceiling. He was trying very hard to look like someone who should be sitting by a fireplace smoking a pipe, with little success. Although close to seventy, his facial features still displayed the gentle curves of youth.

Marsal sucked on his pipe and blew a smoke ring. "What is it you wish to know? I am the chief guide; there is nothing I do not know."

Mike looked at the children, all busy eating now, then looked back at Marsal. "I have to get inside."

Marsal smiled and tapped his pipe on the ashtray. "Impossible, surely you must know that."

"Not . . . I don't mean by the front door."

Marsal leaned forward, his head nodding ever so slowly. "Ah, yes, he said you would come."

Mike's scalp tingled. "Who? Who said I would come?"

Marsal smiled very broadly and rubbed the fingers of his right hand together, as if he were attempting to remove day-old dirt. "Monsieurs Washington, Hamilton, and Jefferson. You know them, monsieur?"

Money—again money. That's all it took.

Marsal leaned forward and spoke at a whisper. "As you can see, I have many mouths to feed. There is another way in, yes, but it will cost you."

His wife came into the room. Marsal renewed a rigid posture and smiled at her.

"Charles has soccer practice today," she said, speaking

this time in English, which Mike appreciated. "You said you would take him."

Marsal nodded and said, "Yes, okay."

She looked at Mike with a piercing gaze. "The caves are closed. Jacques has told you the caves are closed?"

"Yes, I know."

She left hesitantly, casting a measured glance at her husband.

When they were alone again, Marsal said, "One thousand francs. That is the cost. Is that agreeable?"

Mike didn't have a thousand francs, not on him. "Yeah, yeah, I can pay that. Half now and half when we come back. Is that okay?"

In what Mike thought to be a remarkable concession, Marsal leaned back and said, "Yes, that is agreeable."

Using Marsal's Jeep, they left just minutes later. They drove through the town of Montignac, past a sign that said LASCAUX, FIVE KILOMETERS, and pressed on to the other side of the mountain, keeping it always on their right, eventually leaving the asphalt highway for a bumpy, overgrown trail that even the four-wheel drive Jeep struggled with. On the highway the sun had been hot and restful, but here they were protected by a canopy of tall trees, for which Mike was grateful. He didn't want to feel the lethargy of a summer's day. He wanted to be alert, ready to react to what would probably be a series of mindplays the closer he drew to his adversary.

The path abruptly ended a quarter mile or so from the base of the mountain. Marsal stopped the Jeep and got out. "It's only a short climb now," he said. He hoisted a thick rope onto his shoulder and tested two heavy-duty flashlights. Then he donned what was essentially a miner's cap and handed one to Mike. They came equipped with waterproof lights. Mike strapped it under his chin and Marsal checked to make sure it was on tight.

Marsal's promise of a short climb didn't hold. More

often than not they were on all fours, scrabbling for purchase, and the insects had become almost intolerable, doing whatever they could to distract them just when the climbers needed their concentration most. Exhausted, Mike stopped about halfway up and took a drink of water from his canteen, letting some dribble down his chin. Marsal didn't notice that Mike had stopped; he kept climbing.

"Wait up," Mike yelled after him. He screwed the cap back on his canteen and watched as Marsal took a right and all but disappeared behind a thick choke of underbrush. After repositioning his own load of rope, food, and water, Mike hurried after him. Marsal was waiting, pointing at a spot just ahead thirty feet or so.

He smiled. "We're here."

Advancing to the spot, they found what appeared to be only a rodent hole, certainly not large enough for a man to enter.

"This is it?" Mike asked.

"Yes, this is it."

"How the hell are we going to get in there? Christ, do we want to go in there? Damn thing can't be more than six inches across!"

"We enlarge it," Marsal offered with a shrug.

Mike looked at him curiously. "Enlarge it, shouldn't it . . . wait a second here. You have been here before, right? I mean, you just covered it over or something, right?"

Marsal took a small pickax from his knapsack. "But of course, many times. Step back, please."

Mike did as asked and watched Marsal begin to widen the hole. A couple of minutes later it was easily large enough to accommodate a man. The dirt had disappeared inside the hole, which in itself indicated enhanced depth and width. Mike poked his flashlight into the hole; it was wider a few feet below the surface, much wider, skewering the earth at about a thirty-degree angle, like a straw in a milkshake.

Marsal held his hand out, indicating that Mike should

lead. "It is best, I think, to go headfirst, with your helmet light on."

Mike flipped the light on and reluctantly scooched down in, using his elbows like feet.

As daylight disappeared behind them, eclipsed by a slight bend in the tunnel, Mike discovered, to his very great concern, that the hole was getting smaller. His helmet light pierced the dusty gloom, offering nothing but the promise of a very long crawl, and what appeared to be a tunnel whose diameter was steadily diminishing. He stopped and turned his head a half-turn. "You sure about this, Marsal?"

He thought he saw Marsal smile. "You sound worried, monsieur."

Mike returned that smile. "Yeah, a little."

"Not to worry, we'll be there soon."

But Mike did worry—furiously. He had all too real visions of being trapped, of dying here, of tons and tons of dirt suddenly collapsing around him. And death would not visit him with merciful swiftness. The process would be slow and excruciatingly painful. He would grope and scratch like someone who's awoken in a coffin, clawing for a way out. It was precisely that thought that seemed to bolster his waning strength. He moved quickly now, his elbows rubbed raw beneath the wool shirt. Small chunks of dirt, worked free as his helmet scraped the tunnel roof, blended with a baste of sweat and formed mud that worked into his eyes, making it difficult to see. Time and time again, he had to stop and hack dust out of his lungs, which only made his head throb more. And what made it all seem somewhat ludicrous, was the prospect that Marsal just might be his very able adversary, that this was all just a trick. Maybe Marsal went second just so he could take out that little pickax and close the damn tunnel up behind them! Then what would he do? Die, that's what! But although these were very real concerns, fifteen minutes or so after they entered the hole, he found something else to think about—he thought he heard a waterfall. "Hear that?"

Silence. Then. "Yes, I hear it," said Marsal, his tone one of surprise.

"What is it?"

"I don't know, I . . . water?"

Mike's breath suddenly quickened, his heart triphammered. He didn't know? How could Marsal not know? If he'd been in here before, like he'd said . . . He moved furiously now, his shirt torn at the elbows and forearms, letting his blood onto the tunnel floor. Propelled by fear, he didn't notice the sound of water strengthen. He didn't notice the tunnel abruptly end; he barely had time to take note of his free fall, a fall that lasted at least two seconds before he landed on his back in the pond that had collected behind the waterfall. His lungs emptied as he hit the water, and when Marsal, kicking like a man without a bicycle, clipped Mike's head with a hiking boot, he almost lost consciousness. Instinctively, Mike thrashed to the surface, his vision offering only splotches of light tracing along a rocky wall or dancing on falling water. With chopping, panicky strokes, he swam to the edge and pulled himself up onto a foot-wide rim, letting his legs dangle into the water as he leaned forward and gasped for air. But as he refilled his lungs, he realized his next problem—he had a violent case of the shakes. Whereas before he had been sweating profusely, now he was shivering. And in his haste to get out of the water, he had pulled off his knapsack. It bobbed on the surface of the rippling pond. He still had his helmet though, that was a stroke of good luck. But he just couldn't stop shaking. Now he saw Marsal on his left, shaking just as badly as he was. Are you my enemy? he wanted to ask. Are you going to kill me? He kept quiet—afraid of the answer.

Marsal wiped the water from his face, took off his helmet, and pushed his hair back, then replaced the helmet. "I tried to tell you about that, about the fall, but you were so fast. How is your head?"

In truth it felt like three pounds of water poured into a two-pound test balloon. "Okay, I guess. God, it's cold as ice in here!"

Marsal glanced around. "Yes, caves are very cold. Wool is good though, yes?"

"I guess."

"Good insulator. You'll be warmer soon."

"I don't think I'll ever be warm again."

"Come." Marsal got up and started toward the waterfall, walking tidily along the narrow rim.

"How are we gonna get out?" Mike yelled after him. He pulled himself to a standing position and looked longingly at his knapsack. "Shouldn't I get that?"

"Come," Marsal said. "I have everything we need."

Problems were cropping up fast. Now he had a big one—how were they going to get out of here? Mike looked up the wall and shined the light on the hole they'd fallen from. Thirty feet minimum. They'd never get out that way. Well, first things first, he decided. Find Beverly, then get out. First things first.

They walked to the right of the waterfall, then through it; the water slammed into his helmet like iron balls on tin. Once they'd gotten through, Mike looked down. Fifty feet away, he calculated. The trip to the bottom, strewn with slick boulders, sapped even more of his strength, but his determination saw him through. With the waterfall off to the right, Marsal took a flashlight from his pack and panned left to right, shining it onto a large, underground lake. For all Mike knew, it could have been the Atlantic Ocean. All he saw was water. *"Mon dieu!"* Marsal said, obviously amazed.

Fascination? No, Mike thought, Marsal had been here before. He'd said so. "Hold on, just a sec . . ."

Marsal turned and looked at him, shining his handheld light into his face. Suddenly he appeared terribly frightened. His body began to convulse, and tears of desperation welled in his eyes. "Get out!" he commanded.

"Something is wrong. So wrong! Get out! Get out!" He fell to his knees. Mike knelt beside him.

"Marsal?"

He was uncontrollable now, his body wracked by powerful, fear-inspired spasms. He dropped the flashlight to the ground. Mike picked it up.

"Dammit, Marsal, snap out of it. I need you!"

But even as he spoke, he knew Marsal would be useless to him. He'd been somehow instructed to lead Mike down here, and that's what he had done. Now his task was complete. There was nothing more for him to do but perhaps subconsciously ponder what had happened to him, to regurgitate it time and time again for as long as he lived.

"Stay here," Mike said. "I'll be back. You'll be all right. Just stay here."

Marsal could only sob.

39

She was back again, back where she had been before she had gone on that ill-advised exploration, for which she now severely chastised herself. She wouldn't move this time. Not again. She'd die if she did, she knew that all too well. She was probably lucky to be alive. A minute earlier, a minute later, and Philippe would probably not have been able to save her. So now, choices were at a premium. She had one—she had to sit here and wait for whatever was going to happen, to happen. And although that kind of inactivity made her feel very much like a condemned woman on death row, she *would* wait. She would trust in Mike, and she would simply wait.

But thanks, she thought, to divine intervention, she was at least able to see now. Not much, but enough to make out crude shapes, the dark water's edge, the darker ceiling high above the lake. From this vantage point, high on the side of the hill, she felt very much like someone with a seat at a play or perhaps a tragic opera. She remembered how Philippe had pulled her face close to his. "I told you, didn't I? I told you that you'd die!" Looking into his eyes, his face, the fire orange and dancing, his face too white, his eyes, mouth, and nose like chunks of coal on an orange-white paper plate, she had felt so very sure that he would kill her then, that he would twist her neck 'til it snapped like dry kindling, or that with one giant effort he would simply lift her head from her shoulders and cast it into the fire. But he hadn't. With sublime gentleness he had lifted her into his arms and carried her out of there. She remembered the slight flex of his knees before he leapt out of the hole. She remembered how he had set her down with such delicacy. And before he left, he added, "No matter what happens or what you see, stay here. What you may see, what you may hear, does not concern you. Only Jean Paul."

Now, looking down at the water, she wondered if perhaps she wasn't being given a test. There was someone down there, down by the water. A man, she thought, a man with a flashlight. The beam had come very close to where she sat, although over that great distance, it did weaken considerably. But even if it had stopped on her, she doubted if she could be seen. Still, test or not, it was all she could do to keep from yelling down.

Here, so far from the sun's rays, protected, wrapped like a child in winter, moving with the lissome grace so common to her kind, Charlotte still felt a certain anxiety. Her fangs were bared, protruding beneath her upper lip and onto the lower, like swords at the ready. Around her, as she walked, was their city. As they had built it. She had studied their tablets, their histories, such as they were. She now knew something of her ancestry. But where were her brothers and sisters now? Why were they not walking with her, strolling through their great subterranean structures, the columned fronts carved into the earth, behind which lay nothing, just monuments to their beginnings, to their life so long ago, before they were forced from the surface? Yes, she knew that much, that this had been a forced migration. But by whom? And when? Thousands of years ago perhaps? More?

Funny, she thought now, that her glistening weapons should be exposed. That she should feel threatened here. Of course, exposing her fangs was simply a natural response. Her altered genetic makeup probably required it, even demanded it. She had to consciously suppress the inclination while in the company of mortals. But not here, among her kind. Not here. She had seen these beasts, seen that they would not, or perhaps, *could* not retract their fangs. She stopped at a stand carved from rock. There were what could have been vegetables on the stand, also carved from rock. At various points throughout these caverns, fires burned. Hated fire, the immortals' worst enemy, save an ashen lance. Why had they chosen to keep fires burning? Why? As a reminder? But, of what? Perhaps like ancient African tribes, they were used for sacrifices, sacrifices to the God who had smote them, who had cast them down to the edge of hell.

She saw one then, in the shadows, futilely attempting to hide behind a pillar. Afraid; he was afraid. She could smell his fear. He appeared, then retreated with equal quickness, slowly retracting his wings, leaving the shadowy curve for her to see. Oh, how she longed to know more about these creatures, about herself. Surely everything to know had not been contained in their so meager "library." Surely there were other places where their history was kept. Pitiable creatures. And enviable, to a point. They certainly required nothing of life but a good meal: a healthy farm animal, or every now and again, a human caught out at the late hour. And the humans would never find these vampires, not here, at least a kilometer below the surface, hidden by a labyrinth of slender tunnels and passageways, most of which led nowhere, indicating at least a modicum of intelligence. Thinking that, Charlotte's desire to know more about these creatures strengthened even more, so when Philippe appeared across this huge chamber, beckoning—an action that prompted a gentle patter from the hidden beasts—she told him that his revenge was at hand, and that he should certainly enjoy it while she would remain and simply browse.

At that, Philippe said, "As you wish," and was gone.

Moments later, the one hidden behind a pillar stepped into the open and moved cautiously toward her.

* * *

Mike's footfalls made squishy sounds in the damp sand. He was cold, but because he'd taken Marsal's suggestion and worn wool, he could tolerate the cold.

Although it certainly appeared that he was alone—save for Marsal—he knew he was not alone. Brissot was out there, somewhere, beyond the spray of light, waiting. Yes, he had decided, that was Brissot himself who had sat down with him at dinner, Brissot who had provided him with hallucination after hallucination. As for Brissot being a vampire, Mike just didn't know. It would, if mythology could be trusted, explain how he still walked the earth after two hundred years. It would, in fact, explain many things. But still, spanning the gap from improbability to probability seemed akin to spanning the distance between sanity and insanity.

But if he is here, Mike thought, where the hell is he? He stopped and pointed the beam at the hill, then up, toward the ceiling. The sand was unbroken, not a clue. And unfortunately, the crest of the hill was either beyond the beam's reach, or the ceiling was the same color as the sand. As he moved further along the lake, Mike found something that further convinced him that Brissot was here; a skeleton, ten feet or so up the hill, picked clean and partially buried in the sand. And where a pocket might have been, lying between the second and third ribs on the right side, a note, written in French. Mike's French was lousy, but he was able to decipher first the greeting, My friend, Maximilien, and then part of the text, something about a good dog. Lastly, he read the name, written in a flowing hand. Philippe.

Servant or something, Mike decided. He crumbled the note and dropped it to the sand. He'd had enough. Quite enough. He turned quickly; light blazed across his field of vision.

Something there? A man?

He turned back quickly. Nothing. "Brissot?" he hollered. "I'M HERE, DAMMIT! TAKE ME AND LEAVE BEVERLY ALONE!"

The silence that followed lasted only a few seconds.

"And I suppose you're here to see that I don't harm her," he heard from the darkness.

"BRISSOT! Where are you, dammit?"

"I'm here." Behind. "I'm here." In front. "Here." To the right, then to the left. "Here and everywhere. Nowhere."

Laughter followed, and Brissot stepped into the light. "I am light and dark. Shadow and detail. And most of all, Jean Paul, most of all, I am your executioner. Most of all, I am that.

"But, of course, an executioner needs an instrument."

Mike's attention was suddenly drawn to an area behind Brissot, very near the lake. Why hadn't he seen it before?

"A trick," he said with a self-assured smile. "More mind games, that's all. One of your goddamned tricks!"

Brissot seemed amused. "Oh, really?" he said.

Mike shined the light onto the guillotine, rising stark and naked there next to the water. The beam traced every detail, the blade throwing off the light like a white, hovering, sunlit bird. Brissot stepped closer to Mike, his skin glowing bright, his eyes brighter. "It's time," he said, his eyes rounded, flaming with hatred and disdain. "I have you, Jean Paul. Death could not hide you! I'll have your head now!" In a movement too quick to be seen, he wrapped a powerful hand around Mike's neck, and effortlessly lifted him off the ground. Mike wrapped that hand with both of his own and tried to remove it, but he was like a child in the clutches of a giant, there was nothing he could do. With his enemy suspended, Brissot began the short walk to the awaiting guillotine. Mike kicked wildly and tried to break free.

Brissot glanced up the hill toward Beverly. "Marie is gone," he said, "but I have our daughter. That will be enough, Jean Paul. We will spend eternity together, she and I."

God, he could barely breathe, barely talk. "A trick," Mike managed, "just a trick!"

Brissot laughed at him, one eyebrow raised. "A trick? You really think so?"

"Damn . . . you!"

"Then I could release the blade onto your exposed neck and nothing would happen. Is that correct, Jean Paul?"

"Yes . . . just a tri—"

Brissot squeezed his neck tighter still, cutting off the last part of the word. Then he looked up the hill and smiled. "Or perhaps it would be better . . . Jeanette, come here. Now. Come here."

Beverly appeared within a half minute, moving zombielike toward them. Not once did she even glance in Mike's direction. She seemed incapable of that, her eyes fixed and unblinking.

Brissot let Mike go. He scrambled to his feet, hurried down the steps, and took Beverly into his arms, her body straining under his hold. Brissot looked down at them from the guillotine. Beverly's eyes never strayed from his, intent as she was on simply moving up the stairs to him.

"Bev, dammit, Bev, it's me, Mike!" he whispered. "It's all a trick, just a mind trick. Don't let him do this!" He stroked her tangled, dirt-caked hair, smelled the stench of age on her dress. So easy to imagine her wrapped by that dress, prone in her coffin, as dead as Brissot.

Brissot laughed. He threw his head back and filled the cave with his bellowing laughter. "A trick?" he said. "You still think it's a trick, Jean Paul?" He stopped laughing. "Then come up here and prove it to me. If, as you believe, this is only a trick, then what do you have to fear?"

Mike probed Brissot's eyes. There was no trick to be seen in there. Brissot believed, really believed, that he stood upon an eighteenth-century guillotine. Mike had to have courage, enough for the both of them. And faith. He looked at the guillotine. It couldn't be real, not here—it was physically impossible. There was only one explanation. Only one. Mike felt his grip weaken; as soon as it did, Beverly broke free and went up the stairs to Brissot, the sound of her feet falling upon wood was very real indeed.

"Come up here, Jean Paul," said Brissot, his arm around Beverly. "My daughter wishes to take your head. You did kill her mother after all, so who better to take your head?"

Dear God, he was going to make Beverly do it! And he was mad now. Sanity had utterly deserted him. But what did it matter who pulled the lever? If this huge instrument of death was real, then it didn't at all matter. And Brissot could kill him at any time, by any method.

That first step toward the guillotine was as difficult as any he had ever taken, but he did take it. And now he moved much more quickly, almost bounding up the steps. Stopping beside Beverly, he took her by the hand and squeezed it tight. He thought he felt her squeeze back. Or maybe not. Maybe it was his pounding pulse that he felt.

Again Brissot seemed amused. "Your head, Jean Paul, kneel and place your head on the block."

Mike looked at Beverly, still staring at Brissot. "Trust me, Beverly," he said, "please trust me." Despite the cold, sweat drenched his body.

He knelt quietly, stretching his neck as far as he could, placing it properly onto the block. The wood felt cold, and he could see lines of dried blood along the side. The light from his helmet cut into the water's edge. For a moment, for one very brief moment, he thought he saw movement on the hillside.

"Good," said Brissot. "Now the lever, Jeanette. Just there." He pointed.

Mike looked up at Beverly. He thought he saw her chest vibrating, as if she were crying.

"Proceed," said Brissot.

Suddenly Mike felt very unsure. What if he was wrong? What if Brissot *had* managed to build a guillotine down here? What if . . .

Adrenaline pushed through him. "NOOOOO!" he

cried, straining to look into Beverly's eyes, catching her gaze just as she pulled the lever, just as the blade started down . . .

"Beverly? Wake up, Beverly, please wake up!"

They were lying on the sand, very close to the water. Mike laughed, he couldn't help it. He'd beaten him! He'd taken him on fair and square and beaten him!

Beverly's eyes fluttered open. She propped herself onto one elbow and looked at him. "Mike? What happened? I can't remember—"

"It's okay, Bev, it's okay. We beat the son-of-a-bitch!"

"We did? How, Mike, how?"

"All that later. Look, Bev, the first thing we have to do is get out of here . . . somehow. Are you hurt?"

She sat up slowly and ran her fingers through her hair. "No, no, I don't think so. I guess I'm okay. What about you?"

"Yeah, I'm all right. A little cold, but—"

Beverly's attention was suddenly diverted. She rose quickly. Mike got up and stood beside her.

Brissot stood about ten feet away, his face washed white by the light from Mike's helmet, his eyes only dark circles. "How?" he asked. "You . . . you should be dead! The guillotine . . . you should be dead!"

Brissot was utterly confused. His gaze drifted left and right, scanning, probing, searching for the reason his enemy still lived; why the guillotine had not removed his head. He stopped scanning and focused on Beverly. "Jeanette," he said, "dear, dear Jeanette!" He stepped toward her, his fangs exposed now.

Mike stepped in front of Beverly, shielding her. Brissot stopped. "No," Mike said, "you can't have her! Jeanette is dead. You hear me, you bastard? Dead!"

Again confusion. Brissot slanted his head slightly, then shook it almost imperceptibly. He looked at Beverly longingly. "No, you're wrong, Jean Paul."

And that was true, but only to a point. Jeanette's blood did flow in Beverly's veins. She was the last of Marie and Philippe's descendants, a blood relative. It was so easy for Brissot to look upon her not as a descendant four times removed, but as his daughter, as Jeanette. For him time had little meaning.

And now it was time to insure that she remained with him always. Time for her to be reborn, to become a child of the night. He moved toward them then, his mouth gaped wide, something foreign and insane on his face. Revenge and hunger and madness all blended, all undeniable.

"DAMN YOU!" Mike yelled. He threw the flashlight at Brissot, catching him on the shoulder. It clicked on and fell to the ground. Not knowing what else to do, Mike leaped at him. But Brissot, ever quick, caught him by the throat at the apex of his jump, enclosing his neck with one powerful hand. Mike pounded the air with his fists, but the pressure on his larynx was too great; light began to fade. His head felt like it would explode; his strength was almost gone. Perilously close to passing out, he barely noticed his free fall as Brissot effortlessly tossed him into the lake, as he somersaulted through the air, landing on his back in the water. Brissot waded in after him, screaming, "Murderer, murderer!" and pulled him out. But as Brissot encircled Mike's head with his hands, preparing to lift it from his shoulders, there began a chant in the huge chamber. "Brissot . . . Brissot . . . Brissot!"

The vampire seemed distracted.

"BRISSOT . . . BRISSOT . . . BRISSOT!"

He dropped Mike into the water and turned. At the same time, Beverly ran into the water and helped Mike to shore.

"Get back, all of you, get back!" Brissot ordered, doing a full circle. "This is none of your concern. I'll sacrifice more of you if you persist."

"BRISSOT . . . BRISSOT . . . BRISSOT!"

Full consciousness came back to Mike. He looked at the

vampire. Was it? Could it be? There was fear on his face, not overwhelming, debilitating fear, but fear nonetheless. The fear a child might show during a storm.

Mike stood beside Beverly and watched as the beasts emerged from the shadows. Twenty, maybe thirty of them pushed closer and closer to the water's edge, moving down the hillside and spraying sand with their four-toed feet.

"BRISSOT . . . BRISSOT . . . BRISSOT!"

"You're pathetic, all of you," the vampire thundered. "Get back before I get angry. Go back! Back into your caves! Back into the earth where you belong. I'm not afraid of you!"

Mike and Beverly could only watch while the beasts walked around them, oblivious, intent only on Brissot, their feet slapping onto the sand. Seconds later they had surrounded their enemy.

Recognizing their chance, Mike and Beverly scrambled up the hillside, only occasionally glancing behind them. Brissot was doing what he could to beat the creatures back, but it seemed that for every two he fought off, three more emerged from the darkness to take their place. Brissot's strength was incredible. Wings, heads, arms, and legs flew in all directions, splashing into the water or thudding onto the sand. But they were a mob, mindless and inspired to only one end—killing their immortal enemy. And in the end there were simply too many, far too many, even for Philippe Brissot. He finally went down, and they attacked, their wings whipping furiously, the chamber shot with the sounds of their gluttony and the death sounds of the vampire. Sounds that seemed to vibrate the very ground beneath their feet. And when they were done, they lifted his shining, naked body high overhead and carried it out of the water, the scene eerily lit by the flashlight Mike had thrown at Brissot, lying near the shoreline. Brissot was still conscious, fully able to telepathically discern their intent—they would burn him. They would toss his body into his own sacrificial fire and be done with him. They had wanted him alive for that. They had wanted him to experience the pain of fire as it probed beneath his glowing white skin, as it bubbled his eyes in their sockets and boiled his useless innards. They would gather around the fire and watch, and sounds of joy would come out of them, sounds that would drown out Brissot's anguished cries. That was what they had planned for their enemy. Within a minute or so they were out of sight, out of earshot, leaving only the sound of the waterfall in their wake, following their plan. Brissot kicked and thrashed as the fire consumed him, his cries thunderous and discordant, coursing through the caves and even causing some lesser tunnels to collapse under the strain. The creatures gathered to watch, surrounding the fire, drawing closer than they ever would have in the past. Brissot's death was an important event in their history, too important not to witness. Or to detail. While he died, two of the beasts recorded the event. First they drew the fire, as they had before, but now, instead of this creature glaring in at their brethren, they drew one of their own kind, one typical of their kind, staring in at the fiery pit. But strangely, blood lust and denial were not written on its face. What these artists depicted then was far removed from such things. If anything could be seen on the face of their rendering, it was a sense of finality, of newness, perhaps. But certainly not denial.

For many minutes neither Mike nor Beverly could move. They knew they would have to sooner or later, but for now they simply held each other; he stroking her hair, she saying thank God, thank God, thank God.

Finally, he cupped her head in his hands and looked at her. "We've got to get out of here," he said, trying hard not to understate the obvious.

"But how, Mike? Where?"

"I don't know, not yet, but there's got to be a way. There's just got to be—"

It was then that the beasts returned. They were at the bottom of the hill, walking near the water, fanning out. One of them stopped and picked up the flashlight, pointing it into his face. The sudden assault made him jump backwards; he dropped the flashlight to the ground and then swatted at it with his foot.

Beverly yelped. Mike covered her mouth and flipped off his headlamp.

"Shhh, maybe they'll leave, maybe . . ."

"Mike, what are we going to do?"

"This way, c'mon, this way."

They moved to the right as stealthily as possible, away from the creatures, working their way along a natural shelf formed between the top of the hill and the ceiling. But the further they went, the darker it got. Soon they would be in almost total darkness.

"Wait, wait, I found something," Beverly whispered. "Take off your helmet and put it near the wall. Go on, do it, Mike!"

"You sure?"

"Dammit, Mike, just do it!" She took his hand. "Here, right here. I found something. I know I did!"

Mike took his helmet off and did as he was asked. There was a hole in the wall here, just large enough for a hand. What lay beyond, he didn't know, but it was definitely worth exploring. He held the light just inches from the wall and flipped it on, surrounding them with a haloed reflection. Finally, sensing they might be on to something, he put the light down—pointed at the hole—and dug along with her. With the two of them digging, the hole quickly expanded.

"Another room, Bev, another room!" Mike said, trying but failing to keep his voice at a whisper.

"Oh, Mike, I think you're right. I think . . ." She saw something then, just off to the right. She stood and tugged on Mike's shirt.

"Bev, c'mon, what're you—"

Mike turned, got up. Charlotte stood a few yards away,

her fangs glistening. Looking at her, Beverly envisioned those fangs sunk deep into the neck of that poor child at the fountain.

"Damn!" Mike said, taking her by the arm. "Dig, Bev, just dig! It's our only chance!"

With all the strength and speed she could summon, Beverly dropped to her knees and clawed at the earth, fully expecting Charlotte to advance on them. But Charlotte didn't move.

"Almost," Beverly said. Her hands were aching and she'd split a nail. She looked back at Charlotte. What is she going to do? she thought. When is she going to attack?

Charlotte looked to her right, at the beasts in the distance, the pathetic, simpleminded beasts. Then she looked back at Mike and Beverly. The hole was almost large enough now. For a moment, hunger mapped her face, but as Mike put his flashlight on the other side of the hole and pushed Beverly through, Charlotte slowly backed away.

Charlotte waited a moment, waited till they were gone, then worked her way back to her confused brood. Pulling one aside, she pointed to the hole left by Mike and Beverly. The beast trundled up the hill and immediately began a repair, filling the hole with dirt and a bonding vomitus composed mainly of coagulating blood, using its tremendous strength to pack it firmly into place. It stopped once, its head canted slightly, to listen to the sounds of escape and to watch the bobbing light in the distance. It resisted the urge to go after them, squealing and grunting its confusion, glancing down toward Charlotte then back through the hole. But finally, its chance was gone, and Mike and Beverly made their way out of Lascaux Cave, climbing into the protection of a hot, sunfilled French afternoon.

40

Charlotte moved slowly up the stairs, toward the bedroom. She had the dress folded over her arm, the one she had worn all those years ago when she had killed Marat, the one most recently worn by Beverly.

Through the window to the left of the bed, she saw the moon. Seeing it she thought of the sun, the blazing sun, as she often did, for there were no suns in her world. There never would be.

She heard movement below, on the first floor. She ignored it and went to the cupboard beside the bed, first holding the dress close to her breast and then placing it back into the cupboard, affixing it precisely onto a wooden hanger.

She remembered tapping on Beverly's window at the Hotel Lafayette. She had watched them make love, actually feeling something akin to embarrassment while she did. She waited 'til they were done, and then pointed to the dress. While she hovered there, she successfully resisted the ancient urge, just as she had when she'd found them in the cave, after Philippe had been killed. She remembered pride at having resisted. She smiled as she remembered Marsal, dazed and frightened, wandering toward them after the hole was patched. At first the Lamia advanced on him, fully intending to drain him of his blood, but hearing her mental command, they had stopped. She had allowed him to leave, had actually carried him to the hole, not wanting to take the chance that his disappearance would prompt a search. She had seen him since at the cafe talking with his friends, trying his best to convince them of what he had seen, where he had been, but he couldn't. His story was a mishmash. Philippe had seen to that. The hole had been filled in, and the people of Montignac now looked upon Marsal as someone a bit off center. Just a harmless old man.

Movement now, on the stairs. Charlotte turned to face the darkened doorway. One of her brood, the one who had first stepped forward from behind the column, stepped into the room. "We go?" it asked in a childlike voice. For the first time in a long time, it had communicated by word and not telepathically.

She remembered this one coming to her in their underground city. It was then she discovered that Philippe had been sacrificing them, that he had been making yearly trips to the caves solely for the purpose of their destruction. They had recorded those events on the walls surrounding his fire. Infuriating. So intensely infuriating. Appropriate that now his end was recorded on those same walls. Their history, their past, was more important than one immortal, an immortal who seemed intent on stifling that past, perhaps ashamed of it. They had gathered around her then, telepathically seeking her permission to kill Brissot. They knew of her friendship with him, and because she seemed less like him, and more like them, they sought her permission. She had hesitated, but had finally given in. Philippe, she reasoned, would be forever filled with the need for revenge. A need that would never die, because he could live forever.

Some of you will die trying to subdue him, she had told them. More would die, they said, if they let him live. Perhaps all of them, eventually. Genocide would be achieved.

She was proud of what she had done, the progress she had made. Three had come to the surface for reasons other than to feed. She had, over the course of the last two months, again instilled in them a feeling of pride in what they were. Or had been. And now it wouldn't be long before they struck out on their journey. But her search for knowledge would reach beyond her own kind. There were others, each breed possessed of different skills, different talents. She wanted to write their history as well, to gather and catalog the entire history of vampires. Perhaps in so doing she might also find out why sunlight was poison to her kind, why pain coursed through her each time she drew close to a church. Why killing a priest meant that aging would begin, as it had for the fabled Martin, the Hunt vampire, who had taken his own life rather than live on uselessly, trapped in a body more dead than not.

She thought about her upcoming journey and smiled, and as a mother might a child, she took the vampire she called, George, by the hand, and together they went into the night.